COURT OF SHADOWS BOOK 1

PLAY OF SHADOWS

SEBASTIEN
DE CASTELL

Arcadia

First published in Great Britain in 2024
This paperback edition first published in Great Britain in 2024 by

Arcadia
An imprint of
Quercus Editions Limited
Carmelite House
50 Victoria Embankment
London EC4Y 0DZ

An Hachette UK company

The authorised representative in the EEA is Hachette Ireland,
8 Castlecourt Centre, Castleknock Road, Castleknock,
Dublin 15, D15 YF6A, Ireland

A CIP catalogue record for this book is available from the British Library

PB ISBN 978-1-78747-145-0
EBOOK ISBN 978-1-78747-144-3

1

Typeset by CC Book Production
Printed and bound in Great Britain by Clays Ltd, Elcograf S.p.A

MIX
Paper | Supporting responsible forestry
FSC® C104740
FSC www.fsc.org

Papers used by Arcadia are from well-managed forests and other responsible sources.

For the dashing and dauntless cast and crew of the Bloomsbury Theatre's 2004 production of *Richard III*. You were Veristors, one and all.

CONTENTS

PART THE THIRD:

THE BARDATTI

PART THE FOURTH:

THE RAVEN

PART THE FIFTH:

THE DUELLIST

PART THE SIXTH:

THE VERISTOR

EPILOGUE:

THE TROUPE

CHAPTER 1

RABBIT, RABBIT

Everyone has a talent, and these days, mine is running. So superb is my aptitude for panicked flight that it almost makes up for my less admirable traits, which include cowardice, poor fencing skills and a regrettable tendency to forget those faults while making bold threats against brutish thugs who suffer no such deficiencies of their own.

'*Run, Rabbit, run!*' my pursuers cheered as they chased me through bustling streets and abandoned alleyways, over one crowded canal bridge and across the next. '*Run down your warren, run up the hill! Run from the Vixen before she makes her kill!*'

The Vixen. Of all the sobriquets adopted by professional duellists in the city of Jereste, surely Lady Ferica di Traizo's was the most apt – and the most terrifying.

I dived under a fruit-seller's stall, rolled up to my feet on the other side and kept on running. What had possessed me to go and challenge the deadliest fencer in the entire city to a duella honoria?

'Faster, Rabbit, faster! You're the one she's after!'

Damn their tune for being so catchy. Merchants shuttering their shops for the night sang along. Scampering children trying to run between my legs giggled their way through their own mangled lyrics. I had to shove aside two young lovers out for a romantic stroll as they hummed the melody while gazing soulfully into each other's eyes.

I dashed through the overcrowded square and into an equally congested courtyard, doing my best to avoid those among my fellow citizens who saw it as their duty to stick out a foot to trip me in anticipation of witnessing a good beating before I was dragged back to court. I'd been keeping up a goodly pace thus far, but I was tiring, and my tormentors knew it.

'*Hide, Rabbit, hide!*' the black-shirted bravos chanted as they closed in on me. '*She's searching far and wide!*'

When I dared glance back, I caught the flickering light of the brass street lanterns glinting off the metal orchid emblems on their collars. The Iron Orchids called themselves a citizen militia, determined to rid the city of petty criminals and other undesirables, but mostly they were street toughs who sold their services to anyone looking to settle a grudge. Alas, Jereste's notoriously feckless constabulary did little to curb their activities.

An orchestra of swashing and clanging accompanied my pursuers as the small buckler shields slung low on their leather belts banged against the scabbarded steel hilts of their rapiers and sideswords. The thump of booted heels on the loose cobblestone streets added an ominous rhythm section.

Saint Ethalia-who-shares-all-sorrows, I swore silently, *help me escape these mercenary thugs! They're going to haul me back to court and dump me in the duelling circle so that fox-faced lunatic who calls herself the Vixen can stick her blade through my heart before mine even leaves its scabbard!*

The Iron Orchids were herding me deeper and deeper into the narrow alleys of the Paupers' Market, apparently determined to keep me from the Temple District where I might beg sanctuary. Fortunately for me, I'd no intention of sleeping in a church tonight.

'Run down your hole, Rabbit, run up to the sky!
Run a little faster, or else you'll surely die!'

'Coming through!' I shouted to a pair of street cleaners wrestling a stinking refuse cart across the street. Grinning in reply, they pushed all the harder to cut me off. No doubt they were hoping for a reward from my pursuers; a coward fleeing a lawful duel always means plenty of coin to go around for those who help bring the fugitive to justice.

Desperation lent my legs the extra ounce of strength I needed to leap high enough for my right foot to reach the top of the wagon's iron-banded wheel. My left found purchase on the edge of the coffin-sized refuse box – but as I jumped across, my toe caught on the opposite edge and I tumbled headlong towards the cobblestones below. Luck more than skill sent me into a somersault that saved my skull, but it came at the cost of a numb shoulder and an unsettling twinge in my ankle.

I started for the nearest alley, my chest heaving now. If any Iron Orchids thought to circle round and beat me to the other side, I'd be trapped. But I had more pressing problems, as it turned out, because my next step had me hissing through my teeth and the one after that tore a howl from me. I'd sprained my ankle and my race was done.

'Rest, Rabbit, rest. It's really for the best!
There's nowhere left to hide – besides,
It's long past time you died!'

I ignored them and their lousy rhymes as I staggered onwards, grabbing at every gate and door handle I passed in search of an escape route. Too soon, though, a dozen shadowy figures appeared at the far end of the alley. The glint of freshly sharpened blades slashed through the darkness.

So close, I thought. Three doors down the alley had been my destination – and, I'd hoped, my one chance at salvation.

'You've bested me, friends,' I said jovially, as if this had all been a jest on my part, even as my gaze sought out some means of delaying the inevitable. 'My word of honour, I'll give you no trouble on the way back to the courthouse. No doubt her Ladyship the Vixen is most troubled by my temporary absence.'

'*Honour?*' the leader of the bravos asked. 'What honour does a rabbit have? And what trouble could he possibly give a pack of hunting hounds? Fear not, though, little bunny, for we have many games yet to play before we turn you over to the Vixen.'

I stifled a shiver. On his best day, an amateur like me – whose principal sword training had been at theatre school and largely devoted to learning how *not* to hit an opponent – might last as long as a minute in the duelling circle against an opponent of the Vixen's calibre. With a sprained ankle and whatever assortment of bruises my escorts intended to inflict before depositing me at her Ladyship's feet? The only chance I'd have to score first blood would be if I drove the tip of my rapier through my own eye socket before she got to me.

My gaze went to the stage door barely nine feet away. It would surely be locked right now, which meant I needed two things: a great deal of noise, and a minor miracle.

Actually, given how terrible my plan was, I would need *two* miracles, and not that minor, either.

'*Rabbit, Rabbit*,' the bravos chanted eagerly, closing in on me from both ends of the alley. Clanging their bucklers with added gusto, the cacophony turned positively thunderous. '*Rabbit, Rabbit!*'

At least the Orchids can always be counted on for something, I thought. *Now I just need them to be even louder.*

'Oh, do shut up, you swollen-sacked fustilarians!' I shouted.

'*Rabbit, Rabbit!*' they roared eagerly, suitably encouraged, and started bashing the steel bosses of their bucklers against the alley walls for added effect. The endlessly repeated chant was paralysing, as if the words were unleashing some ancient spell upon me, transforming me into a cornered hare cowering as he awaits the jaws of the hounds.

Come on, come on! I thought, watching the back of the stage door. *Don't tell me any company of actors is going to tolerate this racket outside their walls?*

The Orchids would be upon me any second now. I couldn't hope to bribe them – my job as a merchants' messenger was no path to fortune – and nor could I roll the dice and challenge my captors to fence me one-on-one here in the alley, since I'd been forced to abandon my rapier a mile back to keep it from slowing me down.

Also, I'm rubbish with a blade.

The squeal of a heavy door grinding angrily on its hinges surprised all of us, especially when it heralded the sweet melody of a roaring bear woken too early from its hibernation.

'What unholy hubbub intrudes upon these hallowed halls?' the outraged voice demanded. 'What halfwit interrupts the sacred work of this city's finest actors rehearsing the most magnificent play ever conceived?'

Wild, curly red hair and a thick beard framed a face better suited to the war chief of a barbarian horde come to sack the city than an actor performing in one of its legendary theatres. The lantern-light leaking from the backstage door lent a flickering glow to a bronze plaque bolted onto the theatre's back wall.

OPERATO BELLEZA
PLAYERS ONLY

I nearly wept in gratitude to the many, many saints who'd ignored my prayers over the years. What moments before had seemed a *truly* terrible plan had, by this tiny interruption, been redeemed into a scheme of unrivalled cunning.

'What the Hells is this about?' one of the Iron Orchids asked. 'You run all this way to hide in a *theatre*, Rabbit?'

'Actually . . . yes!'

Ignoring the pain in my sprained ankle, I sprinted up the three stone steps, ducked under the burly actor's arm and shot into the dimly lit hallway.

'Hey! What are y—?'

I limped as quickly as I could down a long corridor, the damned ankle grinding like broken glass, past closets bulging with costumes and cabinets filled with props. My shoulder hit the edge of the wall as I took a left turn, following as best I could the sounds of promisingly pompous voices. Rounding a second corner, I found myself confronted with a pair of oak doors sagging on their hinges. Heedless of what awaited me on the other side, I barrelled through and into a massive hall where more than two dozen men and women in ill-fitting costumes were milling about as sullenly as if the gods themselves were pitted against them.

Actors, I thought, jubilantly steadying myself. *Now I just need my second miracle.*

A broad-chested woman in a too-tight red velvet dress jabbed her thumb at me. 'Who the Hells is this now?' she demanded. 'Has Shoville hired *more* bloody amateurs for this stupid play?'

Two things I ought to mention at this juncture: the first is that the

Belleza is one of the oldest theatres in Jereste, and one of only three entitled to call itself an operato. This might sound trivial for anything other than calculating the price of a ticket, but there's a far deeper significance to that lofty title. Historical plays staged in the city's operatos are deemed so vital to the spiritual wellbeing of the city that its performers are granted privileges once exclusive to the legendary Bardatti actors and troubadours of old. These rights include exemption from military conscription, immunity from incarceration over unpaid debts and, according to ancient tradition, the right to demand reprieve from certain affairs of honour . . .

Oh, and the second thing? In addition to being an excellent runner, I'm also a superb liar.

I swept back the damp hair from my brow before favouring my buxom saviour with a wink and a smile. 'I'm the new herald,' I announced, venturing deeper into the room and glancing about for a spare costume.

That there would be a herald's part in their play was an educated guess on my part, as most of the Grand Historias are about ancient battles and the reigns of princes and dukes, which meant they invariably needed at least one herald to proclaim their glorious victories.

A tall, skinny fellow about my age, with a hooked nose and ash-brown hair cut in the fashion of a royal page, and dressed to match in doublet and hose, stamped his foot. 'Roz,' he complained to the voluptuous woman in the red velvet dress, 'I thought *I* was playing the herald in the final act! Has that bloody director given away *another* of my parts?'

'Oh, do give it a rest, Teo,' she replied, tying back her brassy-blonde tresses with a scarlet ribbon. 'It's only one line.'

'Well, it was *my* line,' Teo grumbled. 'Why should this guy get—?'

My newfound rival for the most trivial of acting roles was cut off by the return of the red-bearded lummox who'd unintentionally rescued me from the Iron Orchids two minutes ago. 'There you are,' he said.

'Hey, Beretto,' Teo called out, 'did you know Shoville gave this arsehole my part?'

Whatever Beretto was going to say in reply was drowned out by the clanging of weapons as a dozen armed men and women crowded their way into the rehearsal hall behind him. Even though the doors were already open, one fellow kicked it anyway, shouting, 'There's our rabbit!'

Teo and the rest of the players, most of them costumed in fake finery or imitation armour, retreated to the shadows at the back of the hall. As a species, actors are largely immune from such ailments as courage or dignity. Only the one they'd called Beretto was standing his ground.

Without the beard, he would have looked closer to my own age of twenty-five than I'd first thought. The two of us must have looked ridiculous side by side like that: a great red bear looming over a pale, shivering hare.

Beretto folded his arms across his broad chest, observing the proceedings with calm curiosity. 'Fled a duel, did you?' he asked me.

'I prefer to think of it as engaging with the enemy honourably but from a safe distance.'

'How's that working out so far?'

'I think we're both about to find out.'

I limped to one of the weapons racks near the wall, grabbed a longsword and turned to brandish it at the bravos advancing on me. 'Stay back,' I warned them. 'I'll see the blood of all twelve of you consecrate the floors of this hallowed hall ere the first lays a hand on me.'

The leader chuckled when he saw the weapon I was brandishing and patted his thick leather fencing vest. 'Which should we fear more, Rabbit? The fencing skills of a coward who runs from a lawful duel, or the wooden toy he now waves in my face?'

It was only then that I noticed the distressingly light weight of the sword – due no doubt to the fact that the blade was painted wood rather than proper steel. Usually the operatos pride themselves on having authentic weapons for their performances. Apparently business wasn't booming at the Belleza.

I tossed the wooden prop aside and offered up my best approximation of a victorious smirk.

Well, Grandmother, Grandfather, I thought, *now we'll find out if all those acting lessons you paid for were worth the money.*

I took a deep breath and declared, 'What need would I have of a blade, you ill-bred dogs, when we all know performers in Jereste's operatos are exempt from honour duels.'

My unexpected show of bravado was less convincing than I'd hoped. Their leader looked torn between amusement and disbelief. 'What – *you*? An *actor*?'

Now that hurts.

It wasn't entirely a lie. I had, in fact, attended not one but *three* of the city's finest dramatic academies. That I'd been tossed out of all three of them was an entirely different matter.

'Isn't it obvious?' I asked, trying unsuccessfully to make my question rhetorical. I gestured to the motley assortment of actors now discreetly huddled against the back wall of the rehearsal hall. 'Engaged by this fabled company of players, the legendary—'

Oh Hells.

I looked over at the big, red-haired man desperately.

'Knights of the Curtain,' he replied with a hint of a smile.

'The Knights of the Curtain!' I managed to repeat without irony. 'Among these paladins of the stage am I to perform the sacred role of the herald, as all here can attest.' I wiggled my fingers in a dismissive wave at my pursuers. 'So you see, I can't possibly fight some petty honour duel when my talents are needed here.'

The leader of the Iron Orchids cast a dubious glance at the cowering company of actors. 'And you'd all swear to this?'

If only he'd asked that question with a *teensy* bit more disdain in his voice! My gambit relied entirely on the well-founded hatred actors felt for the bravos of this city, who looked down on them as nothing more than pampered, overprivileged prostitutes.

His question elicited nothing but deathly silence.

More honour among thieves than actors, I thought bitterly. Although, to be fair, I suppose barging in on their rehearsal and lying about being a member of their company wasn't the strongest foundation on which to expect instant and steadfast camaraderie.

One of the narrow doors at the far end of the rehearsal hall swung open to reveal a man of middle years with sallow skin and thinning grey hair. His pronounced pot belly was at odds with his skinny, stoop-shouldered frame. But in his eyes – ah, in *his eyes* – there lay a lion waiting to pounce!

Shoving his way through the milling players, he bellowed, 'In the name of Saint Anlas-who-remembers-the-world, *what* is going on in my theatre? I leave you for all of ten minutes and instead of rehearsing, here I find you dawdling about with—'

He arched an eyebrow as he finally took note of the black-shirted bravos infesting his hall. Without a trace of fear, he strode up to their leader, ignoring the bared blades pointed in his direction.

'No admission without a ticket,' he announced, 'and weapons must be left in the cloakroom. The show isn't until tomorrow night, so until then, get your arses out of my theatre.'

Definitely the director, I thought.

The leader of the bravos looked oddly discomfited by the man's officious tone. 'We, sir, are lawfully deputised . . . um . . . deputies.' His fingers reached up to brush the iron flower brooch pinned to the collar of his leather vest. 'We've come to retrieve this fugitive from justice, Damelas Chademantaigne, who must face . . . um . . . justice in—'

The director barely spared a glance at me. 'If what you're so ineptly trying to convey is that you've brought a *criminal* into my theatre, then you'd best have him out of here before I bring suit against your duelling court for wasting my company's valuable and much-needed' – he turned to glare at his players – '*rehearsal* time.'

That's it for me then, I thought helplessly. *Just my bad luck that I've stumbled into the one theatre in the city where the Directore Principale bothers to show up for rehearsals.*

'Right then,' said the leader of the Iron Orchids. He nodded to two of his henchmen, who grinned in response and, with entirely too much eagerness, advanced on me.

'A moment.'

The voice was so soft, so unexpectedly gentle, that it took a moment for me to realise it had come from the burly red-haired man, Beretto. There was an oddly whimsical look in his eye as he stared down at me. 'Your family name is Chademantaigne? Truly?'

'What's a Shad-a-man-tayn?' asked Teo.

'A Greatcoat,' Beretto replied, 'but not just *any* Greatcoat. Our new friend here appears to be a descendant of one of the most celebrated duelling magistrates in history!'

The leader of the bravos took another step, his three-foot-long single-edged sidesword held ready to thrust as his free hand reached for my throat.

I'm not letting them take me, I swore to myself as I prepared for the bite of that blade. *If I must die, let it be in a place like this, where grand tales of courage and daring were once told, not some cold and brutal duelling court.*

But then a strange kind of miracle happened. It wasn't the kind like in heroic sagas, where a magic axe or a great flying eagle appears just when you need it, but far rarer: the actor, Beretto, a stranger with no cause to help an obvious liar who'd snuck inside his home to cheat his way out of a duel, stepped between me and the twelve mercenaries.

Despite their greater numbers, the Iron Orchids hesitated. Their leader, forced to tilt his head back to meet the big man's gaze, warned him, 'Best you back off, *player*.'

'What in all the Hells are you doing, Beretto?' the director asked.

'Forgive me, Lord Director,' he replied evenly, and his right hand reached surreptitiously to the hilt of a short, curved and very genuine-looking blade sheathed at the back of his belt. 'Have you forgotten you hired our new colleague . . . um . . .'

'Damelas,' I supplied quickly.

'Really?' he asked.

I nodded. My given name isn't of any particular consequence unless you happen to know the history of the Greatcoats. Damelas Chademantaigne, my distant forebear, was reputed to have been the first of the King's sword-fighting magistrates to take up the long leather duelling coat that became their mantle of office.

'Right,' Beretto went on, seamlessly, 'as I was saying, Lord Director, you hired Damelas here for the role of the herald, remember? We can't very well put on a historia without one – therefore, with much regret, we must invoke the operato's prerogative to withdraw him from any legal disputes that might interfere with the show.'

The director tilted his head sideways to stare at me. 'I recall no such thing. When did I—?'

'Enough!' interrupted the leader of the Iron Orchids. His underlings were glaring at him dubiously, their expressions suggesting they might be reconsidering his qualifications to boss them about. 'No one gives a fuck about some obscure theatrical entitlement, and no one's going to stand in the way of us retrieving our fugitive. This one's bound for the Vixen's den tonight!'

Beretto stepped aside, and I assumed he'd gone as far as he could on my behalf and now I was properly screwed. I panicked, tried to take my first step on what would undoubtedly be a shorter run than the last, only to collapse while choking back a scream of agony courtesy of my now visibly swollen ankle. I was saved a swift and unpleasant face-first encounter with the oak floorboards when Beretto grabbed the back of my shirt and pulled me upright.

'Well,' he went on as if nothing had happened, 'I suppose if our esteemed Directore Principale has decided that the ancient privileges of the theatre no longer hold sway in the sacred city of Jereste . . .'

The leader of the bravos gestured for him to move aside, then signalled for two of his fellows to take me away – but Beretto's words must have contained some ancient magic incantation, and one even more potent than the sort that turns perfectly courageous fugitives into cowering rabbits, for they transformed the unprepossessing director into a raging dragon.

I half expected him to start spitting fire as he commanded the bravos, '*Step. Back. NOW!*'

The trio of Orchids halted their advance, which was apparently not sufficient for the director.

'Anyone who *isn't* an actor in the Company of the Knights of the Curtain,' he began, every consonant cutting like a sword's blade, 'will answer to me, Hujo Shoville, Directore Principale of the Operato Belleza, the greatest theatre in the greatest city in the world. Make no mistake: before the night is out, I will *personally* see to it that any such knaves will find themselves on their knees in front of the Duke of Pertine himself. By morning, those who dared test my will shall find themselves exiled for ever to that filthy, barbaric wilderness that is the world outside Jereste's fair walls – but not before they have been dragged, bound, gagged and tarred through the streets, so that their fellow unwashed denizens may hurl upon them such refuse as shall clothe them on their final journey into the void!'

You had to admire the unwavering determination the leader of the bravos displayed in his zeal to drag me back to the courthouse: even in the face of the little director's flurry of verbal thrusts, he attempted one last parry. Holding up the metal brooch on his collar, he declared, 'You can't threaten us! We're the Iron Orchids!'

Shoville, who had clearly been a passionate if perhaps melodramatic actor in his own day, grabbed the end of the nearest bravo's blade and pulled it to his chest. 'Then strike, you blackguards – put steel to your words and let's you and I meet the good God Death together!'

Still clutching his iron orchid, their leader stammered, 'But . . . but . . . you said it yourself: this man isn't even one of your actors—'

'I said no such thing!' Shoville roared imperiously. He let go of the bravo's sword and clapped a hand on my shoulder. 'Look closely, you near-sighted nincompoops, for before you stands my latest discovery: a veritable star in the making. My newest protégé, Dam . . . Damo . . .'

'Damelas Chademantaigne,' Beretto offered.

'Shut up,' the director muttered. 'I'll deal with you later.' He advanced on the bravos, forcing them to yield the field or murder him in cold blood, and as the last of them backed out of the rehearsal hall, he declared, with furious conviction and improbable certitude, 'Mark this day, you ignorant poltroons, for I'll lay odds against every pauper's penny in your purses that by this time next year, Damelas Chademantaigne will be the most famous actor in the entire duchy!'

Regrettably, that turned out to be true.

One Year Later . . .

PART THE FIRST

The Herald

In which our

HERO,

having fled a LAWFUL DUEL,

discovers the life of an actor leads to far

DEADLIER TRIALS

CHAPTER 2

THE HERO OF THE ALLEY

Steel clashed against steel, catching the torchlight and illuminating the grim faces of the two duellists. The chime of rapier blades echoed between the crumbling walls that loomed over the alley like old men leaning in for a better view. Soft leather boot heels slapped against the uneven ground as heaving breaths filled the chill twilight air with mist.

'How many times must we cross swords on this same battlefield, you blood-eyed bastard?' asked Prince Pierzi, delivering a thrust with such deadly precision the tip of his weapon could have cleaved the wings from a fly.

His nemesis, Corbier, called the Red-Eyed Raven for his black hair and disturbing crimson irises, batted the blade aside, returning the promise of violence in kind with a trio of rapid ripostes. 'A dozen times – perhaps a hundred? A thousand?'

The prince laughed, deftly parrying the attack without giving so much as an inch of ground. 'Then by all the saints, let this be our last!'

He sank into a long lunge, his rapier darting like the head of a snake at his enemy's throat. But if Pierzi fenced like a saint blessed by the gods, then surely Corbier was the devil himself, beating aside every attack with such force that both blades bent in the exchange.

'Not so hard, damn it,' I muttered, barely audible above the clatter and clang of our rapiers. 'These things aren't cheap, you know!'

My bloodthirsty adversary stepped back and petulantly stamped her foot on the broken cobblestone. 'It's not my fault, Damelas. Why'd you bring such crap swords?'

'Stay in character,' I hissed through my teeth.

'Right. Right.'

The sandy-haired, grimy-faced girl playing the part of Corbier resumed her haughty posture and brought her sword back for a mighty slash. 'And now you die, Pierzi! Among the dead of this hill shall your flesh be picked clean by the cows!'

'*Crows!*'

The Dread Archduke Corbier stopped to glance around for the loose pages of the script, idly scratching at her grubby neck with an even grubbier finger. 'I thought it said cows.'

A cackle erupted from our audience, seated on the chill ground of the alley with their backs against the wall. 'Cows eat grass, not bones, yer stupid child,' said a particularly greasy-faced old man, spraying crumbs from the heel of bread he'd just stuffed into his mouth.

'Don't you go pickin' on our Zina now,' warned Grey Mags. 'Girl's doin' her best.' Gnarled hands halted in their knitting as bleary eyes glared up at me. 'Far too much talkin' in this play, if you ask me, "Prince Pietro", and not enough fightin'.'

Murmurs of assent rose up from motley assembly of beggars, bone-pickers, pigeon-catchers and cheapjacks who stood, sat or simply sprawled across the cracked cobblestone alley.

'Pierzi,' I sighed. 'I'm playing Prince *Pierzi*.'

Grey Mags wrinkled her face. 'Poncey name. Should go with Pietro. Sounds more regal.'

Several of the alley-rats enthusiastically joined in, shouting out names they thought would be even better.

'You can't go making up a historical prince's name,' I insisted, struggling to make myself heard over their raucous debate. 'Nevino Pierzi was the *actual* ruler of this duchy a hundred years ago!'

'Right, right,' agreed Grey Mags, with obvious disappointment. 'So, is it true the actor playin' him – the proper one, mind, not you – is going to conjure his dead spirit right there on the stage? The ghost of Prince Pietro himself, appearing during the show?'

'*Pierzi!* – and that's not really how it wo—'

I was cut off when Zina launched without warning into the next part of the scene. 'And *I* am Archduke Corbier, the Red-Eyed Raven!' she announced, the blade of her rapier sweeping back and forth in a flurry of boisterous attacks. 'At long last will I revenge myself upon you, abdominal Pierzi.'

'*Abominable*,' I corrected.

'Abominable!' she declared proudly. 'In the name of my love, whom you murdered most foul, the bountiful Lady Ajelaine—'

'No, no,' I said, although by then I was forced to fall back under the onslaught of Zina's surprisingly effective slashes. What the girl lacked in skill she more than made up for in enthusiasm. 'It was *Corbier* who murdered Ajelaine – and she was betrothed to the prince. Pierzi's the *hero*!'

'Don't look like no hero to me,' the gap-toothed codger muttered, collecting up the fallen crumbs and popping them into his mouth. 'Full-grown man getting his arse handed to him by a slip of a girl barely ten years old?'

'Twelve,' Zina corrected angrily, pressing her attack with even greater gusto.

'Ha! You're a liar!' chortled Vadris the drug-pedlar. The young man's heavy jowls quivered with satisfaction as he arranged dozens of tiny glass vials on the faux velvet interior of the wooden box strapped against his ample belly. 'Guess you're no better an actor than that floppy-haired bit-player over there is a duellist!'

So much for my efforts to share a little bit of the magic of the theatre with those never allowed inside its walls because they couldn't afford a ticket. Having Vadris there only increased my frustration: the drug-pedlar was a tick in fancy clothes who feasted on the blood of his hosts and left nothing but a nasty itch in return. He pretended to share the camaraderie of the alley-rats, yet never failed to belittle and demean them at every opportunity. There were rumours that he was expanding his business from hawking vials of pleasure-peppers and dreamweed to offering rent-boys and girls to his favourite customers.

'Could pass for twelve with the right make-up, though,' he murmured, eyeing Zina as she continued to harry me mercilessly with her rapier. 'Maybe even thirteen.'

Bile rose in my throat and with it, a reckless fury that threatened to wipe away twelve months of sincere efforts on my part to avoid provoking anyone to stick a blade in my back.

'Keep ogling the girl like that, Vadris, and I'll blacken your eyes for you!'

'Aha!' Zina cheered, her freckled, mud-specked face beaming with victorious mischief. 'That's not the line! Now who's forgetting to stay in character, *Prince Pierzi*?'

'Best you not threaten me or my business, oh "Knight of the Curtain",' Vadris warned me. He rubbed his knuckles on the grey metal brooch newly adorning the lapel of his garish blue brocade coat. 'Joined up with the Iron Orchids, I 'ave. We ain't afraid to fight for the workin' man's right to earn his living.'

Iron Stink-Blooms is more like it, I thought, but managed to keep from saying it out loud. The city was getting crueller by the day. In the poorer districts, there were beatings and even murders every night, and now these damned Iron Orchids were cropping up like weeds on every street corner. *Who in the Hells gave them the right to enforce their so-called 'citizen justice' on those barely surviving at the margins?*

Grey Mags snorted. 'More like fightin' for his right to get drunk and parade through the streets demanding the duke open more alehouses.' She looked up from her knitting. 'Who recruited a lazy lump like you, anyway?'

Vadris looked oddly discomfited by the question. He tried to recover his composure with a smarmy smile, bringing his thumb to his lips in an odd gesture. 'Shhh . . .' he whispered loudly. 'Can't go revealin' the secrets of the Orchids to a bunch of alley-rats now, can I?'

'Ha!' Mags barked, spotting the drug-pedlar's unease. 'You see that? Vadris don't even know who recruited him! Probably some 'weed addict tricked him into giving up a free vial!'

Their laughter enraged the drug-pedlar, who drew himself to his full – if not very impressive – stature and warned, 'Just you wait and see!' Jabbing a stubby finger at each of them in turn, he declared, 'Times are changin' in Jereste. You mark my words: the Iron Orchids don't take no shite from the Violet Duke with his so-called reforms, so you can bet we won't take any from a bunch of worthless alley-rats!' He turned his glare on me, his mouth widening in a toothy grin. 'You think me mates 'ave forgotten about the 'alf-an-ale player who scurried away from a lawful duel? Them "theatrical prerogatives" you hide be'ind? Well, just you remember: they only protect you from the Vixen so long as you're officially part of the operato's company – so guess what 'appens when your contract runs out . . . *Rabbit*?'

My mouth turned dry as dust, but I didn't even get the chance to fumble for a retort because suddenly Zina struck my rapier with such force that it flew from my hand and went clattering on the cobblestones behind me. The worn heel of my right boot slipped and I fell backwards, landing unheroically on my arse. That's when I felt the stinging wound on my forearm where Zina's tip had pierced my skin – and worse, the sleeve of the billowing Lord's shirt I'd borrowed from the costume room without permission. The bright bloom of blood on the white silk filled me with horror, though not nearly as much as the squeal of rusty hinges behind me.

'What in the name of the good Gods Love and Craft is going on out here?' boomed the irate voice from the open stage door.

I looked up at my employer – quite possibly soon to be my *former* employer – looming over me.

'Now, who's this paunchy blatherer supposed to be?' asked Grey Mags, slapping her knitting needles onto the cobblestones in frustration. 'There're too many characters in this play, if you ask me!'

'I, madam, am Hujo Shoville, Directore Principale of the Operato Belleza, home to the Knights of the Curtain and the stage upon which the greatest plays in all of history have seen their finest performances—'

'What, that shithole?' the old man next to Mags asked, pointing to the rear of the theatre.

Truth be told, the Operato Belleza *had* seen better days. The Lords of Laughter in their little *teatro* down the street now drew bigger crowds than the Knights of the Curtain. Even the Grim Jesters were outselling us of late.

I rose to my feet, hastily hiding my bleeding arm behind my back. 'Forgive me, Lord Director, we were just—'

'Is that one of *my* props being swung about willy-nilly by that tangle-haired imp?' Shoville demanded. He reached over to retrieve the rapier, but Zina showed him the sharp end.

'Away, thou villainous valet,' she said, giving the blade a flourish.

Shoville frowned. '*Valet?*'

'Varlet,' I explained. 'Sir, if you'll allow me to . . . You see, we were – that is to say, *I* was – simply promoting tonight's play, as you so often tell us is expected of your actors.'

'By giving away my props so they can be sold for liquor and pleasure-peppers?'

'Don't drink liquor, don't use no drugs,' Zina said, keeping the point at Shoville's belly. 'Don't take no shite from pompous arseholes, neither.'

Saint Ebron-who-steals-breath, I swore silently, *I know you're supposed to be dead yourself now, but if you could see your way to killing me before this gets any worse, I'll be eternally in your debt . . .*

'You. Damelas' – the director turned away from the girl – 'will retrieve my props, make damned sure you polish and straighten the blades, and . . .' He paused and leaned closer, his eyes narrowing. '*Why* are you hiding your arm behind your back?'

He didn't wait for an explanation but grabbed me by the wrist and spun me around. '*Blood!*' he declared, his strident denunciation echoing across the alley as though this were the play's climax. 'You shall have this resewn and cleaned to perfection by a proper seamstress – and from your own wages, mind!'

'But Lord Director,' I stammered, 'that will cost more than my earnings for the week – and my rent is ten days over—'

'One more word, you talentless supernumerary, and you'll be out on the street with the rest of these alley-rats. You think it's hard for me to find another—?' He stopped, only now noticing that all eyes were upon him. For an instant he'd been guilty of forgetting that most ancient showman's dictate: never undersell the skills and reputations of your actors.

Zina coughed and tilted her head at me in an unsubtle reminder of the promise I'd made earlier.

Oh, please, no, not now – he'll terminate my contract on the spot if I dare to ask . . .

Zina's plaintive pout was unwavering.

But I did promise her. However else I'd demeaned my lineage, I wouldn't add to those disgraces by going back on my word to a girl whose future was even bleaker than my own.

I turned to Shoville. 'Forgive me, Lord Director, but I was thinking, this one here' – I pointed at Zina, who promptly nodded to the even smaller boy sitting beside Grey Mags – 'these *two*, I mean, show quite a bit of promise, and you know how we've been having trouble staging the children for the battlefield scene? Well, I thought perhaps you might consider—'

'Have you quite lost your wits, man?' Shoville cried. 'You're telling *me* how to cast my shows now?'

'You wouldn't need to pay them, sir,' I went on, my odds of success shrinking by the second, 'if the two of them could – well, just eat with the cast . . . and perhaps study the actors—'

'*Study*? As if the skill, the craft, the discipline, nay, the *art* of the theatre could ever be learned from mere *players*?' Rising fury was turning his face crimson and I thought for sure I'd gone too far.

But Shoville's feral glare sought out Zina and the little boy she always claimed somewhat unconvincingly was her brother. The pair of them gazed up at the director wide-eyed, with that unique alchemical mixture of despair and hope that only street urchins can truly master.

'Please, your Lordship!' Zina said, suddenly the very embodiment of terrified innocence. 'You don't know what it's like out here on the streets at night – don't leave us to the mercy of the Iron Orchids.' Her eyes filled with tears as she added, 'Or the Black Amaranth . . .'

A pity my own masters at drama school never taught me to deliver my lines so convincingly, I thought.

'The Black Amaranth?' Shoville harrumphed. 'I hardly think the Duke of Pertine's personal assassin goes around hunting alley-rats.' His narrowed eyes suggested that he wasn't fooled by Zina's performance one bit. However, he did need child players for the battle scene . . .

'Well, now.' He took a tentative step across the alley, looking as wary of the cracked cobblestones as if he were walking on slippery rocks in the middle of a raging river. 'Let us see what we have here.'

I felt a brief stirring of hope. Shoville, for all his propensity towards righteous indignation, *loved* actors – he adored them more than the audience, more than the money, more even than the theatre itself.

'You' – Shoville waved a hand negligently at me – 'get inside with my props and see what Neddy can do with that shirt, while I shall see who here is naught but a filthy guttersnipe, and who, perhaps – just *perhaps* – might have the spark the gods gave to those they hold most beloved of all humanity.'

'Saints?' Zina suggested.

'*Actors*,' Shoville corrected. 'Yes,' he said, staring down at her, 'let us determine whether, with the tutelage of a master directore, you might one day be worthy to walk the boards of the Operato Belleza alongside the finest performers of our age.'

'"Finest performers of our age"?' Vadris scoffed. 'Wot – like that russet-haired fop there?' He jerked a thumb at me. 'Who's 'e supposed to be playin', then?'

'Damelas has no fewer than three roles,' Shoville said expansively. 'The humble page, who brings the great Prince Pierzi soup, that his hunger may be slaked. The noble herald who vows to spread word of the prince's triumphs. And a . . .' The director hesitated, struggling to give weight to the third role. 'And a wise crone who . . . who with *great* gentleness and care . . . sweeps the floor of the throne room—'

'Hah!' Vadris laughed. 'A crone?' He shot me a victorious sneer. 'And 'ere you were, pretendin' to be the prince hisself.'

'No small parts, my good man,' Shoville said, although even his exceptional talent for embellishment proved inadequate to sell that particular line.

What little dignity I'd had sufficiently extinguished, I bent down, picked up my rapier, took the other from Zina's hand and climbed the steps to the stage door.

No small parts, I thought bitterly, *but plenty of shitty ones.*

And how long could such paltry roles keep me out of the Vixen's clutches?

CHAPTER 3

THE DRESSING ROOM

Nowhere could the glamorous illusions of the theatre be so easily swept away as in the gloomy corridors backstage. The filthy walls were cracked, chipped and dented from years of clumsy or frantic stagehands manhandling costumes, props and sets from the stores to the stage and back, night after night. The dressing rooms were cramped and musty, the wooden floors worn and stained by generations of actors pacing as they mumbled their lines or bemoaned their lot in life.

Then there were the mice.

I sometimes wondered if the mice at the Belleza had, over the decades, come to emulate the characteristics of their fellow inhabitants. Any time one of us tried to chase them away, they reared up on their back legs and spewed lengthy monologues in sanctimonious squeaking. There were days when their strident little performances were at least as credible as some of my fellow actors' – or my own, for that matter.

Yet for all its deficiencies, I'd come to adore the Operato Belleza and its misfit troupe. Whenever performance time drew near, the place hummed with anxious energy, as if everything the actors and stagehands would do during that brief time between the curtain rising and falling *mattered* to the world outside. The sense of purpose and the camaraderie created by those moments made the tarnished copper tears of a player's wages sparkle like gold.

Of course, not everyone in the company shared in our noble poverty. Although even the smallest of the dressing rooms had to be shared by several actors, there was one, as opulent as a ducal bedchamber, reserved for a single occupant.

Well, most of the time. Even out here in the hall, I couldn't escape the female cooing playing counterpoint to the baritone moans of Ellias Abastrini. I'd come to shut the door – left ajar on purpose, as if Abastrini's grunting lovemaking was a performance from which lesser actors should learn – but as I skulked outside, I couldn't help but wonder what it would feel like to be worthy of such luxurious quarters.

'Makes one dream of becoming a Veristor, doesn't it?' Beretto whispered behind my shoulder.

I nearly jumped out of my skin. 'Did your mother never teach you it's rude to sneak up on people?'

Beretto's boyish grin didn't quite manage to mask his wit and intelligence. 'And what was it *your* mother said about spying on innocent, hard-working actors just trying to get in a good rutting before the show?'

Innocent? Hard-working? 'It doesn't bother you?' I blurted out, then lowered my voice to a whisper; not that Abastrini or his companions would pay us the slightest attention. 'The way he parades his preferential treatment, lording it over the rest of us, as if our sole purpose in life is to serve him goblets of wine on stage and hold his sword for him as he bellows through his *interminable* monologues?'

'Well, I *do* hold his sword for him as he bellows through those very same monologues,' Beretto noted. 'Just as the humble page – that's you, in case you've forgotten – serves him his wine.' He raised a thick red eyebrow mischievously. 'Although I did hear that you handed him a goblet full of stage blood last night . . .'

'He'd got drunk and pissed on the floor of our dressing room an hour before the show, Beretto!'

'And so was justice done.' He clapped a hand on my shoulder. 'You should've been a Greatcoat like your grandparents, Damelas. I can see you now, riding from town to town, bringing the king's justice, righting wrongs left and . . . well, right. Fighting duels to ensure that your lawful verdicts – mostly consisting of forcing evil men to make restitution for pissing where they weren't supposed to – are mercilessly enforced.'

'Someone bring me a brandy!' Abastrini bellowed from inside the dressing room. 'And some fucking pleasure-peppers that haven't gone stale!'

'Why Shoville forces us to submit to that blowhard's every whim . . .' I let the words trail off. What business did I have complaining?

'Because he's a *Veristor*.' Beretto uttered that last word as if it could conjure lightning. He gestured to the door of Abastrini's opulent dressing room. 'He alone possesses the Bardatti's gift to summon the spirit of whichever historical figure the script demands, channelling their essence into himself and lifting our poor performance to magical heights that will leave the audience breathless, knowing that, for a brief instant, they were in the presence of the great Prince Pierzi himself.'

'Brandy!' Abastrini shouted again, even louder. 'And fetch me another rent-girl from the alley – this one's gone all floppy!'

Beretto must've caught my look of disgust. 'Have pity, Damelas. How can the magnificent Abastrini perform his Veristor miracles unless he has first experienced his own . . . spiritual release?'

'I'd channel the damned spirits, too, if they paid me as many silver grins as Abastrini gets each night.'

The temptation to kick in the door and give the bloated bastard a piece of my mind was tempered only by Abastrini's reputation for brawling in his younger days. Even in middle age, the overbearing sod was bigger, stronger and far more brutal than me. But the way he talked about the alley girls . . .

'Let it go,' Beretto warned. 'There's already one duelling warrant awaiting you the day Shoville boots you out the back door. Best not invite a second challenge from within.'

'You know what really gets me?' I asked. 'It's that everyone *knows* there hasn't been a real Bardatti Veristor on the stage in decades. Abastrini isn't channelling Prince Pierzi; he's just changing the lines here and there. And Shoville's just as bad, keeping up the pretence because it lets him charge twice the price for tickets. Even the audience know it's fake, but they're all so desperate to sit around in their "salons" after the show, sipping wine and making their rich friends jealous at not having been there to witness the ghost of Pierzi himself appear before their very eyes on the stage. The whole thing is nothing but a piece of back-alley flimflam.'

Beretto's eyebrows rose to comical heights. '*What?* You're telling me that what happens on our stage *isn't* real? That it's some kind of . . . theatrical *performance*? Come, noble comrade – we must alert the authorities at once!'

'You should save all that talent for the stage, Beretto.'

He was gracious enough to ignore my bad temper. 'Come then, brother,' he said, throwing an arm across my shoulders and leading me down the hall. 'Let's go and run our lines.'

Our dressing room was more of a closet than anything else: deep enough to squeeze the pair of us side by side as we put on our make-up, but too narrow to pass each other without accidental intimacy. A cracked mirror on one wall boasted a narrow shelf underneath for our paltry belongings. Rusted hooks on the opposite wall held our costumes for the night. A single candle provided what little illumination was deemed necessary for two such lowly actors.

Beretto, however, was congenitally incapable of discouragement. 'Run the herald's lines,' he said, waving the script at me. 'Enthral me!'

'"*Lines*"? There's only one!'

'Wrong as usual, Damelas. There are three.' He held up the last page and pointed to an exclamation mark. 'See? They call those little squiggles "punc-tu-a-tion" – and if you expect our esteemed director to renew your contract and keep the Vixen's teeth from your throat, you'd best learn how to deliver your lines with gusto.'

'Fine.' I placed one hand on my heart and raised the other as if to a distant hill. 'Hark, my Lord!'

Beretto nodded, wide-eyed, fanning himself with the script as if overcome by my performance. 'Yes, yes – now we're talking.'

'"Thou hast defeated the enemy's champions with thine own hand!"'

'Bravasa! Fantisima!' Beretto cheered. 'Am I in the presence of a true Veristor? It's as if you've transported me to the battlefield itself! Now, the last line. Light up the stage, my friend.'

Despite my earlier foul humour, I couldn't help but get caught up in Beretto's preposterous enthusiasm, and I trumpeted proudly, '"Henceforth shall I travel these lands and to its peoples sing thine victories—!"'

Beretto's expression fell.

'What?' I asked, reaching for the script. 'Oh, shit – I did it again, didn't I?'

'*Triumphs*, man. The line is "Henceforth shall I travel these lands and to its peoples sing thine *triumphs*."'

'I still don't know why it matters so much,' I muttered, handing the pages back.

'Because anyone can eke out a victory, but a *triumph*: that's proof of a god's blessing. Besides, it's the last line of the entire play. Shoville's going to hang you from your toenails if you screw it up again.'

Saint Anlas-who-remembers-the-world, why can't I ever *get that damned line right?*

'You're a good actor, Damelas,' Beretto said, though it sounded more like admonishment than encouragement. 'Better than that overstuffed arsehole next door getting his prick polished, certainly. Your time will come.'

I stared into the mirror, saw my youth transformed by the web of cracks into a lifetime of scars. The Belleza had begun as a sanctuary to escape a foolishly accepted duel, but it had quickly become a place I cherished: a place I would have liked to call home.

But an actor's prospects are bounded by his talents, and mine had all too quickly reached their zenith. 'I'll never play kings or princes, will I?' No doubt that same tired lament had been uttered by just about every actor in the company at one point or another, yet it stung all the same. 'Never the hero, nor even the villain. I'll always be the cup-bearer, herald or crone.'

'Don't dismiss the herald,' Beretto said, pulling his tunic over his head before dressing himself in his creaking stage armour. 'The audience always pays close attention when he steps onto the stage.' His bearded reflection in the mirror took on a darkly ominous expression. 'After all, when the herald arrives, it almost always means someone's about to die.'

CHAPTER 4

THE WINGS

On a good night, with a full house, the soles of your feet vibrate as you stand in the curtained wings at each side of the stage waiting for your cue. At the Operato Belleza, the carpeted floor to which the rows of seats are bolted is braced with long planks of sturdy billy oak, the same wood used in dance halls to lend the steps of revellers extra bounce. An audience captivated by the play and its players will bob their feet up and down in rhythmic anticipation of the next unexpected revelation, daring sword thrust or passionate kiss; those tremors carry along the billy planks, all the way down the aisles and up the boards underneath the stage to the booted heels of the actors.

The air buzzes on those special nights: the gasps of especially sensitive souls at unexpected frights, the whispers of, 'No, no, please, no—' whenever a favourite character meets their end, or the, 'Yes, yes, now! Tell her!' when the hero and heroine, long separated by calamity or calumny, are at last ready to confess their love.

Upon such glorious winds even the humblest player could fly.

'Barely half a house,' Teo grumbled, shoving past me as he exited the stage after delivering his only line of the night. 'Shoville will lose the licence to the Belleza if this keeps up.'

'Then best we impress those we can,' said silver-haired Ornella, retying the laces of her bodice.

Ornella, the oldest member of the cast by a full decade, had seen her roles wither from daring princesses to conniving duchesses and now to humble serving women, and still she approached every role with the even-keeled step of a soldier marching to battle.

'Don't know why Shoville keeps the old woman around,' Teo muttered in a tone that badly wanted for a good slap across the face.

Like me, he served principally as a supernumerary, playing an unnamed soldier here, a servant there, or sometimes just a dead body needed to fill space during a battle scene. Teo's every groan and grimace before a show conveyed a sense of foiled destiny, that he was meant for grander things. But while the two of us were in perpetual competition for our meagre parts, there was one subject on which we were united.

'Fucking Abastrini,' Teo said, peering past the curtain. 'Bloated bastard's put them half asleep with all his droning. A graveyard's got more life than this crowd.'

Abastrini's reputation as a Veristor may have increased ticket prices and shielded him from otherwise much-deserved criticism of his performances, but it didn't serve his fellow actors on the stage, nor the play itself. Lately the pompous blowhard had even taken to wearing his Veristor's mark on his collar during the show. The beautifully designed silver brooch in the shape of an actor's mask with narrowed eyes and a mouth in the shape of a key was entirely out of place on Prince Pierzi's golden cloak. No doubt Abastrini wanted to prevent the audience confusing his boorish performance with ineptitude rather than some kind of mystical trance.

'Marvellous, isn't he?' Shoville asked dreamily, eyes shut as he listened to Abastrini's fifth monologue of the night. There were only three in the script. 'Simply marvellous.'

'Staggering,' I said, flinching when I realised I'd failed to sufficiently hide the sarcasm in my voice.

Shoville turned, but the reproach I'd rightfully earned gave way to unexpected concern. 'I say, Damelas, are you quite well? You look pale as a ghost.'

'Been feeling a bit off tonight, if I'm honest.'

In fact, I'd been dizzy and disoriented before every performance since we'd launched this new run of *Valour at Mount Cruxia* six weeks ago. Maybe I was suffering from some sort of fever. Maybe it was just the lousy script.

'Well, hold it together, lad,' Shoville advised. 'The herald is a vital role.'

His encouragement would have been more cheering had I not once seen him telling a stagehand who was standing in place of a tree the carpenters hadn't yet constructed, 'Magnificent. A pivotal role performed with sublime conviction!'

Shoville was clapping me on the shoulder, my earlier infractions in the alley apparently forgotten. 'Come now, boy. Give it your all – remember, 'tis your last line that will bring the audience leaping to their feet, a flush of civic pride to their cheeks as they roar out their approbation!'

Chastened by the director's inspiring tone, I determined that this time I would properly repay his faith in me.

Shake it off, Damelas, I told myself. *Your grandmother used to walk into the duelling circle on steadier legs than yours when you take the stage. All you have to do is walk out to your mark, pick up the sword waiting for you, turn to the audience and announce Prince Pierzi's 'noble victory'—*

I thumped my thigh in frustration. I couldn't even get the line right in my thoughts. 'Triumph, damn it,' I swore. '*Triumph!*'

A thunderous bellow filled the stage as Abastrini, in the role of said *triumphant* Prince, drowned out the death knell of the actor playing his nemesis as he plunged the sword into Archduke Corbier's dark heart. The poor fellow playing Corbier couldn't even get out his final words over Abastrini's newly concocted victory speech.

Triumph, I reminded myself yet again. *That stupid word is going to get me fired.*

'Oh, I almost forgot,' Shoville said cheerfully, favouring me with a sly grin. 'You've a guest in tonight's audience.'

'A guest?'

The director wagged a finger at me. 'You know I usually frown upon actors inviting their paramours to our renowned historias – unless, of course, they've purchased a ticket—'

I was simultaneously confused and horrified. 'My Lord Director, if one of the alley-rats—'

'Alley-rats?' Shoville chuckled, giving me what I suspected was meant to be an admiring wink. 'I'd hardly call the radiant vision of womanhood who introduced herself to me as Lady Ferica di Traizo an alley-rat!'

My knees buckling, I grabbed Shoville for support. 'My L-Lord Director,' I heard myself stammer, 'if this is some sort of jest, I promise you, it's in poor—'

'Jest? Don't be silly. I never jest when noble ladies deign to attend one of our performances.' His face took on a curious expression as he tapped a finger to his chin. 'That name, though. Lady Ferica di Traizo. It's familiar – and yet I cannot quite place it. Mind, she certainly possesses a rather . . . feral beauty. Tell me, lad, might this tawny-haired delight consider joining our company? I am sorely in need of a new ingénue . . .'

The nausea coiling in my belly was threatening to slither up my throat, but I choked it down. 'I fear, Lord Director, her interests lie elsewhere, for she is known by a different name throughout the city.'

'And what is this illustrious sobriquet?'

'The Vixen.'

Shoville paled when he heard the name. 'Why in the world would you bring a notorious duellist – a professional *murderer* – into my theatre?'

'That's what I've been trying to tell you! I didn't invite her!

What in the name of Saint Felsan-who-weighs-the-world was the Vixen doing at the Belleza? Ducal law forbade her from coming after me while the duelling writ between us was held in abeyance.

Unless a noblewoman with the ear of the new duke might be able to convince him to overrule that suspension . . .

Abastrini's improvised monologue finally ended with a trumpeted closing line that ought to have come ten minutes earlier.

'Damelas,' Shoville hissed, apparently now less concerned about a vicious killer in the audience than the possibility of the show running even longer, 'that's your cue, boy!'

Sick with fear, I looked down to see the reflections from the flickering flames of the hanging lanterns in the rafters above turn the boards at my feet into a miasma of fire and shadow.

'Go, noble herald!' Shoville thumped me on the back so hard I lost my balance and went reeling onto the stage. 'Make magic happen before our very eyes—'

CHAPTER 5

THREE LITTLE LINES

Silence has no substance, but it does have weight. Some silences are as light and airy as the space between the telling of a joke and the ensuing laughter. Others are heavy, the uncomfortable pause that never seems to end and which slowly drowns you beneath the depths of despair. When an actor imagines death, it is into such a silence he feels himself sinking.

'*Make magic happen before our very eyes*,' Shoville had said.

Apparently I'd done just that, for the theatre had gone so quiet I would've sworn the audience had disappeared. I couldn't tell for sure, because my eyes seemed to be resolutely shut. When I finally summoned up the courage to open them, I had to wait for the blurry scene before me to resolve. That's when I realised something very bad must have happened shortly after I'd stepped out on stage to deliver my final line.

Please, any saints who are listening, don't let me have forgotten to say 'triumphs' again. Also, please let my trousers not have fallen down . . .

The theatre *wasn't* empty, as it turned out. In fact, just as Shoville had promised, my performance had, indeed, brought the audience to their feet. But they weren't roaring with applause or even clapping politely. Instead, the assembled worthies were just standing there in their finery, staring up at me in horrified silence.

I turned to my fellow actors, but all I found in their answering gazes was confusion and shock. Well, most of them, anyway.

'You *stupid* bastard . . .' Abastrini growled *sotto voce*.

Beretto, in the role of Prince Pierzi's favoured lieutenant, put a hand on his liege's shoulder. 'The boy misspoke, my Lord.'

Misspoke? I couldn't even recall having begun my lines.

'See you, how he suffers a grievous wound to his head?' Beretto went on, speaking as confidently as if his every word came straight from the script instead of outrageous improvisation. 'Observe how the lad's eyes fail to perceive us standing here. He is blinded, my Prince, and in his confusion he feared he was witnessing vile Archduke Corbier slaying *you!*'

I watched with the same mute puzzlement as everyone else.

This can't be due to me flubbing that damned 'victories' line – No! – 'triumphs!' – so what in the name of Saint Zaghev-who-sings-for-tears did I say?

Abastrini, as though suddenly filled with divine inspiration, bounded across the stage towards me. 'I see now that you speak truly, my trusted lieutenant. The chaos of battle has robbed the poor boy of his senses. Oh, how the gods do use this foolish messenger to give us all a great warning: we must be for ever vigilant, lest history be distorted by deceivers and malefactors!' He spun on his heel to the audience, arms outstretched in supplication to the gods above. 'The truth must be told, and retold again and again for all to hear, from this day forth, across every generation!'

A few coughs and rather more groans drifted up from the audience to the stage, but most appeared at least somewhat mollified by Abastrini's hasty improvisation.

My career saved by Ellias Abastrini, I thought. *Surely the gods despise me.*

Still baffled by what I'd done wrong, I nonetheless followed his lead. I swung my head left and right, keeping my eyes unfocused. With trembling hands, I reached out blindly. 'My Prince? Is that you? Has your dread spirit come back to haunt this land even as your blood spilled upon its soil sows grief worthy of a thousand lesser souls?'

Over Abastrini's shoulder I caught Beretto rolling his eyes at me.

'Nay, faithful one,' Abastrini replied, his rich baritone rumbling with warmth. 'I am here, alive and *triumphant*. Come to me, boy. Come to your Prince, that he may embrace you.'

I made a show of following Abastrini's voice until my fingers were tracing the contours of Prince Pierzi's armoured breastplate and the distinctive sigils of his house.

Abastrini pulled me into a hug, feigning affection even as he crushed my ribs mercilessly. 'Do you still doubt me, boy? Be there any confusion as to who *I* am?'

I struggled to turn my gasps of pain into cries of joy. 'Gods be good, my Lord, it *is* you!'

With a great deal of effort, I pushed myself free from Abastrini's grasp and turned to the audience, proclaiming at last, 'Thou hast defeated the enemy's champions with thine own hand! Henceforth shall I travel these lands, every day singing of thy righteous victories!'

I caught Beretto's barely audible groan.

Triumphs! Fuck! Triumphs . . .

From behind the back curtain, a jubilant melody began to play as the musicians took up the final song. The actors on the stage, even those playing corpses, rose to sing the chorus as Abastrini and Beretto made a show of ushering me from the stage.

'You little shit!' Abastrini swore the instant we'd passed the curtains. 'Are you so very determined to put an end to your own career? And if so, would you mind not taking mine down with it?'

Beretto rescued me by pushing him aside. 'Leave him alone, man. Look at him – he's grey as a corpse. Probably has some kind of fever. Maybe syphilis.'

'Yes, that's it,' I agreed, bringing the back of my hand up to my forehead – it really was a little clammy. 'Not syphilis, I mean, but fever. A terrible, raging fever momentarily overtook me. That's the only reasonable explanation.'

Abastrini stormed off to his dressing room, leaving the pair of us in the wings while the rest of the cast sang the audience from their seats and out of the doors. The Veristor's displeasure was mirrored in the eyes of every one of my fellow castmates as they exited the stage.

'Saint Laina's tits,' Beretto swore once the two of us were alone. 'What in all the Hells was that, Damelas?'

'I . . . I honestly don't know – I remember Shoville shoving me out onto the stage to deliver the lines. I started feeling sick to my stomach, then . . . I think I might have blacked out for a moment. What did I say?'

Beretto stared at me wide-eyed with disbelief. 'You're telling me that wasn't an act? You *weren't* just quitting the business in the most spectacularly offensive way possible?'

'Beretto, what the Hells did I *do*?'

Shaking his head, his shaggy red beard trembling, he began to laugh. 'Brother, you strode right out onto the stage, picked up the sword and said – with what I should note was your most convincing performance to date – "Foul deceiver! You have lied to your people, murdered your enemy's lover, butchered his children, and now you would slay their father with that same poisoned blade. You called for a herald, you dog? Here stands your messenger! I will travel these lands and see to it that the entire world learns the truth: that you who would make yourself sovereign are naught but the vilest malefactor in all of history!"'

'That's not . . .' I stammered. 'I . . . I would never have said that!'

But in the deepest corner of my thoughts, I discovered an itch of recognition. I had no memory of uttering those treasonous words, but somehow, the lines sparked an eerie sense of déjà vu in me. This hadn't been some petty trick played on me – Shoville would as soon burn down the theatre himself as allow the Operato Belleza to be desecrated with such a prank.

What if Beretto's right, and I'm so sick of hiding from the Vixen that I just unconsciously sabotaged the theatre company that's keeping me from her clutches?

The historias – the sacred plays – were meant to bind together the people of this city and inspire them with the greatness of their shared past – and I had just committed the unpardonable sin of ruining both the play and the reputation of the Knights of the Curtain.

As the disgruntled audience sullenly made for the exits, I noticed one figure just standing there. She was dressed in flowing burgundy skirts under a tight-fitting black frock coat, her head covered by a scarlet winter cowl at odds with the warm autumn night. Even with her face hidden, my eyes, trained as they were by my duellist grandmother to recognise such things, noted the graceful, feral way she moved.

Lady Ferica di Traizo paused to blow me a kiss – no farewell, but a promise that we would soon see each other again.

CHAPTER 6

THE COSTUME CLOSET

I crouched on the floor, knees pressed to my chest, buried behind the mass of costumes hanging from the racks at the far end of the long closet. I used to come here a lot in the months following my provisional acceptance into the Knights of the Curtain, marvelling at the assortment of court gowns, uniforms, suits of tin armour and any number of glittering gossamer shrouds for those playing ghosts and spirits.

After those first perilous nights on stage, stumbling my way through the trifling parts Shoville nervously entrusted to me, I'd discovered a hunger that brought me back over and over to this odd little sanctuary. I'd spend hours rifling through the costumes, imagining myself in the starring roles: the great princes and valiant warriors – even the nefarious tyrants doomed by the gods, who, when played by the right actor, could be imbued with sympathy and even grace. Tonight, however, it was concealment I sought under the ill-fitting tunics beneath a painted sign that read *Pages & Heralds*.

'Just how long do you suppose you can hide from the Vixen inside a costume closet?' Beretto asked, pushing aside hangers and holding out a clay flagon. He swished it at me. 'Come out of there, brother. Let's get bloody drunk.'

Reflex rather than thirst had me reaching for the flagon, but Beretto abruptly pulled it away. 'Actually, probably best to keep your wits about you. You might need to flee the city now that you've ruined its most beloved historia and practically guaranteed that the Knights of the Curtain will lose our licence for the Operato Belleza to our competitors.

Not sure if it'll go to the Lords of Laughter or the Grim Jesters or even – saints forfend – those artless arse-lickers, the Red Masques.'

I buried my face in my hands. 'I've doomed us all, haven't I?'

Beretto took a swig from the flagon. 'Oh, it's not so bad, really. What theatre company needs a home when there are lovely cold streets out there filled with muggers, murderers and those thespian-loving Iron Orchids just itching to applaud our performances with their fists?'

'You really believe the duke would be so petty as to take the Belleza away from the Knights of the Curtain just because one incompetent bit-player screwed up his lines?'

'Well, this Monsegino fellow is new to his throne and I haven't made his personal acquaintance . . .' Beretto reached over to the next rack, labelled *Kings & Nobles*, lifted a hanger bearing a set of ducal robes and dangled it beneath his bearded chin. 'But you did just imply his progenitor was guilty of infanticide in front of a goodly number of the city's nobility. We were performing a historia, so, legally speaking, you accusing Prince Pierzi of murder constitutes bearing false witness. One would imagine that comes with some sort of fine, at the very least.'

A fine. Prison sentence. Possibly my tongue extracted from my mouth with iron tongs.

'By the bloody red fingernails of Saint Zaghev-who-sings-for-tears,' I swore piteously. 'What do I do now, Beretto?'

He drained the flagon, wiped a sleeve across his mouth and indulged in a lengthy series of burps before suggesting, 'You could go with the fever thing. It does get hot under those lanterns. Actors have been known to—'

'No one's going to believe it's because I had a fever.' I started banging my forehead against my knees. 'Saint Dheneph-who-tricks-the-gods, how could I have uttered such nonsense? I don't remember any of it—'

'I suppose you could plead insanity,' Beretto suggested, 'although I don't suppose that will save your career. Or your life, come to that. Insanariums tend to be rather unpleasant places, or so I've heard. I'd stick with syphilis.'

'I doubt syphilis is a compelling legal defence against charges of treasonous slander.' I forced myself to my feet and pushed my shoulders back, trying my best to emulate those brave heroes who always met their fates head-on. 'At least if the duke has me imprisoned for the next twenty years, I won't have to face the Vixen in the duelling court.'

'Unless he decides to forego a trial and send the Black Amaranth after you.' Beretto stared inside the empty wine flagon as if the answer lay hidden there. 'Funny name for an assassin. Amaranths are such pretty flowers. The petals look like little daggers.'

'Beretto, amaranth petals are notoriously poisonous.'

'Still pretty.' He turned back to me. 'Anyway, you could just run, couldn't you? Wasn't that your plan when you first came to the Belleza? Lay low long enough for the Iron Orchids to give up on their hunt so that you could flee the city?'

'It's not that simple . . .'

'Sure it is.' He made a show of pumping his arms. 'You move your arms and legs like this, see? Works best if you do it very fast.' He stopped to wag an accusatory finger at me. 'Unless there's some other reason you didn't run when you had the chance?'

I held my tongue. The duelling writ was still sealed and the fewer people who knew its contents, the better. But Beretto had proven to be a far better friend this past year than I deserved. Keeping silent now would feel like a betrayal.

'I can't leave,' I admitted at last.

Beretto mistook the confession for resolve and grinned as he clapped me on the shoulder. 'I knew it! You're an actor through and through. The siren song of this sacred place has shackled your soul to its—'

'I mean, I can't leave the city, Beretto. Ever.'

His expression became dubious. 'If you're about to claim there's a witch's curse on you . . .'

'The duelling writ I signed against the Vixen? It's a *duella honoria elegis*. Should I flee the jurisdiction without facing her, my second will be legally compelled to take my place in the circle.'

'Who in the world was foolish enough to agree to be your second? No offence, my friend, but you're not exactly the Saint of Swords and the Vixen's never lost a duel. Maybe if your grandmother Virany were still alive – the King's Parry was a legend in the duelling circle. But other than her, who would dare? . . . Oh Hells, man!'

I nodded miserably. 'My grandfather declared himself my second before I could stop him.'

'That's why you never invite him to our performances? Why you keep refusing to introduce me to him?'

'The further away he stays from me, the safer he'll be.'

Beretto's obsession with the lives of the king's travelling magistrates was no secret, and he took umbrage at my insinuation. 'Well . . . I mean, the King's Courtesy might not have been quite the duellist that your grandmother was, but he was still a Greatcoat.'

'Beretto, the man's nearly seventy years old! Paedar Chademantaigne hasn't fought a duel in more than a decade. His hands shake. The Vixen wants to lure him into the circle; that's how I got into this mess in the first place. I got word from a court clerk that she was about to issue a formal challenge against him and the only way to stop her was to provoke her into challenging me instead.'

Beretto picked a long, tattered leather coat from the rack and held it up. 'Why would the finest fencer in the city ruin her reputation by skewering a retired Greatcoat years past his prime?'

'I don't know!' I shouted, unable to contain a year's worth of shame and frustration any longer. 'She hates my family, or she hates the Greatcoats, or maybe Ferica di Traizo is a deranged lunatic who picks out her victims at random—'

'What about a formal apology to her Ladyship?' Beretto proposed, hanging the leather coat back on its rack. 'Tradition dictates the plaintiff in an affair of honour call off the duel when restitution is giv—'

'You think I haven't tried? I've sent a dozen letters – I've offered a thousand promises to prostrate myself before the entire city and praise her name to the gods. Not once have her underlings replied other than to smear the word "rabbit" on the back of the stage door in what I'm fairly certain were the ashes of those same entreaties! I'm fucked, Beretto! Absolutely, gods-damned fu—'

Beretto cut me off with a raised forefinger at the sound of footsteps coming down the hall.

'That'll be Shoville,' he warned. 'Listen, if he yells at you, it's a good sign, so just keep your mouth shut.'

'Right,' I said, smoothing my shirt and straightening my back, though I had no idea what good it would do me.

'If he starts pummelling you, that's even better,' Beretto went on. 'Directors hate looking like vindictive pricks, so he wouldn't push you out of the door covered in bruises in case that makes the rest of the cast sympathetic to your plight.'

'What if he's nice to me?' I asked, though such an outcome was supremely unlikely at this point.

Beretto let out a long, slow whoosh of air. 'If he's nice to you, brother, then you really are fucked.'

A knock at the door, then the creak of the hinges as it swung open. Shoville's expression betrayed neither anger, nor violence, nor kindness. He looked terrified. 'Damelas, I'm sorry, but you have to come with me.'

Beretto stepped in to intervene on my behalf. 'My Lord Director . . .'

I'd never heard him address Shoville by that lofty title.

'Most esteemed and cherished Directore,' he added, pouring even more honey on his words, 'there's something you must know about Damelas before you fire him. He wasn't himself, you see. He fell victim to' – in drunken moments, Beretto fancies himself a playwright. Alas, he's not all that good at it – 'a spell, my Lord!' he declared, becoming increasingly animated as he embellished his tale. 'A hideous, pustule-faced witch— No – no! A warlock! Yes, that's it – a warlock! Bloody Hells, that's good.'

My slightly inebriated defender began gesticulating wildly, nearly knocking over a rack of animal costumes as he stabbed a finger at the rear wall. 'Saw the vile necromancer myself, out in the alley – strange sigils he drew, a circle made of blood poured from the slit throat of a dying cat! "Damelas Chademantaigne," I heard him intone, his voice colder than a corpse's heart. "I curse thee with this most foul spe—"'

'What on earth are you babbling about?' Shoville asked, looking at Beretto as if he hadn't heard a word the actor had said. Our usually jovial director was looking so pale, hands trembling at his sides, that I worried he might be having a heart attack. 'My Lord Director, are you—'

'You must come with me, Damelas,' he repeated. A look of terrible sympathy came to his features. 'There are soldiers waiting in the lobby. The duke's personal guards have come to arrest you.'

CHAPTER 7

THE CARRIAGE RIDE

With perfunctory menace, the duke's soldiers ushered me out of the theatre and into a sturdy black carriage with barred windows. Midnight had come and gone hours ago and the streetlamps had long since exhausted their oil. Silence had replaced the evening's usual raucous revelry. The stumbling drunks had been escorted home by their more sober friends, or left to the disputable mercy of pickpockets and other less savoury malefactors.

I sat in darkness. The guards had ridden ahead on horseback and whoever was driving the carriage refused to answer when I banged on the roof. I twisted sideways on the stiff wooden bench and grabbed the blackened iron bars on my right, knowing I had as much chance of prying them open as I had of turning into a hummingbird and flying out between them.

'Only an amateur tries to escape through the bars,' said a quiet voice opposite me.

I nearly jumped out of my seat. My fists instinctively came up to protect my face. I don't count myself much of a pugilist – no one else does either, for that matter – but when I was a boy, my grandmother had insisted I familiarise myself with the hand-to-hand techniques employed by the Greatcoats.

'Show yourself!' I demanded.

The figure in the shadows sat so still that even now I wondered if I'd really heard anyone speak, or if this was a phantom come to ferry me to the Afterlife.

'Shall we engage in fisticuffs?' she asked. The woman leaned into the meagre moonlight slipping through the bars. A black veil covered her face, but the fabric was gossamer-thin, revealing high cheekbones and a wide mouth. Her smooth skin gave her face the appearance of an exquisitely cast copper mask. When she spoke, however, the smile that came to her lips was all too alive.

'I have my doubts as to your chances,' she observed, covering my pale fist with her much darker hand. 'Your knuckles feel far too delicate for such blunt violence.'

'My Lady,' I stammered, so relieved to find that this wasn't the Vixen come to demand her duel from me that I struggled to compose myself. My grandfather, however, is a notorious flirt, and his own lessons were as rigorous in their fashion as my grandmother's had been.

The merest brush of the lips, Damy – quick enough to entice her if she likes you, not so long as to embarrass her if she doesn't. And no slobbering!

I quickly turned over my travelling companion's hand and kissed the back of it before saying, 'I present myself to you as Damelas Chademantaigne, a Knight of the Curtain, player in the company of the Operato Belleza, and now your servant.'

The woman's smile grew. 'A knight? A player? A servant? I suspect you are none of those things.' She turned my wrist and kissed the back of my hand as I'd done to hers. 'But I do admire your spirit.'

Her lips had been soft on my skin, but her grip on my fingers was disturbingly strong.

'Might this poor spirit learn your name?' I asked.

She let me have my hand back and sat up straight to gaze out the window. 'I fear you wouldn't have time to make much use of it.'

My attempts at nonchalance were chased away by gnawing dread: the alluring features, the dark skin, the preternatural stealthiness and even the unexpected courtesy she'd shown me . . . I was dead certain I knew who was occupying the seat opposite.

For months, rumours had swirled around the city that Firan Monsegino, only recently elevated to the ducal throne of Pertine, had made it his practice to have his enemies assassinated by a beautiful, mysterious woman who would engage the victim in a brief, altogether charming conversation prior to sending them to their gods. The joke – which didn't seem all that funny now – was that while a new and untested duke couldn't afford to be merciful, Monsegino was nonetheless determined to be gracious to his guests, no matter how short a time they enjoyed his hospitality. If there was one person in all of Jereste to fear more than the Vixen, it was surely the woman sitting across from me at this very moment.

The Black Amaranth, I thought miserably. *The duke sent the deadliest assassin in the country to execute me for screwing up my lines in a damned historia?*

'An especially warm autumn we're having, don't you think?' she asked, dipping her fingers through the bars to feel the night breeze.

Watch those hands, I told myself, determined that if this was to be my end, I wouldn't go down without a fight – no matter how brief my defiance turned out to be.

Any defence I might have contemplated was overtaken by a strangled cry from outside the carriage. I peered through the bars and saw, in the streets beyond, a fellow in tanner's leathers curled up on the ground, arms covering his head as a trio of thugs took turns beating him with wooden cudgels and lengths of chain, all the while jeering at him. Even in the near-darkness, I would have sworn I caught the glint of polished grey brooches on their collars.

The Iron Orchids were at it again.

'*Emzy!*' the injured man called out to me. '*Emzy mi! Emzy mi!*'

The words were foreign, but while I didn't recognise the language, their meaning was plain enough.

'Stop the carriage!' I called out, pounding my fist on the ceiling of the carriage. The driver paid me no heed and the horses continued their unhurried clop-clopping along the street. 'Stop, damn you!' I shouted a second time. 'We've got t—'

'The driver will not halt the carriage until we reach our destination,' the Black Amaranth informed me. 'He does not work for you.'

'Then *you* order him to stop!' I yelled, momentarily forgetting that this was not a woman I should be provoking.

Sounding untroubled by my outburst, leaning back in her seat, she said, 'The driver does not work for me, either.'

Outside the carriage, not ten yards from us, the Iron Orchids were proceeding with their beating of the tanner in the same leisurely fashion as the bloody horses kept plodding along.

'Does the duke care nothing for his subjects, then?' I asked.

The Black Amaranth paid my second act of rebellion no more attention than the first. 'What would you do,' she asked, 'if the driver were to stop the carriage and I allowed you to venture out into the night? How would that serve this nameless stranger whose welfare concerns you so?'

'Can't you see? Those damned Iron Orchids are beating that poor bastard half to death!'

'I did not ask what *they* were doing. I asked what *you* would do. I see no sword at your side, nor are you possessed, so far as I have heard, of the necessary skills or inclination to wield a blade when the occasion demands. So again, I ask, how would you go about rescuing the man?'

Her question cut me deeper than whatever knife she no doubt intended on sticking into my belly when we reached our destination. 'I'd . . . I don't know what I'd do. It shouldn't be up to a third-rate actor to defend the helpless in this city! Why isn't your bloody duke doing *his* job and protecting his subjects?'

'He is your duke, too,' she reminded me. 'And perhaps in such unfortunate matters, he finds himself as helpless as you.'

'Oh, please. I've attended a dozen productions of *A Lonesome Lord's Lament*, my Lady – I even played the chamberlain in one production – and it's a poor play indeed. Even if our new monarch is too timid to do his duty, you're supposed to be the Black Amaranth, aren't you? The assassin even other assassins fear? Why couldn't *you* stop those thugs?'

'Because I am not here for them, Damelas Chademantaigne. I am here for you.'

I am here for you.

My breath caught in my throat. The gentle way she'd uttered those words sent a tremble through my limbs, yet for all that, the anger inside me burned unabated. 'If you were sent to kill me, my Lady, then do so now. I have a distaste for predators who play with their food.'

'Truly?' she asked, her voice suddenly curious. 'For a man who fled a duel a mere twelve months ago, you seem in a great hurry to die. Is it hidden valour that makes you reckless, I wonder, or the inability to live with the memory of a single, entirely understandable act of faint-heartedness?'

The carriage rolled on and the sounds of the beating faded, leaving only the echoes of the bully-boys' laughter. They'd have allowed the tanner to slink away by now, slapping each other on the back and commending one another for defending Jereste from the scourge of foreigners, street urchins and other deadly threats to our glorious way of life. Scenes like this one were playing out nightly across the city.

The Black Amaranth was right: had I tried to intervene, all I'd have accomplished would have been to enrage the Iron Orchids, probably ensuring both the tanner and I ended up crippled or dead. When I looked back at her, she was sitting quietly, one leg crossed over the other, gloved hands on her knees. Beneath that comfortable stillness, was she contemplating the moment and manner of my death?

'*If there's no key to your cell and no sword with which to defeat the guard,*' my grandfather would have advised me, '*then fight with your words. You're good with words, Damy, and the right ones can confound the enemy as surely as the sharpest blade.*'

'We were discussing the weather, I believe?' I asked with forced casualness. 'I do believe your earlier observation was astute, my Lady; I myself am finding the temperature unseasonably warm.'

She laughed, and in doing so accidentally revealed something to me. I had never been the most sought-after player in any of the three drama schools from which I'd been dismissed, but I had picked up a few tricks here and there. An actor must develop an ear for accents, and although this woman's Tristian was as flawless as her composure, her laughter carried a hint of something more distant.

'You aren't from this country, are you?' I asked.

At first I wondered if perhaps she hadn't heard me, but then she propped her elbow against her knee and rested her chin in her palm. 'You are most perceptive,' she said at last. 'Paying attention is a useful talent – one lost on most of the residents of this city.'

An interesting choice of words, I thought. How much *use* could my attentiveness possibly be if she were minutes away from driving a stiletto between my ribs? A desperate optimism threatened to overwhelm me.

'Does this mean you're not planning to ki—?'

'But you talk too much,' she observed, watching me so intently now that I worried she might be reading the thoughts scattered in my head. 'And soon we will see whether your wits can outpace your mouth.'

'What do you mean?'

'The events at the Operato Belleza this evening,' she said, as if my interrogation was now beginning in earnest. 'Were you paid to alter your lines?'

'Only the five copper tears I receive as an actor in the comp—'

'Your grandparents were Greatcoats,' she went on, cutting me off. 'The King's Travelling Magistrates were known for their seditious attitudes to ducal powers. Perhaps you seek to follow in their footsteps, raising doubts about the Duke of Pertine's lineage? Or do you really expect his Grace to believe some lost spirit from the past speaks through you?'

'My Lady, I'm no Veristor, any more than I'm a Greatcoat. I'm just an actor, not even a particularly good one. I've no interest in rebellions and, frankly, couldn't care less whether Duke Monsegino's ancestor was a glorious hero, a notorious child-slayer or a one-legged pig farmer. My grand scheme consists of nothing more than keeping myself fed and remaining part of the Operato Belleza's company until the Vixen loses interest in me.'

She leaned closer to me, so close I inhaled the scent of her, and I noted that, unlike almost everyone else in this city, she wore no exotic perfumes or fragrances. Oddly, I found that all the more intoxicating.

'Skilled actors can live long, comfortable lives in this city, I'm told,' she said then, 'provided they learn to play the roles assigned them.'

The carriage came to a stop. When I looked outside the barred window, I was greeted by the façade of a broken-down three-storey tenement that looked as if the only things holding it up were the similarly decrepit buildings on either side. The Black Amaranth had taken me on a loop of the city, only to bring me to the apartment I shared with Beretto, barely a half mile from the theatre.

'Better than being dumped off at a prison,' I muttered.

'There, you see?' the Black Amaranth asked. Her disappointment in me sounded feigned. 'Your senses have deceived your wits and now your lips reveal your naïveté.'

'You misconjugated the final verb,' I said in an offhand manner as I buttoned up my coat.

She appeared confused for a moment, as though reading her own words back to herself, then smiled when she realised she'd made no error, but instead had been tricked into confirming she wasn't a native speaker. 'You made me betray myself.'

I offered her my grandfather's smile. 'How are my wits seeming now, gentle Lady?'

There was no word, no glimpse of a gesture or movement – nothing, in fact, but the sudden cool sensation of steel at my throat.

'Not entirely suited to your circumstances,' she replied.

As quickly as it had appeared, the stiletto was gone, secreted away – I was almost positive – in the sleeve of her gown.

'But let us leave our cavorting for another time,' she said, and reaching over, pushed open the carriage door. It swung effortlessly, proving that not only was I as naïve as she'd said, but also gullible.

'The door was *unlocked*? The whole time?' I asked.

'I told you, only amateurs try to escape through the bars.'

I heard the thumping of the driver's boots as he clambered down from his perch. A moment later, he appeared outside and held open the door for me. His long, mud-stained grey coat had the collar pulled up; that, along with his black felt tricorn hat, masked his features in shadow.

'That's it, then?' I asked the Black Amaranth. 'A few questions and you've determined I'm no threat to his Grace?'

'I don't decide anything,' she replied.

The carriage driver extended a hand to help me down to the street. 'If you'd be so kind as to step outside, sir?' he asked politely.

Too politely.

Carriage drivers – especially those employed by noblemen – earn as little as actors, but they see themselves as a good deal more important. I couldn't make out his face, but his hand on the door was barely a foot away from me and his fingers were clean, the nails perfectly trimmed.

'Sir?' he asked.

His fingers were unadorned, but I could see bands of paler skin between the second and third knuckles where rings had been.

'He does not work for you,' the Black Amaranth had said of the carriage driver. *'The driver does not work for me, either.'*

Duke Firan Monsegino caught my stare and knew his little masquerade was done. He pulled up the cuff of his muddy grey coat, revealing a heavy silver bracelet adorned with metal tubes the size of his little finger. He slid a tiny blue-glass vial from one of those cylinders and lifted it to his lips. Drinking from it made him wince. 'I wanted a sense of the kind of person I was dealing with,' he informed me after fitting the vial back into the bracelet. His tone had become smoother, more majestic, as if to remind me that playing the role of a duke is a little different from playing that of a carriage driver.

'And what did you decide, your Grace?' I asked, stepping out onto the street and bowing with what I hoped was sufficiently convincing obeisance mixed with a touch of derision over his little game.

The duke gave no reply, but acknowledged my bow with a curt nod before climbing back up to the driver's bench at the front of the carriage.

'He likes to see how his people live,' the Black Amaranth said through the window. 'The advisors he inherited from his predecessor are prone to . . . optimism.'

'So he goes out and plays the role of the Affable Inquisitor in *Between Two Midnight Murders*, disguising himself as a carriage driver so he can mingle with the masses?'

The slight rise at the corner of her mouth paired with the barest hint of a shrug conveyed that she wasn't entirely convinced of the duke's ploy. I'm not sure why, but I found this moment of candour – however downplayed – to be utterly entrancing. That entire ride around the city, I'd thought of her only as the Black Amaranth, a mysterious and deadly assassin. But wasn't that a role, too?

'Might I have your name?' I asked her for the second time tonight.

'What does it matter?'

I recalled a line Abastrini had delivered in one of the minor romances the company sometimes performed in between the grander plays. I'd always rather liked it. 'Because a man should know the name of the woman who might soon take his life but has already stolen his heart.'

She looked at me as if trying to decide whether I was the biggest fool she'd ever met or someone playing a more dangerous game than even she knew. It occurred to me that I might need to keep up that pretence if I hoped to survive the night.

'Call me Shariza,' she said at last. 'For as long as it matters.'

I honestly hadn't expected her to answer. I was both surprised and touched that she did.

I gave her a small bow. 'Lady Shariza, allow me to declare that meeting you has been, without question, the highest pleasure of this entire evening.'

She leaned closer to the bars, allowing me to see through her gossamer veil to the dark copper skin of her cheekbones as she smiled. '*That,* I do believe,' she said. 'And for the sincerity of your compliment, along with the other small amusements you provided on our journey, I will offer you one piece of advice: no matter what you have seen or heard tonight, no matter how congenial his Grace or I may appear to you, *never* assume that the danger has passed – because from this moment forth, Damelas Chademantaigne, nowhere in this city is safe for you, and the stage least of all.'

CHAPTER 8

THE ROYAL

The apartment Beretto had graciously shared with me since our first meeting a year ago had little to recommend it. In winter it was too cold, in summer too hot, thanks to the paper-thin walls, which also meant you could hear a man farting two floors down. Late at night, an innocent could learn of every possible sexual position and style without leaving the comfort of his own living room, simply by listening to the running commentary accompanying the endless grunts, growls and groans drifting through the building.

And the smells . . .

Saint Shiulla-who-bathes-with-beasts, *the smells*!

I often wondered how the sign-carver engaged to make the plaque bolted to the front of the building had managed to stop laughing long enough to inscribe the words *The Royal* upon it.

Our pitiful tenement did, however, have two virtues of note: first, a dumbwaiter system that ran from basement to roof, doubtless intended for the original kitchen staff in the basement to provide hot meals to their masters in the above-stairs apartments. Those long-ago cooks had since been replaced by a singularly foul-tempered, if crafty, woman who insisted her lodgers call her 'Mother'. She lived surrounded by an array of devious traps to keep out anyone fool enough to try to filch her supplies, which she would, for a price, supply to the denizens of the Royal. These included the occasional roast chicken (if we were lucky) or some kind of pigeon- or rat-based stew if we weren't. Alongside these – or perhaps because of them – Mother offered large quantities of dubiously obtained liquor and pleasure drugs.

When I'd first moved in, Beretto had introduced me to Mother's 'system', which involved first opening the dumbwaiter door to sniff whatever was wafting up the shaft to assess what was on the menu that night. Next, you would place on the wooden platform the appropriate fee – in a flagon, if we wanted liquor, a saucer for dreamweed, or a bowl, if rat stew was the dish of choice. How much of the requested goods came back up the dumbwaiter was based on how generous we'd been and how irritable Mother was feeling that night.

Mostly we used the dumbwaiter to buy booze after a bad night at the theatre. Beretto tended to get us better deals than our fellow Royal tenants on account of his willingness to bellow outrageous sexual propositions down the shaft. Mother apparently found these endearing.

The second virtue of our apartment was that while the rooms were horribly cramped, those on the top floor were arranged around a single long hallway that made a surprisingly good fencing piste.

'Tits up!' Beretto called out amiably as he knocked the point of my blade out of line.

'*Tips* up,' I corrected in response to his reminder that I had yet again let my point fall too low. 'You seriously think the solution to my problems is to challenge Duke Monsegino to a duel?' Panting from exertion, I kicked off my back heel and attempted another lunge.

'Not the way you fence,' Beretto replied, easily batting aside my clumsy attack with the strong forte of his own weapon. All the while, he drank from the flagon of red he'd inveigled out of Mother. I watched despondently as my roommate tossed his fencing sword into the air, swapped the flagon to his right hand while catching the grip in the other, and proceeded to fight me left-handed.

'And how exactly is showing me up supposed to help?' I asked, struggling to parry the flurry of dainty, almost lazy attacks Beretto sent my way.

'Stop *pretending* to fence and just fence, Damelas,' was his customary slurred rebuke, followed shortly thereafter by the sloshing of the flagon.

Whoever scored a point had to keep drinking until the other scored on him. The longer you held the flagon, the drunker you got and, presumably, the sloppier your technique became, thus offering more opportunities for your opponent to score.

Beretto tended to get very, very drunk during these bouts.

'You're actually a good swordsman, you know,' he said.

I attempted an envelopment, bringing the point of my weapon around Beretto's blade in a semicircle to attack against his outside line. 'I'm a terrible swordsman,' I said as Beretto turned his point to follow mine, thus disabling the envelopment and allowing him an easy thrust to the inside of my forearm.

'No, no. You're good. Or you could be good, if you'd stop pulling your attacks at the last instant. You're not going to hurt me with a blunted tip, Damelas.'

'I'm not holding back!'

'You're a good actor, too,' he went on, batting away my protestations as casually as he was parrying my thrusts, 'but you overthink everything. You keep trying to *play* the part instead of *becoming* the character. You let the script control you, when the lines should be no more than servants to your performance.'

'I doubt anyone thinks I let the lines control me tonight.'

Beretto stopped suddenly, dropping his own point entirely. 'You must've stumbled onto something, Damelas – something about the vendetta between Pierzi and Corbier that our new duke doesn't want made public.'

Seeing an opening, I tried a quick lunge, only to have my blade disdainfully knocked away. My grandmother would have clipped me upside the head for falling into such an obvious trap, followed by a lengthy recounting of her own duels as a Greatcoat. I could almost imagine her there, leaning against the wall behind Beretto in her long brown leather coat, watching my eyes, searching within for some spark of the daring that had made her famous.

I'm sorry I was never able to live up to your expectations of me, Grandmother.

'What could the duke possibly fear in the fumbled lines of a failed actor?' I asked Beretto. 'I'm no Veristor.'

'Neither's Abastrini, but that doesn't keep him from getting laid three times a night.' A lurid grin came to Beretto's bearded face. 'Speaking of which, tell me more about this entrancing Black Amaranth of yours.'

I sighed. Mentioning her at all had probably been a mistake. Describing her looks certainly had been. Beretto lived in a world where beauty, love and nobility of purpose were largely interchangeable concepts, and he foresaw no complications in goading me into pursuing a romantic relationship with a trained killer. 'Best I can determine, Lady Shariza is some sort of foreign spy or assassin that Monsegino hired to be his personal bodyguard when he came to Jereste and took the throne.'

'A wise enough move when you think about it,' Beretto observed. He ceded ground, only to then stretch out into a long lunge that resulted in yet another point against me and another hearty swig of wine for him, before he continued. 'Plenty among the nobility had questions when old Duke Meillard kept the crown from his own daughter in favour of her nephew. And then we have these Iron Orchids flouting all Monsegino's efforts to curtail the booze and drugs flooding the city.'

The damned Iron Orchids again. Everywhere you found misery in Jereste these days, there you'd find those smirking thugs. Until a few months ago, they'd been little more than packs of arrogant, proud-of-being-working-class arseholes who'd pocket a few coins rounding up fugitives for whatever reward had been posted down at the courthouse. Lately they'd started behaving more like an informal militia, patrolling the streets at night and laying the boots to alley-rats unable to find anywhere else to sleep, or immigrants rumoured to have done something no one could remember to a victim no one could name.

Beretto took an extra swig from the flagon and grimaced. 'Too bad Mother's not one of them – then she might get us the good stuff, eh?'

I ignored the question, for Beretto was drunk enough that I might actually have a chance to score against him. I went for a triple bluff: first a feint to his shoulder, then a disengage down to his thigh and finally the true thrust to his chest. The big man ignored the first two false jabs entirely and when the third came, encircled my blade with his own before jerking down hard and sending my sword clattering to the floor.

'I hope your flirtations with the lustrous Lady Shariza weren't as transparent as these clumsy feints, brother.'

'Oh, for the saints' sake,' I swore in frustration. 'The woman's a cold-hearted killer, as bad or worse than the Vixen herself! If the gods love me, they'll keep me from crossing paths with either of them again!'

'You're not fooling me,' he said, eyes sparkling with mischief. 'You were ensorcelled by her, weren't you?'

There was no point in arguing with the sentimental lummox when he had that much booze in him. Especially when he was right.

'Ensorcelled *and* intimidated,' I confessed.

'Ah, see? That's the sign of true love, right there!'

The distinctive groan of the third stair above the landing leading to our floor caught our attention and we stopped to listen to the timing and character of the steps slowly climbing the stairs.

'You think it's the Bulger?' I asked, pressing my ear to the door separating the hallway from the stairwell.

'That pervert? You'd think he'd know by now that stuffing whatever food or valuables he's stolen from us into his underclothes looks *nothing* like natural . . . arousal. But no, it's not the Bulger.' Beretto tugged the rounded wooden cap off the tip of his steel blade. 'Sounds more like the Pin.'

The Pin wasn't a fellow tenant. In fact, no one had ever seen him. There were occasional reports of his footsteps treading the stairs on the very night someone died, although a body might not be found for some hours, or even days. But his handiwork was never in doubt: the Pin left nine-inch-long needles buried with surgical precision in the backs of the necks of his victims, all of whom were modest, working folk, rather than nobles whose power and privilege should, by all rights, make *them* the target of professional killers. The Iron Orchids had started claiming the Pin worked for the duke. *'Instillin' fear into the common man to keep him from risin' up and takin' back what's 'is,'* they would announce whenever there was a new victim.

My hand shook as I popped the wooden cap from my own sword and took up position to the right of the stairwell door. My job when some reprobate tried to break into our apartment – which was more often than should be reasonable for two impoverished actors with nothing of value to steal – was to quickly turn the handle on the door and swing it open before the would-be invader knew anyone was about. Beretto handled the rest.

'Bloody Hells, man!' Shoville squealed when he found the very sharp tip of a fencing blade pressed against the ball of his throat.

The director tried to bat the sword away, but Beretto was already spinning it in a half-circle and returning the tip to its original target.

'You don't suppose he's the Pin, do you?' Beretto asked.

'Doubtful,' I replied. 'If the Directore Principale of the world-renowned Operato Belleza was a nefarious midnight murderer, you'd think we would've been his *first* victims.'

'Good point.' Beretto removed his weapon and tossed it through the open doorway into our small living room, where it landed on the threadbare couch. 'What in all the Hells are you doing out at such an hour, Shoville? I would have thought you'd still be on your knees offering more coin and prostitutes in exchange for the mercy of our illustrious Veristor.'

Shoville ignored Beretto's drunken impertinence, staring back at the two of us, uncharacteristically shame-faced, until we led him into the apartment.

'I did try to placate Abastrini,' the director admitted after refreshing himself from Beretto's flagon. 'I spent *hours* begging him – even offered him my share of the profits on the production. But Ellias has always been implacable. He threatened to quit the company if I ever allow Damelas another speaking part.'

'That's me done for, I suppose.'

I glanced around the apartment. I'd never had much affection for it, but now it felt as precious to me as any duke's palace. Foul as the place was, it cost a small fortune, even splitting the rent with Beretto. No director would keep an actor who couldn't even play a herald, which meant I would be out on my ear with nothing but a duelling writ awaiting me.

Maybe I can survive on the streets the way the alley-rats do, I thought. *Hide out for a decade or so, until Grandfather gets so old even the Vixen won't want to bother duelling him.*

Of course, that begged the question, *then what?* Move to the countryside and find work in the fields? I didn't have much cause to believe I'd be any better at picking wheat than I'd been at acting. I wasn't even sure if one picked wheat. *Plucked? Harvested? Threshed?*

'I'm afraid the whole company is done for,' Shoville said, holding up a rolled piece of parchment. The red wax seal had been broken. 'A woman dressed all in black delivered this to me an hour ago – I was in the process of plying Ellias with drink at a ludicrously expensive bar.'

Shaking the scroll, he shared its contents without bothering to unroll it. 'By order of Duke Firan Monsegino, our production of *Valour at Mount Cruxia* is ended as of tonight.'

'Damn all the saints, Shoville – I'm so sorry – this is all my fau— Hold on . . .'

What did he say?

'Didn't you say you were at some bar? How did the Black Amaranth know where to find you?'

Shoville gave a shudder. 'Didn't even think to ask. Now I'm even more terrified of her.'

'Was this foreign bloom, who even now grows within the once barren garden of our Damelas' heart, as irresistible as I imagine her?' Beretto asked, giving a knowing bob of his head. Not even the prospect of poverty could wilt his incessantly optimistic licentiousness.

The beleaguered director looked up at Beretto as if he'd forgotten he was standing there. 'I thought you preferred men.'

Beretto spread his big hands in his customary rendition of a penitent's helpless plea to the gods. 'I'm an actor. I love whomsoever the script requires.'

'Well, that's all very well, but we still have a problem,' Shoville replied. 'We have been given seven days to mount a new play, with a new script, and this one comes with troubling prerequisites.'

'Prerequisites?' I asked. 'What "prerequisites"? Is there . . . ?'

The question died on my lips. I'd been about to ask Shoville if there was to be a part for me in the new script. What kind of louse was I to even think of asking such a thing? The Knights of the Curtain had given me a home, protected me from the duelling laws that should have thrust me onto the Vixen's blade a year ago. All I'd done in return was bring misery and discord to heap upon their own troubles.

Beretto tried to rescue me from my own knavishness. 'What Damelas meant to—'

'I know precisely what he meant to ask,' Shoville said, though he wasn't sounding nearly as infuriated as I would have expected. 'That is, in fact, our dilemma. Damelas, the duke has specified that you no longer be permitted to play the role of the herald.'

'Well, that's not so bad, then,' Beretto said, slapping me on the back. 'He hasn't asked that you be cut out entirely – all we have to do is work on Abastrini until he relents and—'

'Abastrini's not the star of the show any more,' Shoville said, unrolling the scroll as if even now he couldn't believe what was written there. 'Prince Pierzi is no longer even the principal character. By *suggestion* of the duke – which is to say, his *absolute fucking command* – Damelas here is to lead an entirely new play, starring in the role of . . . Archduke Corbier.'

'Wait, *what?*' I stammered, convinced I'd somehow misheard him. 'But . . . but Corbier's the *villain*! He's *always* the villain. He's so reviled we don't even have him on stage until the last act, and then it's usually just his corpse—'

'Think of it this way,' Beretto offered. 'At least if you're playing a dead body, you won't have to worry about forgetting your lines.'

'You're not listening, you fool,' Shoville shouted, and it looked like he was trembling in panicked fury. 'We are commanded to stage a play *featuring* Corbier. We must write the archduke as the tale's protagonist and Damelas will have to play him for *the entire show*.' The duke's edict slipped from his fingers and drifted to the floor. 'Once word of this new play gets out, the mob will come with torches to burn down the Operato Belleza – probably with the doors chained from the outside and us still on stage.'

Lady Shariza's parting words returned to me: '*From this moment forth, nowhere in this city is safe for you, and the stage least of all.*'

And she was right, too: Firan Monsegino, the newly crowned Duke of Pertine, had just turned the Operato Belleza – my only refuge from the Vixen – into a cage.

Even Beretto looked shocked as the implications of this new predicament dawned on him. He patted my shoulder awkwardly. 'Tits up, brother. Tits up.'

PART THE SECOND

The Star

In which our

BESEIGED ACTOR,

climbs higher in the ranks,

ALL THE WAY TO

THE HEAVENS,

only to find the air rather thin up there . . .

CHAPTER 9

THE DIGNITY OF ACTORS

Every actor, no matter how humble, quietly dreams of that improbable day when fickle fortune will, at long last, smile upon them. Like a gleaming crown, the lead role will be graciously bestowed. Rich costumes – *new* costumes – will be fitted to their exact proportions. The entire city will gossip over their newly discovered genius, speculating on exotic origins and romantic affiliations. And when opening night arrives at last, wealthy patrons will queue for hours, desperate to bear witness as the city's newest obsession takes to the stage and utters their first astounding lines . . .

'New pages *again*?' I groaned as a dozen more hastily written sheets were deposited on top of the pile teetering on the battered table.

'You think this is easy?' snapped Shoville, hovering unsteadily over me like an exhausted vulture. 'Rewriting an entire heroic saga in seven days to feature the bloody *villain* as the lead?'

I squinted. My eyes were so tired I could barely read the lines, but I needn't have gone to the trouble: these weren't new pages at all – just another rewrite of the damned prelude.

'The prelude is important!' Shoville insisted when I tried to point that out. 'Must set the right tone at the start, or else the audience—'

'Forgive me, Lord Director, but I fear it's what happens *after* your finely crafted prelude that matters. You know, when the audience notices the entire cast milling around the stage in silence because they haven't been given their lines?'

In the week since Duke Monsegino had commanded this ill-omened experiment in theatrical sedition, everything had gone to seven Hells. Poor Shoville had been struggling to mangle the old Prince Pierzi script into a story told from Corbier's perspective, but despite his valiant efforts, none of the scenes made any sense. This in turn sabotaged the rehearsals, for which everyone except Beretto blamed me. In fact, except for when they were spouting their newly butchered lines, most of my fellow players were refusing to speak to me at all. Meanwhile, word around the theatre district was that both the Lords of Laughter *and* the Grim Jesters were preparing to petition the duke to grant them the charter over the Operato Belleza.

I made every effort to live up to the new role for which I was both unsuited and undeserving, spending every spare moment of the day – and night – researching in the operato's archives. Despite poring through dozens of leather-bound chronicles, biographies and stacks of crumbling, yellowed scripts filled with long-gone directors' scribbled notes, all held together with fraying string, I'd found precisely *nothing*. There were no grand insights into Corbier's past, no clues as to what had driven him to murder and sedition. The infamous Red-Eyed Raven was like a ghost: a confused lunatic who'd spent his youth devoted to his country, until, at the age of twenty-six – the same age I was now – he suddenly slaughtered his best friend's wife and children in an inexplicable bid to make himself prince.

Somehow, I had to contrive a credible performance, otherwise the operato would be a laughing-stock, the Knights of the Curtain would be ruined, and I'd be back on the streets, where the Vixen would surely be waiting for me.

'Which saint's toe did I step on to get myself in this mess?' I mumbled aloud.

Low, rumbling laughter broke the silence and I spun around in my chair to discover Abastrini, clad in white fencing gear, leaning casually against the doorframe at the entrance to the archive. Even with the jacket struggling to contain his girth, he looked formidable.

'So, *Lord Director*, you still propose to hold this sputtering candle flame up to the sky and demand the rest of us pretend we are witnessing the birth of a star?'

Shoville buried his hands in his pockets. The Directore Principale might run the company, but it was Abastrini's wrath the cast and crew alike feared most. 'Now, Ellias,' he began timidly.

'When exactly was it you cast aside the last shreds of your integrity, Hujo?'

An angry flush came to the director's cheeks. 'What exactly are you implying?'

Abastrini swaggered into the room, his unsteady gait suggesting he was already deep in his cups. 'You think we don't know you've been taking bribes?'

'Bribes? I'd never—' He huffed and puffed through a series of barely coherent denials.

I wondered why he bothered denying it. Everyone knew old Duke Meillard used to grease the palms of theatre directors to encourage the staging of those especially patriotic historias which happened to advance his own political interests. It was the price of doing business in the duchy's capital city.

'I do what I must to keep this company together,' Shoville admitted at last. 'How else do you think we afford the luxuries you demand, *Master Veristor*?'

Abastrini grabbed the lapels of Shoville's rumpled frock coat. 'I play the actor's game, *Lord Director*, not the politician's. Not the *sycophant's*.'

'Let me go, Ellias,' Shoville warned.

But Abastrini ignored him. 'Now we've a new duke on the throne – a jumped-up foreigner who demands we put on this farce to serve his own personal intrigues – and who does he turn to? Hujo Shoville and the eminently corruptible Knights of the Curtain, of course.' Abastrini spat on the dusty floor between the two of them. 'So I ask again, Hujo, when did you decide to put the dignity of our company up for sale?'

Shoville was a small man, hardly intimidating, save for his ability to shout stage directions like a general on the battlefield, but he shoved Abastrini back with both hands, forcing the portly actor to let go of him.

'Oh, how I do love to be scolded by drunken bullies whose sense of honour is entirely dependent on lines stolen from plays they barely remember.' Shoville's indignation lent fire to his words. 'You wonder about *my* integrity, Ellias? I traded it away for arses on seats the day my partner in this venture stopped reaching for the truth of the Veristor's art and instead began grasping after its rewards!'

Abastrini's meaty fists clenched and I began to worry I'd soon have to intervene – or try to, at least. From the feral look in Abastrini's eyes, the real problem would be getting him to stop once he'd struck the first blow.

'So that's what this is all about?' Abastrini jabbed a thumb at me. 'You resent my success so much that you stab me in the back and allow this . . . this incompetent charlatan to play at being a Veristor?'

I rose from my chair, cringing at the squeal of the wobbly legs against the floor. This small act of defiance brought me dangerously close to Abastrini's daunting bulk. The stench of sour wine and the salty musk of barely contained barbarity filled my nostrils.

Slowly, carefully, I reached across the desk to a heavy brass paperweight of an actor on a pedestal delivering his lines to the heavens. If I hit Abastrini fast and hard, I might be able to knock him unconscious. On the other hand, if I struck too hard, I risked cracking the man's skull open. Then again, if the blow were too weak, it would be my own blood spilled upon the pages of this damned stupid script.

That left me with only one other option. Fortunately, cowering was something of a specialty of mine.

'I would *never* claim to be a Veristor like you, Master Abastrini,' I said, praying to Saint Birgid-who-weeps-rivers to help me soothe the man's pride before it was too late. 'I swear to you, this is all a mis—'

'Oh, don't get me wrong, boy,' he said, cutting me off. 'It was a *brilliant* ploy.' He abruptly released Shoville and turned to pace along the narrow chamber rows of musty bookshelves.

Flooded with relief, I set the paperweight back down on the table. If Abastrini was about to launch into yet another monologue, surely his ire was dissipating . . .

'One must admire the miscreant's cheek, if not his cunning,' the Veristor began, as if a full house were hanging on his every word rather than Shoville and I, glancing at each other in sympathetic unease. 'Using the insignificant role of the herald to concoct those bizarre lines on stage, knowing they would cause a stir among the nobles in attendance' – Abastrini paused for effect – 'not especially clever, admittedly, but *daring*? Yes, we must confess it so. Now, persuading your confederate in the Ducal Palace . . .' He stopped, tapping his lip as if in deep thought. 'That woman, the copper-skinned foreigner who turned up at the tavern with the duke's decree – how did you meet her? She's rather arresting, so I can see why she was able to so quickly seduce the duke to your cause.'

For no reason I could fathom, I began angrily defending the reputation of a woman I barely knew. 'While I'd never met the Black Amaranth before that night, I can tell you that Lady Shariza deserves a damn sight more respect, you ignorant, bloat—'

Shut up! the saner part of me screamed silently, *shut UP! This is how you put the Vixen on your scent in the first place!*

I tried to start over in a more genial tone. 'I swear to you, to the uncaring gods above, that I *never* concocted any such scheme. This isn't some ploy to take over the show. I'm just—'

The veteran actor waved away my denials. 'Please, let us have no lies between us. We're to be brethren of the stage, after all.' His thumb and forefinger played with the mask-and-key brooch pinned to his collar. 'Fellow Veristors, eh? However this all came to be, we must now form a bond, you and I.'

A thought occurred to me then: a simple, elegant way to win my nemesis to my cause. I fumbled through the pile of books to find one of the biographies of Corbier.

'Would you consent to guide my performance, Master Abastrini?' I asked, holding up the battered tome. 'Under your expert tutelage, I might have some small chance of not entirely embarrassing the company.'

Abastrini smiled – the tolerant, encouraging smile of a master illusionist watching a child attempt his first card trick. 'Guide you? Teach you? Why, of course, my young apprentice.'

He tore the book from my hands, and flipping through the pages negligently, announced, 'The Veristor's art is simple enough, really. Where others *read* the histories, you must *live* them in your heart.'

Tossing the book down unceremoniously onto the floor, he pointed first to the stack on the table and then airily at the shelves all around us. 'Find every reference to your subject within these pages, seek out every detail, every subtle nuance. Travel a thousand miles in every direction, speak to the descendants of every man or woman who knew Corbier a hundred years ago. Listen, learn, meditate; pray to the gods for inspiration. Drug yourself until madness creeps into the corners of your mind.'

He placed his hand on my shoulder, then leaned in to whisper in my ear, 'Abandon food and drink for three days until you feel a devil's breath upon your neck. Commit acts of heroism and depravity until not even your own mother would recognise the empty shell of a man you've become. And then, when there is nothing left inside you but a maddening, obscene intimacy with your subject, then my young Veristor . . .' He patted me on the cheek. 'You'll still be a talentless hack who shouldn't be trusted to channel the spirit of a dead alley-rat, never mind Archduke Corbier.'

'All right,' Shoville said, pushing the actor away. 'You've had your fun, Ellias. Now, assemble the cast; we need to run through the play before—'

'I gave them the afternoon off.'

In the silence that ensued, you could almost feel the heat rising from the director's collar. This was tantamount to a declaration of war on Abastrini's part. 'Is this the day, then, Ellias?' Shoville asked. 'Are you making your move to take the company away from me at last?'

Abastrini snorted. 'Oh, don't be so melodramatic, Hujo. I'm saving this misbegotten venture of yours from your own incompetence. There's no play without Corbier, yet here you are filling the boy's head with pages of pointless speeches and volumes of irrelevant histories until his actor's soul becomes trapped within those wasted words.' He grabbed me by the shoulder again, this time squeezing painfully. 'The role is in the *body*, not the script. The lad can't simply recite the lines, he must *live* them.'

'What does that even mean?' I asked, a sudden tightness in my stomach suggesting I wasn't going to like the answer.

'It means, boy, that despite being noblemen, Pierzi and Corbier were soldiers, not scholars. Men of blades, not books. We must get you fighting ready if you're to portray a warrior upon the stage.' Abruptly, he released my shoulder and turned to go. 'Broadsword practice in one hour. We have three duels in the play, so we'd best get you ready for them.'

Saint Zaghev-who-sings-for-tears, but he's right: Corbier was one of the best swordsmen in Jereste's entire history – and he's about to be portrayed on the stage by an actor known only for running away from his first duel of honour.

Abastrini's laughter trailed behind him on his way out of the archives.

CHAPTER 10

PRACTICE SWORDS

There are any number of insults one might expect to hear while being pummelled to death with a wooden sword: '*Die, you worthless piece of maggot pie!*' is a perennial favourite, although '*Cough up your coins, canker-blossom!*' has made a resurgence lately among Jereste's legions of muggers, bully-boys and bravos aiming to fill their purses with other people's copper tears or silver grins.

Outside some of the less sophisticated drinking establishments, one might even hear, '*I know you're not him, moron, but you look like that rat-faced bastard and that's damned well good enough for me!*'

What I *hadn't* anticipated was being beaten senseless with a wooden practice sword while being repeatedly exhorted to, 'Say the sodding lines, you incompetent measle!'

There was something perverse and yet entirely in character for Abastrini to be pounding me into paste on the rehearsal room floor while simultaneously criticising my acting.

'All right!' I cried out, flat on my back and shielding my face with my own battered weapon, one hand on the grip and the other on the blunt wooden blade as Abastrini endeavoured to chop it to bits. 'I'll say the line! I'll say the bloody line!'

'Then do so, you flat-mouthed foot-licker!'

'*The saints will sing* . . . umm . . . oh Hells—'

Remembering lines seen in passing just an hour ago while contemplating my imminent demise was proving to be a bit of a problem.

With a feral growl, Abastrini flipped his own sword and, holding it by the end, swung it like an axe so the crossguard would catch my blade. An instant later, my only means of protection clattered to the floor several feet away.

I'd always taken Ellias Abastrini to be little more than a pretentious, overfed, under-talented buffoon upon whom Fate had happened to bestow the unearned prestige of being a Veristor in a city that unjustly idolised such individuals.

He turned out to be much more than met the eye.

Abastrini was, first of all, an outstanding fighter. On stage it had all looked so . . . well, *rehearsed*: the elaborate duel scenes, the melodramatic charging into battle with a dozen other actors pretending to rush a hill, shaking painted wood or plaster weapons at imagined hordes of enemy fighters . . . Anyone could do that – or so I'd always believed, until I had to try it myself.

Abastrini's talent with a blade, together with those preposterous stories he always told about having served in the ducal army in his youth, had gained much credibility during the hour he'd spent knocking me about the rehearsal room with staggering ease and no apparent effort on his part.

Worse, though, he turned out to be – well, if not a *great* actor, then at least a *committed* one. Somehow, he'd memorised all of Shoville's hastily composed lines with little more than a glance at the pages and was now effortlessly reciting them. At this moment he was giving a terrifyingly convincing impression of being the true Prince Pierzi come to get revenge upon his nemesis.

'Say the damned words,' he snarled. 'Say them or I swear I'll—'

Like an unearned blessing from a tender-hearted saint, the line came to me at last. '*The people will sing my name through every street upon your death, Pierzi!*'

Abastrini pretented to be driven back by Corbier's longsword thrust, giving me a brief moment to catch my breath. '*And how shall you hear their song when I've chopped the ears from your head, Corbier?*'

'You're saying it wrong,' I noted absently, kneeling to pick up my sword. I checked to make sure the chipped blade wasn't about to snap in half. Now that we were trading lines rather than blows, the suffocating panic that had been assailing me began to ebb.

'What did you just say to me?' Abastrini demanded.

It surprised me that he'd misread the script so badly. 'The Pierzi line is, "No songs hears a man without ears." And he didn't say it like you did, like he was angry. He laughed, as if the whole thing was a big joke.'

Abastrini's eyes narrowed. 'Have you lost your senses? Did I crack your skull and not notice? I've been playing Pierzi for years, and this line Shoville's lifted is *exactly* the same as the old play – and besides, how on earth would a talentless supernumerary like you know how to deliver the prince's lines? You've never played the part, and so far as I've been able to tell, never paid the least attention when your betters were doing so.'

'I must have heard someone saying it,' I muttered, only that wasn't true. Every other actor I'd ever seen play Pierzi did it exactly the same as Abastrini. But for some reason, that enraged, bombastic delivery felt . . . well, *false* somehow. The long, sleepless nights bent over the histories of Pierzi and Corbier had left me with the sense that their feud had been less one of bloodthirsty melodrama and more . . . more a friendly competition between brothers gone terribly awry. Of course, none of that explained why I'd just denigrated the acting of a violent narcissist to his face.

'I'm sorry,' I said, mustering as much sincerity as I could as I went to replace my wooden sword on the rack. 'I'm not feeling myself today. Perhaps we should leave off the duel scene for now.'

Unfortunately for me, the Veristor had other ideas. 'You tremulous little turd!' he howled. 'You ruin my show, worm your way into my script – and now you have the gall to tell *me* how to deliver *my* lines?'

I barely had time to notice Abastrini's white-knuckled, two-handed grip on his wooden sword before he brought the blade high above his head and launched into the next scene, cutting mercilessly and ceaselessly at me without even giving me time to deliver my own lines in return.

'*And do I, Pierzi, son of Petrovian, upon the loathsome husk of thine body lay my claim upon all the devils of thy soul—*'

'Abastrini, *stop*!' I shouted, backing away as quickly as my feet would take me from the maddened Veristor's swinging blade.

'For crimes most foul do a foul death demand!'

'Please, I'm not ready! Just give me—'

With surprising speed, Abastrini slammed the flat of his blade into my stomach. I doubled over in blinding pain, only to have thick fingers grab my hair and force my head back up.

'*Let this verdict an answer give in the name of those voices silenced,*' Abastrini intoned, laying his blade on my shoulder in the way of an executioner awaiting the command to lop off a condemned man's head.

'*Those twin babes, their murders unspeakable, shall at last mark the end of your perfidy. Let their twice-blessed flesh, corrupted by your foul touch, their innocence, taken by yo—*'

A chill spread through me, but it wasn't fear this time. Something far colder took hold – so cold that Abastrini's wooden blade on my shoulder felt like a burning torch setting ablaze the words that now slipped unbidden from my lips.

'*Speak not of those children to me, Pierzi. Never again utter their names, nor invoke their memories – for the truth, however deeply buried in your lies, will cry out from my sword, and this bloody blade will be made holy as I carve the indictment of child-slayer so plainly upon your worthless hide that even the rats and ravens will leave your corpse untouched!*'

Abastrini lurched back as if struck by a blow. 'What did you just say?'

All at once – and far too late – my senses returned to me. An ache in my hands caused me to look down and see that my fists were clenched so tightly that my fingernails had dug into my palms.

'I . . . I'm sorry. I think my fever has returned. I've been reading those books over and over, I just need a little sleep. If I could have a moment to rest?'

A slow smile crept up from the corners of Abastrini's mouth. He nodded his head knowingly as the tip of his sword bobbed in the air between us. 'I see what you're doing now – it all makes perfect sense!'

'Really, I just need to sit a while and get my head togeth—'

'You putrid little schemer,' Abastrini spat. 'You've been rewriting the script yourself, haven't you? You're letting that fool Shoville shit out his endless pages of twaddle, but on the night, you're going to alter the story and force the rest of the cast to play along!'

'I'm not, I swear, if I could just—'

'And why wouldn't you? Once the curtain goes up, the Veristor runs the show and everyone else must follow. You'll throw away the director's script and make Corbier the hero simply by changing a few lines.'

'That's never been my . . . Please, put down the sword and let me—'

Abastrini stared down at his weapon as if he'd forgotten its existence. A snarl, low and rumbling, erupted from somewhere deep in his chest. He raised the sword up high, one hand on the pommel and the other on the blade, only to bring it crashing down against his raised knee, smashing it to pieces. He tossed the remnants away and grabbed me by the neck.

'You haven't a shred of respect for the art,' he snarled. 'You have no skill, no talent, no love for this sacred place save for what pathetic rewards it can bring to your worthless existence.'

The sour scent of stale wine filled my nostrils as I tried to protest, but I couldn't draw breath. I tore futilely at the fingers fast around my throat, and when that failed, I tried clawing at Abastrini's face, but I couldn't reach past those meaty arms. The rehearsal hall became blurry, contracting as my vision narrowed to a hazy tunnel through which I could see nothing but the fury in Abastrini's eyes.

He thinks he's the hero, I realised too late, no longer able to fight back. My limp hands rested upon my assailant's forearms as consciousness began to drift away from me. *I'm the villain of Abastrini's tale, and we've reached the last line of his script.*

The strange thing was, his uncontrolled lunacy revealed the talent I'd always lacked: the ability to commit to something – *anything* – with such savage intensity that, for those brief hours upon the stage, an actor was overtaken by a madness so profound that only the applause of the audience could cure the disease. I thought I could hear that clapping now – but it turned out to be coming from inside the rehearsal hall.

As if a spell had been broken, Abastrini's eyes changed as wrath dissipated and sanity returned. The hands around my throat loosened. Desperate gulps of air brought relief so intense I would've fallen to the floor had Abastrini not been holding me up by my neck.

'No one ever told me stage plays could be so violent,' said a figure so close behind Abastrini that at first it sounded as if the distinctly feminine voice had emerged from between his own gritted teeth. Then Lady Shariza's face peeked out over his left shoulder as she rose up on tiptoes. 'It's almost enough to make a girl consider a change of career.'

Breath returned to my lungs, clearing my vision, and I saw the glistening tip of a stiletto pressed against the bulging vein in Abastrini's thick neck. He tried to pull away but the blade followed him. 'Who in the name of Saint Laina-who-whores-for—'

'I've never been fond of hearing that particular saint's name invoked in my presence,' Lady Shariza said. 'Might I suggest another? Ethalia-who-shares-all-sorrows, perhaps? I'm quite certain you'll soon be requiring the services of the Saint of Mercy yourself, Master Abastrini.'

The strong fingers at last unwound themselves from my throat.

'There's a good boy,' Shariza breathed.

The slender steel blade disappeared.

Abastrini opened his mouth, no doubt ready to unleash one of the elaborate insults for which he was legendary, only to suddenly jump two feet off the ground, yelping in pain, grabbing his buttock and scrambling to get away from the source of his discomfort.

'Run along now, Master Veristor,' she said, wagging the stiletto at him like a reproving finger. 'You can play with Damelas tomorrow – if you learn to behave yourself in the meantime.'

Abastrini, looking as if he was torn between fear and humiliation, stopped when he reached the doors and turned his baleful glare – the cause of many a cast member's nightmares – upon Lady Shariza. 'You're the one who calls herself the Black Amaranth, aren't you?'

'I call myself nothing at all, a practice others would do well to adopt.'

There was something deeply terrifying in the casual, almost distracted way she spoke, but Abastrini refused to be cowed. 'I recognise you for what you are, *Dashini bitch*.' Those last two words came out with so much venom, I half expected green mist to spew from Abastrini's mouth. 'I'd heard the Greatcoats had put the sword to your kind – I wonder what they'll do once they learn they missed you?'

Shariza shrugged. 'Don't believe everything you hear, Master Veristor. Besides, the question you should be asking yourself is whether, once *you're* gone, anyone will miss *you*?'

Abastrini slammed a heavy fist against the doorframe, making the wooden casing shudder, and stormed out of the rehearsal hall.

'Oh my,' Shariza said. 'Was I supposed to leave the last line to him? I'm afraid I'm new to this acting business.'

I was about to warn her not to antagonise the man further, but at that moment my legs gave out. My hands grabbed instinctively for the nearest support, which, regrettably, turned out to be Lady Shariza herself. With greater strength than I would've expected from one so slight, she managed to keep us both on our feet.

'You theatre types,' she said, holding me up even as she pretended to be pushing away the advance of an overeager lover. 'You've barely made a woman's acquaintance before you're taking liberties with her virtue.'

She helped me across the room to a chair, then proceeded to examine me, searching for signs of a head wound – or possibly just mental derangement.

Even sitting down made my head spin. I tried to steady myself by focusing on my unexpected saviour, noting that today she had dressed in black fitted trousers and a loose burgundy shirt beneath a dark leather vest. The thigh-high black boots and the narrow-bladed sword scabbarded to her belt gave her the look of one of those free-blade fencers who wandered the streets at night provoking rich men into reckless – and generally fatal – duels.

'You saved me,' I said.

'Is that what I did? My apologies if I overstepped my bounds.'

She smiled, and my gaze traced the curve of her lips to those high cheekbones, then along the line of a nose that, I saw now, had been broken at least once. From there, my attention was drawn to the barely noticeable wrinkled skin on either side of eyes so dark they could almost be mistaken for black. With an actor's instinct for scrutiny, I looked past all that beauty she possessed and all the danger she posed until at last I decided that, while I couldn't swear to it, I was *almost* positive her smile was genuine.

'You look at people too closely, Damelas,' she said quietly, looking away. 'That is neither polite nor wise.'

I felt my cheeks flush, never a good look on me. 'Forgive me, my Lady, for any offence I've given.'

'No, I meant only that . . .' She shook her head before muttering something in a language I didn't recognise, but suspected from her tone involved a great deal of swearing. 'I must go,' she said at last.

An unwise impulse had me rising to my feet and taking her hand. 'What brought you to me?'

I half expected to find a stiletto at my own throat, but the blade remained hidden. 'As it happens, this play now lacks a herald for the final act. I thought perhaps the role might suit me.'

The glib reply masked something troubled underneath. 'It's the smallest part in the entire play,' I countered. 'And I doubt you'd take to the life of an impoverished actress. The duke sent you here to protect me, didn't he, Lady Shariza?'

She looked down at the hand still holding hers. 'The Black Amaranth.'

'What?'

She wouldn't meet my eye but gently turned my palm to stare at my uncallused fingers as though she had found a litter of tiny, helpless animals in her hand. 'Better that you think of me as the Black Amaranth, not Lady Shariza.'

The Black Amaranth: a name to inspire fear, not friendship.

'We two play our respective roles,' she said, 'but neither write our own parts.' She kissed the back of my hand as I had done to hers on the night of our first meeting. 'It would be best for both of us if you ensure tonight's performance is to his Grace's taste.'

She let my hand fall, pivoted on the ball of her booted foot like a dancer and walked towards the doors.

Hers had definitely been a suitably terrifying line on which to exit a stage, and yet that reckless part of me that was apparently determined to get me killed called out, 'Abastrini named you Dashini.'

She stopped, keeping her back to me. 'And?'

'They say no man or woman who meets a Dashini lives to tell the tale.'

When she turned, she was holding up a finger to her lips. 'Perhaps the clever ones learn to keep silent.'

CHAPTER 11

THE STEPS

A darkened alley is a strange place to seek safety, but an hour before the show, I found myself seated on the steps outside the stage inhaling the foetid air and staring at the debris littering the broken cobblestones. The autumn rain had seen off most of those denizens who usually passed a few companionable hours there at the end of the day's begging, pickpocketing and hawking wares both tragic and carnal. Night, with its more violent requisites for survival, had not yet descended over the city of Jereste.

There are entirely too many people who feel entitled to kill me, I decided, reflecting on my rehearsal with Abastrini and subsequent rescue by Shariza, so quickly followed by her own implied threat to my life. I looked down at my hands, watching them tremble as if each finger were attached to a string being jiggled by a puppet master hidden in the grey-black clouds above.

'That's a stupid thing to do,' said a voice, startling me.

'Zina?' I asked, peering into the shadows obscuring the other side the alley. The girl had a disconcerting talent for hiding in plain sight.

'Never let them see you shake,' she replied, emerging from behind the unlit lantern-post by the stage door. The district's lamplighters had abandoned this one of late, the cost of oil being what it was.

'I always shake before a performance,' I reminded her. 'Every single time.'

Zina came closer, watching my hands intently as I held them out. She was an odd girl; I sometimes wondered if she was quite right in the head. The fanciful tales of street urchins living wild and free, bounding over rooftops as they fled the hapless pursuit of the watchmen, pausing only to laugh as they held up the spoils of their latest crime for all the world to see, disguised a truth far less enchanting.

A child who began as a babe on the streets of Jereste would first be used as a prop by beggars seeking handouts from wealthy couples walking by. Seeing the chilled bundle tightly held in the beggar's arms, they would imagine their own precious offspring and seek to banish that vision with the clink of a few copper tears, sometimes even a silver grin. When the child was three or four and still cute, they would beg alone for the best returns. By seven or eight, they stopped being objects of pity and instead became irritants to be kicked away if they got too close.

After that? Once a boy or girl reached the age of twelve, the beggar-masters would decide their fate, depending on whether they had the skills and temperament to make a passable thief or the looks and docility to serve as pleasure artisans. Those like Zina, who suited neither, often found themselves in a dark room late one night where, at the beggar-master's behest, a surgeon would remove a limb or two and at least one eye, leaving them pathetic enough that they might return to begging.

Zina refused to steal, though, and in my occasional bouts of arrogant self-righteousness, I repeatedly warned her never to be lured in by those like Vadris the drug-pedlar, who claimed the life of a pleasure girl was much like that of an actress: she'd be admired, adored and treasured.

Saints be blessed, at least Zina's too smart to believe those lies.

She was different from the other alley-rats. While most bragged or boasted about their latest thievings, Zina listened, picking out those useful insights hidden within the noise. When others preened and pranced about, she watched, noting any tiny details that might have practical use for survival. These past few months she had taken to sharing those insights with me.

'When they see you shake,' she said, grabbing hold of my hands to stop the trembling, 'it creates a stirring in them.'

'When *who* sees me shake?'

She nodded to her right, as if there were shadowy figures standing there watching us, but the alley was empty. 'Them. The cutpurses.

The kidnappers. The jack-snatchers who'll slit your throat so they can sell your corpse to the medical schools for study. The midnight bravos who'll do it to make a reputation for themselves. If you watch very close, you'll see them lick their lips whenever they spot someone who's scared. That's called *salivating.*'

She waited for me to correct her use of the word, and when I didn't, she nodded, pleased with herself.

'They're like dogs smelling fresh meat,' I whispered, almost to myself.

'You're wrong. Dogs don't bite for pleasure.' She let go of my hands and watched as the shaking resumed. 'I'm worried about you, Damelas. You're not suited to this life.'

Not suited to this life. Saints, the girl fears for me when it's herself she should look out for.

'I'm sorry I didn't manage to get you a job, Zina. I'd hoped Shoville might—'

'He said I've no talent.' She cut me off before I could object. 'The directore wasn't cruel about it – and he gave me three tears and half a grin. And he says Tolsi shows promise. He's letting him sleep in the props room at night now, so long as he keeps things clean.'

'What about you, though? That abandoned old wreck of a tenement where you sleep is far too crowded.'

'The Orchids cleared us out,' she said with a nonchalant shrug. 'Said they were commending it for a neighbourhood refuse.'

'You mean commandeering. But *refuse*?'

She pursed her lips and wrinkled her nose, thinking. 'Might'a said *refuge*?'

I started to laugh, but the mirth died quickly as my guts clenched. How dare the Iron Orchids take away the place where two score or more of the city's most impoverished and vulnerable had found sanctuary for themselves? For what? Some stupid command post where they could plot which group of refugees or paupers to attack next?

'They're posting this around town,' Zina said, producing a large, crumpled sheet of paper from the layers of rags she wore.

I took the poster from her, feeling the smooth texture between my thumb and forefinger. This was pure linenstock, finer and more durable than the crumbly pulp used for theatre scripts – and much more expensive. I unfolded it and read the large black-letter words at the top. 'Juridas Orchida?' I had to rack my brain to remember the archaic Tristian my grandmother had subjected me to in order to translate.

'*Juridas* used to mean "articles of justice",' I said aloud, 'and *Orchida*—'

'"The Orchid Laws",' Zina said authoritatively. 'That's what the men posting these around town are calling them.'

The rest was written in the more conventional modern Tristian most of us spoke. There were seven edicts inscribed in rich black ink. I began reading them aloud to Zina, but the commandments sounded so preposterous it was hard to take them seriously. '"Vagrants of low morals are to be banished from our neighbourhoods"? What's that even supposed to mean?'

'Refugees,' Zina replied. 'Unwed mothers. Petty criminals.' She pointed to herself. 'Beggars.'

I went down the rest of the list, which read like a litany of every bully-boy's complaints about the world. 'Usury' was to be banned, meaning money-lenders could be beaten for charging more interest on loans than 'good honest folk' felt they should pay. The selling of ale at higher than the usual price was similarly criminalised – as was the closing of taverns before first light.

'A bigoted drunkard's idea of justice,' I murmured.

'Look at the last one,' Zina said.

I followed her finger to the bottom of the page. 'What is "theatrical blasphemy"?'

'The Iron Orchid told me it meant, "Such plays, performances, songs or stories which demean the noble history of Pertine or otherwise offend the conscience of right-thinking citizens everywhere".'

'Well, here's what I think of a bunch of drunken thugs who go around . . .' I was about to rip up the paper when my eyes caught the last line, printed in red ink with thick letters at the very bottom. '"Let he who would set himself above these laws be crowned in iron"? What does that mean?'

When Zina didn't reply, I looked up at her face. She'd gone pale.

'Zina? What's wrong?'

'The Orchids caught a thief last night – a foreigner, they said. They . . . they drove iron spikes into his skull.' She reached up on tiptoes and tapped my left temple, then the centre of my forehead, then the right. 'One for each Orchid present, so they're all part of it. Looked like an iron crown when they were done.'

'Saint Zaghev-who-sings-for-tears,' I swore, 'that's *ghastly*!'

'They hung his body from a lantern-post before he was even dead,' Zina went on. 'Blood dripped down from his eyes. Like tears, I guess.'

Could there be any sound so chilling as a child speaking dispassionately of torments that would surely haunt the dreams of battle-hardened soldiers? How was any of this even possible? How had unaffiliated bands of thugs become so organised – and yet, at the same time, become even more feral?

You'd think Duke Monsegino could take a break from making my life hellish to deal with the monsters infesting his own capital city.

But that thought sparked a new one twice as terrifying: *what if the reason the Iron Orchids are so well funded is because they're secretly working for the duke, ensuring the common folk are too busy hiding to question why a foreigner sleeps inside the Ducal Palace of Jereste?*

A drop of water struck me on the forehead, followed by the swift pitter-patter of rain falling throughout the alley.

'Where are you staying tonight?' I asked Zina.

'I've got places I can go,' she said defensively. 'Vadris offered me a corner in one of his rooms if I agree to begin my training as an artisan.'

I grabbed the girl by the shoulders, determined to make her understand the danger she was placing herself in. 'How many times have I told you, Zina? A pleasure artisan is *not* an actress! Don't be fooled by Vadris and his false promises. He'll make you—'

She wriggled from my grip. 'I know what a pleasure artisan is, Damelas. I'm not stupid.'

'Then you'll come and stay with me and Beretto tonight. No arguments. You'll have to make do with on a rug on the floor next to the sofa where I sleep, but you'll be safe.'

Of course, if Mother found out there was a third tenant in our apartment, she'd raise the rent, and just as quickly throw us out on the street if we couldn't pay.

You'll figure something out, I told myself. *Maybe if this new play goes well, Shoville will consider a modest raise?*

Zina, ever wary of charity, dismissed my offer. 'I've enough to cover a week's share at another squat in the tanners' district.' She wrinkled her nose. 'If I can stand the smell.'

'Shoville's coin won't last you long,' I warned.

'I've got other money.'

I suspected she was blustering. I hadn't seen her begging for weeks. At her advanced age, the beggarmasters would see it as a waste of a street corner; they'd beat her until she either fled or became so pathetic she might actually earn them a few copper tears.

'*Vadris offered me a corner in one of his rooms . . .*' she'd said to me.

'Zina, tell me where you got this other money.'

At first I thought she wasn't going to answer. She was an obstinate girl, and my attempts to look out for her sometimes pushed her away and she'd not speak to me for days or even weeks on end. I was about to apologise when the flat line of her mouth cracked into a wicked smile. 'Beretto.'

'*Beretto?*'

Her grin was positively devilish. 'Sometimes when you leave the theatre before him, I stand outside looking hungry and I tell him you said to wait there because you had something for me to eat. He gets this terribly ashamed look on his face and then passes me a coin or two and says you left it with him to give to me.'

'He . . .' I burst out laughing. This was *exactly* the sort of ruse that would work on Beretto – and several times, apparently. 'You wretched little schemer—'

The costuming bell chimed inside the theatre, calling the actors to get into make-up and regalia for the performance an hour hence. I held my hands out once more and, feeling Zina's eyes upon me, willed them to stop shaking.

'Better,' she said. 'How do you feel?'

Terrified. Ashamed. Incompetent.

'Unconquerable,' I replied, letting the word rumble from low in my diaphragm so it would echo across the alley. I stood up, shoulders back, chest out, chin up. One of the few lines Shoville had scribbled that I actually liked came to mind. '*Now shall all witness my tale of Dread Archduke Corbier, and the world will tremble at the telling.*'

Zina giggled at that, a small, girlish sound that gave me hope.

'Come on,' I said, opening the door and beckoning her inside and out of the rain. 'You can watch from backstage with your brother.'

'But only the cast and crew are allowed inside the theatre without a ticket – that's the rule.'

She was right, of course, and Shoville would no doubt berate me for such a violation of the operato's long-standing rules. But I was sick and tired of playing the rabbit to everyone's foxes – the duke, the Vixen, the Iron Orchids. The Hells for all of them. Perhaps I *was* nothing more than prey being batted around by scavengers fighting over who got the first bite. But until those teeth actually dug into my flesh, I was going to use this opportunity to bring whatever joy I could to those whose lives contained little of it.

'Rules? Have you not heard, dear child?' I asked in a tone so haughty it would have done Abastrini proud. I took Zina by the arm and escorted her inside as if she were a great lady. 'Damelas Chademantaigne is the star of this show, and it's past time this city learned what that means.'

CHAPTER 12

DRESSING THE PART

Let he who would set himself above these laws be crowned in iron.

Those words haunted me as I navigated the narrow passages of the Operato Belleza, and it was clear I wasn't the only one to have seen the poster. I'd had to ignore the press of players and stagehands alike, all demanding to know what the hells my plan was to keep them from losing their jobs or getting arrested once the curtain fell on this treasonous new play.

Shoville rescued me, after a fashion, dragging me by the collar into the costuming room. 'Quickly now,' he urged, yanking at my shirt. 'We've little enough time before the curtain rises.'

He seemed oblivious to the fact that his manic assistance was making it that much harder for me to get into costume. After politely pushing his hands away, I donned Corbier's fitted black trousers, supple leather shirt – the purple dye still stained my chest from yesterday's dress rehearsal – and the long, sweeping cloak that kept threatening to trip me up on stage.

'You need another hole in that belt,' Shoville observed, now seated cross-legged on the floor and mumbling through the needle between his lips as he adjusted the hem of my trousers, half pulling them down in the process. 'Saints, lad, when was the last time you ate?'

'Yesterday evening, I think.' I looked down at the balding patch on the back of the director's head. 'Sir, might I ask why *you're* hemming my trousers? Where's Neddy?'

'Quit the company,' he replied, hastily pushing a needle through the folded fabric to shorten the leg to the proper length. 'As did Marta, so you'll be doing Corbier's hair and make-up yourself. Don't get over-enthusiastic with the styling oils, either, because we're running out and there's no money for more.'

No wonder the cast and crew were on edge. 'The finances are that bad?'

Shoville kept up his sewing with surprising deftness. 'Haven't been drawing the crowds we used to. We've enough to buy lantern oil and cover half salaries for tonight. I haven't checked on ticket sales yet – couldn't bring myself to, if I'm being honest. A last-minute rush will get us through tomorrow. If not, well, it comes down to how long the members of the company will keep showing up to a theatre that can't pay.'

The director's stoic fatalism shoved what was left of my self-worth over a cliff. 'I'm sorry, Lord Director. All of this . . . I wish I hadn't butchered the herald's lines so badly. I really don't know what came over me.'

The push and pull of needle and thread stopped. Shoville looked up at me, a hint of suspicion laid bare in the arch of his eyebrow. 'Are you certain about that, lad?'

'What do you mean?'

'I mean that it's a far distance from flubbing a word or two in a line to declaring the entire history of the duchy's greatest hero to be a fabrication. Come now, you aren't still clinging to that bit of nonsense about some sudden fever overtaking you?'

I searched for an answer that might allay his scepticism, but I hadn't yet found words that fit the truth, nor could I bring myself to lie to this man who'd been so kind to me.

Shoville took my silence as an admission of guilt and returned to his hemming. 'Wouldn't be the first time an actor staged a bold gambit to alter his fortunes. Abastrini once pursued an affair with a married woman and made sure they got caught so the husband would challenge him to a duel. Just so happened the fellow was on the outs with Duke Meillard. Half the city came out to witness the duel – including the duke.'

'Abastrini won, I take it?'

Shoville nodded. 'Next night, the theatre was packed, absolutely packed – but that was only the beginning of his plan. Halfway through the second act, right in mid-speech, Abastrini fell into a Veristor's trance, suddenly snatching the role of Pierzi away from the man we'd hired from the Grim Jesters specially to play it.' The director chuckled. 'Now *that* took some fast improvising on the part of the rest of the cast.' He bit off the end of the thread and tied it in a tight knot. 'There we are,' he said, patting my leg. 'Time for you to put your face on, Archduke Corbier.'

I was leaning against a sewing table, so when Shoville rose, the two of us came eye to eye. I was shamed by the mistrust I found there.

'My Lord Director, I swear to you by every saint, living or dead, even the made-up ones, that this was no ruse on my part to win a role away from Abastrini.'

Shoville looked genuinely surprised – and even a little hurt – by the denial. 'I wouldn't be angry, lad. If our new duke approached you, perhaps through that woman of his, made certain promises in exchange for your service to him . . .'

'Why would Duke Monsegino come to me? I'm an unknown actor – and for that matter, why would he even engage in such a scheme in the first place?'

Shoville chewed on his lower lip a moment. 'Do you know what they call him at court?'

'"His Grace"?'

The director smiled. 'No, lad, the nobles, the courtiers. Hells, even the ruffians on the street. Behind Monsegino's back, they all call him "the Violet Duke".'

I'd heard the nickname a time or two, but never given it any mind. People always had petty slurs and nicknames for whoever was in charge.

'Pretty flowers, violets,' Shoville went on, putting away his sewing kit. 'Have you ever seen one?'

'In paintings and picture books, I suppose. Not up close.'

'That's because violets aren't native to Pertine.' Shoville tapped a finger to his nose. 'You understand?'

'So when they call Monsegino "the Violet Duke" . . .'

'It's not solely because of those disturbingly violet eyes of his. Monsegino's an outsider – a foreigner.' Shoville shook his head wearily.

'I doubt even the saints can explain what possessed Duke Meillard to pass his crown to Monsegino instead of his own daughter. He's left us with an untested duke who must now gain the love of his adopted people. Perhaps this is all some roundabout scheme to play the patriot, to prove his loyalty to the duchy's history?'

'Lord Director, you really think Duke Monsegino paid me to utter that slander on stage, then secretly ordered us to go further and centre a new play around Corbier, all so he could then shut us down?'

Shoville took down a wide black leather belt from the wall and fastened it around my waist. 'I wouldn't blame you, lad. Only . . . whatever you and his Grace have cooked up, I would beg that you consider our theatre – our company. We players . . . we have a duty to the *truth* of things – not just in the historias, but . . . well, I suppose I'm talking nonsense now. All I ask is that, if this really is the end for the Knights of the Curtain, give me a little warning, if you can.'

The director's sympathy, even in the face of this hesitant plea, was heartbreaking.

'My Lord Director, on my oath as a player, I would never . . .' But I couldn't finish the sentence. There was no point. Nothing I could say would convince this man, whose sense of decency and loyalty I'd come to admire deeply, that this wasn't all a self-serving scheme on my part.

Shoville saw my distress and put up his hands in surrender. 'Ignore me, lad. Ageing theatre directors are prone to flights of fancy.' At the door, he turned to offer a smile so unconvincing it belied his own years of experience as an actor. 'Perhaps there's a simpler explanation than any of us have considered.'

'Which is?'

'Beretto believes you're hiding something from the rest of us.'

The prick of this minor betrayal stung deeper than it should. Beretto was the best friend I'd ever known. That he would harbour secret doubts about me . . .

'What exactly am I supposed to be hiding?' I asked.

'Talent.'

I started to laugh, thinking this had been another of Beretto's jokes and that Shoville had misunderstood, but the director looked deadly serious as he handed me the jewelled scabbard and painted wooden blade that went with the Corbier costume. 'You let Abastrini beat you black and blue in sword practice, and yet Beretto claims that you're a far better fencer than you let on – which one might expect from the grandson of two famous Greatcoats.'

'For the love of all the saints,' I shouted, unable to stop myself, 'I'm *so* sick to death of for ever being measured against my grandparents! No one ever mentions my mother, the blacksmith's apprentice who died in childbirth, or my father, who abandoned us both days before – no, it's always the King's Parry this and the King's Courtesy that, and how I'm named after the *legendary* Damelas Chademantaigne, but I'm no Greatcoat, Lord Director. On that score, you, Duke Monsegino, the Vixen – and, in fact, this entire city – can rest assured!'

Despite my bellowing at near-Abastrini levels, Shoville pretended to be casually scrutinising the Corbier costume one last time for flaws. I could sense he was searching for something else, though.

'You pretend to faint-heartedness,' he said quietly, 'yet I've seen you stand up more than once for the alley-rats outside – even at the risk of your own hide.'

'I promise you, Lord Director, my cowardice is earnest and well-proven.'

Shoville shook his head. 'And this.'

That's all he said. '*And this.*'

'Sir?'

Again, the director went silent for a moment, staring at me with such intensity I felt as if I were being stripped bare.

'You play the parts I give you with mediocre competence,' Shoville said at last. 'And yet, you're a far better actor off the stage than on. In unguarded moments, you speak with greater eloquence than Abastrini on his best day. You listen more carefully. You *see* more deeply.'

The director's words were eerily reminiscent of Shariza's words: '*You look at people too closely, Damelas.*'

'Those things hardly make one a great actor,' I protested.

'You want something to fear, lad?' Shoville asked as he walked back to the door. Outside, the bustle of actors and crew pushing past each other became louder as they started making their way to the stage. The director gave me one last, searching glance, then said, 'What should really scare you is that those are the exact attributes one might expect of a true Veristor.'

CHAPTER 13

THE SPEECH

The opening night of a new play is a frantic affair. Sets only recently built are nervously inspected by the carpenter, who stands in the wings silently praying none of her creations will come crashing down on the heads of the actors – or worse, upon the audience. The costumer sees for the first time a hundred flaws in the fit or seams or hems, only now realising that fabrics meant to glimmer like gold reflect only a dull brown under the stage lights. While ushers race up and down between the hard wooden benches at the back and the expensive plush chairs nearer the front, seating the audience, actors run lines they've barely had a chance to learn. And the director, well, he mostly runs around in circles.

'Barely a third of a house,' Shoville moaned, pacing a groove in the boards in the wings. 'Not even enough to cover expenses.'

'We're still getting paid, though, right?' asked Teo.

The director shot him a look that would normally have quelled the entire cast, but now only set them to grumbling. The Knights of the Curtain weren't an especially large company, and as their reputation had diminished, so too had their numbers. There were twelve principal players: Abastrini, who played the kings, dukes and princes; Beretto, the ever-loyal warrior; the once lauded Ornella, whose silver-haired beauty hadn't diminished nearly so much with age as the roles she was given; twenty-five-year-old Roslyn, with six children at home, a player only because it was a more lucrative use of her rosy features and ample bosom than her other options. Likewise, Ezio, Luticia, Fedarei, Madaline – they all had their typical roles to play.

The bit parts went to the supernumeraries: ever-surly Teo, always convinced he was destined for greatness, and Bida, who, when not serving as Roslyn's understudy, was everything from a page to a tavern strumpet. Now little Tolsi would join them in spending their days anxiously hoping for one of the principals to break an ankle or show up too drunk to perform. Until tonight, I had reckoned on permanently remaining among their number.

None of my fellow supernumeraries were cheering my unexpected advancement. Instead, the entire cast, along with the dozen or so crew who remained, were all standing in a loose circle, nervously staring at me.

'Your big moment's arrived, brother,' Beretto said, jostling me with an elbow.

'What are you talking about? The curtain's not up yet, and I don't come out until the second scene.'

'The speech, man, the speech!'

Hells! The opening-night speech . . .

The lead player always delivered a speech to the rest of the cast before the first performance: a unifying, rallying cry meant to banish nerves and summon conviction. But what speech could I, of all people, possibly give? *Sorry I got you into this mess?*

I suppose I could always apologise for that one spectacularly screwed-up line, which had brought us all to the brink of ruin.

Better to just wish them luck and raise the curtain. But as I opened my mouth to speak, someone else beat me to the punch.

'Is that fear I detect inside the hallowed walls of the Operato Belleza?' came a deep rumbling voice: a siege-engine being rolled up a hill in preparation to smash through the walls of a fortress. Abastrini strode right past me to take what should have been my position at the centre of the cast.

Beretto began to protest, but I tugged on his arm. 'Leave it. I doubt he'll do more damage than I was about to.'

'Fear?' Abastrini demanded a second time. 'In the eyes of this legendary company of players?'

He was dressed in his Prince Pierzi armour, even though he wasn't due to wear it until the second act, which meant in a minute he'd have to run off and swap it all for the court robes needed for the opening scene.

'What is this nameless dread that strikes terror within the impregnable hearts of the Knights of the Curtain?' he asked.

When no one spoke, Abastrini stamped his foot hard against the floorboards. 'Speak, cowards!'

'The house is only a third full,' Teo said warily. 'We all know that means a bad night. People stop paying attention to us and start looking at the empty seats next to 'em. Ain't long after that they start thinking about leaving.'

Abastrini's eyes went comically wide. His fingers clawed at his mouth in mock dread. 'People might leave during the show, you say? Oh, the horror of it all!'

'We've got a reputation to maintain in this city,' Roslyn said more firmly, almost bursting out of the midnight-blue gown of Lady Ajelaine. 'And mouths to feed at home.'

Abastrini waved a hand in the air as if banishing the thought. 'Then whore yourselves to the stragglers after the show. More than a few patrons would gladly pay to bed the Lady Ajelaine. Just remember to have the gown cleaned in the morning.'

'No actor of this fine company would *ever*—' Shoville's furious denunciation died on his lips. Even he knew full well that some had taken up such offers in the past – including Beretto, who was now shamelessly grinning at me from ear to ear.

Abastrini shoved the director out of the way. 'We are *actors*,' he proclaimed, his voice sliding down to the bass register, so low he made the boards quake beneath our feet. 'Ours is the *sacred* art, the only one blessed by the gods.' He raised a fist towards the ceiling. 'Even now do they look upon us, waiting for our play to begin. Did you not hear the thunderclaps outside the theatre? The gods grow impatient, so eager are they to witness our performance.'

Teo, normally not one to put up a challenge, tossed his copy of his pages on the floor. 'With this shite script?' He held out both hands, palms up, alternately lifting one and the other with each sentence. 'Corbier's a monster. Only, maybe he's not such a bad man. Wait, yes, he's definitely a villain. Except, maybe he was just maddened by love. Only . . .' He spat on the pages on the floor. 'Nobody can even make any sense of what the play's about any more.'

Abastrini walked over to the discarded pages, his boot heels hammering against the floorboards, knelt down to retrieve them, then returned to his spot in front of the cast. To everyone's shock, he began ripping the paper to shreds.

'You think I care about the quality of the script any more than I care about the size of the audience?' Without waiting for an answer, he hurled the bits high into the air. The scraps rained down on all of us. 'We. Are. Actors!' Abastrini shouted. 'We do not *fear* the audience. We do not *fret* over money. We do not *falter* because of bad lines.'

He reached back down to the floor and picked up a handful of torn strips of paper. He matched them together and read the line aloud. 'And here now, do I this night, commit such acts as my sins command, though it pains me to do so, and yet with delight do I proceed, with my very soul laughing, weeping, waxing, waning.'

'See?' Teo asked. 'It's total bollocks. Don't make a lick of sense.'

'Now look,' the director intervened, trying in vain to piece back together some shred of his own dignity, 'I had only days to write something that would satisfy the duke's demands while keeping us from—'

'AND HERE NOW!' bellowed Abastrini.

The cast and crew backed away from him as if he'd gone mad, and I wondered if the wide-eyed expression of enraged glee on his face was proof that losing the lead role really had driven him from his senses.

He began to stride the boards backstage in a zealous fervour, hands opening and closing so hard you could see the whites of his knuckles. 'And here now, do I *this night,* commit such acts as my sins command.' He smashed a closed fist against his own chest as he looked up to the heavens for mercy. 'Though it pains me to do so . . .'

He stopped suddenly and held up just one finger. A smile crept over his face, even as his eyes remained pools of anguish. 'And yet . . . with delight do I proceed.'

A soft, almost whispering chuckle broke from his lips. 'My very soul laughing . . .'

He stopped, then looked away downstage towards the curtain, as if two little boys cowered there, awaiting the axe. Tears filled Abastrini's eyes. 'Weeping.'

Determination appeared in the tensing of his shoulders as he plodded towards the curtain with increasing speed. 'Waxing.'

Just before he reached the imaginary children, his hands reaching out to snap invisible necks, he turned back to the rest of us and, near collapsing in despair, finished with one final, tragic word. 'Waning.'

I stood there, dumbfounded by this daring interpretation of the jumble of words Corbier was to utter in the third act – a line I hadn't been able to find any usable meaning in until this very moment. The rest of the cast stared likewise at Abastrini, awestruck not only by his performance, but by the way his actor's heart refused to yield to the hopelessness of the company's dire circumstances.

'I am an actor,' he said simply. 'I do not care how poor or grand the lines on the page. I will give them life and meaning through my art, which is more sacred than words. I do not care how many people sit in the theatre. Through my art, which is more sacred than fame or money, I will turn them into hawkers who will run shouting to their friends of what they missed tonight, and tomorrow, I promise you, this house will be full.' He began walking, briefly taking each person's hands in his before moving onto the next. 'I do not care if my part be large or small, for when I tread these boards, however briefly, I know only that the gods will look upon this vessel of their holy art . . .' He finally came to me and, taking my hand in his, squeezed it. 'And they will smile.'

But the smile Abastrini gave me – the one only Beretto and I could fully see – was as artful as any part of his performance, for it was a smile that said, *This is what a* true *actor can do. What you yourself will never achieve. And should you happen to die on stage tonight by some accident, no one will blame me, because what they will remember most is the grace and honour I showed you before the performance began.*

'Knights of the Curtain!' Teo roared, beaming with youthful pride.

Ornella, forty years his senior, slender as a beanstalk, had a warrior's smile on her lips when she pumped her small fist in the air. 'Knights of the Curtain!'

'Knights of the Curtain!' the others cheered, thumping each other on the back, cast and crew alike – all save one figure who I noticed standing alone at the far side of the stage.

The Black Amaranth leaned casually against a pillar, dressed in the herald's uniform of brown leather riding trousers beneath a blue and black coat with a silver sash across the chest. She'd added one small detail to the costume: a long curved knife in a red lacquer scabbard that I'd never seen in the props room. When she caught me staring, she winked at me.

Beretto observed the eerie exchange and whispered, 'My brother, this is one night you'd best remember your lines.'

Easy to say, I thought, still watching Lady Shariza. *But which lines are the ones she wants to hear, and which are the ones that will get me killed?*

CHAPTER 14

HIGH ART

Shoville, visibly heartened by Abastrini's speech, made a point of hugging each and every member of the cast and crew, no matter how menial their role, offering his own words of encouragement and support. I'd managed to evade his burst of enthusiasm by taking my place in the wings, peeking past the angled black curtain at the audience and wondering if the Vixen was out there patiently awaiting the failure of this new play. There was no sign of Lady Ferica di Traizo tonight, though, only the faces of surly nobles staring up at the stage in gloomy, irritated silence.

Beretto's heavy hand clapped me on the back. 'Don't let their sour faces trouble you, brother. Behind those squinting eyes and tight-lipped scowls, they're all bursting with anticipation to witness your performance.'

'Really?'

'That, or they're curious to see what happens when an unknown actor takes to the stage and commits treason by portraying the duchy's most notorious usurper and child-killer as a hero.'

'Your inspirational speeches are really coming along,' I said, turning to pat him absently on the shoulder.

Beretto, now garbed as Pierzi's principal lieutenant, rubbed his leather-gloved hands together excitedly. 'Ah, Damelas, this is what the theatre is meant to be: controversies! Intrigues! Black, bloody feuds that spread from the stage to the streets and beyond!'

'You realise that sounds horrendous, don't you?'

'Theatre is life, Damelas – not the dull, plodding day-to-day, but those moments that rile up a man's soul and make him demand justice from a world that has forgotten the very meaning of the word!'

A pair of stagehands pushed past us with the golden wooden horse upon which Abastrini would later 'ride' onto the stage.

'You're the one who should've been a Greatcoat, not me,' I said, watching as the great steed creaked and swayed to a stop.

'I tried,' Beretto replied. 'Spent every silver grin I could scrape together and travelled all the way to Castle Aramor to beg an audience with the king. Twice.'

'What happened?'

'He told me not to return a third time unless I'd got it through my thick skull that justice was more than just a rousing song; that a magistrate needs a greater purpose for rendering verdicts than enjoying the sound of his own voice.'

'That was . . . that was terribly cruel of him.'

'Ah, well. We can't all be descended from legendary Greatcoats, you know?'

I hated it when Beretto brought up my ancestry. It felt like a rebuke, like the way my grandmother used to stare at me sometimes when she returned home from her judicial circuits, wondering if in her absence her grandson had finally proved himself worthy of his lineage.

The scent of too much perfume heralded Roslyn as she glided towards us. She looked stunning tonight in the Pertine-blue velvet gown, fitted at the waist and hips, with the long blonde Lady Ajelaine wig, for once perfectly coiffed, and the special maschiera-paints applied to her face more generously than usual.

Indigo-shadowed eyes turned to Beretto. 'Darling,' Roslyn said in a soft, sultry voice, 'kindly fuck off.'

Beretto harrumphed at being so casually dismissed, but as he left to take his mark for the first scene, he gave me a lascivious wink.

'I should get out of your way, too,' I said, trying to squeeze past her without accidentally brushing up against her bosom and earning myself a slap.

She pushed me back with a brightly painted fingernail that somehow got between the buttons of my shirt to poke at the bare skin underneath. 'Not quite yet. I'd have words with you, Chademantaigne.'

'My Lady?'

She smirked at that. 'No more a lady than you're a lord, but I like the sound of it.' She shooed me further away from the curtain, into the shadows of the wings. 'Now, let us discuss our scene.'

'Which one? We have three together.'

She looked as if she was deciding whether to laugh or slap me across the face. 'The kissing scene, *obviously*.'

My already uneasy stomach roiled violently. I hated that scene: the lecherous Corbier comes upon an unsuspecting Lady Ajelaine playing a love song while pining for her long-absent Prince Pierzi. The lyrics, cleverly composed by Shoville from the letters and diaries attributed to the historical Ajelaine, gave voice to her dread over what devastation the Archduke would wreak upon her beloved homeland should noble Pierzi not return.

Clever, but hardly the stuff of high art.

It didn't help that the company's forest set was shabby from overuse, nor did I enjoy having to spend half the song standing behind unconvincing bushes making a show of leering at the unwary Ajelaine. The two of us might as well be performing in a pleasure house's *fornicatio* rather than in a historia at the grand Operato Belleza. Frankly, it was a huge relief when, just as Corbier was about to move on to his assault upon Ajelaine, Abastrini in his fine golden armour burst upon the scene to save his lady love, bellowing his outrage and sending me scurrying into the wings like the gap-toothed, wart-nosed villain of a children's story.

'Don't rush it,' Roslyn said.

'Rush what?'

'The kiss – in rehearsal you barely pecked me on the lips before fleeing the room.' She gestured to the curtain; the audience beyond were beginning to rumble with annoyance at the late start. 'I want to do something a little different tonight – give the punters a bit of a show. Something to talk about in their parlours in the morning.'

'A show?' I asked. 'What kind of "show"?'

'Oh, don't look so innocent.' Roslyn edged closer to me. 'I just want to let Ajelaine show a bit of . . . well, unpredictability – as to which man she truly desires, you know?'

'*Unpredictability*? Are you mad? Corbier tried to rape her!'

Roslyn's shoulders rose and fell in a display of profound indifference. 'Just because that's what Shoville put in the script, doesn't mean it's what really happened. Nor does it mean you and I need to play it that way.' She bit her lip seductively. 'You ask me, Ajelaine was a lot more wild and wicked than the historias give her credit for. I'm certain she'd've preferred a rebel like Corbier over some self-important, domineering prat like Pierzi. Besides' – she leaned in and whispered in my ear – 'the better the show we give them, the more likely you and I are to earn a few extra coins after the curtain falls.'

Saint Ebron-who-steals-breath. Did she truly intend to enrage half our paltry audience in hopes the two of us could then prostitute ourselves to the other half?

The irony was that Ajelaine was the one with royal blood in her veins – no doubt why her suitors were so eager to wed her. Yet while the historias immortalised the men as '*Prince* Pierzi' and '*Archduke* Corbier', Ajelaine was always merely 'Lady'.

And now Roz intends to combat that particular injustice by playing her as a licentious tart. Outstanding.

Roz gave me an appraising eye. 'You know, in that get-up you're quite the handsome devil, Damelas Chademantaigne.' She reached out a finger and traced the line of my jaw. 'I think there's more Corbier in you than you've been letting on.'

'Perhaps it's best if we stick to the script . . .'

She rolled her eyes. 'Oh, don't be a wilting daisy. I'm not going to molest you on stage. We don't even have to change the words – just lend them a little spice.' Without warning, she grabbed hold of my purple leather shirt and pulled me closer. 'Come not to me seeking love, Corbier,' Roslyn reached a hand to grab the back of my head, fingers interlacing my hair, 'for it is not love that awaits you here.'

She drew me into a kiss so hard I felt the press of her teeth against my lips. I tried pulling away, as much from surprise as indignation, but she held me firm. Only after Roslyn had thoroughly explored the inside of my mouth did she finally release me. In a husky, lurid variation on Ajelaine's traditionally dulcet voice, she whispered, 'There. That's not so bad, is it?'

That's definitely not *in Shoville's script*, I thought, feeling oddly out of my body.

For her part, Roslyn looked pleased with herself. 'Yes,' she said, straightening my shirt, 'that will do nicely. We'll have the audience talking about that kiss all through the third act.'

'But we . . . what about the duke—?'

Roslyn wiped a thumb across my lips, taking with it a rather bright streak of red lipstick. 'Don't fret, Damelas. Give yourself to the moment and let Corbier be Corbier.'

She pushed me away just as the musicians at the back began the opening song and the curtain started to rise. As she left to take her mark, she gave me a final wink and said, 'Besides, Duke Monsegino demanded this new play. He must be expecting *something* to be different.

CHAPTER 15

THE FIRST ACT

From the moment I took the stage, unruly drops of sweat began to drip down my forehead. The lanterns hanging from the ceilings seemed to be heating the air more than usual – or perhaps it was simply the fiery glares coming from the audience members. Barely a third of the house, just as Teo had said, they were leaning forward in their seats, looking as if they were waiting for a noose to slip around my neck and the floor to drop from beneath my feet.

Everything around me was painfully bright. That, too, I blamed on the lantern light reflecting the masses of emeralds, diamonds and even shimmering blue romantines adorning the throats, ears, wrists and fingers of the aristocrats presently gracing the Operato Belleza with their sullen presence.

It's like having the sky beneath me rather than above, I thought, mesmerised by the gemstones shining like many-coloured stars, winking promises of unseemly rewards to come if the performance pleased the audience, and warnings of dire consequences should we fail.

But the first scenes unfolded with almost magical grace and poise. The battles were thrilling, the soliloquies enchanting. I made it through all four of my appearances without flubbing a single line of Shoville's deliberately ambiguous script. Moreover, my delivery, if not remarkable, was at least credible.

The rest of the cast were doing even better, adjusting to the twists and turns of the new play far better than in rehearsal. Some of them even looked to be enjoying themselves. Once or twice I dared to hope Abastrini had stopped resenting me in my role of Archduke Corbier.

Things were finally looking up for the Knights of the Curtain, and for me.

Then came the damned kiss.

As directed, I skulked in the shadows of the flimsy trees painted in unconvincing greens and browns. Half my attention was focused on not snagging my cloak on the fake branches, as I made a show of leering at Roslyn playing 'Ajelaine's Lament' on her lute. I felt like an idiot.

In contrast, Roslyn was incandescent. She'd never been a particularly skilled musician or a powerful singer, but tonight the raw passion in her voice was bewitching. She had the entire audience – front of house and backstage – entranced. You could almost imagine it really was Lady Ajelaine sitting there at the edge of the forest outside Pierzi's mighty fortress. Her voice poured out such longing for her absent prince that her despair filled the air, which made it easier for me to imagine myself as Archduke Corbier, lurking so near the object of my desires and yet unable to touch her.

That was the first sign something was going wrong.

A terrible sort of doomed love awakened in my chest, more potent than I'd ever felt before. I was in agony, every nerve in my body demanding to hold her, as if nothing else could soothe the ache inside me. I poured that pain into my silent performance, watching Ajelaine, listening to her song, lusting for her with increasing recklessness.

Then, just as she reached the final verse of the song and I prepared to rise, Roslyn's performance fell apart. Her voice, so insistent moments ago, lost the melody. Her hands kept strumming the lute, but the chords were muted, lifeless. She turned to face me.

What is she doing? I asked myself, confused, terrified I'd missed a cue or forgotten a line. I'd been too busy researching Corbier to eat; was that why I was suddenly so light-headed?

Ajelaine wasn't supposed to see me in the shadows, but Roslyn, as she mouthed the final lines of her song, stared right at me, making it obvious to everyone that she could see Corbier crouched there. Worse, the look in her eyes wasn't one of surprise and terror, but of melancholy longing, as if she stood upon the shore gazing at an island too far to reach.

The lights dimmed and the shadows spread across the stage. *What in all the Hells are the crew up to now?* I wondered helplessly. Was this some petty act of revenge to throw me off my game? *Is this why Roz kissed me earlier? To trick me into making a mockery of my own role in the play and transforming Corbier from brutish assailant to comical, lovesick fool?*

However bitter that conjecture, it made perfect sense. I had come to the Belleza an outsider, a thief come to steal their roles, and what else had I done this past year to earn my place in this family of actors, save to endanger their lives and careers? And yet, when I glanced up at the dimming lanterns, I could see the brass covers were still fully open.

Why is it so dark?

I shivered from a chill breeze I hadn't noticed before. It wasn't unusual for the air to move in strange ways on Belleza's stage. The arrangement of the set, the vents to keep the auditorium from getting uncomfortably hot, the movement of the players – they could all cause unpredictable gusts of wind to sweep through the theatre.

It's just dizziness, I told myself, but the stage was growing darker by the second. The squeaking of the lanterns, the creaking of the boards, even the coughing and muttering of the audience grew distant, like echoes from somewhere far away. Soon all of it disappeared, except for the final words of Ajelaine's song, ringing clear as a summoning bell.

At Summer's End,
At Night's Fall,
Pray not my Love,
Ignore my Call.

The last note was a whisper so close to my ear that Ajelaine could have been right beside me.

And the world went black.

CHAPTER 16

THE KISS

At first there was only the last note of the song, hanging precariously in the air like a teardrop from an eyelash, waiting to drift down cheeks already damp from the mist. The sensation of moisture clung, dampening his skin, fogging his breath. Corbier opened his eyes to find that it had been raining all day and now, at twilight, the mists had floated in from the lake, slicking the grass with heavy dew.

His boots were heavy with mud, from the long ride through the marshlands as much as the hours waiting here under the shadows of the trees at the edge of the field. In the distance, a mighty fortress loomed over this tiny patch of green like an angry father, its parapets clenched fists preparing to mete out punishments upon the child who'd dared to disobey his commands.

Ajelaine.

She was waiting for him – she *had* been waiting for him, for hours. There had been a message – a promise – brought in secret by those whose loyalties they both trusted. As much as one could trust anyone these days . . .

'What is he doing?' a voice muttered.

I stumbled back a step, suddenly aware of the audience. They gazed up at me like row upon row of unquiet ghosts believing the living had come to stage performances for their benefit, that they might while away the long hours of eternal damnation. When I looked down at my feet, I saw both the ground *and* the stage. When I pressed down with the heel of my boot, I felt both the softness of the turf and the solid boards. I glanced up to find both a grey-blue clouded sky, just dark enough for the first stars to blink into wakefulness, and beyond it, the painted ceiling of the Operato Belleza, its hanging lanterns swaying gently from their chains.

And just a few feet away was Roslyn, in her cheap blue gown with paste jewels around her neck—

—and Ajelaine, who disdained such frippery, her leather riding trousers worn from much use, her own boots muddy, hair more chestnut than gold, tied back so as not to hang down upon the lute she held in her arms as she stared back at me.

'Raphan?' she asked.

In the script it was always 'Corbier' or 'the Dread Archduke' or 'the Red-Eyed Raven'. But Ajelaine had just called me Raphan . . .

From behind me came another voice. 'The line, lad!' Shoville whispered urgently. 'Give them the line: "I come for you, and none shall stay my hand."'

I tried to comply, but my mouth refused to utter the words. I stayed where I was, hidden in the shadows of swaying trees, the leaves tickling the short black whiskers on my cheeks. I felt Shoville try to push me from behind to take my place at centre stage, but I didn't move, because the scene playing out before me wasn't the one Shoville had written.

Ajelaine wasn't alone.

'A woman of sorrows,' I called out loudly, turning to the auditorium as I shifted into voca déosi, the voice of the gods, where one actor acts as narrator for the audience, rather than playing the scene on stage. 'Every day she comes to this place. Every day she sings that same song.'

'What are you doing?' demanded Shoville from the wings, quiet enough that only I could hear him.

'Two men,' I declared, even louder. I pointed to the opposite side of the stage where Roslyn stood alone, masking her confusion by idly plucking the strings of her lute and waiting, as the others must surely be, to find out what on earth I was up to. 'Loyal lieutenants of Pierzi's personal guard,' I went on, 'confidants he trusts – not merely with his own life, but with beloved Ajelaine's honour.'

'Seven Hells,' Shoville muttered, and I heard the clomping of his feet as he ran behind the back curtain to grab whoever he could find to take up the new roles.

Roslyn, bless her actor's soul, picked up the cue without hesitation. 'I know you're there,' she said, not deigning to look behind her. 'You're always watching, aren't you?'

A moment later, Teo and Beretto, still dressed in their shoddy armour from the opening battle scene, walked out on stage. When I blinked away the sweat at the corners of my eyes, I saw in their place two very different men: refined officers, elegantly clothed in Pierzi's colours. 'We . . . merely seek to protect you,' Teo mumbled awkwardly, even as the broad-shouldered man who shared his place on the stage, the one who'd walked upon the grass beneath the darkening sky, uttered words that were similar, yet infused with barely hidden scorn.

'The forest is a dangerous place for a woman alone when night falls, my Lady,' Beretto said more confidently. His own choice of words and demeanour were astonishingly close to those of his shadow, who also had a head of thick red hair, though with a considerably more neatly trimmed beard.

Roslyn refused to look at them, and so too did Ajelaine, who hastily slid a notebook covered with green leather into a canvas bag at her feet. Was this a diary she meant to hide from prying eyes?

'A castle can be a dangerous place for a woman alone, too,' she said. Or perhaps it was Roslyn who'd said it and Ajelaine had given a completely different response? It was becoming harder and harder for me to distinguish between events transpiring on the stage and those which had taken place outside that castle a hundred years in the past.

Perhaps the closer we match what really happened, the closer the two worlds will become . . .

In the past, Pierzi's lieutenants were trying to step around Ajelaine to get a look at whatever she'd been doing. I tried to peer closer myself, to somehow pierce the veil and see what so troubled the two men, but was jolted back to the stage when Roslyn played the line for a joke, holding up her lute and with a laugh, saying, 'Besides, I come here well-armed, my Lords!'

But next to her, the real Ajelaine had drawn a narrow-bladed smallsword from the scabbard at her side. 'Here be all the defence a woman needs, my Lords.'

While Pierzi's guards looked upon Ajelaine with a mixture of uncertainty and contempt, Beretto and Teo stared at me, waiting.

They need to know what to do next . . .

I turned back to the audience, wrenched in two as some part of me continued to gaze at Ajelaine. It was like being a puppet whose strings were being pulled by two different masters.

'It is the game we all play,' I announced to the audience, 'one of subtle threats and promised punishments held in check until the return of the prince. For though all know Pierzi's love binds him utterly to Ajelaine, what is less certain to those at court is her fidelity to him.'

Murmurs erupted from the spectators, floating like the mist above the grass. An urgency prickled at the back of my mind, warning me that this strange moment was coming to an end.

'As ever,' I went on, 'the game ends with the two guards leaving Ajelaine alone, knowing that for all her defiance, she will soon return to the castle and to her private chambers, as much a cell as a refuge.'

Beretto and Teo began to turn away, but the two lieutenants in whose place they stood did not.

'But first,' I announced, stopping my fellow actors in their tracks, 'her minders offer one last warning.'

Teo looked utterly baffled, but Beretto, a born improviser, picked up the thread. 'We but do our prince's duty, my Lady,' he said, reaching a hand to touch her arm with indecent familiarity. 'As e'en the brightest star dims before celestial powers.'

Close, so close! I thought, amazed by how near Beretto's extemporaneous line had come to the words echoing from the past. But Pierzi's man had said the last part differently: '*For even the loveliest pertine bows before the Court of Flowers.*'

What was the Court of Flowers? A poetic metaphor to warn Ajelaine that she couldn't hide behind her beauty, or some other archaic nonsense? And why had she been so determined to keep that notebook from them?

The glint of a small, round device on Beretto's collar distracted me, but when I peered across the stage, he was wearing the same armour he'd had on since the start of the play.

That emblem wasn't on Beretto's collar, I realised, struggling to separate the superimposed images of the man I knew so well from that of the stranger on stage with him. *It was on the lieutenant's. Saints help me, I can't keep track of what I'm seeing or hearing any more!*

I tried to focus my vision deeper into Ajelaine's world, but Roslyn pulled me back when she abruptly shrugged away Beretto's hand. This time, when she spoke, she did so with the exact same words Ajelaine had uttered: 'I know my duty, sir, as I know my own heart.'

The two courtiers turned and walked away, whatever was on their collars now hidden from view. Beretto and Teo trailed after them like shadows.

Roslyn turned to face me, our scene together coming at last. Tears were falling down Ajelaine's cheeks as both women waited for me. I could feel the audience's eyes watching me, but something deeper stirred inside my chest: a restless desire, refusing to be contained. My mind, no longer able to hold two worlds within its grasp, let go of the plodding, day-to-day existence of Damelas Chademantaigne and reached out for the glorious dreams of a man far more passionate. I took my first, precarious step out of the shadows towards Roslyn.

The stage disappeared completely, the audience banished. There was only Ajelaine now, standing there, shining like the sole light of the universe as she awaited Corbier.

A second step, more insistent this time, with words to match. 'You claim to know your heart, my Lady. Then surely you know mine, for ours was ever one.'

A sob broke through Ajelaine's lips as she rushed towards him.

He experienced soaring happiness, and the absolute certainty that all-consuming love was within his reach.

A third step—

—but this one never touched the soft, grassy ground . . .

I tripped on the hard, unforgiving wooden surface of the boards. A grunted command backstage was quickly followed by the screech of pulleys shutting the lantern covers above.

The stars winked out. Darkness enveloped two worlds.

I fell.

And fell, and fell, and fell.

CHAPTER 17

THE APPLAUSE

'Up, man! Up!' Beretto commanded.

Strong hands gripped me under the armpits and I found myself yanked to my feet, no longer sure where, when or who I was. A roaring filled my ears.

'Are we under attack? Are those siege-engines?' I asked, my throat raw as if I'd been shouting for hours without end.

'Siege-engines?' a more familiar voice asked.

Ajelaine? No, it had to be Roslyn.

Only, it was neither. Lady Shariza had taken my other arm. She and Beretto were holding me up. A dark red fog filled the field in front of me, thick as . . .

No, not fog, I realised. *That's the stage curtain.*

Beyond that scarlet barrier, angry shouts and the stamping of feet were shaking the theatre.

'Are you sure we're not under siege?' I asked.

Beretto gave me a grin. 'Might as well be. Come on.' He ushered me closer to the curtain. 'Time to take our bows. You and Roslyn gave rather a remarkable performance tonight, my friend.'

I resisted. 'The rest of the play . . . How did you all perform it without me? How long was I out?'

'A few minutes, no more,' Beretto said. 'Shoville halted the play. I suspect the audience may be wanting their money back, to say nothing of what Duke Monsegino will do to us when he hears about this.'

'Quickly now,' Shoville said, pushing and prodding everyone into positions for the bow. 'Brave faces, everyone!'

With a nod to the stagehands, the director signalled for the curtain to rise.

The entire audience were on their feet, and though they filled only a third of the house, still every eye was cast upon the stage, searching for the cause of their unrest. When they found me, their clamour died out and a hundred of Jereste's most illustrious citizens stared at me in mute silence.

Hells . . . did they like it? Hate it? What's happening?

Shoville shoved me forward. Roslyn was suddenly at my side and the two of us stepped out to the front of the stage. She grabbed my hand, leading me into our bows, once, twice, thrice.

I started to step back but she crushed my fingers to keep me in place. 'Keep bowing until they fucking applaud,' she whispered.

As we bowed for the fourth time, I took the opportunity to look behind us. I'd lost track of Lady Shariza. She was now standing a few feet back with the rest of the cast. Her frown was anxious – a state to which she was clearly unaccustomed because her features appeared entirely unfamiliar with how to frame the expression. Her attention was focused on a spot near the back of the auditorium.

She's waiting for something. A signal . . .

I turned to the silent crowd, seeing nothing unusual, only the usual extravagant clothes and jewellery glinting under the lights in the expensive seats; further back, the dull greys and browns of more drably attired patrons.

That's where Shariza keeps looking, but for what?

A brief flash of silver—

A blade? No, it had been small and round. A coin, then?

When I looked back at Shariza, her right hand had disappeared behind her back, as if she were about to take a bow with the rest of the cast. But actors traditionally bowed with the *left* hand behind and the right forward. That's when I remembered what she kept sheathed at the back of her belt.

Saint Ebron-who-steals-breath . . . The Black Amaranth has just been ordered to execute me right here in public!

By instinct more than intent, I drew the stage sword from the scabbard at my side. Roslyn gripped my other hand tightly, her angry glare demanding to know what the Hells I was doing. I was wondering the same thing.

A wooden stage sword in the hands of an amateur against the steel blade of a Dashini assassin?

All those hours my grandmother had spent teaching me to fence, hoping I would one day show the courage to fight for myself, insisting I could be a skilled swordsman if only I would try a little harder . . .

I hope you're watching now, Grandmother.

The audience, anticipating some grand flourish to complete my performance, suddenly broke out of their stunned silence. From the clamour they'd been making earlier, I'd expected outrage, threats, satisfaction demanded, but instead, they were . . .

Saints, they're clapping!

The applause was thunderous, rich and poor alike roaring their approval of the performance – cheering for *me*?

'Brava! Bravasi! Bravalisimo! Ultimi magnificanto!'

Not once in my brief career at the Belleza had I witnessed such unbridled adulation, nor conceived of ever being its cause.

At least I'll die a star of the stage.

I shook free of Roslyn's grip and spun to face the Black Amaranth, grim determination rising up in me. Every day of the past year it had felt as if a pack of bloodthirsty hounds were stalking me, held at bay only by sheer luck and the kindness of a company of actors who'd given me a home. Now the hounds were done waiting, and so was I.

Shariza came forward, right hand still secreted behind her back. In a blink of an eye, that dagger of hers would slide from its scabbard to be sheathed in my heart. I brought my gold-painted wooden blade up high. A diagonal slash was my best hope of forcing her back just long enough for Beretto to realise what was happening and intervene.

There was a momentary break in the applause – almost a hiccough – as the audience noticed the actor playing Corbier was about to attack the poor herald. I couldn't worry about my reputation for gallantry right now. As Shariza bridged the distance between us, I braced for the sudden sharp pain of a dagger being plunged between my ribs.

Her eyes widened, just a fraction – then she gave a tiny, almost imperceptible shake of her head.

One thing my grandmother taught me: never hesitate in a duel. I swung my sword down, hard and fast as my muscles would allow, hoping through sheer physical force to make up for my weapon's lack of sharpness.

With depressing ease, Shariza caught my wrist before it dropped below my shoulder and took my other hand in her own. Before I knew what was happening, the two of us were twirling on the stage, hand in hand, leaving the wooden weapon clattering to the floor.

Peals of laughter exploded from the audience. It must've appeared to them as if Shariza and I had launched into an impromptu waltz. The musicians at the back of the stage kicked off into a merry tune, soon drowned out by even more wild applause from the crowd.

I glanced down at my chest, still expecting to see the hilt of her dagger, but there was no blade, no blood.

What happened to her weapon?

'Over there,' Shariza said, pretending to let me lead even as she turned me round so that I was again facing the cheering audience. There, three rows from the back: a coin being held up that was no longer silver, but gold.

The signal's changed!

After a few more rousing turns, Shariza gracefully thrust me back into the arms of a confused and irritated Roslyn. The audience laughed again at the bewildered look that passed between the two supposed lovers.

'What the fuck is going on?' Roz demanded.

'Quiet yourselves,' Ornella warned from the wings, still garbed in the bland grey gown and wimple of Ajelaine's serving woman. 'Something's afoot.'

Her words were prescient, for the applause stopped abruptly.

Roslyn gasped and a heartbeat later yanked me down onto bended knee in the customary obeisance due the Duke of Pertine.

And there he was: Duke Monsegino, rising from his seat near the back, removing a plain grey cloak and floppy traveller's hat that overshadowed his angular jaw and smooth, elegant features. His left hand was pocketing something.

The bastard saw the audience applauding and halted the assassination . . .

'My worthy Director,' Monsegino began, his rich tenor ringing out through the theatre as if he were delivering his own opening lines, 'this is indeed a clever innovation you've brought to the operato, splitting the play over several nights.' He gave a musical chuckle. 'Especially in that it now requires us, your entirely enchanted and – dare I say? – *captive* audience, to pay for each evening's performance if we wish to enjoy the privilege of experiencing this remarkable tale in its entirety.' He wagged a finger at the stage. 'Rather sneaky of you, Lord Director.'

The other nobles in attendance laughed along, though nervously, as many hadn't yet determined if the duke was about to express his displeasure at this obvious grab for coin.

Monsegino allowed that uncertainty to hang in the air a good long time before he finally said, 'I, for one, will eagerly return tomorrow.'

The entire audience erupted, the shouts of 'Hear, hear!' and 'Brava, Bravisima!' as much in relief as enthusiasm. The duke turned on his heel and the crowd scampered back to make way for him. They followed him up the aisle towards the exit like the train of a long, glittering bride's cloak.

When Roslyn led the whole company in a final bow and held it as the audience departed, I asked in a whisper, 'What on earth happened after we kissed?'

She shot me a wry grin. 'We never got that far. You passed out before our lips touched, you flaccid pansy. Certainly did the job on the audience, though. Apparently passion withheld is even more enticing to these fancy aristos than seeing it fulfilled.' She reached out a finger and touched my lips. 'Pity. For a moment there, I felt like I really *was* Ajelaine.'

The chattering gaggle from the nobles died down as they fled the building for their salons. The entire cast and crew were left on the stage sharing stunned glances, all save Shariza. The Black Amaranth had disappeared without a word.

She saves me, she nearly kills me, and then she's gone again.

Giddy from relief and exhaustion, I found myself mumbling the old children's game: *Friend, lover, spouse*, imagining myself tugging the spiked, poisoned petals from a black amaranth as the words changed into *Friend, lover, cold-blooded-assassin-who-plans-to-murder me; friend, lover, cold-blooded-assassin-who-plans-to-murder me—*

My confused reverie ended when an elderly usher burst into the auditorium and ran down the aisle wheezing, 'My Lord Director – what do we do? We've sold out the performance!'

'For the saints' sake, Jario, calm yourself,' Shoville urged, descending the stairs from the stage to place a soothing hand on the old man's shoulder. 'We had but a third of the house—'

But Jario was shaking his head. 'No, sir, I mean we've sold out *tomorrow's* performance.'

'Excellent news,' Beretto proclaimed. 'Let Pertine's finest shower us with their grati—'

'No, you great oaf,' Jario interrupted, momentarily forgetting his place in the company. 'They're demanding more seats and we don't have any – that's what I'm trying to tell you. *Everyone* here tonight? They're *all* insisting on tickets for their friends and family. Lady Vendaris wants *ten*! And by the time those at the back of the queue got to me, we'd completely sold out.' He looked helplessly up at Shoville. 'They're threatening my ushers, sir – they're saying if we deny them tickets tonight, we'll find ourselves hanging from posts and crowned with iron spikes on the morrow!'

Shoville rubbed at his jaw, his gaze going to the rows of empty seats. 'Sell another . . . let's say fifty tickets. In the morning we'll put in extra seats. We'll use the aisles. Charge extra – another five grins apiece – for the "exclusive seats".'

Jario looked dubious, but he dipped his head before panting his way back up the aisle to write out more tickets.

Shoville turned to me. 'Well, lad, you certainly left an impression on the great Houses of Pertine. What took place within these walls tonight will be the talk of the town within the hour.' He patted my shoulder, adding cheerfully, 'By every saint and every devil, I pray you have something equally compelling for us tomorrow.'

'Don't suppose there's any chance we'll be getting a proper script, then?' Teo asked, still visibly irritated at having to improvise the guard role that had been thrust on him in the midst of my . . . what? Vision? Seizure?

He stalked over to me, still scowling as he asked, 'Or are you just going to make it up as you go along again, leaving the rest of us looking like fools trying to catch up?'

'Ah, stifle your whingeing,' Beretto boomed. He turned to the rest of the cast, glowing with pride. 'Brothers and sisters, *that* was acting: no script to hide behind, no endless rehearsals that reduce us to moving like gears in a clock. I swear, for an instant it was as if we were really there, upon the edge of that forest in the middle of nowhere.'

'It was outside a fortress,' I said absently.

'Even better!' Beretto thumped me on the back. 'Perhaps we'll take the action *inside* this fortress of yours tomorrow, yes? Or a battle scene – swords drawn, sides chosen, as glorious love and tragic destiny hang in the balance?'

'I . . . I don't know. I had no idea what I was doing,' I confessed, unwilling to deceive the cast and crew whose lives I'd thrown into chaos. 'Honestly, I've no inkling what happens next.'

'Perfect.' Beretto raised his arms and bellowed, 'Knights of the Curtain: together we came, united we fought, as one we triumphed – so now let's all get fucking drunk!'

Cheers of approval rose up from the cast, even the perpetually sullen Teo. Hands clapped backs and pinched backsides, bawdy suggestions were made – and accepted – as the Knights of the Curtain strode from the theatre, heads high, singing as if they were warriors fresh from the battlefield rather than penny players headed for the nearest tavern.

No one noticed that I had stayed behind.

Can this really be the same stage where I stepped into another world entirely, as real as this one, where a woman named Ajelaine looked upon me with such adoration as I'd never imagined possible?

Once word spread of my performance, the citizens of Jereste would demand to know what other lies filled their history books. If Prince Pierzi wasn't the hero the legends made him out to be, what did that say about the dukes whose right to sit the throne owed to a now-suspect bloodline? What did it say about his descendant, Firan Monsegino, the man who'd commanded this new play and yet could lose his crown over it?

What game are you playing, your Grace?

The thud of heavy footsteps drew my gaze and I realised too late that one member of the cast remained, waiting in the shadows of the curtains. The feral look in his heavy-lidded eyes suggested he'd already been drinking heavily and, I suspected, contemplating the cause of his decline in status.

'My Lord Abastrini,' I mumbled, trying to back away but already up against one of the prop trees, 'truly, I never meant for any of this—'

Before I could proceed further with my awkward apology, Abastrini's meaty fingers grabbed me by the collar and lifted me until I was on the tips of my toes.

'Please, Abastrini, can we not discuss this like civil—?'

But the actor held me there a second longer in silence, then, without a word, let me drop. He strode off the stage and out of the theatre.

I was reaching up a hand to adjust my collar when my fingers brushed the surface of something hard and metallic – something that hadn't been there before: a tiny silver actor's mask with narrowed eyes and a mouth shaped like a key.

CHAPTER 18

THE ACTORS' BRAWL

Midnight had come and gone by the time I finally stumbled out the stage door of the Operato Belleza. The rest of the Knights of the Curtain were long gone, and like an idiot, I'd completely forgotten the centuries-old tradition followed by rival companies when an actor wins a role to which they deem him unworthy.

'*Saint Forza-who-strikes-a-blow!*' I swore as the door latched behind me.

There had to be a hundred actors crowding the alley. Fully half the Lords of Laughter had shown up to deliver the ritual beating, along with almost the entire Fellowship of Grim Jesters. The Red Masques, a tiny company with hardly more than half a dozen players – and no prospects whatsoever of holding dominion over a theatre as grand as the Operato Belleza – had come in force, wearing the outmoded lacquer masks portraying the gods and devils from their old-fashioned mythic stage plays.

'Ill-met by moonlight, Laredo,' I called out to one of them. 'Did you really think I wouldn't recognise you beneath that silly mask of Argentus when you were at my door not three weeks ago, begging a meal and a bed for the night after your show got cancelled.'

The big-bellied brute, his face hidden beneath the grinning, avaricious features of the God of Coin, spun what looked suspiciously like a sock filled with stones round and round. 'That was before you made yourself famous slandering the city's most beloved hero and embarrassing the rest of us. So the question now is, will anyone recognise *you* after we're done?'

'Thought you could get away with pretending to be a Veristor, did you?' asked Pink Mol, leader of the Grim Jesters. The voluminous woman had earned her name from the colour of the 'magical' make-up she'd bought from a travelling pedlar which had, in what everyone agreed was a rather magical way, stained her cheeks a permanent bright rosy pink.

'Look at him, wearin' that Veristor's mark on his collar,' said Gin Bruti of the Lords of Laughter, pounding a beefy fist into his palm. At nearly seven feet tall and wide as a horse cart, he wasn't so much a beast of a man as just a beast. 'The Bardatti got rules about posing as one of the sacred actors. Them as break 'em gotta pay.'

Murmurs of assent followed his verdict, but a small voice piped up to offer a dangerously cavalier dissent. 'Like any of you lot would recognise a true Bardatti if they were bashing your brains in with a lute.'

Seventy-seven Hells and a thousand screaming demons!

'Zina, get out of here!' I shouted.

Ignoring my command, the girl climbed up to join me on the steps and jerked a thumb in my direction. 'Damelas is too a Veristor!'

'I'm really not,' I said, desperate to placate the crowd before things got out of hand. 'This is all just a big misunderstanding.'

Usually, the 'rivals' blessing' was more a ceremonial hazing than an actual drubbing: a few players would come by, deliver half a dozen smacks to the head, hold you down and maybe – *maybe* – piss on you as a reminder of your proper place in the universe. Avoiding it only made it worse later on, so it was best to get the ritual over with and suffer the indignity with as much good humour as one could muster. Tonight, the mood felt very different.

I really wished Zina wasn't there. Nobody was laughing at me; instead, the palpable antagonism in the air chilled me to the bone. I couldn't run back into the Operato Belleza, either; as the last person out, I'd set the door to lock behind me.

'Look, friends,' I said soothingly to the mob, 'you really don't want to do this—'

'Oh?' Pink Mol was spinning a bludgeon around and around on its chain. She sounded distressingly sober tonight. 'Why's that, then?'

'Because eighty against one are staggeringly unfair odds. It makes you a miserable bunch of villains and me the hero of this story. You don't want to make *me* the hero of the story, do you, Mol?'

That set them laughing, but still no one was backing away. Apparently, appealing to their sense of dramatic irony wasn't going to work.

Why is everyone so damned furious with me for something that's not my fault?

'So what's the plan?' Zina asked, no longer sounding quite so confident. She was clutching my hand.

Had I thought it would do any good, I might have pleaded with Pink Mol to let the girl go, but I doubted there was even a copper tear's worth of compassion in this crowd tonight. I would need to come up with a different ploy.

'You go low,' I whispered to Zina. 'Sneak under their legs and then run as fast as you can. Find Beretto, tell him what's happened. He'll likely be with the rest of the cast and crew at the Lucky Liar on the corner.'

Zina was eyeing the approaching mob dubiously. 'What can Beretto do?'

'Bribe the city guards to break up the fight before things get out of hand.' *I hope.*

'What are you going to do in the meantime?' she asked.

As I'd done many times before, I reached deep inside myself, searching for a scrap of my grandmother's daring – that reckless yet cunning swashbuckling spirit that had served her so well as a Greatcoat and a duellist. I didn't find it, though. I never had. So instead, I summoned my grandfather's irreverence and pasted a hopefully convincing madman's grin on my face as I replied, 'Me? I'm going to go high.'

I vaulted from the top step, leaping as high as my legs would take me, before landing on the heads of our would-be assailants and scrambling as fast as I could over them, kicking at the angry hands grabbing for me. It was like trying to swim over a mass of wriggling, screaming eels.

'Damn it to all Hells!' one of the Grim Jesters swore after my boot had caught his jaw. 'Somebody grab that bastard!'

Hands were awkwardly swatting at me, trying to find their grip, but I just kept clambering over the mass of bodies as fast as I could, praying a hundred silent prayers that one saint or other would assist me to magically reach the other side and get a running start out of the alley.

'You're letting him escape, you idiots!' Gin Bruti shouted, knocking his neighbours aside with those mallet-like fists of his. 'Get out of my way!'

'Ow, damn you!' Pink Mol bellowed back. 'You nearly broke my fucking nose!'

There was a lot of shouting, and this time, not all of it was directed at me. With so many trying to assault me, I took plenty of jabs, of course, but these were mostly glancing blows. When a solid punch at last caught me on the jaw, I felt an odd sense of relief; after the constant tension and unfulfilled threats of deadly violence I'd endured over the past week, to *actually* be getting my arse kicked felt weirdly reassuring.

I spared a glance for Zina, but she was no longer on the steps, so hopefully, she'd run home to safety. Things were going to get considerably worse any moment now; while half a dozen fights had broken out between members of the mob – actors always remember their long-running feuds when blood runs high – cooler heads were now taking charge.

'Get his arms and legs,' Pink Mol shouted above the rest. 'Don't try to take 'im down yourself – just grab whatever you can and hang on!'

Within seconds I was pressed against the alley wall, all four limbs restrained, and the debate had turned to who got to punish me first.

'I'm the one got us the contract,' Laredo of the Red Masques complained.

Contract? Someone's paying these fools to beat me up?

'And part of that deal was we were to keep our damned mouths shut about it,' Pink Mol warned, pairing her words with a hefty backhand that nearly knocked the mask off Laredo's face.

'Mol's right,' one of her fellow Grim Jesters declared, 'and 'sides, she's the one got us organised, so we Jesters oughta go first!'

I gasped for air, winded from a surreptitious elbow to the stomach someone had snuck in. 'Friends, players,' I wheezed, 'let's settle this like actors: whoever can present the best monologue on why theirs is the career I've most damaged should get to go first.'

Instantly people began shouting arguments in various poetic meters on how the upstart's outrageous hubris had traumatised them – until Gin Bruti forced his way to the front of the pack.

'Think you're so fucking clever, don't you?' he asked, thick fingers digging painfully into my jawbone.

'Honestly?' I mumbled. 'Until tonight, I considered myself rather clueless, but you lot have given me cause for optimism about my intellectual poten—'

My glib retort was cut off by a brutal punch to my chest – not anywhere soft and vulnerable, but straight to the muscles on the left side, where it should've been hardest to hurt someone. I felt like I'd been struck by a battering ram.

'You feel that?' Gin Bruti asked, and when I nodded, panting, he promised, 'Now I'm gonna do that to your face, and none of us are gonna hafta to worry about you taking the stage again tomorrow night and discrediting our profession.'

Being hit in the face is any actor's worst nightmare. The eyes and eyebrows, the mouth, these are the locus of the player's art. Also, nobody hires an actor who looks like he's been run over by a horse cart.

'Do it,' I spat, surprising myself.

Between Abastrini nearly choking me to death and the Black Amaranth awaiting the duke's cue to skewer me, maybe getting pummelled so badly I couldn't perform was the best chance I had at surviving long enough to figure out what in all the Hells was happening to me.

Gin Bruti smiled, a big, idiotic grin that revealed a surprisingly healthy set of teeth. He opened his mouth to speak just as a brick landed on top of his head and broke in half. A cloud of filthy crimson dust crowned his bald pate.

The alley went silent as Gin stared at me, the confused expression on his face wordlessly asking, *Why would you do this to me? I thought we were friends?*

Then the big man fell unconscious to the ground.

'Up there, look!' someone called out, pointing up to the rooftops. There, thirty feet above us, balanced on the roof of the building opposite the Belleza, was a diminutive figure standing beside a stack of bricks.

Zina?

'Best you come down now, love,' Pink Mol urged with blatantly false sweetness. 'If I have to come up there, I'm not going to be gentle.'

A second brick came hurling down, missing Pink Mol, but landing on Creave Reaver of the Grim Jesters next to her. Those nearest shuffled about, trying to get away, but Zina's aim was dead-on and each brick found its mark.

'How many times must we cross swords on this same battlefield, you blood-eyed bastard?' the girl shouted.

Mad child, I thought, impressed that she'd remembered the line. Had it really only been a week ago that the two of us had staged our version of Pierzi and Corbier's duel for the alley-rats?

Pink Mol was less dazzled by Zina's performance. 'That's enough, little girl!' she shouted, arms overhead to protect herself from more falling debris. 'I din't come here to hurt a child, but I will if—'

'Among the dead of this hill shall your flesh be picked clean by the cows!' the girl called down, pairing her words with another brick that crashed onto Mol's foot, setting the big woman to howling.

'*Crows*,' I shouted back.

'Cows sounds better!'

Pink Mol was a hard woman; neither a broken foot nor the impending threat of a cracked skull were enough to dissuade her. 'You're all alone up there, you nasty brat, and you're running out of bricks!'

Not only that, but the Red Masques counted acrobats among their company and they were already making for the alley wall, nimble fingers and toes finding easy purchase in the gaps in the failing mortar. They'd soon reach her, but heedless, the girl hurled her last remaining piece of artillery at the nearest one before calling down to Pink Mol, 'At long last will I revenge myself upon you, abdominal Pierzi.'

'Abomina— Oh, the Hells for it,' I sighed, and kicked out at the man in front of me who'd been too busy watching the acrobats climbing for the roof to notice my boot heel driving into his belly.

'Oh, and who said I came alone?' Zina asked. I looked up, and even from this distance I could make out the wicked grin on her face.

For the barest instant, a stunned silence overtook the shambling battlefield as every head turned towards the far end of the alley, just in time to witness a mass of shadowy figures rushing towards us, roaring with righteous outrage as they crashed into the mob. Beretto, in the lead, was still wearing his fake steel breastplate, armed only with a pewter beer stein from the corner tavern. Shoville, not normally an imposing physical presence but terrifying in his fury, was close on his heels, and behind were more Knights of the Curtain. Ornella might be more than sixty years old, but with her silver hair tied back in a soldier's knot and a pair of tavern knives in her hands, she could have been a warrior out of legend. Roslyn, no longer wearing her too tight Ajelaine gown but instead an equally snug green shift, was brandishing the iron bar she always carried with her to ward off unwanted attention. Even sullen Teo was charging into the fray, wielding rocks in each hand.

And the loudest and most brutal of my rescuers, swinging a broadsword like some gargantuan lumberman chopping down trees, was none other than Ellias Abastrini.

'Away, thou rankest of bunch-backed toads!' he bellowed, dipping into his endless supply of theatrical insults. 'Thou pinch-lipped arse-faces! Thou darest come here? To *our* territory? To attack a member of *my* company?'

'*Your* company?' Pink Mol asked, squaring off with Abastrini. The pair of daggers in her hands looked as sharp as her tongue. 'You fat, overrated sack of dung . . . that whelp stole your role – you should be standing with us!'

With an axe-like sweep of his broadsword, Abastrini forced her back. 'You thunder-thighed strumpet! Know you not that Ellias Abastrini stands ever with the Operato Belleza, the finest theatre in Jereste, fighting always alongside the Knights of the Curtain, the noblest company of actors in all the world!'

I suspected the slurring of his words accounted for his sudden affection towards the company, to say nothing of his willingness to risk his own hide protecting his usurper, but I wasn't about to complain.

A heavy brick landed on the head of the fellow holding my right arm. Evidently, Zina had found a fresh supply. The sight of blood pouring from a jagged wound convinced the man holding my left arm to back away. I shook off my distracted captors and leaped into the fray. I've never been much good with my fists, but then, actors are accustomed to *not* striking their fellow players; on the stage they're all about making their intentions obvious for the benefit of the audience and narrowly missing their targets for the benefit of their scene partners.

My blows weren't missing tonight.

Though my fellow Knights of the Curtain were outnumbered four to one, the Lords of Laughter and the Grim Jesters quickly began to lose interest once they started taking injuries themselves, to say nothing of the mayhem caused by Zina's constant barrage of bricks. The Red Masques kept going longest, but soon enough they too fled, leaving only a few groaning stragglers too dazed to run, curled up and begging not to be kicked any more.

'Who says the theatre is dying, eh?' asked Beretto as he bashed the last remaining attacker in the head with the buckled pewter stein. 'There's life here aplenty!'

I shrugged off the grip of a woman on the ground who was down but still valiantly hanging onto my ankle as she tried to bite me to death. 'The only problem with that theory is that this *wasn't* a performance.'

The company of the Operato Belleza were now engaged in the time-honoured practice of rifling through the pockets of those too stupefied to fight back. Cheers went up every time someone found a coin, but they quickly realised that every coin held up was a shiny new eight-sided gold jubilant worth more than most players earned for a week's performance with a packed theatre.

'Shit,' I whispered to Beretto, as shaken by the appearance of this mysterious loot as the actual attack. 'It must've cost a small fortune to bribe them all . . .'

Beretto chuckled. 'When have you ever known actors to get off their arses unless there was both money and an audience awaiting them?'

I spun around, but the alley was empty save for my rescuers and the mostly unconscious remnants of my attackers.

The contract, Laredo had said.

The corpulent youth was lying unconscious by the wall, one of the first to fall to Zina's missiles. I strode over to him, tore off his Argentus mask and started shaking him awake. 'Who paid you to attack me?' I demanded.

Eyes still unfocused, Laredo brought a fleshy thumb to his split lip and grinned through broken teeth. 'Shh . . .' he whispered before passing out again.

The arrogant gesture sent a chill through me. Hadn't Vadris the drug-pedlar made that same sign when asked who'd recruited him to the Iron Orchids?

'Well, now,' Abastrini said, stumbling up to us. He was favouring his right leg and there was a rip in his trousers revealing a purpling bruise. He was smiling, though, as he held up one of the prized jubilants. 'Who would've thought that Damelas-fucking-Chademantaigne would earn me gold tonight?'

I snatched the gleaming coin from his hand.

'You dare try to steal from me, you—'

'Abide a moment, Master Abastrini,' I said, holding it up to the flickering light of the alley's only lantern. The coin was indeed made of gold, but the relief on the surface wasn't the recently minted image of Duke Monsegino, nor even of Duke Meillard. Instead, it showed a six-petalled flower. An orchid.

'Those arseholes have their own currency now?' Beretto asked.

'I couldn't care less who minted it,' Abastrini said, grabbing it back. 'Gold is gold. Besides' – he flipped it in his hand – 'the way things are going, these may prove easier to spend than ducal jubilants before the year's out.'

'But . . .'

Beretto thumped me on the back. 'A mystery for another day, brother.' His voice rose to echo across the alley as he held up another of the confiscated coins. 'I say we spend some of this orchid gold on the finest wine they'll fetch us, and raise our cups to the valour of the mighty Knights of the Curtain!'

'Hear, hear,' said Shoville. The poor director looked like he'd taken more bruises than I had, but still he strode forward with fierce determination, raised a fist high in the air and shouted, 'For the honour of the Belleza!'

Answering cheers rose up from the rest of the company. Shoville looked up to the rooftop. 'You, girl!' he shouted. To me, he asked, 'What's her name again?'

'Zina, sir.'

'What do you want?' she asked, still holding a brick in her hand and looking rather tempted to drop it on the director.

Shoville jabbed a finger at the debris scattered everywhere. 'Look at this mess! Broken bottles, spilled beer and the evidence of many a Lord of Laughter having pissed himself in our alley. Get down here and do your job.'

'My job?'

The director smiled at me as he shouted, 'Aye. Cleaning up after actors, running petty errands, being yelled at and – only on those rare occasions where pity overtakes my senses, mind you – playing a modest part here or there on the stage. You'll eat with the crew before each performance and share the props room with the boy at night.'

There was a pause.

'Five copper tears a week.'

'A salary?' Shoville shouted, incredulous. 'You expect a *salary*?'

Her brick dropped to the ground and shattered at the director's feet. A moment later she'd swung herself out onto a rusty drain pipe and slid down.

'I'm an actor now,' she informed Shoville. 'A member of the esteemed Knights of the Curtain. You think players of our calibre perform for free?'

'Why, you larcenous guttersnipe!' Shoville began, but the rest us were roaring with laughter, Abastrini loudest of all.

He grabbed the director's shoulder. 'Take her five coppers from my salary, Hujo. I want her for my assistant.'

'You're not the star of the show any more,' Shoville reminded him.

The drunken Veristor shrugged. 'Doesn't change my contract, which means you pay me whether I play the lead or stand at the back of the chorus farting all night.'

'Actors!' Shoville declared, and stormed off into the night. He was followed by Abastrini, leading the whole company in a rousing chorus as they made their way back to the tavern.

Beretto lingered a moment. 'Here,' he said, handing me a second gold jubilant he'd extracted from a groaning Lord of Laughter. 'You've earned a bonus for your own bruises.'

I studied the coin, still baffled by the beautifully raised relief of the orchid on one side and the crest of Pertine on the other. 'Something's not right here, Beretto. Actors hired to *cripple* other actors? Bands of thugs minting their own currency? The duke commissioning a play that can only hurt his already fragile reign? What does it all mean?'

'It means, brother' – Beretto paused to raise the battered stein to his lips, found it empty and promptly hurled it at one of the stirring Grim Jesters, who moaned in response and slumped back to the cobbles – 'that this city of ours may be in deeper shit than we ever imagined.'

I'd come to that conclusion myself. 'Question is, what are the two of us going to do about it?'

The big man scratched at his beard. 'Well, we've already beaten up enough actors for one night. There's not much we can do about the Orchids, and I doubt Duke Monsegino's of a mind to answer our questions. That leaves just one avenue of investigation.'

'Which is?'

A thick forefinger poked me in the chest. 'You.'

'*Me?*'

'What happened to you on stage tonight is almost certainly connected to why you fumbled the herald's lines last week. There's no point denying it any further, Damelas. You're a Veristor.'

Until Beretto had said it out loud, I had been clinging to the faint – admittedly *very* faint – hope that this was all some bizarre series of coincidences. But the memory of Ajelaine, standing on that cool, wet grass outside that fortress, the sound of her voice, the scent of her hair . . . I knew I – or at least some part of me – really had been there with her.

'Come, brother,' Beretto said, laying a heavy arm across my shoulder and leading me away from the theatre district, 'let us investigate this wondrous gift of yours.'

'How do we do that?'

Beretto grinned. 'By consulting the sort of oracle to whom all wise men flock when seeking answers to life's great mysteries. A naked woman.'

PART THE THIRD

The Bardatti

Where a

YOUNG MAN

in search of

ARCANE KNOWLEDGE

finds entirely more of it than he bargained for …

CHAPTER 19

THE DIVINE HERAPHINA

Despite having lived in Jereste my entire life, not once had I crossed the infamous Ponta Mervigli until that night. Located in a part of town even more riven by violence and crime than where Beretto and I lived, the inaptly named Bridge of Marvels spanned a waterway that hadn't existed for a hundred years or more.

The canal had dried up more than a century ago, leaving a wide channel whose only virtue was that it provided a vast swathe of theoretically unowned real estate. Instead of muddy waters, it was now a mile-long maze of dilapidated shacks and shops held together by desperation and whatever splintered wood, rusty metal and frayed rope its denizens had managed to scrounge. Property in Jereste was prohibitively expensive, but since by law no one could own a waterway, a strange, endless bazaar had been allowed to spread along the erstwhile watercourse like a fungus.

And thanks to some obscure law to do with dawn duels fought across them, bridges were by tradition considered *regia negate*, or free from legal oversight. And as no magistrate had ever envisioned the need for regulations, nothing had prevented a bridge no longer over water being converted into a combination bar, brothel, drug den and – if Beretto was to be believed – the place where one could find arcane answers only a true Bardatti could provide.

'A stripper?' I demanded, shouting over the raucous revelry, boisterous applause and occasional outbreak of drunken fistfights filling the crowded common room of the infamous Tavern-On-The-Ponta. 'You brought me to a *stripper*?'

Beretto gave me a disapproving frown over the rim of his mug. 'Let's not be uncouth, brother. The polite term is "unveiler". Her Divine Heraphina is a true Bardatti Danzore of the old ways.'

'Somehow I always pictured Bardatti dancers performing with their clothes on.'

Beretto leaned back precariously on the rickety chair he'd paid a preposterously high fee to sit upon. Such usury was prohibited by the ducal laws governing all drinking establishments in Jereste, but this, of course, was a saints-damned *bridge* . . .

'Pay attention,' he scolded me, swinging an arm round to gesture at the woman gyrating on the tiny stage. For the past twenty minutes, her performance had been leaving her progressively more vulnerable to catching a nasty cold. 'She'll consider such lack of interest a grave insult. Besides, I think she's about to show us the good bits.'

'You know, Beretto,' I said, over the roar of nearby admirers of Her Divinity's latest gyrations, 'given your own romantic affiliations, you spend a great deal of time contemplating, admiring and generally waxing poetic about the female body.'

He grinned, spreading his arms wide and sloshing beer from his mug as he bellowed, 'Beauty in all its forms, brother. Beauty in *all* its forms!'

That conjured up a 'Huzzah!' from the other patrons, who, I had noticed, were highly predisposed to cheering. Whether this was due to the voluptuous, nearly naked woman on stage or because it was long past the hour taphouses should be closed for the night wasn't entirely clear.

'Go on,' Beretto said, pointing to 'Her Divine Heraphina' again, 'tell me this gift of the gods has not made of herself a work of art.'

It was an oddly apt analogy, actually. She was a big woman, all curves and rippling undulations. Her dark hair, glistening with sparkling oils, was so long and thick, she was able to use it to artistically cover her nakedness as she swayed and spun within a circle of candles upon the three-foot-square stage. The flickering flames bathed her in an otherworldly light, while the shadows they cast swayed in time with her dance. A second woman, blonde-haired and sharp-featured, sat sullenly nearby, plucking the strings of her guitar, looking as if she were about to fall asleep – and yet the lament rising up from her instrument was heartbreaking . . .

'Belleza, Belleza!' the audience cheered as another scrap of silk fell away, revealing even more of the dancer's undeniable lusciousness. The gauzy fabric floated onto the guitar-player's head and she scowled threateningly at the dancer. I wondered if anyone else had noticed.

The crowd's vocal approval clearly inspired the dancer, who started spinning faster and faster; the candles sputtered in the breeze of her passing, extinguishing one by one, until suddenly the woman was utterly naked, yet shrouded in darkness. In the gloom I could just make out the glimmer of an intricate silver tattoo below her belly button in the shape of a winged key.

'That's a Danzore's mark,' Beretto whispered, 'worn only by the sacred dancers of the Bardatti.'

'Belleza! Ultimisa Belleza!' the audience cried, bursting into applause. Coins flew through the air to fall like drops of copper rain at Heraphina's lovely feet. She waited, as if unmoved by their generosity, until at last there was so much money on the stage that coins were falling to the floor. Only then did she bestow upon her admirers a smile that made most of them catch their breath, then donned a long crimson cloak that enveloped her entire body before kneeling to pick up the coins one by one. Almost dismissively she tossed a single copper tear to the guitar-player, who caught it neatly in one hand without bothering to acknowledge the Bardatti's questionable generosity.

'Come on,' Beretto said, rising from his chair and hauling me up with him. 'Best we make our way to the Divine before other suitors come calling with generous offerings for a private dance.'

Sensible advice, yet I found myself resistant. It wasn't that I considered the actor's art superior to hers, but for all the dramatic pretensions of her performance, something had felt a little . . . well, contrived. The dance had been captivating, certainly, and aesthetically imaginative in both its movements and staging, but the poetry had seemed to come not from Heraphina, but from elsewhere.

Maybe she's like me and the depth of her performance is due not to her own talent but to some conjured spirit?

Was that all there was to being a Veristor, just becoming a vessel for someone else's story? That's all acting was, anyway: surrendering self in favour of embodying the soul of another. The thought was not a happy one.

'Ah, Heraphina, the Goddess of Love herself,' Beretto intoned, pairing the greeting with a kiss of the woman's cheek. 'Come to arouse the sleeping hearts of mortals.'

She accepted the affectionate gesture graciously, though her eyes went straight for me. Beringed fingers ending in elaborately painted nails reached out and grabbed my jaw. 'Who visits Heraphina in her temple this night? Is it the boy, Damelas Chademantaigne, or the spirit of Corbier, the Red-Eyed Raven?'

'You kn-know?' I couldn't stop myself stammering. 'You can . . . you can *see* him?'

'I am Bardatti,' she replied, one finger of her left hand tracing the silver brooch holding her cloak in place. It matched the tattoo on her belly. 'The gifts of song, story and dance are ours, as is the awareness of those who share in our magic.'

'Is it true, then? Am I really a Veristor?'

Something light, almost insubstantial, struck the back of my head.

I reached back and pulled from my hair a small piece of bread. When I glanced around to see who'd thrown it, all I saw was the queue of admirers waiting to speak to Heraphina, the rest of the crowd, deep in their cups or wolfing down food, and the sullen blonde guitarist still occasionally plucking at her strings.

'You, a Veristor?' Heraphina laughed, twisting my jaw back to face her. 'You are a boy. A fool. A jester.' She leaned closer. Her breath, a mixture of spice and mint, was intoxicating. 'But there is potential awakening inside you, summoned by these dangerous times, for it is the needs of an age that give rise to each Bardatti. With the right training? Yes, you might become a true Veristor, perhaps the first in a generation. Without such guidance?' She pushed my head away. 'A month from now you'll be found stumbling along the streets of this city, drooling over yourself, unable to remember your own name even as you spout the words of a hundred dead voices clamouring for the attention of the living.'

Rising panic flushed the air from my lungs, leaving me weak in the knees.

Beretto interrupted. 'But you can train him, yes?' he asked.

Heraphina tilted her head to the side, watching me like a cat. 'I possess such knowledge that could save the boy from that terrible fate. Yes, I *could* teach him.' Her head shifted to the other side. 'Were I so inclined.'

Desperate relief filled me, but Beretto held me back with a hand on my chest. 'Ah, money,' he said, smiling at Heraphina. 'I'd hoped, Divine One, that your gifts were beyond price.'

'A prize not paid for is seldom valued. Lessons unearned are too quickly forgotten.'

'I would gladly give you all I have,' I promised.

I fumbled for the gold jubilant in my pocket, intending to offer it as a down payment on her instruction, but the thump of something soft colliding with the back of my head prevented me from beginning my tutelage. A larger crust was lying on the floor at my feet. I scanned the patrons in the tavern again, and again found no evidence of the culprit. Except . . . there had been *something*, hadn't there? I resolved to listen more carefully next time.

Heraphina's seductive laughter brought my attention back to her. 'I find a sympathy in my soul for you, Veristor. Long before your present dangers, you wandered as one lost, didn't you?'

'You speak as if you know my past, Divine Heraphina.'

Her gaze became more intent, her dark eyes boring through me. 'I see a child alone – the mother's life extinguished by his birth, the father's spirit broken long before her death. The abandoned boy now looks to his grandparents, reaching for their hands – but those hands are always occupied, gripping weapons of violence. Not soldiers, though. Duellists? But do they fight as so many in this city do, for wealth, for fame, for the settling of scores? No, their blades serve a higher cause: *justice*. I see long coats upon their backs and even longer roads behind them.'

'My grandparents were Greatcoats – Virany and Paedar Chademantaigne, the King's Parry and the King's Courtesy. They were kind to me, but always wished—'

Heraphina cut me off, speaking almost absently, as if in a trance.

'The child's path is not theirs, but he badly wants to make them proud. He fumbles at every endeavour, trying so hard to make something of himself that he becomes nothing at all. He takes refuge in the theatre, where even one of limited talents can attempt, for however brief a moment on the stage, to become someone of note.'

Her words drummed a bleak rhythm inside me, a counterpoint to the sad melody of the guitarist's idle, almost irritated—

There.

I spun around just in time to see the heel of bread flying towards me and caught it in my right hand.

Heraphina's nails in my forearm demanded my attention. 'Is my company already so stale that a crust of bread compels your attention, Veristor?'

'Damelas,' Beretto warned, 'let's not upset our goddess now.'

'A moment, if you please.'

Carrying the piece of bread as evidence, I made my way past the boisterous drunks to a table at the back occupied by a lone woman. She was plucking discordant, almost vulgar notes on the strings of the guitar on her lap. Unruly blonde curls framed a face that I suspected had the capacity for endless expressiveness when she wasn't scowling at me.

I set the heel of the loaf on the table in front of her. 'Pardon me, my Lady, but you dropped this.'

'Ah,' she said, removing one hand from the neck of the guitar to pick up the crust. 'Many thanks. I'd wondered where this had gone.' She threw it back in my face.

I returned the insult with a bow. 'My name is Damelas Chademantaigne. If I'm to drown beneath a sea of stale bread, might I at least know the name of my slayer?'

'Rhyleis dé Joilard.'

Without invitation, I pulled out the chair opposite her and sat down. 'Have I done you some discourtesy, Rhyleis?'

'You have,' she replied curtly, then went back to playing her guitar.

'Perhaps you could explain to me the nature of my offence? Or are you unable to express your anguish without the aid of bread?'

She struck an unpleasant chord, her fingers pressing so hard on the neck that the vibrato it produced resonated painfully inside my skull.

Evidently this was judged sufficient punishment, for she finally laid the guitar on the table and said, 'Your offence is that shared by any lackwit who laughs at a joke that isn't funny and then cries, "Look, there stands a true comedian!", and by every woman who faints at a swaggering prat, however lacking in charm, and wakes from her swooning to ask, "Was that Saint Erastian-who-plucks-the-rose who came to me?"' Rhyleis picked up another piece of bread and flicked it so it struck me square between the eyes. 'And by every gullible fool who watches a woman swinging her tits in his face and says, "At last have I witnessed a true Bardatti Danzore!"'

'Are you saying the Divine Heraphina is not a proper Bardatti?'

'I'm saying she's not even a particularly good dancer.'

I might have taken the barb as jealousy, had I myself not felt something lacking. Only now did I realise that what had made the performance so magical wasn't the dance, but the way the sinuous music wove so perfectly into the movements. Take away the song and the dance would have been uninspired – banal, even. I could still hear the melody in my mind, even though the intricacies of Heraphina's swaying were already forgotten.

'So she isn't a Bardatti,' I said quietly. 'But you are, aren't you, Rhyleis dé Joilard?'

The scowl was only briefly interrupted by the flicker of a smile, but I couldn't mistake her satisfaction at being recognised.

'You see?' she asked. 'Even a half-witted horse will occasionally, given enough chances, stamp out the correct hour.' She rose from the table and grabbed my hand. 'Come with me.'

Beretto ran to intercept us. 'Brother, have you lost your mind?' he called out. 'You're giving offence to the only true Bardatti in the entire city—'

Rhyleis abruptly stopped, turned and shouted so loudly the rafters shook, 'She's *not. A fucking. Bardatti!*'

Every head in the crowded tavern turned to gape at her.

'Oh, the Hells for it,' Rhyleis swore, and dragged me from the room. 'We need somewhere with fewer eyes and ears.' She kicked open the door that led out to the Ponta Mervigli. 'It's high time someone told you what it means to be a Veristor, and why you, Damelas Chademantaigne, might just be the most fucked man in the entire country.'

CHAPTER 20

THE BARDATTI

Rhyleis grimaced at the stench of smoke and beer clinging to our clothes and accentuated by the crisp night air. 'Taverns that serve ale the calibre of that piss ought to be burned to the ground,' she complained as we descended the stone steps beneath the bridge to the bazaar stretching along the dried-out canal.

The ramshackle shops – some little more than crude shelters, others pieced together from the salvaged hulls of sunken barges – offered up everything from brass trinkets and fixtures plundered from those same vessels, to greenish-brown vegetables ingeniously grown in the canal dirt and laid out alongside meats of even more dubious ancestry.

Most common by far were the sleazy, smoke-filled dens of iniquity purveying hard liquors and even harder drugs to the despairing and desperate. I couldn't help but shudder at the sight of droopy-eyed, staggering customers queueing to hand over what little money they had in exchange for a night's distraction.

When did the people of this city become so determined to dull their senses and sink into every oblivion offered them? I wondered.

Since his coronation, Duke Monsegino had put out any number of decrees aimed at curbing the recent rise in the manufacture and importation of endless varieties of dreamweed, pleasure peppers and sleep serums, not to mention those fouler substances used to induce compliance and forgetfulness, but nobody was paying the slightest attention to the Violet Duke's admonitions.

'I take it back,' Rhyleis said, sparing a scathing glance at the drug-pedlars and their patrons. 'Leave the Tavern-On-The-Ponta where it is and burn the rest of this shithole of a city around it instead.'

The Bardatti was a prickly sort, I decided: quick to anger, quick to mock, quickest of all to judge.

'How long have you been playing for the Divine Heraphina?' I asked, hoping to turn the conversation back to her knowledge of Veristors.

She barked out a laugh. '"Divine Heraphina"? You mean Silga Swaybottom back there? Tonight's my first night covering her arse. I thought it best to discover if she had even a glimmer of genuine Bardatti talent before I throttled her.'

'Are you serious?'

She sighed. 'Probably not. The new First Cantor of the Greatcoats takes poorly to wanton acts of murder, even when they're richly deserved. I'll likely have to settle for carving that winged key tattoo off her belly.'

Before I could suggest that might also be a touch severe, Rhyleis turned her fiery gaze on me. 'I'm sick of talentless frauds wandering the countryside, flaunting Bardatti brooches and passing themselves off as Troubadours or Danzores, bilking the gullible. It's time these pretenders paid the price for their deceptions.'

As she shook her fist, I noted a tiny guitar with the neck shaped like a key securing her cuff. All too aware of the Veristor mark at my own collar, I wondered what price Rhyleis might choose to extract from someone impersonating a sacred actor.

'If Heraphina isn't a proper Bardatti,' I began cautiously, 'then how did she know who I was?'

'She didn't, you idiot! That big oaf you hang about with can be found every other night at the Ponta, drinking himself senseless as he drones on endlessly about the "noble art of the player". Everyone there knows him.'

'But the Div—' Catching her glare, I corrected myself, '*Silga* knew who I was. She knew all about my past.'

Rhyleis rolled her eyes. 'Saints, have you never met a professional swindler before? I've only been in this city a week and even I'm bored of hearing about the goings-on at the Operato Belleza. The oddsmakers are taking bets on how many days this play will run before somebody kills you – and there's a side wager guessing the means of your execution. Most are split between the duke hanging you for treason or the Vixen deciding she's tired of waiting and just burying her blade in your belly.'

I tried not to flinch. 'If we could return to the subject at hand . . .'

But Rhyleis was unstoppable. 'Now, *my* money's on you turning up one morning in an alley with half a dozen spikes in your skull courtesy of these Iron Orchids.' She leaned closer to me and whispered, 'Right alongside your new patron.'

'You think Duke Monsegino is in danger?'

'Why else would I have come to this rancid fleapit you call a city? The ambiance?'

'I thought you came to rain unholy terror on those who dare impersonate Bardatti.'

Rhyleis stopped and gave me a wicked grin. 'Well . . . you might say planning Silga's well-deserved demise is more of a hobby. I'm mostly here on a mission for the Trattari.'

It was the second time she'd brought up the Greatcoats. Her sideways glance made me suspect she was goading me for a reaction; calling them 'Trattari' or 'tatter-cloak' would have immediately set off my grandparents. But I wasn't a Greatcoat, and I wasn't going to be provoked.

'First you claim to be a Bardatti, now you're a magistrate, too?' I asked.

She resumed her long-legged stride through the maze of shops and drug dens. 'We're not that different, really. Think of a Bardatti as a more intelligent, dazzling and talented Greatcoat. The Trattari deal with the petty day-to-day disputes over whose sheep shat on whose lawn, while we Bardatti contend with vastly more complex and dangerous matters.'

'Such as?'

She pulled something from her pocket and flipped it in the air. I caught the coin, but didn't need to look to know it was a gold jubilant with an orchid stamped on one side.

'I take it you've seen one before?' she asked, observing my expression.

'Last night – someone handed out a considerable number of these to hire a mob of actors to beat me senseless.'

'Actors?' She laughed. 'They couldn't find a litter of kittens to do the deed?'

Ignoring the jibe, I rubbed the coin, wondering, if I wore all the way through the gold, whether I might find the secret hidden within. That wasn't likely to work, so I flipped the coin up in the air. 'Why does it feel like everyone is playing for the wrong side?' I asked aloud.

'What do you mean?'

I held up the coin, showing the side with the duchy's crest. 'Duke Monsegino is a direct descendent of Prince Pierzi. His reign is already fragile, so why would he risk alienating the entire city by having me stand up on stage making it look as if Corbier was the true hero?' I turned my hand to expose the other side of the coin. 'And the Iron Orchids have been rebelling against every one of Monsegino's reforms – so surely they should be *begging* the Operato Belleza to continue humiliating the duke's ancestor and undermining his lineage.'

'That *does* rather sound as if everyone is playing for the wrong side . . .' Rhyleis took the coin back from me, flipped it in the air and caught it, closing her fingers around it. 'Unless there's a third side you're missing.'

'What do you mean?'

She handed it back to me. At first I thought it was the same gold jubilant as before, but the front no longer bore an orchid, nor Duke Monsegino's visage, as was legally required on official currency. Instead, Rhyleis had conjured up a coin that displayed a woman's profile, her elegant features framed by thick curls held in place by a slender crown.

'Who's this?' I asked.

Rhyleis made a tut-tut sound. 'You don't recognise Duke Meillard's darling daughter? Viscountess Kareija would've been crowned Duchess of Pertine, had her father not named Monsegino his heir just a couple of months before his death. Didn't you know?'

'I'm afraid Duke Meillard failed to consult me on matters of succession, and a poor player is generally concerned only with legendary dead rulers, not mediocre living ones.'

I turned the coin over in my hand. I was pretty sure just being in possession of it could be considered an act of treason. 'Where did you get this?'

'When a new ruler is about to ascend the throne, the treasury begins minting new currency to both celebrate their coronation and add legitimacy to their rule.' She took back the coin. 'Only a few hundred of these were made before they were melted down to make Monsegino's.'

'So why did Duke Meillard change his mind before his death? Isn't the Viscountess younger, even though she's Monsegino's aunt?'

'Yes, she is, and as to the last minute change of heir, no one knows. Meillard took his reasons to his grave. Wait a hundred years and perhaps you can play him on stage and tell us all what the Hells he was thinking, handing his crown to a weakling foreigner like Monsegino.'

That's not entirely fair, I thought. *It's not Monsegino's fault his family kept him away from Pertine most of his life. Did the old duke discover some grave fault with his daughter?*

Since his coronation, Monsegino had set out to prove himself a reformer, limiting the use of debtors' prisons and pushing back against the influx of hard drugs and organised, often brutal forms of prostitution that had infected the city at the end of Meillard's reign, even though many of these same business enterprises profited Jereste's great Houses.

I considered the coin in my hand. Perhaps Viscountess Kareija would have been more sympathetic to the interests of the nobility?

'Do you believe the Viscountess is making a play for the throne, maybe working both sides to destroy her nephew's reign?' I asked.

'I don't know.' Rhyleis' lips pressed into a thin line that suggested she resented the admission. 'The fate of the Violet Duke is his own problem. Yours is uncovering the truth of Corbier and Ajelaine.'

'They've both been dead for a hundred years. Why should it matter?'

'The Red-Eyed Raven's bones may be rotting in his grave, but thanks to you, we might still dig up the truth about him.' She stopped walking and spun on her heel to face me. 'I was at the Belleza last night. I saw your performance.' A gentler, almost admiring tone crept into her words. 'You might well be a genuine Bardatti Veristor, Damelas Chademantaigne. The first we've seen in my lifetime.'

Hearing her words made me wary of the throngs passing us by. Might there be agents of the duke or his enemies or even those damned Iron Orchids among them?

'You speak of it as some kind of saintly gift,' I said quietly.

Rhyleis snorted. 'Saints come and go. Veristors are far more rare, my friend. Bardatti legends tell of sacred actors who could, with a single performance, raise an army to fight their enemies.' She pressed a finger to the swollen bruise on my left cheekbone where I'd caught an elbow from one of the Grim Jesters earlier that night. 'Though in your case, it seems to work in reverse.'

Her glibness stoked the bitter fire already kindled inside me. I pushed her hand away. 'All this "gift" has done for me is to get me into deeper trouble by the day! I don't know how to summon Corbier's memories, and no one can explain whether I'm just remembering events or actually *living* them.'

'So? When I play old songs, it's not to turn the audience's thoughts to the past. It's to bring something back: something that might help them now.' She took my arm as we resumed our walk, the unexpectedly affectionate gesture taking me by surprise. 'We Bardatti are the country's memory. Our gift is to record those truths which others would see forgotten. Our *duty* is to make sure that never happens.'

'You sound almost nostalgic, Lady Rhyleis.'

'The opposite.' For once, there was no mockery in her voice. 'There's a great deal of ugliness in our country's past, Damelas, and no end of bastards who'd bring it back if they could.'

I caught her brief, sidelong glance at me. It vanished as quickly as it came, but it was enough to let me know I'd not met Rhyleis by happenstance, nor was this just a meandering stroll.

'You knew I'd come to the Tavern-On-The-Ponta, didn't you?'

She stopped to inspect the wares of a flower vendor. 'Hmm?'

I pulled her away from the stall. 'You might be a great Troubadour, Rhyleis, but you're a lousy actor.'

She turned on me, her feigned surprise a three-act play that went from shock to dismay and ended with a grand flourish of outrage.

'Don't bother,' I told her, holding up a hand to forestall any further theatrics. 'Allow me to put the pieces together.' I counted the facts off one by one on my fingers. 'You already admitted you'd been at the Operato Belleza.'

'I'm a lover of theatre,' she said dismissively. 'Imagine my disappointment.'

'Second, you said I could be the first genuine Veristor in a generation – and you knew I'd be desperate to find someone who could guide me.'

'And look at you, falling for Silga Swaybottom's mediocre act at the drop of a hat – or was it the dropping of her dress that caught you like a slobbering fish on the hook?'

'Third,' I started as an old man enfeebled by palsy and relying on a cane bumped into me. Before he could make a show of apologising, I stomped on his foot, elbowed him sharply in the stomach and seized the gold coin back from him. The codger, miraculously recovered from age and ailments, took off at an impressive run.

'Third,' I went on, 'you've been feeding me all sorts of sentimental garbage about the greatness of the Bardatti and how we're just like Greatcoats, only better.'

She winked at me. 'Well, that part's true, anyway.'

I wasn't finding any of this funny. 'Why did you come to Jereste, Rhyleis? You said you were on a mission for the Greatcoats but you've been conspicuously vague about the details.'

Her smile gave way to anger, the most sincere expression I'd yet seen from her. She grabbed my arm and yanked me through a group of staggering revellers to a wall covered in graffiti and tattered posters. She tore one down and shoved it at me.

It was the Juridas Orchida, the list of 'laws' Zina had shown me before tonight's performance.

'*This* is what brought you here?' I asked. 'A bunch of idiotic edicts that aren't even legal being proposed by a group of ignorant bully-boys nobody respects?'

'And what happens when a weak and unpopular duke, frightened of his own subjects and pressured by his advisors, decides to pass a few of those laws to mollify those same bully-boys and their supporters? The laws of a nation define its people, Damelas. Change the laws, you change the people!'

She snatched the poster back from me and held it up to the passing crowds, shouting at them like a madwoman, 'Theatrical *blasphemy? That's* what offends you? And this' – her voice suddenly dropped an octave to almost drunken pomposity – '"the rights of the common man to enjoy his drink and drugs shall not be abridged by any ordinance or edict"? Oh, and let's not forget this one: "No money from the common coffers shall go to the wastrel, the vagrant or the foreigner"? How noble of you! How much better your lives will all be once your every venal prejudice is enshrined in law!'

Rhyleis tore the poster in half. 'Is this what passes for patriotism among you louts and thugs?'

Several of those same louts and thugs were now eyeing her up and muttering to each other.

I took the Bardatti by the elbow and marched her away from the gathering mob. As soon as we were clear of the crowds, I whispered, 'As it happens, fully half the population of Jereste consider getting drunk and stoned every night to be perfectly patriotic. And lately they're becoming more and more convinced that offensive plays and songs *are* detrimental to the soul of our once-noble city.'

She rounded on me, snarling, 'And you're just letting this happen?'

'*Me?* What am I supposed to do about it?'

She grabbed me by the lapels of my shabby coat. 'You're Damelas-fucking-Chademantaigne, you idiot – of *course* I was waiting for you to turn up at the Tavern-On-The-Ponta! You should already be out there unmasking whoever's concocting these hideous laws before they take hold and begin to spread elsewhere.'

'I'm an *actor*!' I shouted back at her, horribly aware the two of us were attracting attention again. 'It's not my—'

'Not your job? Your grandmother was Virany Chademantaigne, the King's Parry. You're a direct descendant of Damelas Chademantaigne, the first Greatcoat. Justice and swordplay are in your family's blood. I'm surprised your grandfather hasn't already challenged every one of these Iron Orchids to a duel—'

'He's nearly seventy years old—'

'All the more reason *you* ought to be in the game, Damelas.' She looked up at me through narrowed eyes as if searching for signs of some exotic disease I'd somehow contracted. Her gaze dropped to my waist. 'You're not even carrying a sword – what's the matter? Afraid you'll cut yourself?'

'Do you find it so easy to kill people you disagree with? Because perhaps the disease afflicting my city is what's making us all so quick to draw steel and slit each other's throats over any perceived slight and disagreement.'

She let go of my lapels and punched my shoulder, *hard*. 'When the disagreement is over whether my homeland becomes living Hells for those who *can't* draw steel to defend themselves and *don't* have the luxury of a cushy theatre in which to hide from their enemies, then you're damned right, I find it easy to kill those who would hound and torment "wastrels, vagrants and foreigners" to their deaths!'

I bowed curtly. 'Then may you enjoy your time in Jereste, Lady Rhyleis. Alas, I can't help you with your plan to duel every brute and bully-boy in the city, because as it turns out, I'm *not* my ancestor, nor am I anything like my grandparents. And with the Vixen, the Iron Orchids and quite possibly the Duke of Pertine all plotting to send me to an early grave, I have no need to add you to the list.' I turned and strode away, ignoring her calls for me to stop.

The weight of her disdain at my failure to live up to the example of my grandparents was no great burden. I'd been carrying it my entire life, after all.

CHAPTER 21

THE LOVER

Rhyleis shouted my name again, but between my longer stride and my determination to escape her carping, I was soon lost in the most crowded part of the bazaar. At last I came to a set of stone steps to street level and took them two at a time, keeping up my breakneck pace, ignoring the glaring drunks stumbling in search of a nice warm place in which to piss, pass out or possibly expire. Exhaustion warred with anger and lost the battle as I kept moving, eager for the dubious comforts of the Royal and a return to dealing with my own problems rather than the ones the Bardatti was apparently intent on piling on top.

So engrossed was I in the dreamy thought of cocooning myself beneath a heap of blankets and wishing away this past week, that I nearly slammed into a slender young man who stepped into my path to greet me.

'Well met, my midnight lover,' the fellow said, his light tenor voice dripping with the promise of pleasure and companionship, enhanced by the distinctive aroma of rainberry spice, an olfactory advertisement for those in his particular profession. The handsome youth beckoned me with a curled finger deeper into the darkened alley, further from the light bleeding beneath closed doors on either side. 'Fancy a quick fu—?'

'Fuck off,' I said with a snarl.

The rent-boy put up his hands in surrender and stepped back. 'You needn't gnash your teeth at me, sir.'

Saints, what's wrong with me? I've no business growling at him like that.

I was about to apologise, but the words that came out of my mouth were lower pitched, smoother and deadlier than my normal voice. 'Take no offence, young libertine' – I leaned casually against the corner of a decrepit building – 'for I was talking not to you but to your lady friend.'

'What lady friend?' the rent-boy asked, shifting uncomfortably.

Good question. What am I talking about?

'The one who forgot to blacken her blade before taking to the shadows beneath a full moon.' The fingers of my right hand closed into a fist and I suddenly found myself stalking into the alley. 'The one who is, I fear, going to have a most melancholy morning, should the tip of her blade rise so much as an inch higher.'

What are you doing, idiot? You're bone-tired and half-starved and even on a good day, you probably couldn't take the rent-boy in a fair fight. Now you want to challenge his girlfriend, too?

Inexplicably, I felt not fear but giddy excitement at the prospect of sending this pair of purse-baiters home with black eyes and broken noses. It wasn't only that they'd set out to mug me, but the sheer banality of their scheme: young lovers, impoverished by circumstance or bad choices, the pretty one to lure the patron into the alley so the stronger or faster or more bloodthirsty of the pair can deliver a beating before liberating the valuables.

In a city already crowded with bravos, bully-boys and freeblade fencers, amateurs like this pair would be easily cowed by a few bold words and a threatening posture. Or they would have been, had I not severely and catastrophically underestimated the situation . . .

'Run along now, Stefano,' the woman in the shadows said. 'You've played your part.'

The inexplicable defiance that had led me deeper into the alley fled faster than my breath. *Saint Forza-who-strikes-a-blow*, I prayed, fully aware that any such entreaties were far too late, for I recognised that voice.

She stepped into the light, tall and lean, the fitted dark burgundy leathers clinging to muscles sculpted by a lifetime of mastering the lightning-fast lunges for which she was rightly admired and feared. Her arms and wide shoulders were bare beneath the padded black duelling vest, revealing scars that told the world she wasn't timid in a fight. The eyes were the same deep brown as her hair, which was cut short in a distinctive fashion, with the fringe swept away from her forehead, the sides rising up, almost like the mane of a—

'Vixen,' I whispered.

She looked very different from when she'd turned up at the Belleza to witness my ill-fated performance as the herald. Even that casual appearance had skirted dangerously close to violating the duchy's laws on suspended duels, but to show up here, just a few blocks from my home . . .

On hearing the nickname of his employer, Stefano the rent-boy skittered away from her, slipping on the uneven paving even as he abandoned both me and whatever coin he'd been promised. A wise decision on his part, I thought. Despite her fame, few outside her own social echelon had ever met the Lady Ferica di Traizo face to face, and most of those who had, had known her for only a very, *very* short time.

'My beloved rabbit,' she said, her delicate, musical lilt better suited to a singer of love songs than the deadliest duellist in all of Jereste. She beckoned me closer with a curled finger, her other hand resting on the hilt of the rapier at her side. 'We are long overdue for this dance, you and I.'

CHAPTER 22

THE DANCER

Every city prides itself on being home to *The Greatest Duellist Who Ever Lived!* Like the grandiose claims of theatre companies promising an honest-to-gods real live Veristor on their stage, this was one of those very public lies that no one contradicted because everyone profited from it. The duellist, of course, was paid increasingly higher fees, purses clinking with gold jubilants instead of copper tears. Minstrels hired to laud their near-mythical accomplishments earned their share of silver grins, in turn attracting more clients eager to hire the best. Legal disputes featuring such legendary fencers meant that the duelling courts, the solicitors and advocates all saw higher fees too. So much good fortune to go around . . .

All for a lie.

My grandmother had forced me to read Errera Bottio's seminal text on the subject of duelling, *For You Are Sure to Die*, from cover to cover at least a dozen times. The book's lessons had never left me, and first among them was this: *there is no such thing as the perfect fencer*. Every swordsman or swordswoman dies eventually, and the greater their skill, the more vaunted their reputation, the more likely their end will come at the hands of an amateur.

These might be reassuring words when you're the amateur in question, but Bottio's sage counsel felt distinctly less convincing when face to face with the Vixen of Jereste.

Don't show fear, I reminded myself. *Never show fear to a predator or a duellist.*

My grandmother had been full of such helpful advice during the many hours she'd wasted trying to turn her awkward, nervous grandson into a passable fencer. Only she'd never bothered to explain just *how* I was supposed to disguise my fear.

My grandfather, thankfully, had had more practical counsel. 'Your grannona is a wise woman, Damy,' he'd whispered to me one night. 'Never show the enemy fear . . .' His face had split into a wide grin. 'Show him your heels instead!'

Running away was precisely how I'd ended up at the Operato Belleza in the first place, so perhaps discretion wasn't quite the panacea my grandfather had promised.

The Vixen walked a slow, graceful circle around me. The cracked cobblestones of the alley were, like so many in Jereste these days, littered with shattered clay jugs, foul-smelling refuse and other detritus – and yet every step Ferica di Traizo took was as steady as it was silent.

'The d-duel is still adjourned,' I stammered, 'and m-my contract with the Belleza prohibits me fr—'

'This is no duel, my rabbit,' she said soothingly, still circling. She hadn't drawn her rapier, but that didn't feel all that helpful. Having watched her at the duelling courts, I'd seen the speed with which she could make her weapon appear whenever she desired. 'I was most distressed when you fled our official assignation,' she went on. 'For one in my profession, a forfeit is no better than a draw. People like to talk, you know. They whisper behind your back, speculating: perhaps you secretly paid off your opponent? Clients wonder aloud whether the reach of your blade is a little too short these days to achieve their ends—'

'My Lady, it would be my privilege to reassure every one of your putative employers regarding the depth and sincerity of my cowardice.'

She gave a sorrowful shake of her head. 'Oh, my dashing rabbit, your self-effacing nature wounds me. When I learned you hadn't fled the city, I assumed your intent must be to hide yourself away somewhere, where you would be training relentlessly, studying the arts of the duello, until you could come back to me with grand designs of retrieving your honour.' She gave a playful, almost coquettish little shrug. 'Imagine my disappointment when I realised you really had become . . . an *actor*.'

'You thought . . . ?' I couldn't even bring myself to finish that sentence. The fact that this feral lunatic believed that a man running away from her as fast as his feet could carry him must be planning some intricate, heroic redemption for himself only proved that the two of us couldn't be from the same species.

I'm a rabbit. She's a vixen. This is the way of things, and my fate in this affair was dictated long before I dared challenge her.

So what was left? To die on my feet or on my knees?

Or maybe it's long past time you stopped playing the rabbit and became a wolf instead?

I buried that unruly thought as fast as it was born and, instead, held up my hands in surrender, my mind spinning in search of a way to delay my death even a second longer. 'My Lady, I hardly think your reputation will be enhanced by the cold-blooded murder of an unarmed man. Your enemies will say you feared to face me fairly in the duelling courts once my contract ended and thus took me in the dark with no more honour than the Pin, who sneaks into men's homes to murder them in their sleep.'

She gazed at me with that otherworldly confusion, as if I'd spoken in a foreign language. 'My rabbit, what on earth are you squealing about?' She gestured to the crumbling walls of the alley. 'We are neither in a duelling court nor that tawdry little apartment of yours . . . the *Royal*, is it?'

Perfect. The Vixen knows where I live.

'This is an alley,' she continued, 'and alleys are places not for duels nor murders, but for simple muggings.'

Without a warning, without even a sound, her blade was out of its sheath and I was yelping from the tiny cut on my right cheek.

The quick-draw. The Vixen's trademark.

I cursed myself for not having seen it coming. How many times had my grandmother told me to always watch my opponent's shoulders, not their eyes or their hands, both of which could move too quickly to follow. Had Lady di Traizo desired, she could've slid her point right past my ribs and through my heart. Apparently, she had something else in mind.

'Oh my, does that hurt, my rabbit? There's been such *a rash* of muggings lately – and though rarely fatal, I'm afraid a few cuts and bruises are the inevitable result.'

Her blade whipped out again; this time the flat struck the side of my head.

I stumbled back, vision blurring, balance all but gone. When my fingers went to the injury, I felt no blood, but a nasty bruise was certain.

Four bells rang out in the distance and the Vixen gave a theatrical sigh. 'Alas, I must go. I am, at this very moment, engaged in a delightful evening of cards with several well-known friends halfway across the city. Tomorrow I'll be on the south side – I have a late-night fitting for a new jacket. The day after, of course, I'll be fast asleep after an exhilarating session with a new lover of mine. It's too bad, really. If I were not otherwise so provably occupied, I might have been able to protect you from these scoundrels you'll no doubt keep encountering.'

A simple, but effective, plan, since the outcome would be as inevitable as it was callous. As long as I held my contract at the Operato Belleza, Lady di Traizo couldn't force me into a duel, and were I to be murdered outright, she would be a suspect; even if the crime couldn't be pinned on her, people would talk. But this? Catching me alone and inflicting whatever little wounds and indignities she pleased, always ensuring she had an alibi to cover her tracks?

She'll snare me like this over and over again until I can't take it any more – until one day I'll show up at the duelling court begging her to put an end to my misery.

But why now? If she was so damned determined to destroy me, why had she waited this long to enact her scheme? Duellists were hardly known for their patience.

'Why are you doing this to me?' I asked. 'I never—'

She cut me off, sharp as a knife, although her tone was as pleasant and playful as ever. 'Because your grandmother is already dead, Damelas Chademantaigne. I can hardly dig up the bitch's corpse and kill her a second time. Your grandfather might have made a reasonable substitute, but when I tried to force him into a duel . . .' She wagged a finger at me as if I were an errant schoolboy. 'Well, you know what you did.'

'He's an old man!' I cried out. 'His hand shakes – he's no match for you. Why torment him when you know he can't beat you?'

She gave no reply, just favoured me with that fox's smile of hers.

I couldn't seem to find my footing. My entire body was trembling, waging a war between terror and outrage, between tears and—

Laughter.

Cold, calculated laughter.

The horror grew as I realised the chilling mirth was coming from my own mouth.

'Come then, my quarrelsome little pup,' I heard myself say. My arms spread of their own accord, opening wide, a lover beckoning the object of his desire. 'Pierce my heart with love's arrow, my Lady Fox, but thrust deeply, mind. Let you not stop until your guard shatters against my breast and our lips meet for a final farewell.'

What in the seven Hells is happening to me? I wondered helplessly. *There's no stage here, no script for me to recite – why am I talking like this?*

Lady Ferica stared at me, bewilderment on her face. 'Do you perform a play for me now, Rabbit?'

An excellent question, I thought, but that mad impulse driving me kept goading her further.

'A rabbit, my dearest? Is that all I am to you?' My hands came up on either side of my head, fore and middle fingers bending like long, floppy ears. I stuck my front teeth out. 'Perhaps I am indeed a rabbit, my love, and we all know that ninety-nine times out of a hundred it's the fox who feasts upon the poor beast's flesh.' My arms dropped to my sides and I felt my fingers twitching, aching to pursue a course of action that would surely bring about my end. 'But the more enticing story is that rarest of tales – that one in a hundred in which the rabbit eats the fox, wouldn't you agree?'

Derision was in her gaze, but I noticed those broad shoulders were no longer quite so loose, her steps not so smooth as they had been when this game began. 'If you're hoping these bizarre theatrics are going to rattle me, Damelas, then I fear you've overestimated your abilities as an actor. Look at you – you're not even wearing a blade!'

'Why should I need one, my dearest? Yours looks sharp enough for my needs.'

She gave a stamp of her foot – a fencer's feint to throw me off – and my instinctual fear took hold again. A bead of sweat dripped down my brow. My mouth tasted copper. My heart was beating far too fast to keep up this inexplicable pretence that had taken hold of me. And yet, instead of trying to run, my left leg reached back as I bent at the waist and extended my right hand towards her, just as a courtier might while inviting her to dance . . . or a duellist offering her a quick death.

'To me, my midnight delight,' I heard myself say as calmly and confidently as if the Vixen and I were old bedmates, 'past time we shared that dance.'

Lady Ferica di Traizo took a half step back, just out of reach of my hand. 'You're bluffing,' she said warily.

Of course I'm bluffing, you idiot. Why in the name of Saint Gan-who-laughs-with-dice am I bluffing? Because I'm exhausted and confused, and a few hours ago I played the Archduke on stage and my head's still full of Corbier's arrogant bluster. Only problem is, he was a veteran of nearly a hundred duels and I've never won so much as a fistfight since I was ten.

'Would I dare dissemble before you, Lady Fox?' I asked. 'A question for the ages, one pondered by men and women better trained and better armed than yourself. Though should you wish to divine how it was I so easily turned their fine blades against them, well . . .' Still bent at the waist, I curled a finger and invited her closer. 'I would be happy to arrange for you to ask them directly.'

For a long while she watched me, neither her eyes nor her hands moving even a hair. A lifetime of training and instinct was being confounded by my baffling performance. At last her smile returned, though the line of her mouth was stiff now, a red slash painted on an ivory mask. 'So I was right all along. You *have* been training! Studying ruses and tactics, I imagine? A year wouldn't be enough to ready you to challenge me on skill alone, so instead you've been practising your disarms and deceptions, plotting distractions and sudden attacks? Not a bad strategy for someone in your position. Even the greatest duellist can fall prey to a beginner's trick if she isn't ready for it.'

Lady Ferica di Traizo backed away and gave a quick salute of her blade. 'When next we meet by midnight, my rabbit.'

I smiled at that, knowing the use of the old duelling expression made the strange, reckless spirit inside me like her better. I gave her a fencer's bow, low, but never taking my eyes off hers. 'Until that hour, may you know no harm, my Lady Fox.'

Her elegant, sinuous silhouette disappeared from the alley, leaving me alone and wondering what madness had overtaken me. My shirt was soaked in sweat, my hands shaking and heart thumping, and all the while I struggled to catch my breath, for I couldn't seem to stop laughing.

CHAPTER 23

LAUGHTER

'You said *what*?' Beretto guffawed heartily, slapping a hand against his own chest as if he were in the midst of a heart attack. 'Tell it again, brother! Of such fine music my ears have too long been denied!'

'I told you, I asked Rhyleis why she was push—'

'No, no,' he sputtered, spilling wine down his beard, 'the part where you said to the Vixen – the *Vixen*, Damelas – "What blade should I require, my love, but the one in your hand that so longs to rest in mine?"'

'That's not even how I said it!'

Beretto fumbled around our rickety timber dining table in search of quill and ink. 'It's how you'll be saying it in the new play I'm going to write. *Of Vixens and Rabbits – A Romance of Rapiers*.' He stopped, muttering, 'Damn, that's a good title.'

'This isn't funny, Beretto! You weren't there. I was out of my head. I nearly tried to snatch the Vixen's blade right from her hand! *Lady Ferica di Traizo* – the most famous duellist in the city! Consequences to her reputation be damned, she could've killed me then and there—'

'Ah, but she didn't, did she?'

Beretto abandoned his search for writing implements in favour of a minuscule drumstick wrenched from the unidentified bird Mother had provided for tonight's supper. He shook it at me. 'The Vixen expected to find a rabbit hopping unknowingly into her lair tonight, but in truth, she faced that most dangerous of predators, the beast before whom all others must roll upon the ground to reveal their bellies . . . *an actor*!'

'You're enjoying this far too much,' I said, reaching over to take the remains of the drumstick.

Beretto licked the juices from his fingers. 'And you aren't enjoying it nearly enough, my friend.'

I decided to forego a reply in favour of further risking my life by eating the meal Mother had so generously provided. The meat was stringy and tough and the emaciated pigeon who had provided it had probably been diseased. It tasted delicious.

'Oh, saints,' I moaned after the first swallow, 'tell me there's more of this – I don't remember when I last ate.'

Beretto, regret painted on his features, showed me the empty plate. 'I waited as long as I could, my friend, but a man has needs.' He grinned. 'But tonight, let us break with tradition and beg of Mother's goodwill a second feast.'

He took the plate and sent it down with a pair of measly copper tears.

A moment later a menacing voice called up through the shaft, 'You'll cry me three more tears or go hungry tonight.'

'Two coppers were all I had, beloved Mother,' Beretto cried into the shaft. He didn't dare admit to possessing a gold jubilant. Our fellow denizens of the Royal would break into our apartment nightly in search of our treasure.

'Well, now you have none, and you ain't got no chicken, neither!'

Beretto raised an eyebrow and said – not particularly quietly – to me, 'I have as many chickens as she does.'

'I heard that!'

'Of course you did.' Beretto placed a hand on his heart as he leaned into the shaft and called down, 'How could your hearing be other than perfect, when your divine ears were sculpted by the gods themselves to inspire poets – and such a sonnet I'll write you, my lovely Mother, as none have ever—'

'That's worth four tears,' she called up.

'Four copper tears for a single sonnet?' Beretto asked, surprised.

'Aye. You want me to listen to another one of those silly rhymes of yours, it's going to cost you four tears!'

The sound of her cackling echoing up the dumbwaiter shaft was the stuff from which nightmares were sewn.

Beretto's face took on a peevish expression. 'Fine. I'll come and clean out the rubbish for you in the morning.'

'And scrub the cankers on my feet. They've been aching something awful lately.'

Beretto paled, but like one of the great warriors of old, compelled by honour to charge the hill no sane man would dare, he said, 'Marked.'

A few minutes later, his noble sacrifice had become a fresh roasted bird, and big enough this time to suggest that the morning sun would bring Beretto no joy.

'You are,' I said, wiping the back of my hand across grease-stained lips, 'a truer and more boon companion than ever I knew.'

Beretto leaned back in his chair. 'And you, my friend, have restored my faith in our profession.' He shook his head ruefully. 'After watching Abastrini chew every line like old leather these past years, I despaired of ever being part of a play worth performing. But last night . . .' He whistled through his teeth. 'Last night, I, Beretto Bravi of South Lankavir, stood upon a stage where magic was conjured and the dull-witted cynicism that has plagued our profession too long was banished.'

'Was it really so impressive?' I asked.

'Are you fishing for compliments?'

'No. It's just . . . to me it was all a blur – a haze. Like standing in two worlds at once, unable to see either clearly. I completely forgot Shoville's script.'

'The script? Who gives a shit about the script? What you gave us was so much better than any mere text!' The rickety chair protested when he rose to pace about the room. 'There you were, coming up with those amazing lines, and even better, giving us subtle clues of what the rest of us were to say and do next. It was like . . . it was like you were a conductor and we your orchestra . . . No – no, we were the *instruments*! The most finely crafted violins and vitolas, bursting with new melodies as your bow slid across our strings.'

'Gods, Beretto, listen to yourself – these similes? They're why Shoville never wants to buy your scripts—'

'Pah! Shoville doesn't know talent when it kicks him in the arse. He runs from passion like a cat scurries from thrown water. No wonder his love scenes are so tame . . .' His voice tailed off and a lascivious grin appeared.

'What are you smiling about, Beretto?' I asked, my stomach suddenly queasy – and not from Mother's chicken.

The big man broke out laughing. 'You and Roz – I swear, for a second there, I thought we were going to spend the third act watching the two of you fucking like weasels.' He wagged a finger at me. 'I shall be most disappointed in you, brother, if you don't do exactly that at tonight's performance.'

'I've had enough people threaten me with knives lately,' I reminded him. 'I don't need Roslyn slitting my throat in front of a packed theatre.'

'It *would* make for quite a surprise ending to our play if the legendarily fidelitous Lady Ajelaine should slay Corbier after a raunchy bout of rumpy-pumpy. Now that I think on it, an ending like that might please our public mightily.' He waved a hand in the air. 'But no, I fear Roz would not agree. Oh, and speaking of the devilishly voluptuous one, she wanted me to tell you that you're to arrive at the Belleza an hour early tonight.'

'Why? Has Shoville called another rehearsal?'

'No, Roz wants to practise your kissing scene together. You know, on the off-chance you don't faint tonight before getting to the good part? Looks like she fancies you rotten now that you're not quite so abominable an actor.'

A hearty endorsement, that, and it might even have been gratifying, if I had been more interested and Roslyn less married. Besides, the audience might not take kindly to witnessing vile Corbier and saintly Ajelaine in an adulterous embrace.

'Beretto, I'm really worried about the company – about what will happen to all of us if this play continues.' I set my plate down on the floor and went to stand by the wooden-shuttered window, my thoughts turning back to the encounters with Duke Monsegino, the Vixen, and above all, Lady Shariza, who half the time looked as if she were awaiting the command to kill me, and the other half as if she feared for me. I spread the window slats with my fingers.

'There's a . . . a darkness out there, Beretto. The Iron Orchids are so much worse than we ever knew, and these laws they're proposing? They're cruel and despicable. I don't know why, but after what happened outside the Belleza, with the other companies being paid to attack me, I'm becoming convinced that someone believes the means to stop the Orchids is hidden within the tale of Corbier and Ajelaine.'

'Yes,' Beretto said, thumping his fist against his own chest again, 'yes! *This* is why the gods created the theatre: Art in the service of Chaos! Actors giving shape to the truth until it shakes the very foundations of the world!'

His enthusiasm was beginning to sound perilously close to all that Bardatti bravado and Rhyleis' admonitions that I ought to be out there, rapier in hand, challenging the Iron Orchids, the Vixen and everyone else who dared scheme against my homeland.

'You keep talking about this as if it's all some grand adventure,' I yelled at him, unable to contain my consternation any longer. 'You great *idiot*! Stop preening on about the theatre and the importance of actors – we're called *players*, Beretto, because what we do is just a game . . . only now it's a game that's going to get someone killed—'

'Not if we outwit our enemies and draw them out of the shadows and into the light—'

'*Outwit* them? Are you mad? You think I want to set myself at war with the most powerful people in this city? Whose "wits" am I to rely on, you oaf? *Yours?*'

Beretto's smile faded. His shoulders slumped. 'I'm sorry, brother. I didn't mean to . . . It's just . . .'

For a moment he looked so much as if he were about to cry that I wondered if this was some joke, that Beretto would suddenly jump up and start laughing at my gullibility. But no, spite was foreign to his nature . . .

What's wrong with me? How deep in my bones has Corbier's bitter spirit permeated that I would talk this way to a better friend than I've ever known or deserved?

'Saints damn me, Beretto, I'm sorry.'

He shook his head. 'No, no, it's my fault. I shouldn't be making light of the dangers you're facing – the Vixen, the Orchids, the Black

Amaranth – but . . . . well, it's just that part of me . . . No, forget it. I'm not nearly drunk enough to make sense.'

'Tell me.'

He was silent for a while. When at last he spoke again, his voice was quiet, almost timid. 'I wanted to be a Greatcoat, ever since I was a boy – you know that. I wanted to be the one who rides into danger with naught but a good cause, a sharp blade and a fool's smile. I'm big. I'm strong. I can fight. So why not me? But I spent every penny I had travelling to Aramor, begged King Paelis to let me join his magistrates. "Justice isn't a performance." That's what he told me. "The Greatcoats need duellists and magistrates, not players."'

That wasn't so different from what my grandmother used to fling at me when I refused to practise my sword fighting. 'So it turns out the great King Paelis was an arsehole.'

'No – no,' he said earnestly, 'I mean, sure, I was disappointed – heart-broken, in fact. But it was more than that, because after we'd all been seen, the King took me aside and he said, "The world needs stories as much as it needs verdicts. It wants for hope even more than justice. These times call for Bardatti as much they do for Greatcoats."' Beretto chuckled. 'So I went off to join the Bardatti, only it turned out they weren't interested, either.'

And here I was, grumbling about being called a Veristor – an honour of such magnitude I could scarcely fathom its meaning, never mind appreciate such undeserved fortune. Saints, what a vain, self-important fool I'd been, whining endlessly about a curse that was, in Beretto's eyes, a gift beyond price.

'I'm sorry, Beretto. I've been a fool—'

He waved the apology away. 'Well, fools and jesters used to be actors too, so I suppose it makes sense.' He walked over and put a meaty hand on my shoulder. 'I don't mind, honestly I don't. If my role in all this is to help you become a true Veristor, to stand by your side and knock a few heads out of the way so that you can speak truth to power, well then, I'll count myself as lucky an actor as has ever lived.'

I found it hard to speak in the face of such unearned loyalty.

So maybe now's the time to start earning it.

'I was raised by two Greatcoats,' I said, 'and while I knew almost from birth that I'd never be worthy of such a lofty title, the one thing my childhood with the King's Parry and the King's Courtesy taught me was how to spot those who are.'

I took hold of my friend's hand between both of mine. It felt awkward and contrived and yet exactly the right thing to do. 'On what little honour I have, I swear to you, Beretto, one day I will find the First Cantor of the Greatcoats. I will walk up to him or her and slap them across the face with my glove and say, "Name you Beretto Bravi to the Greatcoats, and do so today, or tomorrow you will face me in the duelling circle and, by steel and blood, will I change your mind."'

Beretto stared at me, mouth hanging open, tears already forming at the corners of his eyes. The man could cry at the drop of a hat. 'Oh, my brother,' he shouted, shaking off my hands to grab me in a crushing hug. More softly he said, 'That would mean so much more if you weren't such a lousy fencer.'

CHAPTER 24

THE INVITATION

We laughed and drank every drop of ale Beretto's obscene promises could wheedle out of Mother until the unpleasant glare of morning seeped through the shuttered windows. As dangerous sobriety began to set in, I declared, 'I'm for bed. Don't wake me until it's time to head out to the Belleza – or if someone's come to murder me.'

'Ah,' Beretto said. 'I *knew* there was something I was forgetting.' He stumbled to the other side of the living room and started fishing in a stack of scripts.

Saint Zaghev-who-sings-for-tears, please don't make me read another of his new plays . . .

'Beretto, you know I love and admire your stories, but—'

'None of your platitudes, varlet. I merely hid the invitation here in case the Bulger came a-burgling while we slept.'

I rose to join him. 'An invitation?'

'Yes,' Beretto said, still shuffling through the pile of paper. 'While you were off wooing half the ladies of Jereste—'

'Most of them being assassins or madwomen, of course.'

Beretto shifted his attention to the bookshelf of well-worn novels. 'Naturally. Anyway, while you were indulging your preoccupation with breasts and awkward fiddly bits—'

'Um . . . you know you've slept with more women than I have, right?'

'—beauty in all things—'

'Yes, well, did they appreciate you referring to their private parts as "fiddly bits"?'

The big man held a book by the spine and shook it. 'Can't be sure. At the time they were screaming my name.' He dropped it and picked up another. 'I'm strangely gifted at making love to women.'

One of these days the saints were going to send a wonderful, good-hearted man to fall madly in love with Beretto . . . and the saints would owe that poor fellow an *enormous* apology.

As he shook the next volume, what looked at first to be a wooden coin with something gleaming at its centre slid out from between the pages. He caught it in his free hand – then displayed the title. 'Of course – *Saint Erastian's Erotic Journeys*. I knew I'd put it somewhere sensible.'

I walked over and took the proffered object, which turned out not to be a coin, but a thin, delicately carved brooch of gilded ebony shaped like a human eye with an iris of gold. I rolled the smooth disc between my thumb and forefinger, marvelling at the exquisitely dark grain of the wood and the way the light of our candles glinting in the gold of the eye made it seem alive, almost as if it were watching me.

'A scholar's mark?' I asked. 'Why would someone leave a pass to the Grand Library for me? And why didn't you mention this earlier?'

'How was I to remember something so trivial when you were staggering in here raving about mad Bardatti guitarists and scaring off the Vixen herself with your raw, unbridled manly disposition? Besides, the library isn't open at night, so it's not as if you could've done anything about it.'

I examined the gold edge of the scholar's mark more closely. It was a thin layer, although you could probably scrape off at least a jubilant's worth, but access to the Grand Library of Jereste was far more valuable, so I'd been told.

'And you've no idea who left this for me?'

'I never saw them, but I can tell you everything you need to know about your would-be benefactor.'

'If you didn't see any—'

Beretto took the brooch from me and flipped it in the air like a coin. 'Do you have any idea how much a pass like this costs? At best – and only if we came into a decent inheritance – a commoner like you or me could afford a copper-trimmed one. Scholars from the academies and visiting professors *might* wear a silver mark, if their institutions were paying. But a *gold* pass?' He flipped it again. 'These are crafted exclusively for the great Houses of Pertine, and that means—'

When I snatched it in mid-air, the shiny golden iris at the centre seemed to wink at me. I pinned it next to my Veristor's mark, then glanced over at the window and the now glaring morning light. The Grand Library would be opening soon. I picked up my coat and headed for the door. 'Someone very powerful desires to make my acquaintance at my earliest inconvenience.'

CHAPTER 25

THE GRAND LIBRARY

Jereste's Grand Library, the largest and most prestigious in the entire duchy, was a monument to architecture, scholarship and hypocrisy. Twelve massive columns surrounded the gargantuan storehouse of lore, one for each of the twelve branches of knowledge held within on hundreds of shelves holding thousands of books. Inscribed in glittering gold letters on the arch above the front entrance was a motto that was itself a testament to sanctimony: *That nothing true may be lost, and all that is known freely shared.*

Shared with all who could afford a pass, to be more precise.

The library warden examining the scholar's mark on my collar kept one hand on the two-foot-long iron truncheon that served as both badge of office and the means of dispensing with unwanted visitors. His gaze flitted between the gold-edged ebony brooch and its bearer's clothes. I endured the scrutiny with what dignity I could, all too aware that a quick change of shirt and splash of water on my face had done little to dampen the odours acquired during the actors' brawl and later worsened by my encounter with the Vixen.

'How'd you come by this, then?' the warden asked, pinching the scholar's mark between thumb and forefinger.

Anticipating the question, I'd prepared what I believed to be the most effective response. 'None of your fucking business.'

After all, even the truth wouldn't have satisfactorily explained my possession of the scholar's mark. 'Someone gave it to me' would have invited the question of *who*, and the lack of a credible reply would have convinced the warden that the brooch had been stolen and the miscreant in possession of it a liar, a thief and possibly a murderer. He would summon his fellow guards and soon thereafter I'd be suffering a repeat of last night's unpleasantness, this time without any twelve-year-old brick-hurling street urchins to come to my rescue.

The warden locked eyes with me, twitching his truncheon as if doing so would shake the interloper before him into revealing the origin of this gold scholar's mark, but I didn't blink. I'd stood up to the Vixen last night – admittedly, it was under Corbier's influence, but I still wasn't about to go scurrying away because a bored library warden didn't like the look of me.

Some claimed there were more wardens in the Grand Library of Jereste than there were guards employed by the Ducal Palace, and while the duke no doubt hoped this was not the case, no one could doubt that these armed guardians of knowledge took their role as protectors seriously and prided themselves on their merciless enforcement. I'd been told they carried truncheons instead of bladed weapons to reduce the chance of harming a book or scroll on those occasions when they found it necessary to bludgeon a patron into unconsciousness.

'There's a placard inside the front doors, and at the top of the stairs for each floor,' this one said, finally removing his thumb and forefinger from my collar. 'You follow those rules when handling the books and you won't have any problems. Break one of them and we'll break something of yours.'

'Hardly my first time here, friend,' I lied glibly, striding past the warden.

'We'll be keeping an eye on you,' he called out.

Guess it's not only actors who feel the need to get the last line.

Once through the arch and into the sprawling, centuries-old building, I paused to catch my breath, my senses overwhelmed at the scale of the library, surely as magnificent as any palace. Each circular floor had rows of long, curved shelves, forming colonnades around a central avenue where supervising librarians sat at gleaming wooden desks, watching the patrons perusing books or filling in the sheaves of forms necessary for access to the rarer tomes kept at the top of the building. What kind of life must it be, surrounded daily by so much knowledge? Science, art, mathematics, philosophy . . . A person could spend their life here reading novels filled with tales sacred and profane, imagining other possibilities for their future.

My fingers reached up once again to feel the scholar's brooch, only to realise I'd instead gone to the Veristor's mark pinned to the other side of my collar. Had that been mere instinct, or was Corbier's influence even now guiding my hand?

I made my way to the historical section on the second floor and searched for everything covering the period a hundred years ago when the conflicts between Pierzi and Corbier had dominated the duchy's affairs. I felt an unexpected surge of pride when I found only a few books which weren't already in the Operato Belleza's own library. It was a matter of honour that the historias presented by the Knights of the Curtain were the most authentic of any company in the city.

Well, until I'd got involved, at any rate.

I carried three hefty leather-bound volumes to one of the reading desks, their back-bending weight reminding me how exhausted I was. The prospect of spending the entire day poring over them, before rushing back to the theatre for another dreadful performance – sure to end in further disaster – left me nauseous.

Tits up, brother, I imagined Beretto saying in that infuriatingly optimistic tone of his. *I'll bet one of these books has a terrific last line you can deliver right before they hang you.*

Hours later, barely able to focus, my single momentous discovery was that the number of spelling mistakes made by scribes reproducing a text increased the closer they got to the end.

So far the only book that had provided any real insight into the Raven's life was a medical text, probably misfiled because of its title: *Observations Of Ocular Maladies, Being An Account Of Certain Peculiar Conditions Of The Eyes Such As Those Of Prelate Urdius, Archduke Corbier, And Other Notables*. Corbier's eyes had been blue until shortly before his seventh birthday when, overnight, the irises turned dark red. The physician who wrote the book believed this was due to an illness that caused the blood vessels in the eye to swell and rise to the surface; he suggested this could have been ameliorated with the use of certain illicit herbal remedies. Of course, his hypothesis directly contradicted the far more popular theory that Corbier was a demon-spawn who'd chosen to at last reveal his vile nature.

The physician's less supernatural speculations were mildly interesting, but brought me no closer to understanding Corbier the man. I turned to the next book on the pile, but found my attention drawn not to the words, but to the odd little drawings squirming along the margins of the pages like trails of insects: weaponry, fierce beasts, and, in some of the more obscure tracts, what looked like poorly disguised decorative genitalia. This being Pertine, of course, illustrations of flowers and vines were everywhere. Mentions of marriages got roses, and the blue pertine showed up wherever a coronation was discussed. None of it was proving to be particularly illuminating.

But when I came across the adornments in the third book, *The Garden of Majesty*, a slender volume by one Sigurdis Macha, my curiosity was piqued. The handwritten journal, bound in cracked, dark green leather, purported to recount the 'Glorious Deedes of the Noble Lineages of Pertine', but it read more like thinly veiled parody.

'*. . . of such fertile seed did Margrave Lurius the Mighty bloom that one almost wonders whether the good God War was its source, rather than his father, who was said to be eighty at his son's birth and was known to have suffered an unfortunate amputation of his noble staff several years earlier. Truly is the potency of the ruling classes herein proved,*' I read aloud, ignoring the disapproving stares around me.

A later passage was even less circumspect: *How playful are the noble souls of this city, how merry. How often we find those in power and those who seek it almost like children grasping at each other's toys.*

Such innuendo was typical of satirical biographies; there were any number of similarly salacious plays. What surprised me were the passages inferring ducal corruption. The marginalia suggested grey lilies entwined around golden crowns, but the longer I stared at them, the more I was convinced they were actually orchids.

Iron orchids, perhaps?

The flaw in my clever theory was that the date inside the front cover of *The Garden of Majesty* was nearly a century ago and the Iron Orchids first appeared in Jereste only a few years back. And who was this Sigurdis Macha anyway? The name was surely a pseudonym; what loving parents would call their newborn 'Cutter of Weeds' in archaic Tristian?

My stomach rumbling, I pushed the book aside.

Twilight was only an hour away and I would soon need to race back to the Belleza to get into my costume and memorise whatever mangled lines Shoville had added to the script. And there was that 'rehearsal' Roslyn had in mind for the two of us . . .

What a colossal waste of time this turned out to be, I thought, staring down at the stack on the little reading desk and cursing whoever it was who'd left the scholar's mark for me in the first place. Then my eyes landed on *The Garden of Majesty* again. I flipped through the pages once more, examining the orchid drawings, but there was nothing hidden there that I could see. Only when I gave up and closed the book did I notice the discreet *Vol. I* inscribed at the bottom of the spine.

'Have you any more books by Sigurdis Macha?' I asked an elderly librarian stationed at the centre of the concentric colonnades of polished oak shelves. 'Specifically, the second volume of *The Garden of Majesty*?'

The hawkish-faced woman at the desk glanced up with a smile that faded when she got a look at me. 'Students given the privilege of entering the library should know better than to expect others to do their work for them.'

'I'm an actor, not a—' I stopped, doubting she cared about such distinctions, and instead unpinned the ebony and gold brooch from my collar and handed it to her.

If the warden had been dubious about my right to be here, the librarian was positively disgusted. 'Fucking noble Houses,' she swore as she turned it over in her fingers. 'Which wastrel lord gave you this in payment for sucking his cock? Or was it a tip from some bitch damina for licking her arse pleasingly?'

She tossed the mark back at me before turning away to begin digging through the huge leather-bound registries. After a minute of angry flipping, she informed me, 'Sigurdis Macha was a barely literate smut merchant who probably needed four drinks to string three words together. No doubt why he wrote only one book.'

My heart sank. Macha had been the only writer of the period to offer something more intriguing than grandiose praise and platitudes.

'. . . which he split between two volumes,' the librarian added.

'Wait, what? So there *is* a second book?'

'Volume,' she corrected me, squinting at her leather-bound registry. 'Yes, here we are: *The Court of Flowers* by Sigurdis Macha.' The librarian rolled her eyes. 'Someone should've told that talentless hack that writers of satire have a solemn duty to avoid pretentiousness.'

I reached for the registry. 'The second volume – it's really called *The Court of Flowers*?' But before I could see the listing myself, the librarian wrenched the registry back, the curl of her lip suggesting she wasn't above biting a patron's hand, should the need arise.

'Try that again and I'll call the wardens and have them tear off both your arms and toss them out the front door,' she warned, adding, 'Hardly worth losing a limb over a book so banal that no publisher would waste the paper on it.'

I stared at the worn volume in my hand. 'You're telling me I'm holding Sigurdis Macha's *original* journal?'

The librarian tapped a finger on the listing in her registry. 'Which should tell you how worthless it is. Says here that after Macha's death, the text was declared seditious and not to be reproduced on pain of imprisonment.'

My fingertips drifted across the cracked leather. The cover had probably been as green as emerald a century ago, but time and handling had stained it a darker, forbidding olive colour. Something about it was oddly familiar, although I was positive I'd never seen it before.

'What about the second volume, then?' I asked the librarian. 'Where can I find *The Court of Flowers*?'

She gestured dismissively towards the aisle that led to a wide marble stairway guarded by one of the wardens. 'According to the registry, the second volume is in the restricted section. But I wouldn't get your hopes up. The wardens will flay you alive and use your skin for vellum before they let some pissant viscount's prostitute mount those stairs.'

I let the insult go and pinned the brooch back on my collar. 'I suspect this might smooth the way.'

She shrugged. 'Perhaps. I couldn't care less either way.'

I was about to leave, but curiosity made me hesitate. 'You're very free with your thoughts on the nobility. Aren't you worried someone might report you?'

One corner of her mouth rose in a smirk. 'You think I fear those toothless wastrels and their overfed bodyguards? More likely I'll wake up one night to find the Pin standing over my bed with his poignard already buried in my throat, or someone'll spread a rumour I've got foreign blood and the Iron Arseholes will crown me with spikes through my skull, leaving me hanging from my own balcony for passers-by to ogle as the blood seeps from my eye sockets.'

'You're not frightened of either possibility?'

'Look around, rent-boy. The good God Death has more than his share of ways to feed his hunger these days.' The old woman pulled the neckline of her shirt just low enough to reveal a mass of bulbous red sores. 'The Scarlet Waste, they call it. Feels like rats crawling under my skin at night. It's not contagious, so they let me continue working here. I'll be dead long before anyone bothers to arrest me for some trumped-up crime or another – and long before you'll get to see that book you're after.'

I was awed by this woman, so pragmatic in the face of such a horrific and surely fatal disease. 'I'm sorry, my Lady,' I said at last. 'I wish you a peaceful passing.'

That earned me a halfway genuine smile. 'I imagine my death will be as peaceful as any soul may hope for in such troubled times, gentle whore. As peaceful as any of us deserve.'

CHAPTER 26

THAT WHICH GLITTERS BRIGHTEST

I'm not one of those people who can bend others to my will. Never having known the influence that comes from being born into wealth, I was enjoying the prospect of pointing to a brooch on my collar and having men of violence bow and scrape before me.

'What do you mean I can't enter?' I demanded, tilting the scholar's mark so that the gilded edges would catch the lantern light. 'I've got a gold pass!'

The senior warden guarding the restricted floor offered up what could best be described as tolerant disdain. 'Gold gets you in the library once a day. Don't let you into the restricted athenaeum.'

I kept tapping the pin on my collar as if it were a bell that could magically awaken the warden's sense of awe. 'But what else is there?'

Someone standing behind harrumphed to indicate that I was blocking the way. The warden pushed me aside with one hand, and with the other, beckoned forward the richly dressed man also waiting to get in. At first glance, the fellow's eye-shaped brooch looked identical to mine – until the light from the enormous lantern hanging above us glinted off a green stone in the centre of the iris.

'Was that an emerald?' I asked, once the man had gone in.

The warden smiled as if a child had just asked if there were numbers larger than three. 'Emerald. Sapphire. Ruby. Diamond.'

'*Diamond?* But what else is left once someone can enter the restricted section?'

'Oh, plenty of things. Librarians will do private research for those bearing sapphire passes. A ruby pass gets you a scribe to copy the unrestricted books.'

'And diamond?'

The warden pursed his lips. 'Truth be told, I've never seen one, and I'm not entirely sure what it allows. All I know is that if someone ever shows up with one, all us wardens are to clear the library at once while a clerk fetches the chief librarian.'

Saint Anlas-who-remembers-the-world, I thought, *whoever knew there was a secret hierarchy of library patrons out there?*

I started pondering what other enigmas were being kept from prying eyes – and what could possibly be so seditious in the work of an obscure author like Sigurdis Macha that it warranted being kept under lock and key?

'Please,' I begged, 'I just need to look at the second volume of *The Garden of Majesty* – two minutes with it and I'll be gone.'

The warden stroked the short truncheon hanging from his belt. 'The only thing open to negotiation, sir, is the manner of your departure, not the timing.'

So ended my career as a budding scholar of historical puzzles. The last thing I needed was more bruises.

But as I turned to leave, I heard someone whisper, 'If it is a garden of majesty you seek, oh Veristor, you shan't find one in this barren desert.'

I spun around, searching for whoever'd spoken, but all I saw were rows of shelves on either side and the warden barring my path.

'What did you say?' I asked.

'I said the only thing open to nego—'

'Right, right. Clever turn of phrase, that.' I turned to seek the owner of the mysterious voice, which I noted had been pitched theatrically low.

Someone's trying to be sneaky. My mysterious benefactor, perhaps?

I traced a path along the nearest of the massive curved bookcases, almost positive I could hear someone shuffling on the other side.

'Hello?' I asked, quickly pushing several volumes out of the way to create a three-inch gap. I caught a glimpse of loosely braided coral tresses, but when I walked to the end and round to the other side, the row was empty.

'Who's there?' I demanded.

'A ghost, perhaps?' This time the voice came from a set of shallow shelves behind me. When I turned, a pair of green eyes locked with mine through the gap between books. The pinching at the corners suggested an unseen smile.

'Who are you?' I asked.

'A friend,' came the evasive reply. After a theatrical pause, the voice added, '. . . perhaps.'

'Was it you who left the scholar's mark for me? Because it hasn't helped me one bi—'

But she was gone again.

'I've no time for childish pranks,' I called out, which elicited a roar of '*Hush!*' and '*Shhhh!*' from the reading desks lining the far wall, followed by angry whispers threatening dire consequences if I didn't shut up. The *whoosh* of books being shoved aside made me spin around. This time my tormentor had made her own gap, revealing a pair of berry-red lips framed by plump cheeks and chin painted with the alchemical sigils used by those actors who lower themselves to performing in cheapside occultatoria. Despite the elaborate stage trickery used to craft the illusion of foreign mages performing supernatural feats, these . . . . entertainments . . . generally ended with half the cast naked and writhing together on the stage. I wasn't especially proud of my career as an actor, but at least I'd never had to perform in an occultatoria.

I had things to do and was out of patience. 'Either reveal yourself or leave me alone,' I said.

She pushed more of the books aside, and kept beckoning me closer until my face was pressed into the gap – whereupon she reached a hand through, gripped the back of my neck and pulled me into a kiss.

It was, as such things went, a pleasant kiss. A man of greater integrity might have stopped it sooner, but I was tired and confused and really, people rarely offered me kisses. Her tongue danced playfully with mine as her fingernails traced gentle circles on my neck. I was so caught up in the moment that I failed to notice her pushing aside the books on a lower shelf until she'd slithered her other hand into the top of my trousers.

'Stop!' I said, pulling away.

'What's the matter?' she asked. 'Afraid we'll ruin the books?'

'Among other things.'

'Well, you're no fun at all,' the woman informed me. There was a pronounced street accent to her words. 'I fancy the real Archduke Corbier wouldn't turn away such an opportunity.' She pushed aside more books and pressed her chest forward. 'How much would you wager he'd seize the moment with both hands?'

Beneath the playful words, I noted her delivery was too smooth, too rehearsed. The cheapside rent-girl act and ribald tone weren't quite enough to mask a highborn Pertine accent.

I made my way back along the shelves, expecting her to evade me once again, but when I rounded the corner, she was waiting for me with a sultry smile on her lips, hands on her generous hips.

I extended my right leg back and, bowing deeply, I stretched out a hand to her. 'I would address you properly, my Lady, but I must first beg the gift of your name.'

The entrancingly pneumatic noblewoman crossed her arms and leaned negligently against the shelves, the pale red, almost pink, braids of her hair dangling over one shoulder. 'So where's this "lady" you're talkin' to?'

She doesn't like being caught out, so this is a competition for her. But who else is playing? Surely not a trifling actor. No, someone closer to her own class.

I kept my silence, still bowing, forcing her to acknowledge her rank.

'Clever,' she said at last, giving up the game. She took my hand and, just as Shariza had done, turned it and kissed the back as if she were the courtier and I the noble. 'But wouldn't a true Bardatti Veristor already have divined my identity?'

A friend of Ferica di Traizo's, perhaps? But I quickly rejected that idea. Flirting with the lower classes wasn't the Vixen's idea of entertainment.

So, not an enemy, I decided, *nor a friend, either. Someone who intends using me for their own ends, yet prefers the illusion of alliance.*

My mask of nonchalance nearly fell apart when the answer came to me, but I refused to let her see my shock.

'I aim for no title higher than that of actor, my Lady.' Before she could pull her hand away, I echoed her action, kissing the back of it. 'But would the name of your family win me some small measure of your esteem?'

She looked surprised and the false accent vanished, her words now sharp as a blade, her smooth delivery making her sound almost poetic. 'Let us see, then, Damelas Chademantaigne, whether you share the investigative talents once ascribed to your grandmother, the King's . . . *Thrust*, I believe they called her?'

Lately it had become everyone's hobby to throw my grandmother's name in my face at any available opportunity, as if my grandfather had been nothing but some lowly servant to her grander destiny. I wasn't especially impressed with the casual insult, either.

'Virany Chademantaigne was dubbed the King's *Parry*,' I corrected, then allowed myself a lengthy – insolent – pause before adding, 'your Grace.'

Her shoulders stiffened, her lips pressing to a flat line.

Got you!

'You elevate me to a position I do not hold,' she said.

I bowed low a second time. 'Forgive me, but I assumed that as your cousin is a duke . . .'

'Then you are twice misinformed, my handsome Veristor, for Duke Firan Monsegino is my nephew, not my cousin, and I, alas, a mere viscountess.'

Since she was so delighted with my apparent error, I decided to give her the triumph she so clearly desired. Gazing at her, I stammered, 'B-but . . . you can't be Kareija Meillard – you're far too young and beautiful to be *anyone*'s aunt.'

'My eldest brother's wife gave birth to Firan shortly before my own mother—' The victorious smile gave way to a frown. 'Which you already knew, didn't you? And after all the hours I spent on my disguise?' One well-manicured finger touched her made-up lips, then traced a line over the abundance of exotic beads around her neck and down to the belt encircling her waist. 'Are you sure you aren't a true Veristor, Damelas Chademantaigne?'

I bowed at the compliment. 'Merely a player, with a player's instincts. In truth, Viscountess, given how rarely you have been seen in Jereste since your nephew's coronation, you could have easily passed unnoticed without disguise.'

'Where would the fun be in that?' Her finger drifted up to the low-cut neckline. 'Am I so unconvincing as an actress?'

I kept the disdain reined in; it wouldn't do to push so well-connected a woman too far. But there was something almost contemptuous in her portrayal of those for whom such feigned sensuality was a necessary tool for survival. 'Nothing that should trouble you, Viscountess, although your performance does suffer from a condition endemic to those of high birth.'

Green eyes narrowed dangerously. '*Do* enlighten me, I pray you.'

Shut up, Damelas! Just shut up and smile—

But my treacherous mouth was already open. 'Like all nobles, you think that spending your days diverting yourselves with schemes, intrigues and petty seductions makes you an actor.'

Anger and outrage flashed across her face, and for a moment I feared she was about to summon the wardens . . . Then the coquettish smile returned to her lips. 'So, no part in your new play for me, then? How does that old saying go? "When a Veristor takes the stage, all who witness must join the play"? Come, Master Chademantaigne,' she took my arm, 'let us leave this dull and dreary place for brighter avenues, where you may beguile me with your Veristor's insights into my many deficiencies.'

With that, she led me across the marble floor to the stairs, ignoring the wardens staring at us and no doubt wondering what a patron wearing an ebony and gold mark was doing with a common strumpet on his arm.

Is no one in this city who they appear to be?

CHAPTER 27

THE VISCOUNTESS

The late afternoon sun glared down upon us, the blinding rays like sycophantic court toadies reflecting their master's grandeur into the eyes of his subjects.

'Oh, I had forgotten how Jereste gleams in autumn!' Viscountess Kareija said as we passed an elaborately carved marble fountain with a golden crown shooting water into the air so it could rain elegantly down upon the blue pertine flowers surrounding it. She took my hand and leaned against my shoulder. 'Come, Master Chademantaigne, let us wander these streets together and forget about those intrigues the world seeks to impose upon us. Just a man and a woman, strolling together, seeing the sights as tourists might, playing—'

'Playing for time, my Lady?'

'Why, whatever do you mean?' Her downcast eyes were full of innocent rebuke.

'You seek to delay me, my Lady, when I am due at rehearsal to prepare for tonight's performance. Is it it that you wish to stop the tale of your ancestor's enemy being revealed to all upon the stage?'

'You are cruel in your suspicions,' she said, jutting her chin out petulantly, 'and all too free with accusations against your betters.'

'All I desire from my betters is that they should leave me alone.'

'Why, Damelas,' she laughed, 'I do believe that is the single most naïve statement I have ever heard – and from an actor, no less!'

Kareija's hand was light in mine, yet I felt like a dog kept at heel by its leash. She rested her head on my shoulder as we resumed our stroll along the boulevard. 'Now, my audacious Veristor, pray tell, how do you know I'm not here on my nephew's behalf?'

Her coral-coloured curls tickled my jaw. The warmth of her body next to mine was as intoxicating as her perfume. How long had it been since a woman wanted to walk arm in arm with me down the street? And yet Kareija's presence made me think only of another whose touch I found myself unexpectedly longing to feel again.

Perhaps Shariza follows us even now, waiting for a sign – either to kill me, or to save me from whatever scheme the viscountess has in mind for me.

'I possess no secret knowledge about your relationship with Duke Monsegino, my Lady,' I admitted as she led us into one of Jereste's abundant public gardens. 'I know only that his Grace would not send his beloved aunt to dally with a mere actor when he already has an agent at his command more suited to the task.'

'The Black Amaranth.' The venom in Kareija's voice was unmistakeable.

'The Lady Shariza,' I corrected.

She let go of my arm and walked to an ornately carved oak bench. She sat and patted the spot beside her. Obediently, I joined her.

'Best not fall in love with a Dashini, my clever Veristor. The Black Amaranth – and that's the only name that foul weed deserves – almost certainly intends to murder you before this is done.'

That hardly makes her exceptional of late, I thought, but what I said was, 'Again, my Lady, I must protest at this delay. I'm expected at the Operato Belleza, and if you are not working against your nephew's interests, then you must allow me to—'

'Has Firan told you of his abiding love of the theatre?' she asked abruptly. Seeing my confused expression, she added, 'I'm surprised. I thought perhaps that was why he'd taken such an interest in you.'

'Admiration for the performing arts appears to run deep in your family, my Lady.'

She either missed the jibe or intentionally ignored it. 'Oh, my father *adored* the grand theatres. That's why Jereste has so many players gainfully employed in the great operatos. But Firan . . . ah, poor Firan.' She tapped a finger on my knee. 'The very moment he saw his first historia – about another of Pierzi's legendary exploits, as I recall – Firan was besotted. You can't imagine the screaming fits when he failed to convince his parents to let him renounce his titles and become an actor. At first I thought he was simply being a wilful little boy, until the night he made me accompany him. Ah, the dandies, the comedias, the tragidas, and above all, the historias – I confess, I too fell in love with all those elaborate sets, the costumes, the players . . .' Her finger drifted up my thigh. '. . . Some players in particular.'

Although Beretto might suggest otherwise, I'm not actually a celibate monk. The stirring I felt at the touch of this voluptuous noblewoman was maddeningly intense. But this wasn't genuine flirtation, merely another lazy exercise of power, hardly different from her earlier implied threat to summon the city guard. I resented my own arousal.

'You're doing it again, my Lady,' I said.

'Doing what?' she asked.

As respectfully as I could, I picked up her hand and placed it on her lap. 'Putting on a performance instead of answering my questions.'

She sighed. 'Are all Veristors so dreary? Go ahead then, Damelas. Ask what you will.'

I unpinned the ebony and gold scholar's mark. 'Why did you have this sent to me? What was I meant to find in the Grand Library?'

For a long time she gazed silently at a nearby flower bed where butterflies danced among the petals. I had the oddest feeling that for all her game-playing, Kareija wished she could have been one of those butterflies and flown away.

'An absence,' she said at last.

'An absence?'

She turned to me, and for the first time, all her masks – the actress, the seductress, even the noblewoman – vanished. 'You spent the whole day searching for insight into Corbier's history, but what did you find? Nothing more than the usual torrid accounts of his villainy: stories copied from other tales copied from rumours until gossip has become legend and legend poured like molten iron and hardened into the very foundations of our city.'

She was right, of course, except for the lone book containing a madman's rantings against the nobility of Jereste, written not long after Corbier's death and decorated with illustrations which might be orchids.

'The second volume of Sigurdis Macha,' I said. 'When first you spoke to me, you implied I wouldn't find that book in the restricted section. Why not? The wardens are merciless when it comes to the theft or destruction of books from the library, aren't they?'

She stared at me with that subtle, secretive smile, as if the answer should already be obvious to me, but she hadn't been able to stop fiddling with her hands when she thought I wasn't paying attention.

She's afraid. This whole act of hers, disguising herself to go slumming among the lower classes, the petty seduction when it's obvious her attraction is feigned – this is what the nobility always do, masking their fear with games of intrigue.

'My Lady, no one could have walked out of the Grand Library with a volume from the restricted section. Not me, not you, not unless . . . Ah! The diamond scholar's mark!'

Ever since the warden had mentioned it, I'd wondered who could possibly possess such a treasure. The answer should have been obvious from the start: the one person who could command the *entire* library to be cleared out any time he wished.

'But why would Duke Monsegino—?' I stopped when I noticed the pressing of Kareija's lips. It wasn't her nephew who'd removed the book. 'Your *father*? Duke *Meillard* stole the second volume?'

She looked displeased. Perhaps she'd hoped I would've given up pressing the issue before reaching this point, so distracted was a mere actor meant to be by her charms.

I ignored the warning in her eyes and pressed on. 'Duke Meillard, ageing, ill, soon to give up his throne, has a moment of doubt. Why – some old rumour, perhaps? A family tale he's ignored his whole life? But now, so close to death, he comes across Sigurdis Macha's *The Garden of Majesty* – a book filled with illustrations of orchids wrapped around crowns – and he decides to steal it.'

'Now who's putting on a performance, Damelas? But please, do continue. I am your most captive audience.'

You're also far more anxious than you'd like me to believe, I thought.

'Was it very much later that your father declared Firan Monsegino his heir, my Lady? He'd have had to have moved quickly, after all – the Ducal Mint had already begun pressing coins with your crowned profile on them. But why would he pass over his own beloved daughter for her nephew, who was practically a foreigner?'

'That's enough now, Master Chademantaigne,' she warned, rising from the bench.

I produced the gold coin with the orchid pressed into one side. 'And the moment Duke Meillard is dead, these "Iron Orchids" go from being ruffian troublemakers to writing and enforcing their own so-called "laws" upon the poor and immigrant population of this city. That's what's behind all this, isn't it?'

Kareija started to turn away from me, but the truth was so close, like a butterfly on a flower, just waiting to be netted.

I grabbed her arm. 'Your father didn't turn against you, did he, Viscountess? Duke Meillard knew something about the Iron Orchids, something dangerous. He uncovered a secret in the second book of Sigurdis Macha's rantings – a book that I'm now quite convinced was not coincidentally titled *The Court of Flowers*—'

Kareija pushed at my chest. 'Unhand me, Damelas! Are you some back-alley thug, to paw at me so?'

I let her go, aware my behaviour would have got me soundly thrashed by my grandmother. 'Forgive me,' I said, putting up my hands to show I meant no threat. The coin in my right hand glinted in the harsh sunlight. 'I meant no offence, my Lady, but I must know – who or what is the Court of Flowers?'

Kareija walked away, but I chased after her. 'What did Duke Meillard discover about the Iron Orchids that made him so afraid for his daughter that he chose instead to give his throne to a virtual stranger? Please, my Lady, this is my life and the lives of my fellow actors you're playing with.'

Her pace became more determined. 'You are too clever, Master Chademantaigne, yet beneath your wit and scorn is none of the wisdom I'd expected from a man with the good sense to flee a duel he knew he could not win.'

'Which means *what*, precisely?'

The theatre district's clock tower struck five. We were only a few blocks from the Operato Belleza, but thanks to her games, I'd missed my early rehearsal with Roslyn.

'I *wanted* you to uncover Corbier's absence in the historical records,' Kareija replied, leading me into the road without looking. I had to yank her back to avoid her being crushed by a horse and cart whose driver reprimanded us with a volley of extensive and descriptive threats.

She shook off my grip a second time and continued forging her way through the increasingly crowded streets. 'I hoped that if you saw for yourself the efforts our city has made to bury the secrets of the Iron Orchids and their masters, the Court of Flowers, that you'd refuse to aid Firan any further in his mad quest for the truth.'

'But my Lady, *why*? If you love your nephew, why wouldn't you—?'

I stopped and stared at the Operato Belleza just ahead, trying to see what was causing the commotion outside the stage door. All I could see was a mass of people blocking the side alley.

This time it was Kareija who grabbed *me*. 'My father understood politics and intrigue. He knew the limits of a duke's power. What does it tell you, that he stole and destroyed the one book which might have given Firan the answers he now seeks?'

There was something important in what she was saying, but I turned back towards the theatre and the shouting of the crowds.

Kareija's fingernails dug into my arm. 'You *must* listen to me, Damelas! The axe my father feared for me now dangles above my nephew's neck. Firan has always been obsessed with the tale of Corbier and Pierzi and that obsession now sees him beset by enemies from within and without his court.' She had finally dropped the pretences now, and her games. 'I love my nephew, Damelas, as I love my home, and I will do whatever I must, whichever plots and schemes are necessary, to protect him and, above all, this duchy.'

Shouting turned into screaming outside the theatre and a sickening feeling rose inside me, like hands squeezing my intestines. 'My Lady, why did you delay my coming to the Belleza today?' I asked.

What might have been genuine grief – or perhaps shame – came over Viscountess Kareija's ashen features. 'It was you they wanted,

Damelas. Had I let them have the actor upon whom Firan's apparent favour shines, my nephew's enemies at court would have seen it as a sign of his weakness and begun to move against him. I couldn't allow that to happen.'

It was you they wanted . . .

I flung off her grip and pounded across the street, shoving through the horde of gawkers until I broke into the gap the rabble had left in front of the stage door – and saw the object of their sick fascination.

The sight cut my knees out from under me.

I stumbled to the ground, my gaze focusing only on the filthy cobblestones beneath me. I prayed more fervently than at any other time in my life that I'd been mistaken, but the steady back-and-forth creaking of the lantern-post put the lie to that false hope.

Barely able to breathe, I forced myself to look up. First I saw the bare feet, the shoes already stolen. Blood trickled between the toes. My eyes traced those crooked paths up pale legs and soiled dress, and higher still, past the slackened jaw and matted hair, to the five iron spikes impaling flesh and puncturing bone, letting all the promises of life and love leak away for ever.

I heard footsteps, growing louder as they approached. I felt Kareija's fingers touching my hair for a brief instant. 'The play's the thing, Damelas,' I heard her murmur. 'The play's always the thing.'

By the time I turned around, she'd already gone.

CHAPTER 28

THE THIRD SIGN

Roslyn dangled from a frayed rope barely a foot in length tied to the lantern-post by the stage door of the Operato Belleza. Around her neck hung a wooden sign bearing a mocking rejoinder in red paint: *Let actors give us merry tales, lest we make them melancholy.* Her body swayed in time to the groaning from the curved iron pole bearing her weight and the wailing from the crowd witnessing this depraved coronation. The late afternoon sunlight glistened off the blunt ends of the five iron spikes hammered into her skull.

I wanted to flee, to shut my eyes and pretend I'd never known Roslyn, never walked the stage with her . . . never shared a kiss.

No, I thought, rising to my feet.

I shoved back the gawkers, returning their snarls, daring even one of them to make a move.

I won't look away, I swore to myself and whichever gods or saints could be bothered to listen. *Not now, not ever again.*

I turned back to Roslyn, clear-eyed and cold-hearted, determined to commit every last detail to memory. She was wearing the blue Lady Ajelaine gown, which was odd because she'd removed it last night before going to celebrate with the others. The only reason she'd had it with her was because she wanted to fix a loose hem on the sleeve.

Which means they caught her on the way home.

Roz had always been meticulous about removing her stage make-up at the end of every performance, but her face was covered in a thick layer of gaudy maschiera-paints. Blue irises had been painted within ovals on her closed eyelids to make her look like she was staring down at the crowd in the alley. The hideous lipstick smile smeared on her face perversely distorted the gaping mouth that was still crying for help, even in death.

They wanted to make a mockery of the woman she was, I thought, wishing for the first time in my life that I had a sword in hand and an enemy before me.

There were other cruelties to catalogue: her fingernails were broken and torn, which meant Roz had fought her attackers, yet I could see no trace of blood or skin beneath what was left of her nails. She'd always struck me as a formidable woman, confident, savvy, imperturbable. She would have gone for soft flesh, had there been any to reach, so the men who'd attacked her must have been wearing armour, and helms, too, or leather hoods of some kind.

Cowards, I thought. *You didn't want anyone seeing your faces, only those damned iron orchid brooches.*

I read the wooden sign again, its mocking words: *Let actors give us merry tales, lest we make them melancholy.*

Had it been only yesterday that I'd dismissed the absurd new Orchid 'laws' when Zina had first shown me the poster, especially the prohibition against 'theatrical blasphemy'? But this sign bore the real message the Orchids were sending to the Knights of the Curtain: end the seditious rehabilitation of Archduke Corbier and return to performing the pacifying historias of brave Prince Pierzi. Never again question the past – and *never* dare to put the truth on stage.

Why does the story of a long-dead nobleman matter so much? What in Corbier's tale is so threatening to those in power?

I whirled on the crowd behind me. 'Who did this?' I demanded.

Some backed away further, a few glared at me defiantly, but no one answered.

'One of you cowards must have seen them hanging the body here,' I yelled, knowing I was making a spectacle of myself, unwilling to stop. 'Come on!' I bellowed, taking another step towards them, daring anyone to make a move against me. 'Do I have to beat it out of you? Is that the only way to make you care about anything other than your own damned—'

A woman's hand tugged on my arm. 'Come on, Saint Damelas-who-shouts-at-crowds. Time to go.'

I recognised the unmistakeable mockery in that melodious voice. 'Leave me alone, Rhyleis.' I shrugged off the Bardatti. 'I'd have thought you'd be pleased. I'm finally going to do what my grandmother would have done. I'm going to beat the living Hells out of these people until someone tells me who butchered Roslyn!'

'Right now it's *your* life I'm concerned with, you idiot.' She grabbed my hand and tried to open the stage door behind us, but when she found it was locked, she started hauling me towards the main entrance. 'Whoever did this wants to see the fear in your eyes,' she explained. 'Standing in a crowded alley and challenging half of Jereste to a duel is decidedly the wrong message.'

'Maybe it's exactly the *right* mess—'

She stopped just long enough to slap the back of my head. 'Do you not get it? *You're* the one they want, Damelas, and when they couldn't get to you, they killed the actress instead. You think they won't murder someone else you care about next? Maybe that big oaf who brought you to the tavern last night?'

Saint Ebron-who-steals-breath – if they took Beretto . . .

Dumbly, I followed Rhyleis as she pushed through the onlookers crowding the alley. A few people tried to bar our way, pointing at me and making noises about *answers being required.* Rhyleis stared down some; others she hit with her guitar, apparently unconcerned about the instrument I had assumed would be sacred to a Troubadour. Once the guitar shattered, she used the sharp broken end of the neck to threaten the mob until they parted for us.

'You broke your guitar,' I observed impassively. My rage had faded, leaving me in a fog of confusion and guilt. Whenever I closed my eyes, I saw the hideous smile painted on Roslyn's face.

'You'll buy me a nicer one,' Rhyleis replied. She sounded more irritated than frightened.

We were moving so slowly that it felt as if days had passed before we finally reached the front entrance, which was presently being guarded by several big men and women brandishing clubs. They stood beneath the Operato Belleza's great arch above the main doors, barring anyone from trying to get in.

'Looks like your director's hired a few bravos to guard the Belleza in case someone else decides to come in search of players to string up from lantern-posts,' Rhyleis observed.

'That's him,' one of the men called out, pointing at me, and his companions moved to surround us, clubs at the ready. Only then did it occur to me that someone could just as easily have hired the bully-boys to beat me – and anyone with me – to death.

'What do you think you're doing?' Rhyleis asked. She was staring at my arm across her chest.

'Um . . . protecting you?'

She tilted her head. 'Normally I'd ask why on earth you would imagine yourself qualified to defend me, instead of the other way around, but right now I'm more curious about whom you intend to protect me from.'

I looked down at my arm, embarrassed. Such pretentious gestures were the province of the old courtly romances, not actors who flee from honour duels.

Was that you, Corbier? Is this your idea of chivalry, you pompous bastard?

No reply was forthcoming, but the guards were now ushering the two of us inside the theatre. Shoville caught sight of us, and shouting, 'Thank the saints!' he strode over to me and began patting at my arms and torso as if searching for hidden weapons. 'You're alive,' he said, 'and you look unhurt.'

'Unhurt?'

'The others are in the rehearsal hall . . .' He finally noticed Rhyleis. Looking her up and down, he asked, 'Who is this?'

'Your new guitarist and orchestra leader,' she replied, holding up the broken neck of her instrument as if that were proof of her new position.

'We don't need a guitar-player and our musicians are perfectly capable of sorting themselves out, thank you very mu—'

'Your musicians are hacks,' Rhyleis said, talking over him. 'I've known deaf-mutes who could better carry a tune and keep a stricter rhythm. Besides, you're going to need my skills tonight if you hope to keep the audience from setting the theatre on fire.'

'She's a Bardatti, sir,' I explained. 'You can tell by the confusion and irritation you're feeling right now.'

Shoville stared at me for a second, then searched me a second time for signs of wounds. 'Whatever. I don't have time for this right now. Just get to rehearsal so we can start—'

'*Rehearsal?' Has the man completely lost his wits?* 'Lord Director, did you fail to notice one of your actors hanging from a lantern-post in the alley?'

Shoville looked stricken. 'The mob won't let us take her down. They fear reprisals from the Iron Orchids, and the city guard are refusing to disperse the crowds. I sent word to the duke, informing him that we had no choice but to abandon the play—' He reached into his shirt and produced a rolled-up piece of parchment with a broken wax seal on it. 'His Grace's reply was delivered by that woman – the spy or assassin or whatever she is.'

I took the little scroll and unfurled it to find just two lines, written in a fine hand in rich black ink. The first line read, 'From his Grace, Duke Firan Monsegino, his heartfelt condolences.'

The second was even shorter: 'The show must go on.'

PART THE FOURTH

The Raven

Wherein our

BELEAGUERED RABBIT,

finds his TEETH *at last . . .*

MUCH TO HIS CHAGRIN . . .

CHAPTER 29

THE WARNING

'I want to do something a little different tonight – give the punters a bit of a show. Something to talk about in their salons in the morning.'

Roslyn's words wouldn't stop echoing in my head. Every time I glanced around the crowded rehearsal hall, I expected to find her spectral form floating above us, a ghostly queen crowned in iron, the spikes protruding from her skull warning of the fate awaiting any actor foolish enough to believe their art made them special. Safe.

The air inside the hall tasted heavy, ashen, as if Grigo, our grizzled one-handed pyrotechnics expert, had been setting off smoke-pots and flash-jars for a battle scene. But Grigo was sitting hunched in a corner, wiping away tears with his forearm, his mumbling lost amid the general cacophony of shouting, wailing and clomping of feet. The Knights of the Curtain shuffled about like confused horses whose newly dead riders had not yet fallen from the saddle.

'Why haven't the city guard taken her down yet?' Teo demanded, slamming his fist into his palm as he stared out of the window at Roslyn's bare feet swaying back and forth like a clock's pendulum.

'She's just hanging there like a sack of meat,' Cileila said. Her voice was oddly airy for a woman nearly as tall and broad as Beretto. The carpenter hadn't appeared to notice that her big, strong hands were clenching and unclenching, almost of their own volition. 'Can we not pull her down ourselves? We have ladders – I could fashion a coffin for her. We could make sure she's decent before her family sees her . . .'

It was the longest speech the notoriously taciturn carpenter had made all year.

Her words were answered by a bottomless growl: Abastrini was standing beside the window, looking ridiculous and impotent in the golden Prince Pierzi armour he'd donned for the rehearsal. 'The Iron Orchids hide among the witnesses,' he said, upper lip curled as he stared at the crowds below. 'They wait to mark any who would dare desecrate their art.'

Cileila stamped a heavy-booted foot against the floor. 'What do you mean, "desecrate their art"? How can you call what they did "art"?'

Abastrini gestured towards the back wall and the auditorium beyond. 'Last night we put on our production.' He tapped a finger against the window. 'Today they have offered their own in response.'

'Saint Birgid-who-weeps-rivers protect us,' Grigo swore, still crouched in the corner. A dozen others took up the futile prayer.

'Why is this happening to us?' Bida cried, wiping her tears with her long blonde hair. She was barely twenty years old and far more of a match for the Ajelaine depicted in the histories than Roslyn had ever been. We all knew how precariously close Shoville had come to casting her in the role.

'This was my fault,' the director whispered.

'On that we finally agree,' Abastrini said. His voice was cold, callous, utterly devoid of his customary melodramatic delivery. He left the window and began walking slowly towards the man who had once been a brother to him, if the stories were to be believed, just as Beretto was now to me.

'The lives of the cast and crew are in the hands of the Directore Principale,' Abastrini said, visibly baiting Shoville. 'You should have hired bully-boys to guard Roslyn last night, but as usual, you penny-pinching pustule, you did nothing.'

The accusation struck me as unfair – who ever heard of an actor being given a bodyguard? But Abastrini's pace was increasing as he approached Shoville, a siege-engine about to crash through gates too old to resist.

I stepped between them, fully expecting to be bowled over by Abastrini's bulk, but in the end it was only words that he hurled at

Shoville. 'You damnable canker!' he bellowed. 'You allowed our Roz to play Lady Ajelaine not as the chaste, demure, devoted wife of Prince Pierzi the audience demands, but as a wanton slut – nay, a whore!'

'Roz was no whore,' Shoville answered back, even as he withered under Abastrini's towering bulk. 'She played the part true and I'll not have it said otherwise—'

'*You* know that and *I* know that, you blasted dung-weasel!' He swung an arm out to point at the outer wall of the rehearsal hall. 'The nobles of this city who name their daughters after the virtuous Ajelaine? The Iron Orchids who claim her favoured flower as their symbol? *They* don't know that! What they saw last night was an actor portraying their sainted heroine as the illicit lover of a rebel and a child-slayer—'

'O may the Gods of Love and Craft forgive me,' Shoville begged, falling to his knees. '*What have I done?*'

It wasn't you, I thought. *It was me.*

A choking silence fell over the hall as we drowned beneath the unbearable truth of Abastrini's words. Roz had meant her performance to be a mischievous wink to the crowd's more salacious fantasies, a ribald jest to lure chuckles and lightly disapproving tut-tuts from the audience. Nothing more would have come of it, had I not unexpectedly transmuted her pantomimed lust into something purer, something far more dangerous: a kind of testimony . . . testimony someone in this city would not abide.

'Roslyn's death was a warning,' I said. 'Whoever commands the Iron Orchids wants our play stopped – that's the price for our safety.'

The doors at the end of the hall slammed open as Beretto stormed in. 'Which is precisely why we must continue,' he thundered. 'We will show these jumped-up thugs what happens to those who threaten the players' art!'

To me, it was as if the great God War himself had descended upon us.

Others were less awed.

'Fuck your "art",' Teo snapped. 'Some of us have families.' He ran to Shoville. 'Lord Director, I beg you, cancel the play. Close the theatre tonight – close the Belleza for ever, if you must!'

Shoville's eyes were downcast, his lips moving as if silently practising a soliloquy. I understood then that what Teo was demanding had been the director's intent all along; he simply hadn't yet found the courage to say the words out loud.

'Don't do it, Lord Director,' Beretto warned. 'If the Knights of the Curtain bend to the will of the Iron Orchids and their ilk, soon every theatre company in Jereste will be tamed.'

'*Tamed?*' Teo laughed, and others followed suit. 'You do realise none of us are actual Knights, don't you? We don't wage war against our enemies any more than the Lords of Laughter sit in palaces and hold court. We're *players*! We speak whatever lines we're handed in hope of nothing more than a full house and a heavy purse.' He threw his hands up in the air. 'Who among us gives a fuck whether or not we're to be "tamed"?'

The backhand I'd been expecting moments ago finally made its appearance, but it was Teo who went stumbling to the floor, one palm to his already reddening cheek.

'*I* care,' Abastrini said with uncharacteristic calm. '*Actors* care.'

A few of those present muttered assent, but there wasn't much conviction. Those mumbling their disagreement didn't dare do so loudly, in case they attracted Abastrini's attention.

At the far end of the hall, I noticed Rhyleis balancing an ink bottle on one bent knee as she scrawled something into a small leather book.

Probably writing a song about our plight, came an uncharitable thought, *with no concern about how it will likely end for the rest of us.*

'Enough!' Shoville said, struggling to regain control of his company even as he avoided Abastrini's gaze. 'I am still Directore Principale of this operato and I will risk no more lives on Duke Monsegino's mad endeavour. We close our doors tonight – and for ever, if need be.'

Murmurs of relief swelled – until a single voice, so eerily calm it brought silence to the entire hall, reminded us that our destinies were no longer ours to choose.

'Close these doors tonight and by tomorrow you'll find yourselves chained to the walls of a place far more dangerous than any theatre,' Lady Shariza said.

CHAPTER 30

THE UNDERSTUDY

No one had noticed the Black Amaranth enter, but there she was, leaning against the back wall, dressed all in black. A slender rapier I hadn't seen her wear before now hung from the belt of her long brocade coat.

'Dashini *bitch*,' Teo shouted, 'it's you and your duke who march us down the road to the seven Hells!'

Teo's ill-considered words set tensions in the room afire. Grief and rage momentarily overwhelmed reason and self-preservation as the angry cast and crew, throwing caution to the wind, turned on the duke's personal assassin, lining up shoulder to shoulder so she couldn't escape. They stalked towards her, some armed with stage props, others with nothing more than clenched fists, all growling like a pack of hounds—

—then they fell silent.

The blade of her rapier was as black as her garments, and everyone could see the tip pressed so firmly against Teo's Adam's apple that surely the tiniest twitch of her wrist would open his throat.

'Of late, I find the men of this city overfree in calling me "bitch",' she observed. 'Should anyone else wish to speed their way to the grave, they need only to address me thus one more time.'

'Stop—!' I shouted, clawing at shoulders, trying to pull people out of the way before someone decided to outflank Shariza and matters went from appallingly bad to utterly catastrophic.

'You're siding with her?' Cileila demanded. The heavy carpenter's mallet was no prop and her scowl made it clear she was ready to use it.

'It wasn't Lady Shariza who killed Roslyn to silence us, but the Iron

Orchids,' I reminded them. 'Somehow, when we're all on that stage, we become a danger to their interests – though the saints alone know what those interests might be.'

Ornella, who'd been standing silently against the wall, spoke for the first time. 'Perhaps if we understood why Corbier's infamy or Pierzi's glory was so vital to those interests, we might devise a way out of our predicament?'

In the fading afternoon light, the silver-haired actress looked younger than her years, reminding me of Lady Ajelaine as I'd seen her outside Pierzi's fortress. Ornella had probably played that role hundreds of times in decades past, but the unwavering gaze with which she returned my stare now suggested those performances would have been altogether different from the demure portrayals fashionable these days, or the sultry depiction that had proved fatal to poor Roslyn.

A question began to itch at the back of my mind like a misshapen key grinding inside a rusted lock: *what if both are wrong? What if Lady Ajelaine wasn't—?*

'Damelas?' Beretto asked quietly, coming up behind me.

'Hmm?'

'Is there some reason you've been ogling Ornella like a demented pervert for the past few minutes?'

I turned away, embarrassed. 'Forgive me, I haven't slept in—'

'Speak, Veristor,' Rhyleis said, her voice cutting across the hall. She was staring at me.

They all were.

'Really, it's nothing – it's just . . . for a moment there, I thought . . .' I looked back at Ornella, but all I saw now was an ageing silver-haired woman – handsome, yes, but no ghost from the past come to haunt the present. 'Honestly, I'm just tired.'

It was a feeble lie. I think the others would have let it go, but a strange thing happened then: Ellias Abastrini, the man who'd so recently and convincingly threatened to beat me to death, walked over and put a hand on my shoulder. 'I know little of the Veristor's art,' he confessed, which was a dangerous admission for someone who'd built his career on that particular fiction, 'but an actor must heed their instincts. What are yours telling you?'

Whatever I say now will only give false hope to these men and women whose livelihoods – and lives – are at risk because of me.

But they were all waiting on me, and I found I couldn't lie to them.

'What if Roslyn wasn't killed solely because the Iron Orchids couldn't get their hands on me?' I asked.

'What do you mean?' Shoville asked, a fire coming to his cheeks. 'Would you accuse poor Roz of having dealings with such ruffians? I'll not hear such slander – do you hear me? I'll not—'

Ornella put a hand on his arm. 'Damelas is the last person to spread gossip or innuendo, Hujo. Let him finish.'

Shoville grumbled something under his breath, but settled. He never could raise his voice to Ornella.

'Our Lord Director is right,' I said. 'Roz was too canny – and she cared too much about her family – to involve herself in anything reckless or criminal.'

'Then why is she dead?' Teo asked.

'What if . . .' I almost couldn't bring myself to suggest it. 'What if she was playing her role *too* well last night? Not the bawdy winks and seductive poses during the opening scenes, but later, outside the fortress, when I . . . when the play changed.'

'Her performance *did* change,' Beretto agreed. 'All of ours did as we tried to follow your cues.'

Teo and Abastrini nodded thoughtfully, but I could see doubt in Shoville's expression. Still, the more I gave voice to this strange thought I was having, the more convinced I was that it might just be true.

'What if it's not Corbier's story the Iron Orchids want to keep from being revealed, but Ajelaine's?' I asked. 'What if somehow she's th—'

'Yes!' Beretto interrupted suddenly, clapping his hands together, excitement reddening his cheeks. 'Yes, damn it – *she* is the key to this. Think about it: Lady Ajelaine has always been at the centre of the war between Pierzi and Corbier – all the battles and the intrigues, the fight for the crown – all of it! Damelas is *right*, by all the saints virtuous and venal – this is no tale of princes vying for a throne. It's a love story. It's *her* story!'

A ripple of surprise went through the room and the anger that had filled the hall minutes before trickled away as everyone began speculating on what this might mean for the play.

A love story, and a truth someone wants to keep buried that can only be uncovered if we continue the performance . . .

But that would require someone to play Lady Ajelaine.

All eyes turned to Bida, who was shuffling nervously from foot to foot.

'I-I'm sorry,' she stammered, 'but I can't. N-not now.' Her hands were unconsciously cradling her still-flat belly, but she'd made no secret of her current condition.

'My father is ill,' Dalca said quickly. She was a strapping girl, but she'd understudied Roslyn's roles before. 'He's barely hanging on – who will care for him if I'm hanging from a post with spikes in my skull?'

They've all got people they love, families who depend on them. I shared a disheartened glance with Shoville.

'I will perform the play alone,' I announced.

Nervous guffaws filled the room at my ridiculous suggestion, but I persisted, 'It's been done before . . .'

Admittedly, a solto fabulata was a poor sort of a play: sitting through a performance from an actor interacting with an imaginary cast was like watching a madman talking to ghosts, but it would keep all eyes – and weapons – focused on me. Hopefully that would leave the rest of the company untainted by whatever outrage I provoked.

I can do this, I thought. *Tonight, I will step out onto that stage and give Corbier his moment beneath the lights. I will let him utter any heretical treason he wants, and when he's finally done? I'll turn tail and run as fast and as far as my feet will take me. I've always been an excellent runner, after all.*

I could almost feel the fear in the hall dissipating, leaving room for the grief for Roslyn that would follow, but an instant later, even that feeble hope was dashed.

'The duke will not allow a solo performance,' Shariza said quietly. 'He requires this play to continue with its full cast. The audience must be convinced that what they are witnessing is revealed truth, not the rantings of a desperate actor more concerned with hiding his fellow players than in uncovering what the past has to tell us.'

Teo opened his mouth to contradict her, then closed it again of his own volition, no doubt remembering the sensation of her blade against his throat.

'Fuck it,' Beretto said, puffing out his chest and spreading his arms wide. 'I'll be your Lady Ajelaine tonight.' He cocked his hip and wagged a finger at me. 'Just you watch where you put your hands during our kissing scene. And put some *passion* into it for once!'

Beretto's ribald suggestion elicited some nervous chortling, but laughter didn't change the dilemma we were facing.

'Beretto, pretty as you are, I think it better if I play the Lady Ajelaine,' Ornella said, pushing her way to the front. Her chin was high and she ignored the dubious stares from her younger castmates. 'It was not so long ago that women had to fight to play our parts. We faced beatings and worse for taking the female roles away from young men flaunting make-up and skirts. I'll not now relinquish this ground my sisters battled and bled to take.'

'Ornella . . .' Shoville began, but she ignored him and came to me.

'I'm not as pretty as Roslyn,' she said to me. 'When the kiss comes, you'll have to imagine me as I was in my younger days.'

I took her hand and bowed over it. 'I will do no such thing, my Lady. I will see you exactly as you are, here and now, and I will be as grateful for that kiss as if it had come from the lips of Ajelaine herself.'

She gave me a crinkled smile. 'Fine words from such an untried youth. Is it Damelas who flirts with me, or Archduke Corbier?'

'I don't care who's flirting,' Shoville interrupted, an angry red flush staining his cheeks.

Seeing the anguish fused with ire on the director's face brought a sudden flash of intuition to me. *He's in love with Ornella,* I thought. *Yet I've never seen anything happen between them – is the poor fool even aware himself?*

Catching my stare, Shoville's cheeks flushed even darker and he turned his glare on Lady Shariza. 'Kindly inform his Grace that no actor of my company will play the role of Ajelaine,' he declared. 'I am the Directore Principale of the Operato Belleza, Commander of the Knights of the Curtain' – he stabbed a finger in the direction of the window – 'and not one of these brave women will I toss to those wolves out there. Do you hear me? *Not one!*'

Shariza left her spot against the wall and stepped silently towards Shoville, a sleek black cat stalking a wary mouse. I let go of Ornella's hand, prepared to intervene, though I had no idea how I might stop the Black Amaranth. That's when I caught the sly look in her eyes and the ever-so-slight upward curve of her lip.

She's known all along it would come to this. She's just been waiting for the rest of us to arrive at this exact moment . . .

'"Let fall a dozen towers,"' she said, her accent suddenly a near-perfect match to Roslyn's interpretation of Ajelaine. '"Bring forth a hundred armies and still I will remain in this place awaiting his return. Though the heavens rage with thunder above me and the ground crumbles beneath my feet, still will he find his Ajelaine standing firm, unmoved, her love not a cloudy dream to gaze upon beneath a summer sky, but the hard rock of devotion that neither bends nor breaks, no matter that the ocean rages against it until the last grain of sand in time's hourglass is spent."'

Shoville, wide-eyed, gestured for one of the stagehands to bring him the script. He riffled through the pages, then glanced through the lines. 'You know it? All of it? All of Lady Ajelaine's part?'

'"What matter such sentimentalities to any but a wishful child? You speak of love as if t'were a shield, but though arrows may not puncture love's devotions, still do they pierce flesh, and need no fine words to do so."'

'Hey, that's the lieutenant's line,' Teo said. 'You learned *my* part, too?' He sounded genuinely concerned that he might lose yet another role to a fledgling actor.

'I know your lines as well as I know Ajelaine's,' she replied, 'as I do Pierzi's and Corbier's and the second crone who brings the soup in the third act.'

'You memorised the *entire* script?' Shoville asked, still glancing at his pages in disbelief.

'I'm a spy, Lord Director. This is hardly the first time I've had to become someone else at short notice.' She turned to Ornella and held out her hand. 'Forgive me, warrior, but this battle is to be mine.'

Ornella reached out and gripped her forearm, greeting her as two soldiers might. 'I am too old for vanity,' she replied, 'but speak the role true, young lady. Play what games you must for your duke, but do not embarrass this company, else it's me you'll answer to.'

The fierce pride in those words spread through the cast and crew, putting steel in our spines. The Knights of the Curtain would not give an inch more ground to those who had silenced Roslyn, and not even the sight of her still-swaying corpse would bend them now.

This is exactly what Duke Monsegino wanted, I realised then. *It's just as he wrote in his note: the show must go on.*

As everyone began to shuffle out of the rehearsal hall, I noticed Rhyleis was carefully wrapping up her pen and ink before closing her book.

The Troubadour rose to her feet and stretched languidly before locking eyes with Lady Shariza. 'Dashini,' she said, pouring an alehouse's-worth of scorn into that single word.

'Bardatti,' Shariza replied.

And that, apparently, was all they had to say to one another.

Rhyleis left with the theatre's four musicians in tow, following her like a squad of infantry into battle. I wondered if they were accepting her leadership because she was a true Bardatti Troubadour, or because they didn't know what else to do.

Shariza took my hand, the intimacy of the gesture at odds with the press of people brushing past us. 'It's better this way,' she said, when at last we were alone.

'What way?'

She held up my hand between hers and pressed it to her chin. 'Whatever happens out there, whatever price must be paid for what my duke has demanded, I will not see you pay it alone.'

I'd heard any number of tales about the Dashini, how deadly and devious they were, but my grandparents had never mentioned any who tried so hard *not* to kill.

'Why risk your life with mine, my Lady?' I asked her. 'We are not lovers and you owe me no debts. I am an actor – not even a particularly good one – and you . . . you're the legendary Black Amaranth. Half the men in this city would drop instantly to their knees out of adoration or—'

'Or fear?' she finished for me.

She smiled at me, and I wished that somehow, in some other life, I might have been given the opportunity to learn all her many expressions.

'You look at me too deeply, Damelas Chademantaigne.'

'I'm sorry, I didn't mea—'

'*That* is why I'm staying,' she said, cutting me off. 'Because even though you distrust me and doubtless despise what I am, you are always courteous. I was told you were a coward who fled from a duel and a liar who insinuated himself into this theatre to hide behind its walls, yet whenever another life is at risk, I've watched you place yourself between it and danger. Most of all, though, I want to be here because when I'm with you, I find myself wearying of intrigues and dark deeds, and I am beginning to wonder if Beretto might be right.'

'Beretto? Right about what?'

She kissed the knuckles of my hand before letting go and turning to leave the rehearsal hall.

'Perhaps this really is a love story.'

CHAPTER 31

THE SECOND ACT

Never before had the Operato Belleza been so packed. Every seat in the house was occupied, even those the crew had been constructing late into the night. The creaking balcony floor above moaned in complaint as twice as many people as it had been built for jockeyed for the best positions.

At last the stagehands raised the eighteen-foot-long poles to ignite the wicks of the brass lanterns hanging from the ceiling. The lights sparkled off the jewellery in the audience, setting a sky's worth of stars glittering. There were no paupers or last-minute punters tonight, no cheap seats, no complimentary tickets for friends or family of the crew. If any of Pertine's nobility were absent, it could only be because they were dead, their rotting remains not yet discovered inside their huge mansions.

The stench of the living was almost as bad tonight: sweat mixed with a hundred different perfumes wafting up to the stage, a fug of florals, citruses and spices mixed with the musks of men and animals. Already sweating in the excessive heat, the audience were unwilling to relinquish their carefully chosen finery, so the odiferous cloud lingered in brocades and furs.

What should have been an energised atmosphere felt almost lifeless: there was no gossiping or chattering, no bouncing of feet on the floor nor wiggling of arses on uncomfortable wooden seats – only five hundred pairs of eyes, staring at the stage, waiting.

They're like an army of the dead come to judge the living, I thought, as spooked by the unnatural silence as the rest of the crew. The stagehands were gripping the curtain cords so tightly their knuckles were white, their palms so sweaty that the ropes threatened to slip just when the moment came to pull. The cast clutched at their pages, lips repeating the same lines over and over, just in case the scrawled ink letters had somehow changed shape at the last minute. Often they looked pleadingly at me, silently begging me to offer some clue as to what would happen next.

I responded with my best, most reassuring smile, which elicited only expressions of sheer dread from my fellow players.

'Just follow the scene as it's written,' Shoville urged us all, coming over to place one hand on my shoulder and the other on Abastrini's. 'We begin on the field at Mount Cruxia, where Prince Pierzi and Archduke Corbier are meeting in secret among the bones of the dead for a final attempt to negotiate a truce between their Houses before blood stains this hallowed ground once more.'

'We know the damned script, you fool,' Abastrini said.

Shoville was so distracted and anxious that he barely noted the insult. 'Yes, yes,' he mumbled, squeezing my shoulder like a man hanging from the edge of a cliff. 'Get the opening right and then whatever happens next is up to the gods.'

'I will do my best, Lord Director,' I promised. 'You've my oath on that.'

Poor Shoville, I thought. *All he ever wanted was to bring the Operato Belleza back to its glory days. Now all his labours have been washed away by a tide of events beyond the control of mere theatre directors.*

I needed to do better tonight for Shoville, for all of them. I'd had enough of being swept up in the madness of this Veristor's curse that had placed everyone – this family I was beginning to feel a part of – in such cruel jeopardy. Archduke Corbier would indeed appear on the stage tonight, but it would be the Corbier that *I* chose: one convincing enough to walk the knife's edge between Duke Monsegino's obsession with authenticity and Shoville's placating script; one who artfully weaved between comfortable myth and unpleasant truth. The audience would be a little bored, perhaps, but those threatened by yesterday's performance would be reassured of their power tonight.

The nightmare would come to an end, at least for now.

'It's time.' Abastrini brushed down Pierzi's gleaming golden armour. 'Just do your part,' he said grimly, 'and I'll do mine.'

'Ready, Veristor?' Shoville asked.

Not in the slightest, I thought, but he deserved better, so I replied, 'At your cue and by your command, Lord Director.'

Steeling himself, Shoville tugged at the bottom of his rumpled white shirt to straighten it and gave a curt nod to the crew. The players shuffled into the wings, ready for Pierzi and Corbier's opening dialogue. I followed the Black Amaranth's gaze, which was trained on one particular seat in the audience.

The stagehands strained, the ropes tautened, and the curtain rose smoothly – to a deafening silence. There was no opening applause tonight, only those hungry stares.

It's going to be fine, I told myself. For some reason, I remembered my grandfather, watching my grandmother drawing her blade from its scabbard as she entered the duelling circle: '*Smooth as silk and twice as soft*,' he would always say.

I stepped out on the stage, Abastrini close behind me.

And everything went to the seven Hells.

CHAPTER 32

THE LOVE STORY

The stage was gone, the set with it. Rich red curtains had given way to a pale grey Midsummer's mist. Cileila's newly painted wooden pillars representing the stone columns at the gates of the ancient battlefield of Mount Cruxia had vanished too, along with the audience.

The air, oppressively hot just moments before, was now freshened by a cool breeze wafting past Corbier as he climbed the rope to a luxuriously appointed bedchamber. The mingled smells of sweat and clashing fragrances had yielded to the scents of wax candles and rose petals filling the room. The silence that had reigned over the theatre was banished by the quiet laughter of the young woman sitting on the edge of her bed and writing in the leather notebook on her lap with a feathered quill.

Ajelaine.

I'm in the wrong part of the play entirely, I realised with a start. *Corbier never appears in Ajelaine's room – the others will have no idea what's going on!*

I forced myself to focus not on the scene before me, but the one I'd left behind, trying to see the stage, to feel the hot, humid air inside the theatre and hear the voice whispering furiously behind me, 'What the fuck are you doing?'

What was I doing?

'Stop pushing me back!' Abastrini was demanding.

Saint Dheneph-who-tricks-the-gods, let me escape this spell before it's too la— There!

A kind of haze was filling Ajelaine's chambers, and through it I could just make out the Belleza. My fingertips could feel the hammered tin of Abastrini's fake armour even as my nostrils inhaled the aromas of beeswax, rose petals – and most of all, the scent of *her*.

Ajelaine.

Concentrate . . . you can do this. You just need to make these two tales fit together. The scene is meant to take place at Mount Cruxia, but the stage is dressed with gravestones . . .

I opened my mouth and, ignoring the instinct to speak softly to the ghostly woman before me, instead deepened my voice to make it resonate throughout the theatre. 'Is this your bedchamber I have risked so much to enter, Lady Ajelaine? Or the graveyard of my dreams?'

I heard shocked intakes of breath among the audience.

Please, all you saints and gods, let them believe that this bizarre juxtaposition of set and setting is just a bit of theatrical metaphor.

'Without you,' I continued loudly, gesturing to the elaborate splendour of the room no one but I could see, 'all these fine tapestries and furnishings are naught to my eyes but dust and bones, for without your love, the world is a graveyard to me: a reminder of battles lost and battles still to lose.'

I walked to centre stage, playing for time so my fellow players could try to make sense of the cues I was trying to give them.

'I see no bed here,' I bellowed, sweeping my arm around, 'no hearth to bring warmth to my skin. Even the light of your candles cannot reach me without your eyes to illuminate them.'

I heard the faint squeal of lantern-covers closing just as the world around me went dark, and hoped the audience wouldn't notice the scraping across the boards as the set was hurriedly adjusted.

'Gods help me,' I called out, wailing to cover the noise, 'for I am blind without your love, Ajelaine!'

Silence. Emptiness. Seconds ticked by, each one slower than the last, until . . .

'Then open your eyes, my Raven, for my love is always with you.'

The lantern-covers overhead slid back, allowing light to sweep onto the stage, revealing a four-poster bed enclosed in violet silk curtains sitting between the gravestones, creating the illusion of a tiny island of life and opulence stranded amidst a sea of death and desolation.

Gods willing, the audience will find all this terribly artistic, I prayed.

A lute began to play from within the bed curtains, triggering an unexpected but overwhelming urge inside me: I *needed* to open those curtains, to see the woman awaiting me there. I strode across the stage and drew the silks aside so that I – and the audience – could see within.

The *oohs* and *aahs* at the sight of Shariza in her costume quickly faded from my hearing, for it wasn't the duke's enigmatic agent I saw now but Ajelaine herself: indomitable, audacious, despairing Ajelaine. She wore her hair loose. She'd once draped those long, sun-kissed chestnut tresses over Corbier's eyes, laughing as she swore the dreaded Red-Eyed Raven's irises had turned gold at her touch. Those delicate fingers, callused at the tips from endless hours plucking the strings of her lute, had once spent many hours entwined with Corbier's. And those *lips* . . .

Corbier had risked his life so that he might taste those lips one last time, no matter the price.

She's so real, I thought, mesmerised by the sight of her – and the scene dissolved again, fading into the mist that was drifting in through the window, and my own world was lost to me again. All I could see was the past, and in Ajelaine's gaze, a desire as powerful as my own.

'Are you real?' I asked – and realised that somewhere in the mundane world of the Operato Belleza, Lady Shariza was having to contend with my idiotic utterances.

Bad enough she had to learn an entire script in the first place; now she'll have to improvise a whole play with me.

'I am a ghost,' Ajelaine replied, rising from the bed, the gossamer-thin silk nightgown clinging to the curves of her body. She spread her arms. 'All the petty prettiness of this chamber is naught but a coffin for my bones, this castle a graveyard that houses the dreams you and I have lost.'

Deep inside me, a furious passion stirred: not merely lust, nor even pure love, but a reckless fire demanding to burn bright against all the darkness that had taken hold of our lives.

'You have but to take my hand, beloved ghost,' I said, 'and find that two wasted souls brought together are more than enough kindling to bring back the spark of life to both.'

Shariza rose and offered her hand. I bent down to kiss it, to greet her in the traditional way, but Corbier refused to wait and suddenly I was standing tall, pulling her to me, my hands going to her waist, my mouth meeting hers.

No! I howled to the spirit inside me. *Shariza is not yours to play with, not some prop to bring back the memories of lost love – you will do nothing without her consent!*

Corbier's spirit, so much brighter than my own, threatened to consume both of us, but I held firm against his will and a moment later felt a gentle brush against my right cheek.

I noted subtle differences between Lady Ajelaine's fingers and Shariza's, even as the slight upturn of their smiles overlapped, weaving them together. 'Then prove with your lips what your words promise, my Raven,' they said as one.

She kissed me then, and through the mist I heard the audience gasp. In none of the historias did Ajelaine willingly join with Corbier. The Raven was always the leering villain come to ravish the passive victim while she cried out for her true prince to save her. Instead, here was Ajelaine – *Shariza* – drawing me to her with such ardour, the like of which I had never known before.

My fingers slid through hair that was one moment straight and fine as silk, the next thickly curled. I revelled in both.

A voice like my own, but deeper, more confident and utterly suffused with grief, pleaded with me, *Let me have this moment, I pray you.*

I allowed the kiss to continue a few seconds more before I forced it to end.

'My love?' Ajelaine asked, peering into my eyes so intently I felt like an intruder on another's most private moment.

What happened next? I asked Corbier. *Why did you risk coming to Pierzi's home?*

As if in answer, words came effortlessly to my lips. 'I came to take you from this place,' I told Ajelaine. 'Flee this prison with me while we still can.'

'I cannot,' Ajelaine cried, 'for I will never abandon my two sons. Pierzi loves them only as mirrors of himself, as remembrances of his own past and the future he sees for his bloodline. They are sweet boys, and gentle, and I will not leave them to wither and die from such paltry love as my husband has to offer them.'

Shariza had no way of knowing what Ajelaine had said, which meant I would have to feed her the lines – but at least I knew where to start. Without relinquishing her hands, I dropped to my knees and declared, 'I know you must fear for your two sons, so young and so gentle.'

Without missing a beat, Shariza followed the cue brilliantly. 'What love the prince holds for our children is only those few pitiful drops he has not already drunk for himself.'

Angry mutters pierced the mist surrounding us. No surprise to find some in the audience were not happy with those words.

What did you do? I demanded of Corbier. *You had to have known she wouldn't abandon her children. What was your plan, damn you?*

Corbier answered through my lips. 'I would never see you separated from your children, Lady, nor would I love them an ounce less for all that they are his. I came with a treaty – a gift. I will offer Pierzi everything he desires: my titles, my lands, even my claim to the ducal throne – mine, and my heirs. I will bend my knee to him and he will finally have the right to call himself prince, the title he so arrogantly took for himself. He can marry someone else, have a thousand children by a thousand concubines if he so pleases. I will give him everything – *almost* everything – he has ever wanted.' Corbier held her hand to my cheek. 'And in exchange, I ask only one thing – that for which I yearn every minute of every day.'

Ajelaine bade Corbier to rise, and Shariza, almost as if she too could see the past, pulled me upright.

'Then you understand your enemy no better than he understands me,' the two interposed women declared, 'for Pierzi, to have *almost* everything is no different to having nothing at all.'

Shariza's line was so close to Ajelaine's that my breath caught in my throat.

A cold, cruel smile came to Corbier's face in the past, and to mine now. I patted the hilt of my rapier. 'Then *nothing* is what Pierzi will have.'

Ajelaine shook her head sadly and Shariza must have caught the sudden turn in my expression, for she did likewise. 'There is no future for us, my Raven.' Ajelaine's hand reached out to clasp the back of my neck and pull me closer. 'Only this last hour together.'

Shariza in her turn, gazing into my eyes, said, 'This must be our last meeting, then . . .'

Corbier's desperate, tragic longing overwhelmed my will to resist and I found myself tugging my shirt over my head and casting it aside. I kicked off my boots, then removed my sword belt – and even here, a world away in Ajelaine's chamber, I could hear the sudden gasps from the audience. That far-off part of me who remembered who I was, what *this* was, wondered how far Shariza would let it continue.

Stop, I told Corbier, *this cannot happen. Not here, not now.*

The reply I heard inside my head was filled with such sorrow it brought tears to my own eyes. *You don't understand*, he told me. *It didn't happen. It couldn't.*

What? Why—?

The answer was like a chilled knife passing between my ribs, for from within Ajelaine's bedchamber in the past, I heard the creak of a doorknob turning.

Because he is already here.

CHAPTER 33

THE PRINCE

I had to fight to keep my awareness in my own world so that I could cue my fellow actors, that we might together bring to life the heart-wrenching truth of what had happened to Corbier and Ajelaine. In the past, I bore witness to the unfolding of that unbearable tragedy.

'What is it?' Shariza murmured from the bed, so quietly only I could hear.

'Hark! Whose footsteps approach your door?' I replied in my stage voice, sending a palpable wave of surprise and anxiety through the audience.

In Corbier's world, the door swung open to reveal not one but three figures standing in the hallway without. I leaped from the bed, scrambling to grab the discarded scabbard and draw Corbier's sword. Shariza rose too, and grabbed at my arm to restrain me.

She called out her best guess as to what I was seeing. 'The prince has come . . . Oh Corbier, flee this place – let not this chamber become your coffin!'

I pulled away from her, as Corbier did in the past, and brandishing a similar weapon in both eras, we both demanded of the intruder, 'Why do you bring the two of them here, Pierzi, you coward?'

In the wings, Teo and Beretto, dressed as guards, prepared to enter the room alongside Abastrini, misunderstanding my stupidly vague instruction.

Fool! How are they to play the right parts if you don't give them the proper cues?

Waving my sword in what I devoutly hoped was a heroic manner, I ran to the edge of the stage, keeping my point in the way so none of the three could enter. 'Let the children go!' I shouted. 'Remove the blindfolds about their eyes and send them back to their beds where little boys may find hope in dreams. You and I will go to the courtyard, that one of us may make our own bed upon the cold, hard ground and the other will at last rise from the nightmare that has ever been Pierzi and Corbier!'

Distantly I heard the muffled chaos backstage as Shoville struggled to fulfil the scene Corbier was setting for us all – but the boys were not yet seven and there was no one in the company who could—

'Are they not *my* sons?' Abastrini demanded as he entered stage right, unwittingly repeating the very words Pierzi was speaking in the past. He kept one hand outstretched, out of view of the audience, as if holding someone there. 'Is not their place beside their father?'

A moment later he ushered in Zina and Tolsi, hastily torn strips of cloth tied around their eyes. With Zina's hair bound back, she looked as much a boy as Tolsi.

'My doves!' Shariza shouted, racing to them, but Abastrini, guessing that Pierzi would not have allowed that, drew his own sword and held her at bay.

Kill him! Corbier urged. *Kill this pig here, as I could not then!*

No, I resisted. *You want the tale told, then tell it to me as it happened, not some pathetic revenge fantasy.*

In the half-world of Ajelaine's bedchamber, Pierzi pulled the crying boys into the centre of the room.

'Why do you drag them about like mules?' I demanded of Abastrini, echoing Corbier's words to Pierzi. 'Do you not care that you terrify your own children?'

Abastrini's eyes narrowed for just a moment as the implications of my words awakened his actor's instincts: *a true player must know the human heart and all its winding ways*. In that moment, Abastrini set aside the vain, pompous preener he'd been for so long, and I finally understood what it looked like when an actor worthy of the name took the stage.

'You call them *my* children,' he bellowed, his words an eerie mirror of those Pierzi was screaming at Ajelaine, 'just as I have done these past seven years, never questioning, never doubting.' He turned the two youngsters away from the audience, towards Shariza. 'Tell me, was I a fool?'

He's magnificent, I thought, brought almost to tears by the clash of raw fury and heartache in Abastrini's words.

But too soon I was pulled back to Corbier's world, where Pierzi was grabbing at the children's blindfolds. With my left hand out of sight of the audience, I tried to signal to Abastrini, hoping against hope he'd understand what to do.

'Mine, you claim, most esteemed of wives?' Pierzi asked in the past, the deep baritone of his voice breaking with a grief that bordered on madness. 'You lie to me – to your husband? To your *prince*?'

And as the blindfolds fell away from the children's eyes, I realised what had brought Pierzi to his wife's room in such a rage that he'd scarcely noticed she was in the embrace of his most hated enemy.

Corbier couldn't bring himself to describe what he'd seen, but I had no choice. 'Their eyes,' I cried, 'the boys' eyes—'

Abastrini, instantly understanding, cut me off, giving voice to almost exactly what Pierzi himself was saying to Ajelaine a hundred years before. 'Blue as yours, they were, Lady Wife, blue as the honey-dove who sings from the branches of our favourite oak in the gardens. Blue since the day they were born. But not today. Today their true colour shines through, just as my dearest friend's eyes were so befouled when he turned seven. Then was Corbier's devilish nature revealed to us all – and now see: are these boys' eyes not red as blood?'

The sharp intake of breath from the audience was like a wind rushing through the theatre as they saw the history of their duchy being torn apart.

Abastrini gave Zina and Tolsi a gentle push, signalling they should stumble towards Shariza. In the past, Pierzi shoved the boys so hard they fell to the floor. I heard the awful crack as the slighter of the two struck his head on the hard stone.

'Oh, faithless heart!' Abastrini shouted, his words overlapping eerily with Pierzi's. 'You call them doves, but in truth, they are ravens!'

The boy who'd struck the floor looked up, blood trickling down from the cut on his forehead, his gaze unfocused, confused, as if he was seeing me there and not Corbier.

He can't possibly see me, I thought. *I'm not here. These are just Corbier's memories – aren't they?*

Then I saw that Ajelaine was looking at me strangely, too.

What's happ—?

'My lieutenants!' Pierzi called out, shattering my concentration.

Heavy footfalls heralded the arrival of the same two armoured men who'd chided Ajelaine outside the fortress. They came storming into the chamber.

I spun towards the wings as if startled, catching Beretto and Teo's eyes. They reacted instantly, drawing their swords and striding onto the stage. The audience roared their dismay, an ocean of anger crashing down upon the auditorium.

'The children were *Corbier's* – Ajelaine loved *him,* not Pierzi!' someone yelled, as if no one else had been paying attention.

But there were other protests, too, and these sounded far more dangerous for the Knights of the Curtain.

'Lies – treasonous lies! This is black, bloody sedition,' another shouted, and more took up the cry.

But for all their protests, not one of them moved, sitting as if chained to their seats. No matter whether they were entranced or outraged by what was happening on the stage, everyone in that theatre – including us – was desperate to know what happened next.

And with Corbier's weeping voice in my ears, it was down to me to dredge the horrors of the past into the present. Using every piece of stagecraft we'd ever learned – and several we made up on the spot – we players brought to life those events taking place in Ajelaine's chambers.

And in doing so, I made every single person in that theatre a witness to murder.

CHAPTER 34

THE RAVENS

Pierzi's sword was still in its scabbard, but his hand rested on the hilt and Corbier had seen too many times the lightning-fast draw that could summon his falchion into action.

Pierzi was just as aware that Corbier's rapier had the reach of him, but with his most loyal lieutenants at his back, though he might take the first wound, the end of the fight would never be in doubt.

I stared at the lieutenants, trying to focus on something glinting on their tunics, peeking from beneath the studded leather armour, but Corbier kept pulling me back.

I tried desperately to breach the wall of hatred lying between them.

'I beg you,' Corbier cried, 'let me take them from you, these ravens you so despise. We will leave this city tonight and ride far from this duchy, *your* duchy, never to return. You have always said you were the better man, Nevino, the more fit ruler for this duchy. Prove it now . . . my Prince.'

Corbier had sworn never to call him prince – that he broke that vow even as he invoked Pierzi's first name was enough to shake him from his rage.

'Your Highness?' one of the guards asked.

Prince Pierzi gazed upon Archduke Corbier, then upon the two boys clutched in their mother's arms, and some shred of the man he'd always claimed to be broke through the unyielding iron of his desire for vengeance.

'Send for parchment, quill and ink,' he ordered one of his lieutenants. His eyes still fixed on Corbier, he said, 'You will renounce your title, your lands and your wealth. You will declare with your signature and seal that I am your liege-lord, now and for ever, and you will command all those who supported your false claim to swear themselves to me.'

'I will,' Corbier promised, tugging the silver Archducal brooch from his collar. 'With this emblem, I will seal the decree.'

'You will leave the city tonight,' Pierzi went on, 'and tomorrow you will leave my duchy. By the end of the week, you will be on a ship away from this country, never to see Tristia's shores again.'

'I will do this, and I will praise your name until I die.'

Pierzi ignored him. 'You will take the foul offspring you have hidden inside my home, who ate from my plate and warmed themselves at my hearth.' His glare went to Ajelaine. 'And she who wed herself to me when a hundred others more beautiful, more faithful, would have taken her place, she who lied to me, whispering her devotion even as she laughed behind my back—'

'My Prince,' Ajelaine started, a plea of shameful regret in her voice.

The instant she spoke, Corbier knew her interjection for a terrible mistake. The sincerity of her remorse was no balm, but a bee's sting that roused Pierzi's anger.

The prince's eyes narrowed, as if he'd been in a dream and only now awakened. The sound of her voice, like a melody remembered, brought a cold, cruel smile to his lips.

'*She* stays.'

'No,' Corbier pleaded, 'do not bind your heart to one whom you never loved, Pierzi; she was never more to you than the means to the throne. Let Ajelaine come with me and you may marry anew, have sons and daughters to cherish, a woman you can truly love.'

One of the prince's lieutenants whispered into his ear and again my eyes were drawn by a glint at his collar. When I tried to force Corbier's head to turn so I could see what was hiding in those shadows, the world began to shift out of focus, as if there were limits to how far I could stray from the path to which Corbier was bound.

Let me see, damn you . . .

But I was yanked back when Pierzi repeated, with the force of an iron gate slamming down, '*She stays.*'

Corbier shouted, 'Nevino, you must not—'

'I agree,' Ajelaine interrupted. She was holding the boys tightly, as if already saying goodbye. 'I will stay with you, my Prince. I will serve in whichever way pleases you – only let the boys go.'

Pierzi did not smile, just dipped his head once.

The bargain was made, the future sealed.

For a moment the vision froze, leaving me confused, unable to let the others know what they should do next.

Help me here, I asked Corbier silently. *I don't understand – if you made a deal with Pierzi, then what happ—?*

Abide, the Archduke whispered.

All was motionless in the present, and in the past, except for the sound of Corbier, weeping uncontrollably. Not knowing what else to do, I began to signal to the stagehands to let loose the curtain cords, to bring the night's events to a close – but he resisted me.

No, he said, still weeping, *abide. Let them see why they are right to call Corbier a murderer.*

And suddenly I was back into Ajelaine's chamber – the audience, my fellow players, the theatre itself, nothing but a distant memory. The crushing weight of Corbier's grief washed over me.

She made the bargain. It was her choice, not mine. She warned me all along that to be denied even the tiniest sliver of his desires was the same for Pierzi as having nothing at all. I knew she was right – all I had to do was keep silent – but I couldn't.

I felt the single syllable drop from my own lips: the one word which altered the course of history.

'No.'

The man holding parchment, quill and ink let them fall to the floor. The ink bottle shattered, sending a river of black across the flagstones.

Pierzi smiled, the look of a man freed from the chains of his own conscience. 'So be it.'

Before a sound had even escaped Ajelaine's mouth, the deed was done.

Corbier had extended his blade, aiming for Pierzi's heart. The prince had not yet drawn his weapon, but he wasn't as unprepared as he'd appeared, for the tip of Corbier's rapier sent up a screech of sparks as it scored the steel breastplate hidden beneath his fine silk shirt.

I'm dead, I thought, catching the flash of Pierzi's curved falchion. But instead of steel piercing my chest, it was Pierzi's boot that struck, hooking my knee, taking my feet out from under me to send me tumbling to the ground. The wind *whoomphed* out of me as I landed on my back against the hard stone floor, looking on helplessly as the falchion blade swept above me.

Twin sprays of blood arched through the air.

Ajelaine's scream was earth-shattering – but only for an instant, for Pierzi, seeing her coming at him with a dagger in her hand, had knocked it aside – and his blade found a new sheath in her soft belly.

'Oh ye gods—' Pierzi cried like a man who'd regained his senses too late. '*What have I done?*'

My head turned and I looked at the little boys, still clutching their throats where the blade had parted flesh. Ajelaine was on her knees, the falchion buried to its hilt in her belly. She was reaching a hand towards Corbier, but it wasn't love I saw in her eyes now, only crushing despair.

'Fly, you foolish Raven,' she whispered, blood dripping from her mouth. 'Let me die knowing some part of my heart still lives.'

Her soft words drove Corbier to action. He rose to his feet, pulled down the curtain from the bed and threw it over Pierzi and his men like the shroud he swore would soon clothe them for eternity. Without looking back, he leaped through the window, his hand clutching the rope he'd used to climb up less than an hour before, when the world was still a place of daring and mischief, where joy was more than a jester's false trick.

He slid down the rope and my palms burned from the friction, though Corbier felt nothing. He'd left behind any shred of the man he'd once hoped to be.

As his heels struck the flagstones of the courtyard below, Pierzi's voice followed. 'Fly away then, Raven. Let the price she paid purchase a few years more of misery for you. Close the door on the past once and for all and leave this place for ever.'

Corbier gazed up at his former friend, who was looking down on him, still as a statue, even as his lieutenants more carefully climbed down to give chase.

Was that regret in the prince's gaze, or pity – or shame, perhaps? It no longer mattered.

'A generous offer,' Corbier called up to him, 'but as you see, I have no wings, only these red eyes of mine you have mocked for so long.' He laughed then, a bitter sound. 'My whole life I have sought a cure, that my eyes might be as blue as when we were boys together. Yet now I find I do like the red tinge they lend to all within my sight; they show me the world as it truly is: a place where blood reigns everywhere, even when we do not see it.'

'Will you lead your army to Mount Cruxia, then?' Pierzi asked. 'My forces are twice your number. Your treason will bring death to your followers and misery upon this duchy, as even now, enemies gather on our border, seeking to steal the lands of our ancestors for their own.'

'What cares the crow for borders? What cares the rook for armies? Ajelaine is dead. The children I never knew were mine are dead.' He slammed a fist against his heart. 'And here I find Corbier too is dead. Only the Red-Eyed Raven remains.'

Before the two lieutenants had reached the ground, Corbier had fled across the courtyard. When he reached the gate, he turned and raised a hand in salute. 'Where the raven flies, death always follows.'

Those words must have haunted Pierzi as they had haunted Pertine for a century, but it was Corbier's final glance at the two lieutenants that chilled me to the core. The distance should have been too great, the night too dark, but perhaps Corbier's famed red eyes were more acute than my own, for in that moment I finally recognised the glinting emblems attached to the smirking men's collars.

They were iron brooches, fashioned in the shape of orchids.

CHAPTER 35

TICKET SALES

The curtain dropped.

The sudden shock sent me reeling backwards, and only Beretto's steadying hand kept me from falling.

'Tits up, brother,' he said encouragingly. 'The real show's about to start.'

A riotous clamour filled the theatre, confounding my senses. My head was spinning and I couldn't focus my eyes; all I could see in front of me was a waterfall of crimson blocking out the world.

'Beretto, something's wrong,' I whispered loudly, panic tightening my chest. 'I've got Corbier's affliction – everything looks red as blood—'

Beretto smacked the back of my head. 'You're staring at the curtain.'

I rubbed at my eyes. My galloping breath slowed to a canter and I could see clearly again.

Beyond the velvet wall, the notoriously reserved upper crust of Pertine society sounded as if they were losing their collective minds, judging by the incoherent shouting and arguments echoing around the hall. On this side, everyone was staring at me, apparently waiting for some signal as to whether they should hoist the curtain to take a bow or sneak out of the stage door and make a run for it.

Stage door, I thought. *We should all definitely be making a run for it.*

But Beretto had other ideas. 'Rejoice, my sisters and brothers,' he boomed, his deep baritone cresting over the furore, '*that* was the show of a lifetime! For a moment there, I would have sworn I felt inside me the very spirit of the miscreant I was playing!' A fresh trumpeting outburst pierced the curtain, but he ignored the clamour. 'Although I grant you, our performance was not, perhaps, the one our esteemed patrons were expecting—'

He ducked away from those attempting to pummel him to silence and I took over.

'Glad you're finally developing a talent for understatement,' I said, pushing away Teo, who looked as if he was contemplating leaping on Beretto's back. 'Your sense of timing could still use some work.'

My breath caught in my throat when I saw Shariza approaching from the wings. She'd already shed Ajelaine's gauzy nightdress in favour of a sturdy leather jerkin and trousers. Both the curved dagger and long, slender rapier were at her side and her hand moved between them as if she couldn't decide which she would draw. Her dark eyes were fixed on me.

Will it always be like this between us? I wondered, the sight of her momentarily deafening me to the clangour beyond the curtain.

Despite the danger, my thoughts returned to the moment I saw her sitting on the bed, beckoning me; the scents of the candles and rose petals – the smell of *her*. When she looked at me, did her Dashini training war against the same flood of emotions?

'Saint Gan-who-laughs-with-dice protect us,' Shoville swore, signalling for the stagehands to raise the curtains at last. 'To your marks, everyone.'

As we shuffled into our assigned places, Shariza pushed her way to the centre and took my hand in her left, Abastrini's in her right. It was an outrageous breach of protocol, but a clever instinct: the three of us displaying such cordiality might – just *might* – remind the audience that the many outrages they'd witnessed this night had been nothing more than a piece of theatre.

'Smile, all of you,' Shoville commanded. 'Smile as if your lives depend on it!'

The curtain rose, but our audience barely noticed, for they were too busy debating theories and trading explanations – all of which apparently necessitated a great deal of shouting and wild gesticulation, wailing and weeping. Some were pleading for calm, while others issued rallying cries for violence. One poor fellow was desperately trying to restrain his wife, who'd drawn a bejewelled blade from the sleeve of her dress and was threatening to slit the throat of her neighbour, who looked so similar she had to be a sister.

'I don't understand,' Teo said from behind me. 'Is this a good thing or a bad thing?'

'Well, they're all talking about us,' Beretto replied. 'What else can a troupe of players ask for?'

Not finding ourselves hanging from lantern-posts with spikes coming out of our skulls would be a nice start, I thought, but not even that hideous image could banish the more sinister thought that was presently haunting me.

'I saw something in Corbier's memories,' I whispered to Beretto. 'The two lieutenants – Pierzi's men – they were wearing the same brooches we've seen on the Iron Orchids!'

Beretto kept his smile pasted firmly in place for the oblivious audience. 'How could that be? The Orchids only started up a couple of years ago. Besides, they're working-class thugs, not proper soldiers.'

Nor had there been any record of such symbols being part of Pierzi's House regalia in any of the dozens of histories I had consulted in the Grand Library.

What if I've been hallucinating Corbier's world the entire time, concocting this dream from my own fears and confusion? Maybe what the legends call Veristors were really no more than eloquent lunatics spouting delusion – or worse, their own political philosophies?

Amid the sea of madness in the stalls was a lone island of calm at its centre: Duke Firan Monsegino was still in his seat, still wearing his silly traveller's cloak and broad-brimmed hat. The sight of him there, untroubled by the chaos the play had unleashed upon the audience, awoke a reckless fire in my belly.

'My Lord Duke,' I called out, projecting my voice to drown out the clamour of the crowd.

Shariza hissed and squeezed my hand painfully hard.

How is someone so delicate so strong? I paused to wonder, but the memory of Ajelaine and her children so cruelly slain burned inside me. 'Might a poor player know, your Grace, if tonight's entertainment was to your liking?'

Stillness swept over the audience as they realised that an actor – a mere performer – had defied convention by daring to call out the duke in front of his nobles.

Duke Monsegino rose, removing the hat from his head. He held my gaze a long while before saying at last, 'I found the performance . . . illuminating.'

I returned his cynical reply with a mockingly small bow. 'How kind that you shou—'

'A bit melodramatic for my tastes, however,' Monsegino continued smoothly, cutting me off. His eyes swept the audience all around him, showing that his displeasure wasn't limited to the performances that had taken place on the stage. 'I do hope the finalé will bring back some of the stately dignity for which this hallowed theatre is renowned.'

Shoville scurried to the front of the stage. 'Of course, your Grace – the very plan indeed! We shall—'

'No,' I interrupted.

Again Shariza squeezed my hand, this time pressing her fingertips against small bones so painfully I almost cried out before managing to release myself.

'"No"?' the duke asked. 'But we have witnessed only the first two acts.'

'It's a two-act play, your Grace. *The Tragedy of Corbier and Ajelaine*: a tale of such sorrow that to add to it would only force their suffering upon the good people of your duchy.'

The duke chuckled, but somehow the laughter never made it to his eyes. 'I am quite certain, Master Veristor, that the men and women of Pertine are made of sturdier stuff than you credit them.' He turned to his nobles. 'What say you, friends? Have your hearts the strength to survive the ending to this sad tale?'

The crowd enthusiastically cheered the duke's name, as much to demonstrate their loyalty as signal their assent. I doubted their sincerity on both fronts.

Monsegino turned back to the stage and this time focused his gaze on Shoville. 'My Lord Director, can I assume that at the next performance – shall we say . . . hmm, what? Two days hence? – we shall at last witness the climax? For I'm sure we are all looking forward to your own special staging of the Battle of Mount Cruxia.'

That set off renewed roars of agreement from the audience.

'Who doesn't love a good bloodbath?' asked one old codger whose gilded coat hung loosely on his crooked frame.

The younger noblemen on either side cheered raucously.

Shoville glanced helplessly at me, then bowed to the duke. 'Why, of course, your Grace – all goes according to our script.' He wagged a finger daringly. 'No hints, though. You'll all have to come back the night after tomorrow to witness the finalé of . . . *The Last Days of the Red-Eyed Raven*!'

'Damn,' Beretto muttered behind us. 'Good title.'

A slight woman in the audience called out, 'But there was no performance on the schedule for the day after tomorrow! We've had no chance to buy tickets! I wish to purchase mine now – and for my sister and her husband.'

'No doubt so she can lord it over them,' Beretto quietly speculated.

'My good lords and daminas, gentlemen and ladies,' Shoville called out, no longer able to hide his despair, 'you see we can fit no more seats in this theatre. We cannot sell you more than one ticket apiece.'

'Why not?' a stately, middle-aged man in expensive finery asked, pushing past his fellows to saunter down the one remaining aisle towards the stage. 'If a ticket is worth more to me than another, well then, let silver be the measure of our desire.' He doled several coins from his purse into his palm and tossed them onto the stage with a supercilious smile. 'Or *gold*.'

Before Shoville could speak, the entire audience started rushing the stage, shoving each other in their efforts to offer up their money first. Among the coins clattering everywhere were jewels, hastily pulled from ears or necks or fingers.

'Saint Ebron-who-steals-breath,' Shoville muttered, and gestured to the ushers to start writing out tickets while we kept the loot from rolling off the stage.

'Have any of you ever even seen that much money in one place?' Teo asked, wide-eyed and breathless, as we watched the mayhem.

I felt a tap on my shoulder and turned to find Rhyleis holding the guitar Shoville had reluctantly provided. Unlike everyone else, she appeared neither troubled by recent events, nor greedily excited by the largesse being showered onto the stage.

'I was wondering, Master Veristor, if you might provide some insight into the next scenes so that I can compose something suitable for the musicians to play during the climax.'

'How like the Bardatti,' Shariza observed, her words thick with derision – and yet I could have sworn a trace of anxiety lay beneath. 'To think *anyone* will care what the musicians are playing when the mob comes with torches and ropes.'

Rhyleis grinned. It wasn't a pleasant grin. 'Ah, the Pink Pansy – or is it the Beige Tulip? Shouldn't you be off stabbing someone in the back?'

'Oh, this is wonderful stuff,' Beretto interrupted. 'Let me fetch paper and quill so I can get some of this down: a Bardatti and a Dashini begin as mortal enemies, sworn to each other's destruction, only to discover they're long-lost sisters at the end. A comedy, I think . . .'

The wordless stand-off was broken by Shariza, who nonchalantly dropped her hand to the hilt of her rapier and announced, 'I must away. The duke will have orders for me – and no doubt for all of you.'

'Run along then, dear,' Rhyleis said sweetly. 'Wouldn't want your master to have to whistle for you twice, would we?'

Shariza ignored the slight, but after she left, I took Rhyleis aside. 'You realise if she *is* a Dashini, she can kill you a hundred different ways before you even notice death has come for you?'

Rhyleis snorted. 'A Dashini getting the better of a Bardatti? Are you too trying your hand at comedy, Damelas Chademantaigne? Because you're not very good at it.' She plucked a few notes on her guitar. 'I could play a melody that would make the Black Amaranth forget her own name, or whistle a tune that would have her sinking to her knees, pissing her trousers, while weeping with such sorrow as to make the most hardened killer worthy of pity.'

Even an amateur actor recognises braggadocio when he sees it. For all her boasting, Rhyleis was almost certainly full of shit.

Beretto, however, was utterly captivated. 'I must say, brother,' he declared, beaming at me, 'out of this entire collection of impressively homicidal damsels you've been courting, I find this foul-mouthed one the most enchanting of all.'

Rhyleis stepped up to the big man, holding her guitar as if about to club him with it, for all she was dwarfed by his size. 'Refer to me as part of anyone's *collection* again, you bumbling melodramatist – you incoherent chewer of scenery – and you will discover that those other women are no more dangerous than a stubbed toe compared to what *I'll* do to you.'

Beretto's smile disappeared. His shoulders squared, fists clenched. He gazed down at this slip of a woman who'd just threatened him.

Despite his gentle nature, Beretto wasn't one to take such direct challenges lightly. More importantly, I'd never seen him tolerate anyone, regardless of their beauty, accusing him of being melodramatic.

Suddenly he winked at Rhyleis, then turned to me. 'Oh, I do adore this one, brother. May I keep her?'

Rhyleis groaned before turning to one of the stagehands. 'You – Grigo? Strange name. You should choose another. In the meantime, guard this instrument with your life. It's a sacred artefact more valuable than this theatre – more than this whole city, in fact.' She tossed her guitar negligently through the air and turned her back on poor Grigo, who looked like he was about to have a heart attack as he scrambled to catch it with his one remaining hand before it could hit the floor.

'That's the same crap guitar Shoville's had gathering dust backstage for ten years,' Beretto observed as Grigo cradled it, sweating.

'Perhaps, but now it's been played by a Bardatti.'

Smiling, she took my hand, then reached for Beretto's and led us towards the rehearsal hall. 'Come, my pretties. You owe me a meal and something to drink. And then the three of us will discuss how we're going to save the country.'

CHAPTER 36

THE CONGRETTO

Buying a simple meal proved more challenging than any of us had anticipated. The entire city was buzzing with talk of the Operato Belleza's shocking new historia, to say nothing of its outrageous and possibly treasonous lead actor. Over the past year, I'd grown accustomed to being derided as 'the Rabbit', the cowardly fugitive who'd fled an honour duel to hide behind the walls of the Belleza like a frightened child burying himself beneath his mother's skirts. After tonight's performance, however, my long-overdue fight with the Vixen seemed to have been forgotten. Now people referred to me as 'the Veristor' and spoke in hushed tones of the man who'd conjured the notorious Corbier back from the dead to wreak vengeance upon the living.

None of which actually improved my reputation.

The moment I stepped outside the Belleza, someone started shouting, 'There he goes, the Red-Eyed Raven himself!' Every time I tried to squeeze my way into a tavern to buy a beer, I was accosted by some drunk grabbing at my shoulder and shouting in my ear, 'Come on, your Grace, surely you can afford to stand your faithful subjects a drink?'

Beretto invariably slammed the drunk's head down on the bar, while Rhyleis disarmed the fellow's enraged compatriots with a joke so ribald even the hardest-hearted among them collapsed in riotous laughter, and the three of us made our escape – and sadly, without any beer.

But it was those who *didn't* cajole or curse who were troubling me the most: grim-faced men huddled in corners, eyeing me as they whispered to their comrades. Far too many of them wore iron emblems pinned to their collars.

'What I don't understand,' Beretto began after *finally* taking a break from singing outrageously bawdy songs with Rhyleis – the two of them had bonded over a shared love and encyclopaedic knowledge of what they gigglingly referred to as *the sublime poetry of the perverse* – 'is how you could have seen those brooches on Pierzi's lieutenants a century in the past, when the Orchids only appeared a few years ago.'

'This time,' Rhyleis said, absently shaking the near-empty wineskin she and Beretto had snatched from the last tavern we'd fled.

'What do you mean, "*this* time"?'

The Bardatti hummed softly to herself, then paused to drain the skin dry before launching into a hauntingly intricate lament.

'No crown, no sceptre, howe're brightly they shine,
Gainsay our rights, as holy as thine.
Thy pertine is comely, o'er the garden it looms,
But gaze all around you, at sturdier blooms.

A Court of Flowers rises up,
Petals unfold,
Their stems are steel,
All covered in gold.

So go thou gently, oh prince.
Cease your roaring, oh Lion,
Else the morrow may find you,
Crowned with orchids of iron.'

'Pretty melody,' Beretto said. 'What's it called?'

'No one knows for sure; only that one fragment remains.' She nodded to me. 'I'd forgotten it myself until last night's stroll along that cesspit canal beneath the Ponta Mervigli. I believe it's an old dolacrimo – a funeral song.'

My chest clenched as if a cord tied around my heart was being pulled tight. It wasn't pain, exactly, more of an unexpected burst of . . . *irritation?*

'Are all Bardatti so musically illiterate?' I asked, taken aback by the venom in my own voice, 'or are you one of the especially stupid ones?'

Did I just—?

Rhyleis spun on me, grabbed the lapels of my threadbare coat and demanded, '*What* did you call me, Player?'

'I'm sorry,' I stammered, 'I don't know why I—'

My teeth clamped shut so quickly I nearly bit my own tongue. A second later, my mouth betrayed me once again. 'Don't peck your beak at me, you chattering hen. What Troubadour worth the name can't recognise the lyrical structure of a congretto?'

Rhyleis eased her grip as indignation gave way to confusion. 'A congretto? Corbier is telling you the verse *isn't* from a dolacrimo?'

'I've no idea what Corbier is saying,' I groaned. 'This isn't the same as when I'm on stage with the other actors and the sets and the audience. When that happens, I slip into his world – I can see and hear everyone else, and feel whatever he's feeling. It's as if I'm experiencing his traumas alongside him.'

'And when you're *not* on stage?' Rhyleis asked.

I resumed my slow walk down the narrow alley, recalling my misadventures barely a dozen blocks from here. 'When the Vixen ambushed me last night, I started saying the kinds of things Corbier would've said to her. My hands were positively *itching* for the hilt of a rapier. It was like my entire body had become convinced – *utterly convinced* – that I could take her in a fight.'

Beretto was looking worried. 'Brother, you know how I always say you're a better fencer than you think? Well, you are, truly, but against the Vixen . . .'

'I know. *I know*. Fortunately, most of the time – I suppose when I'm not panicked or terrified – Corbier's presence is nothing more than a few stray memories, and the odd sarcastic comment when something irritates him.'

'Well, apparently he's not fond of congrettos – whatever those are supposed to be.'

'Rebellion songs,' Rhyleis explained. 'Congrettos are a blend of simple lyrics and catchy melodies meant to arouse the passions in common folk and rally them against their Lords during times of oppression.'

'Catchy?' Beretto laughed. 'Lovely as it was, that tune of yours is positively labyrinthine! Not to mention that we "common folk" rarely go in for such florid phrases as' – he placed one hand on his cocked hip and raised the other to the night sky, mimicking the comical poses of courtly poets – '"thy pertine is comely, o'er the garden it looms".'

'That's why we assumed it was a lament,' Rhyleis said, frown lines marring her forehead. 'Listen to the transition from consonance to dissonance halfway through the phrase . . .' She whistled the tune again, and even I could tell there were too many notes and the movements between them too subtle for the average crofter or labourer to remember after just one hearing.

The Bardatti's lips pursed into a vexed line. 'The melody's definitely too ornate for a traditional congretto. Something like that could never spread from village to village on its own.'

Which would seem to defeat the purpose of a peasant rebellion song in the first place, I thought, but before I could raise the issue, a chorus of triumphant voices rang out from the entrance to the alley behind us.

'There they are! Let's give Archduke Corbier his crown!'

On any other night those words would have set my limbs to trembling. Instead, I watched helplessly as my right hand shot across my body, reaching to grip the hilt of a sword that wasn't there. Despite the lack of a weapon, I found myself spinning on my heel to face my enemies, a mocking challenge coming to my lips.

Whatever cutting insult Corbier was about to deliver was cut off when tree-trunk arms grabbed me around the middle and hauled me backwards down the alley towards a narrow path between two buildings.

'Get your paws off me, you lumbering bear!' I heard myself growl. Once we were out of view, I wrenched myself free. 'What do you think you're doing?'

Beretto tilted his head. 'Saving your idiot life, it appears. Did you not hear them talking about "crowning" you?'

I turned back towards the alley, more eager than ever to face the curs who dared hunt the Red-Eyed Raven. 'Then stand and fight with me, you overgrown ninny! There can't be more than six of them—'

Beretto unceremoniously shoved me further along the alley. 'You appear to have forgotten something, brother.'

'Which is?'

'You're rubbish at fighting.'

Oh shit, I thought, as Corbier's momentary influence faded away and I stumbled into the darkness after the others. *I really am, aren't I?*

CHAPTER 37

THE CITY ABOVE AND BELOW

Beretto led us out of the alley and down a set of stairs into a pitch-black nest of winding stone passages beneath a building that stank like an abandoned tannery. The three of us linked hands to keep together – and to stop me running back into the alley like a suicidal idiot.

'What's wrong with him?' Beretto asked Rhyleis. 'Why is Corbier's influence over him growing?'

For the first time since I'd met the mischievous, flamboyant Bardatti, her voice betrayed genuine concern. 'I don't know. The ways of Veristors are unknown, even to other Bardatti. I suspect some part of him *wants* to be more like Corbier.'

That nearly set me laughing out loud. *Why in the name of all the saints living and dead would anyone* want *to become a bloodthirsty swordsman so maddened by his lust for vengeance that he doesn't care if he gets himself – or me – killed?*

Beretto was ushering us up a sloping path and into a tiny enclosed courtyard. Rhyleis and I looked around in vain for an exit – until Beretto pointed into the shadows where two crumbling walls joined. By the time I'd noticed that the gaps where the mortar had fallen out offered a viable, if precarious, ladder, Beretto was halfway up, finding hidden hand- and footholds with suspicious ease.

He reached the top, grabbed hold of the edge of the roof and hauled himself up and over before turning to offer a hand to me, then Rhyleis, who was hard on my heels.

'Can't help but think you've been here before,' I said accusingly.

'Once or twice—' he admitted, then, more sheepishly, 'All right, possibly more – but there's nothing naughty about it. This place used to be a very respectable brothel.'

'Used to be?'

'Well, until the Orchids took it over a couple of months ago.'

'You've dragged us into Orchid territory?' Rhyleis asked. 'Is everyone in this town possessed by a suicidal spirit?'

'Ah, but therein lies the genius of my plan,' Beretto said, even more pleased with himself than usual. He wiped his dusty hands on his trousers. 'The Orchids converted the brothel into another one of their dreamweed dens.' With a grin he pointed down at the rooftop. 'Inside, it's so foggy with sapphire-coloured smoke that anyone managing to summon up the strength of will to come out here will assume we're hallucinations and go back to their imaginary orgies. I reckon we're as safe here as anywhere.'

The three of us got down on our stomachs to peer over the edge. Three storeys below, the half a dozen Iron Orchids who'd been chasing us were prowling the maze of alleyways, brandishing weapons that occasionally caught the dim light of the crescent moon in the sky above. Not one of them thought to look up.

Beretto chuckled softly. 'Dumb fuckers. They'll never think to search one of their own dens. We could stay up here all night – after all, there's dreamweed smoke going for free, if you fancy it.' He rolled over onto his side and gestured at the pale blue fog emerging from the vents in the roof, then gave Rhyleis a lecherous leer. 'Although I'm open to other amusements . . .'

'Come then, you overstuffed warthog,' the Bardatti said, pushing herself to her feet. 'Get your kit off and show me an instrument worth the playing before asking for a tune.'

'Show you?' Beretto stammered, rising awkwardly. 'Um . . . show you what?'

'You claim to be enamoured of me, so let us observe the *magnitude* of your adoration.' Mischievous green eyes trailed from his face to his chest, and down still further. 'Hurry now, I await proof of your affections.'

'Umm . . . I never said I liked you *that* way,' Beretto mumbled.

I had to clamp a hand over my mouth to keep from bursting out laughing. *And so the great lecher Beretto meets his match.*

Now that the immediate danger of metal spikes being hammered into my skull was past, I decided to leave Beretto and Rhyleis to their bizarre courtship. I stopped to pull off my boots before padding silently along the edge of the roof, following the movements of the armed bravos below.

Will morning see some other poor fool beaten half to death? I mused bitterly. *Or will the sun's rays be glinting off the tips of another iron crown dripping blood down a face frozen in terror and agony? How far are we going to allow the weeds to grow before the garden is lost to us?*

'What's that?' Rhyleis asked.

I turned. 'Nothing, I wasn't—'

'You were mumbling something about gardens.'

I gestured out over the grey-brown field of rooftops atop rundown shops and apartments, taverns and tenements, all lining the streets of Jereste like rows of decomposing crops. 'Week by week, block by block, the Iron Orchids are taking over this city. Bands of thugs are spreading like rotting underbrush, becoming stronger every day. Now they're even writing their own laws. How long before Duke Monsegino, weak as he is and already threatened by his nobles, is forced to enact them? How long before the very roots of our society are so tangled up in those of the Orchids that everything we've ever loved about this place dies on the vine?'

'Those are rather a lot of metaphors about vegetation,' Beretto said. 'And that's coming from *me*.'

'If it's this majestic garden you're worried about losing,' Rhyleis said, balancing daringly on her tiptoes near the edge, 'stop wasting time on the weeds and start rooting out the gardener.'

'An Emperor of Orchids?' Beretto suggested, the look in his eyes implying he was only half in jest. 'Hiding beneath the soil, sending forth his commands on tiny petals?'

I turned away and gazed out across Jereste. My whole life I'd been criticising it, and only now was I coming to realise how deeply I loved my city. Where else in the country were actors treated like sacred messengers of the gods, and mere plays capable of turning society on its head?

'What if Duke Monsegino is behind it all?' Beretto asked suddenly. 'He's weak and foreign, unpopular with his subjects. Maybe he fancies having a private army?'

'I doubt it,' I replied. 'Can you see him arming a rabble made up of thugs and bully-boys, who promptly start riling up the populace against his reforms? No, whoever's leading the Orchids is working *against* the duke, that much I'm certain of.'

'Then Monsegino is screwed, and so are we,' Rhyleis said.

'What do you mean?'

She paused a moment, then finally answered, 'The Black Amaranth.'

Beretto whistled through his teeth. 'Rhyleis is right: surely the duke must have ordered Lady Shariza to find and kill the Orchids' leader – and if she really is one of the last living Dashini assassins, the fact that she's failed can only mean the enemy is even more devious than we guessed.'

'Which I could believe,' Rhyleis continued, 'were the Orchids themselves not such utter fucking morons.' She pointed to the alley below. 'Look at them, running rampant through the streets, following orders they barely understand, issued by no one they could ever name.'

That sparked a thought. 'Vadris – the drug-pedlar who works the alley outside the Belleza? – Grey Mags challenged him on who recruited him to the Orchids, and though he tried to hide it, you'd swear he had no idea.'

Beretto chuckled deep in his chest.

'What is it?' I asked.

'Wouldn't it just be perfect if it turned out the militant thugs and corrupt nobles of this city were all caught up in a game of "drunken whispers"? Passing messages and launching intrigues and never noticing that not a one of them had ever met their own leader?'

'The damage they do is real enough,' I pointed out. 'If this doesn't st—'

The clang of steel against stone put a stop to my ruminations. We heard the rattle of a something – a buckler, maybe – rolling down the cobblestones, followed by swearing as its owner, presumably, chased it down the alley. His comrades were laughing at his misfortune, hurling jibes after him.

We leaned cautiously over the edge.

'More Orchids?' Beretto whispered.

I nodded, my jaw aching from the way my teeth were grinding together from biting back Corbier's desire to scream at these men, to face them, sword against sword, but the bravos passed us by, never thinking to look up.

'Perhaps we ought to consult Corbier? He might know who planted these foul orchids in our garden.' He reached out and started tapping me on the forehead. 'Hello? Your Grace? Might you come out to sing for us a while? We've got a few questions.'

I batted his fingers out of the way. 'It doesn't work that way. It's . . .' My tongue twisted, searching for words to describe sensations I could barely understand and couldn't control at all. 'I don't think Corbier is a ghost or spirit haunting me. He's more like . . . like a box of half-remembered memories. Bad ones, mostly. When the box opens, I fall inside and every thought I reach for turns out to be another of Corbier's recollections. He doesn't take me over, not like that. It's more like part of my own mind fills with those memories and . . . recreates whoever Corbier was at the time when our last performance ended.'

'So when Rhyleis sang the congretto . . .'

'I heard the same words you did, the same notes, but sung by someone else. Corbier remembered it as an annoying ditty this idiot minstrel in poncey clothes sang at some margrave's ball. But that's all it was, a passing annoyance – no buried secrets, no grand revelations, just a bad taste in my mouth.'

Beretto patted my shoulder. 'That's one shitty magical talent you have there, brother.'

Rhyleis bridled at our casual dismissal of what she no doubt saw as a magnificent Bardatti ability. 'The Veristor's gift is to uncover buried truth. It's not some parlour trick to make it easier for the two of you to get laid by whichever half-witted nobles jangle their—'

'Wait,' I said, cutting her off. 'You said congrettos are rebellion songs, right? Composed to rally the peasantry in revolt? So why would a margrave allow one to be performed in his home?'

Rhyleis stopped scowling at me long enough to reply, 'He wouldn't. Not even in jest.'

'Could you sing it again?'

The complex arrangement of melody and words rolled smoothly off her tongue.

'No crown, no sceptre, howe're brightly they shine,
Gainsay our rights, as holy as thine—'

'There,' I said, stopping her, 'the "rights" the song talks about – could they be referring to those belonging to the *nobility*, not the lower classes?'

'I suppose. That would certainly make the line "as holy as thine" less blasphemous,' she conceded.

'Keep going,' I urged her.

'Thy pertine is comely, o'er the garden it looms,
But look all around you, at sturdier blooms—'

Rhyleis halted of her own accord this time. 'Traditionally that term – "sturdier blooms" – was used as a metaphor for the working classes, who like to think of themselves as hardier than the pampered nobility. But it's out of place, given the next stanza:

A Court of Flowers rises up,
Petals unfold,
Their stems are steel,
All covered in gold.'

She stopped singing again. 'This is the only mention in any Tristian song I've ever heard to a "Court of Flowers". Steel and gold are usually references to the armies or wealth of foreign rulers who might seek to undermine the country.'

'The Court of Flowers!' I repeated excitedly. Now that I was more or less free of Corbier's influence, the coincidence of that turn of phrase matching the one used by Pierzi's lieutenant in the past and appearing in the Sigurdis Macha book whose second volume had been stolen from the Grand Library took on new significance. I recounted all this to Beretto and Rhyleis. 'What if it's more than just a poetic metaphor?' I pressed them. What if this "Court of Flowers" was used as an implicit threat that the ducal family could be replaced if the duke himself doesn't fall in line?'

'Of course!' Beretto exclaimed, jabbing his forefinger in the air as if this was proof of some long-proclaimed political theory of his own devising. 'That would make this so-called "congretto" less of a call to arms for the common man and more of a—'

'—ransom demand,' I finished for him.

The final lines of the song came tumbling from my mouth.

'So go thou gently, oh prince.
Cease your roaring, oh Lion,
Else the morrow may find you,
Crowned with orchids of iron.'

'Indeed,' Beretto said. As quickly as it had come, his enthusiasm faded, replaced with melancholy as he sombrely repeated the last line. 'Crowned with orchids of . . . with orchids of iron.' His voice cracked at the end. 'Poor Roz. Poor, poor Roz. Tortured and killed for no reason but to terrify a mere company of players.'

'The crowning wasn't to scare *us*,' I said, annoyed with myself for having missed what should have been obvious. 'The Iron Orchids *don't* care about a bunch of actors – *we* can be replaced. Roslyn's death was a message for Duke Monsegino.'

'An interesting way to deliver it,' Rhyleis said, playfully punching Beretto in the shoulder as if she could tease him from his grief. 'What do you suppose this message is meant to convey?'

I couldn't answer. I'd stretched what little information I had as far as it would go, and the anger that rose up in me was my own this time.

I wished for once that I carried a rapier like the bravos of Jereste so that I could draw it from its scabbard and slash the air in futile rage, or brandish it at the moon, shouting idle threats to the night sky. But I'd not picked up a real blade since I'd laid aside my sword when I'd fled the duel with the Vixen.

Besides, everyone knows a sword slows you down when you're running.

Only, I was so very tired of running, tired of being afraid, of being bullied by dukes and thugs alike. Perhaps it was time I stopped running. Perhaps the world ought to know that the blood of two Greatcoats ran through the veins of Damelas Chademantaigne and that *did* mean something.

Please, all you restless saints, make it mean something.

I turned to Rhyleis. 'The congretto – can you compose one yourself? Only with different words?'

Her eyes narrowed. 'I'm a Bardatti Troubadour, moron. What do you think?'

I laced up my boots. 'We'll write it on the way,' I said and slid my legs over the ledge before turning to begin the climb back down.

'On the way where?' Beretto asked, descending more nimbly than his bulk would have suggested.

'The Ducal Palace. We're going to persuade Monsegino to reveal everything he's been hiding from us about the Court of Flowers.'

'It's past midnight, Damelas. How exactly are you going to convince the palace guards – not to mention the duke himself – to grant you an audience in the middle of the night?'

I waited to answer until Rhyleis had dropped the last few feet to the ground. I pasted a confident grin on my face and, taking some small pleasure in playing, just for once, the cavalier hero, announced, 'Why, the same way actors have been seducing their way into the bedrooms and boudoirs of wealthy patrons for centuries. We're going to write his Grace a love poem.'

CHAPTER 38

THE GATES

Two pairs of iron gates separated the Ducal Palace of Jereste from the city. The first were set in a colossal arch of blue-enamelled brick, the top of which served as a guard house for the sentries, who could gaze down through strategically placed arrow slits at those who came begging entry into the massive courtyard where Jereste's civic festivals were held. Courteous even at such a late hour, the sentries were perfectly willing – after a brief recitation of the legal penalties for seeking entry under false pretences – to open the gate to those asserting vital business with the duke.

The second gate was where our real problems began.

'Our hosts don't look pleased by our arrival,' Rhyleis observed, glancing behind her at the heavy bars now imprisoning the three of us inside the courtyard. We'd been instructed to wait there until the guards at the second gates returned to either wave us inside or escort us to the beheading blocks beneath the massive statues of Death and Coin.

'D'you suppose that line you wrote about "withered ducal sceptres left flaccid by spectres" might have been a bit . . . ungenerous?' Beretto asked.

I agreed, although I'd lacked the courage to say anything myself, just handed the folded sheet of paper to the bleary-eyed chamberlain with instructions to put it into the hands of Duke Monsegino himself and no other. That was more than an hour ago, and I was starting to wonder if perhaps we'd pushed our luck too far.

Rhyleis shrugged. 'Everyone's a critic these— Oh, Hells.'

A dozen guards in pertine-blue tabards over hastily donned armour, spears in hand and crossbows strapped to their backs, were marching loudly down the passage towards the gate. They looked entirely displeased with us.

'It's all right,' I told the others. 'Unhappy guards is a good sign.'

My grandfather used to say that if a Greatcoat ever met a soldier who *wasn't* grinning at the prospect of beheading him, he'd know he'd left Tristian soil.

A large woman with short-cropped blonde hair was leading the troop. She was almost as big as Pink Mol, with a grimace twice as unfriendly. The moment she reached the gate, she stopped and held up a fist. The twelve soldiers behind her clanked to an immediate halt.

'I am Captain Terine of the palace guard,' she said bluntly.

'Terine?' Beretto asked. 'Did your parents mean to name you after a meal of slow-cooked vegetables and meat, or after the silver bowl into which said repast is placed to cool?'

'Not helping,' I said.

'I'm hungry. We never had supper.'

'When I give the signal,' Captain Terine began, ignoring our exchange, 'the gate will rise. You will walk six paces forward and wait there as my soldiers take up position beside and behind you.'

And that way we'll be neatly boxed in on all sides. I glanced back at the first gate, wondering if we might be fast enough to race across the courtyard and climb over before we were impaled by crossbow bolts.

'Should you attempt to flee, you will be executed on the spot,' Captain Terine informed us, catching my eye. I suppose I did have a reputation for panicked flight. 'Attack me or any of my guards and you will be executed. Offer bribes, threats or insolence—'

'*Insolence?*' Rhyleis repeated incredulously. She stepped up to the bars separating us from the armoured giantess on the other side. 'Know you this, Guardswoman – and I grant such courtesy only by the sense of charity tradition bids me to offer fools on starry nights – that I am a Bardatti Troubadour. Attempt to command me, menace me, cajole me or stare at my arse too long in a way I find displeasing, and I will compose a tune that will drive you mad with lust for the nearest barn animal. So great will your obsession be that not even these tin-plated fools behind you will be able to stop you from racing around the city naked in hot pursuit of the nearest goat or sheep, against whose buttocks you will rub yourself insensible while declaring your eternal love until your throat dries out and your voice cracks like old clay.'

'If you're still deciding which of the lovely women you've been consorting with lately to wed, brother,' Beretto whispered, 'may I suggest the Black Amaranth? A Dashini assassin seems the safest choice at this point.'

Captain Terine stared wide-eyed at the Bardatti, who stood barely as tall as her chest, apparently overawed by the detailed nature of the threat. 'You are Bardatti? Truly?'

Rhyleis paused to give me an I-told-you-so glance before turning back to the captain. 'I am.'

The captain raised an armoured fist and instructed her lieutenant, 'Make sure to shoot the annoying little one first.'

Finally the guards found something to smile about.

The three of us stepped beneath the iron spikes as they were slowly raised, before advancing the requisite six steps towards the steel spearheads facing us. Our escort clanked into position around us, spears held parallel to the floor to keep us penned in.

The Captain gave a signal and the phalanx lurched forward like a siege-engine on rusted wheels.

You'd think by now I'd have grown accustomed to being threatened and ordered about, but saints, I was tired of bearing witness to indignity being heaped on injustice. Or maybe Archduke Corbier was whispering in my ear, bridling at being treated like a commoner.

The world is positively stuffed with arseholes, I thought. *May all the gods keep me from becoming one of them.*

The guards kept up their steady, rattling march through the palace's gaudily decorated halls, affording plenty of time to admire the many, many works of art depicting the glory of Pertine made manifest through its glorious rulers.

All twelve soldiers came to a dead halt, stopping so suddenly that I stumbled headlong into the man in front of me. He turned his head an infinitesimal amount, just enough to convey both my utter irrelevance and the assurance of excessive violence should I touch him again.

Captain Terine banged three times in ceremonial fashion on the imposing set of double doors. A moment later, they opened smoothly, without so much as a creak, to reveal what I took to be the ducal throne room.

'By his Grace's command,' the captain began, standing tall, and so broad in the shoulder that she blocked my view entirely, 'I bring before you Master Beretto Bravi, a Knight of the Curtain.'

Beretto leaned over to whisper to me, 'I quite like how she says it. Do you suppose she fancies me?'

'Have you yet again forgotten your romantic interests lie elsewhere?' I asked.

He shrugged. 'She seems a gentle soul. I'd hate to disappoint her, is all.'

Captain Terine, either not hearing or not caring, continued her introductions. 'Rhyleis dé Joilard, a Bardatti, known among her order as Sharptongue.'

That took me aback. How was it this ducal guardswoman knew more about the Troubadour than I did? Then I realised Rhyleis had probably signed her full name – along with several other grandiose and self-bestowed titles – at the bottom of the 'love song' we'd sent to Duke Monsegino.

Let's hope my clever plan really is clever and not just Corbier's unhelpful influence.

'And finally,' Captain Terine began, and I wondered if the gruff edge in her words revealed an eagerness to get the introductions over with so she could get on with my beheading, 'the Veristor Dam—'

She was cut off by a new voice, a light, airy one whose dulcet tones did nothing to hide the cruelty beneath, like the whisper of a courtesan breathing seductions in your ear even as she slides the blade ever so gently between your ribs.

'The Veristor Damelas Chademantaigne,' the woman waiting for us in the throne room announced, my name and title dancing on her tongue. 'I hope no one present will take offence, but I know him by a different sobriquet, a token of the special affection in which I hold him close to my heart.'

Captain Terine and the guards stepped aside, making an armoured tunnel through which I could now see our hostess as she smiled at me with more ardour and need than any lover ever had.

'Hello, my rabbit,' said her Ladyship Ferica di Traizo.

An entire year I'd spent trying to hide from her in both my waking life and my nightmares. Now it appeared that my cunning plan to intimidate the duke had just delivered me, Beretto and Rhyleis into the waiting arms of the Vixen of Jereste.

CHAPTER 39

THE LOVER SCORNED

Rabbit. Rabbit. Rabbit. The word gnawed at me, echoing in my mind until that casual, almost affectionate jibe hardened into a dread realisation: *She's right. I am a rabbit.* My breath was coming in ragged gasps, my heart already racing as my body demanded I flee as fast and as far as my legs could carry me.

So what happened to showing the world that the blood of two Greatcoats runs in the veins of Damelas Chademantaigne?

I couldn't tell if this scornful new voice in my head was Corbier or the inevitable manifestation of my own shame. Either way, it wasn't helping.

I never asked to be this way, you arsehole, I replied. *It's not a choice I made.*

Isn't it? I wonder, is it the prospect of your flesh being parted by your enemy's blade that so frightens you? Or might it be the sight of her *blood dripping from the tip of your own sword?*

Shut up! I raged silently. *You don't know anything about me – you're long dead, and frankly, the world was better off without you.*

The sneer that came to my lips definitely belonged to someone else.

The dead leave their mark upon the living, Damelas Chademantaigne. Where is the influence of your grandmother, the valorous Greatcoat who fought a hundred duels and lost only one?

The question cut me as sharp as the tip of a smallsword across the cheek. Had Virany Chademantaigne been standing here toe-to-toe with the Vixen of Jereste, any shaking in her hands would have been the loosening of her muscles in preparation to strike the first blow.

My grandmother is dead, I replied bitterly. *You need lose only one duel for that.*

The taunting voice in my skull was unrelenting. *Where is your grandfather, then, who could bluff his way past half the devils in Hells and trick the others into taking his side?*

Were Paedar here, the trembling of his lips would have been the first twitch of a smile, masking the schemes he'd be planning, playing upon his opponent's vanities and insecurities to subtly alter the game board, one piece at a time, until every move favoured him.

He's old now, and alone. He sits at home waiting for death to reunite him with my grandmother.

But Corbier's voice – and it *was* Corbier's, I was sure of it now – had all the sympathy and compassion of a raven nibbling on a corpse's eyeball as he whispered, *A man who carries neither his grandmother's spirit nor his grandfather's heart ought not be so quick to refuse the gift of my counsel, for I promise you, Damelas, blood will be spilled upon this floor tonight.*

'Draw me a circle upon this floor,' the Vixen commanded. 'And someone find my rabbit a rapier suited to his height. Nothing too heavy, mind—'

'Lady di Traizo—' Captain Terine began.

'Margravina, actually,' the Vixen corrected her. 'Didn't you hear? Duke Monsegino's aunt, Viscountess Kareija, has this very night persuaded her nephew to sign an accord with my family. We may have been disgraced these past fifteen years, but we've never been short of money. As it happens, we have many, *many* private soldiers in our household, and Kareija wisely concluded they would be most helpful in keeping his Grace's head attached to his shoulders in the coming days. Duke Monsegino wasn't pleased, but he came around eventually. He's off explaining the new arrangement to the – well, I suppose we must refer to him now as the *former* Margrave of Sorveau.'

She set her gaze on one of the guards and gestured to a table laden with flasks of wine and silver-rimmed goblets. The man barely hesitated before running to fill one for her. Captain Terine looked displeased, but forbore to admonish him in front of the newly minted margravina.

The Vixen smiled. 'There, see how quickly we all adapt to our new stations?' She turned back to me. 'It is as if the Gods of Love and Death themselves wish to bless my ascension, for even as I idled here awaiting the duke's return, they sent you to me, my beloved rabbit, that I might end my duelling career with one final flourish.'

I felt Beretto shifting closer to me, sensed his hand drifting to his dirk, even as his eyes passed over each of the guards to see if any were close enough for him to grab one of their spears. Rhyleis had a hand in her coat, no doubt ready to produce some exotic Bardatti weapon secreted there.

The Vixen, sharp-eyed as ever, caught both movements and her cheeks flushed with delight. 'Oh my, an actor and a minstrel preparing to unlawfully draw weapons on a margravina in the ducal throne room? What fun this is going to be – I can barely wait . . .' She waved a finger and as one, the guards pointed their spears at Beretto.

I watched in awe as he stood by me, refusing to back up even a step. What makes a person so steadfast in their friendship, in their beliefs in what is right and what is wrong? And Rhyleis – who I'd met only yesterday – stood with us, ready to fend off the guards with . . . what? A devastatingly sharp poem? It was beginning to look suspiciously as if the two of them were ready to die for me.

And die they will, Corbier's dry voice observed, *if you huddle behind them, shivering your little bunny tail as you await the Vixen's teeth.*

'Stop!' I shouted, stepping in front of my absurdly steadfast friends – and coming perilously close to being speared through the heart by an overeager guard.

Ferica di Traizo laughed. 'So eager to dance, my rabbit? Surely you would not strike a lady in so boorish a fashion?'

I hadn't even realised I'd raised a clenched fist – was that Corbier's doing? And what on earth was he hoping to accomplish? I was reasonably skilled at stage fisticuffs, although that meant only that I was particularly good at *not* hitting people.

Corbier wouldn't shut up. He just kept egging me on. *It's not so hard: you bat away the spear with the palm of your left hand, spin counter-clockwise and follow the shaft. Drive your right fist into the guard's nose between the gap by the steel cheek-guard of his helmet – he'll try to grab you, of course, so his fellows can stab you in the back, but you just need to duck under his arms and come up the other side, where you'll be close enough to this Lady Fox of yours to strike her in the throat with your elbow. Crush the windpipe and—*

'Shut up, and damn you to every Hell that'll take you!' I bellowed.

Ferica tut-tutted at me. 'Now, now, my rabbit. Such coarse language? Where is that devil's tongue of yours that so brilliantly humiliated me in front of the entire duelling court last year, leaving me no choice but to drop my suit against your grandfather to accept your challenge instead?'

'He's a seventy-year-old old man, no threat to you even in his prime, yet you would have murdered him without cause!'

The whimsical smile fell away, and for just a moment, Ferica di Traizo's soul was laid bare. Her features were so cold, so devoid of humanity, that it was as if a corpse were addressing me. 'Did you know it happened right where we're standing?' she asked.

'My Lady, whatever your griev—'

'My *grievance*? Shall I recount for you my life's sad tale, my rabbit? How Virany Chademantaigne' – she spat out the name with such venom I couldn't stop myself flinching – '*ruined* my mother? How she slandered her and rendered false judgements against her in public? How she invoked trial by combat to uphold her malicious verdict?' The Vixen tapped a finger over her left breast. 'How the King's Parry put six inches of steel through my mother's heart – just here?'

My grandfather had told me the story – but not like this. I caught the crucial lie in the Vixen's recounting. 'Lady di Traizo, it was *your* mother who issued the challenge. She was the one who deman—'

But the Vixen, oblivious, was pacing a semicircle on the marble floor. 'The spray of her blood reached all the way to this spot right here, where her young daughter, only twelve years old, had been waiting impatiently for her mother to finish her silly business at court so she could take her home.'

She looked back at me. 'What better beginning could there be to a tragic revenge story?'

'Please, these vendettas serve no—'

Corbier's voice cut me off. *You waste your words, Player. She does not see you. She sees only her past unfolding before her, again and again.*

As if to prove the Raven's point, the Vixen continued softly, lost in remembrance of a childhood long gone, 'Mother had refused a hundred times – a *thousand* – to teach me fencing.' Her voice and the way she moved were unnaturally wistful. 'Duelling wasn't a suitable career for a damina's daughter, she insisted.' She pivoted on her heel, spinning like a child. 'But your grandmother took care of that, didn't she? My mother's title was rescinded, her ancestral lands given to the peasants she'd been wrongfully accused of mistreating.' She began a damina's flourish, but instead, moved seamlessly into a lower-ranked lady's curtsey. 'So the dilemma of how I might become a duellist was solved for me by the King's Parry – and all it cost was my mother's life.'

The sincerity of the Vixen's portrayal reminded me how easily history could become twisted, the myth growing with each retelling. In truth, Heilana di Traizo's story was far crueller – and more common – than her daughter suggested. A landlord of brutal efficiency, Heilana had starved her farmers and their families, and when the desperate mothers had banded together to seek justice from the Ducal Court, Heilana had had their children locked in a barn and threatened to set it on fire unless they withdrew their claims.

I'd been a child myself at the time, but I'd snuck down the stairs late one night and heard my grandfather begging my grandmother to bring the matter before Duke Meillard. And I'd never forgotten the way she had laughed, wondering aloud when in Duke Meillard's entire reign had he *ever* ruled against a noble House to whom he was beholden?

That was why a Greatcoat had to take the case.

But that wasn't the entire truth either, was it? Dukes weren't unfeeling monsters sitting on luxurious thrones playing with stacks of gold jubilants; they were weak, dependent on the wealth and armies of their nobles, who methodically wound their influence like pretty silken cords around and around the duke's neck. If his decisions threatened their interests, they tugged on those cords, choking off his attempts before any displeasing edicts could be issued.

Is that why you broke the line of succession, Duke Meillard? Did you grow to hate your throne so much you couldn't abide the thought of your daughter being imprisoned upon it?

'Ah,' said Ferica di Traizo. The mock sadness showed her mask was firmly back in place. 'I see my rabbit grows bored with this dull recitation of my family history.'

'No, my Lady,' I started quickly, forcing down Corbier's contempt, 'please, I mean no offen—'

She reached into a pocket of her gown, took out a gold jubilant and held it up. 'The red-bearded fool and the minstrel attempted to draw weapons on me. Kill one of them for me. I don't mind which.'

Two guardsmen stepped forward, spear points dipping down. Another pair unstrapped the crossbows from their backs.

'Halt!' Captain Terine strode forward and grabbing the two crossbowmen by the shoulders, practically hurled them bodily back into line. 'We are soldiers of the Ducal Palace of Pertine, not hired bravos to unquestioningly execute the orders of any noble who flashes a coin in our faces!'

'Soldiers with families, one presumes,' the Vixen said. 'Wives, husbands, children – that sort of thing.'

Look at the faces of the guards, Corbier urged me. *See how they fear the wrath of the Lady Fox more than their commander, or even their rightful ruler? This is the price of the Violet Duke's weakness. Any second now, one of them will do as the margravina demands, calculating that her support will ensure their survival. The minstrel or the player will die unless you act—*

'Enough!' I shouted.

The Vixen glanced at me briefly, then immediately returned her gaze to the guardsmen. 'I have an excellent memory for faces, and I believe my proclivity for *holding grudges* is well established.'

At that, Beretto pulled his dirk and Rhyleis produced a tiny, finger-length blade from inside her coat.

Captain Terine shouted orders for everyone to stop *right where they were*, but her guards, using the excuse of seeing weapons drawn to ignore their captain, prepared to attack—

It was all happening too fast! My friends were about to die and I wasn't even carrying a damned rapier to help them!

But I didn't need steel to save them, I realised. There had always been a way to put an end to this cruel madness. I'd run and hidden for an entire year, bowed and scraped as long as fate would allow, but that time was done now. No more running. No more rabbit.

I forced my hands to relax. Sweeping my right hand behind my back in a flourish, I bowed low, not in the way of an actor, but as one noble addressing another.

'Gracious Lady,' I announced, projecting my voice throughout the room.

Everyone turned to me and I favoured them all with a mocking rendition of a courtier's smile. 'It would be my greatest delight, *Ferica*,' I declared, addressing her with intolerable familiarity, 'if you and I were to at last consummate our *affaire*' – I looked up just long enough to wink at her, letting that word hang in the air a perilously long time before finally adding, 'of honour.' I glanced pointedly at Beretto and Rhyleis, then sighed theatrically. 'Alas, the presence of these two players would distract me, lending you an unfair advantage.'

What precisely are you trying to accomplish? Corbier asked.

Well, I've addressed her as an equal, insinuated that I could beat her in a fair fight and implied she wants to have sex with me. If that doesn't piss her off enough to put her off her game, nothing will.

The easy smile Ferica di Traizo habitually wore shifted, revealing the Vixen's feral appetite beneath. 'You're saying if I allow your friends to leave, you will duel now, of your own free will, foregoing any last-minute appeals?'

'Brother, what are you—?'

I cut Beretto off with a hiss and made a grand gesture to the row of windows on the other side of the throne room looking onto the courtyard. 'You and I can watch together as the Actor and the Troubadour take their leave of us. The moment they pass the outer gates, our dance can begin.'

Ferica di Traizo stared at me, predatory eyes narrowed, seeking the trap, but anticipation quickly overcame caution. 'Marked!' She practically screamed the word in ecstasy and went skipping across the throne room to take a scabbarded rapier down from the wall. Examining the elaborately engraved hilt, she cried, 'Oh, my rabbit – my darling rabbit, no lover has ever offered such pleasure as you are about to give me.'

CHAPTER 40

THE SECOND

I really did have a plan of sorts. First, I needed to get Beretto and Rhyleis out of the palace to prevent Ferica di Traizo from concocting some pretext to kill them after the duel was over. The second part . . . well, that was going to be less pleasant.

You mean to taunt her, don't you? Corbier asked. *Put on foolish displays of grandiose stage-fencing techniques, grand swooping gestures to no avail so she can bat you about a while, relishing your incompetence?*

Some animals like to play with their food, I replied.

And should her delight momentarily overcome her caution, you hope to then attempt a genuine blow, praying some saint grants you such extravagant good fortune that it lands somewhere other than your own foot?

See, when you put it that way—

Something hard pressed into my stomach. One of the guards was shoving the hilt of a scabbarded rapier at me.

'Looks about the right length,' the man muttered, sounding as if he were having a debate with himself. There was a lot of that going around lately.

'Margravina di Traizo, again, I must protest this outrageous behaviour,' Captain Terine said, making one last effort to keep blood from staining the gleaming marble floor. 'Duelling inside the palace walls is beyond irregular—'

'On the contrary,' the Vixen replied, her attention still fixed on me, 'were my mother here, she would happily remind you of its rich and bloody tradition.'

'Brother . . .' Beretto warned, putting a hand on my shoulder.

'Get out of here,' I whispered to him. 'Take Rhyleis and get back to the Belleza, quickly as you can. Oh, and tell Shoville I might be late for tomorrow's rehearsal.'

'Where is the bloody Duke of Pertine?' Beretto demanded. 'Surely he wouldn't allow this to continue?'

'No doubt where such men always are at times like these,' Rhyleis said, still holding her finger-blade at the ready. 'Anywhere but where you need them.'

Beretto caught her glance and I thought I saw something pass between them. I had the terrible feeling that what I'd spotted was a remarkable – and entirely reckless – pact that neither would abandon me.

'I stand as *secundi* for Damelas Chademantaigne,' Beretto turned and shouted. 'Should he fall before the matter is settled, I will pick up his blade and finish this foul affair once and for all!'

'I, too, will remain,' Rhyleis announced with no less extravagance. 'As a Troubadour of the Bardatti, I invoke my right to witness any judicial matter of my choosing.' Her scathing glance swept over the Vixen. 'And to chronicle it in song and story for all time.'

'Marked!' Ferica shouted triumphantly before I could gainsay my friends' idiotic demonstrations of loyalty. To Beretto she asked, 'And does your brave service as Chademantaigne's second extend to the duel to follow this one, as well?'

'What?' Beretto asked.

No matter what Ferica di Traizo's new rank might demand of her, a vixen would not change its nature for a title.

'The duke will never allow a newly named margravina to challenge a poor old man to a duel,' I insisted.

Ignoring me, one of the guards produced a nub of chalk and began drawing a circle on the pristine marble.

Ferica walked its perimeter daintily. 'I rather think I won't have to challenge him at all, will I? Even as mediocre a Greatcoat as "The King's Courtesy" – and what sort of a name is that, I ask you? – will surely feel the need to avenge the death of his beloved grandson.' Her gaze caught mine and suddenly I found it hard to breathe. 'And such a death it will be, my rabbit.'

What have I done? Of course my stupid plan isn't going to work. She didn't even need to set a trap for me – I walked into it myself!

Beretto was saying something to me, urging me to plead some excuse to delay in the hope that the duke might return and put a stop to this, but his voice was sounding ever more distant as my ignominious death grew closer. I tried to draw the rapier the guard had handed me, but the hilt slipped from my grasp and the blade slid back into the scabbard as if trying to flee the scene. Frantically, I rubbed my sweaty hands on my thighs before attempting to draw the weapon again.

I could help you, you know, Corbier offered with placid indifference.

How? You're just a faint collection of stolen memories. Irritating memories, true, but still—

I felt the Red-Eyed Raven's smile twitch on my own lips. *Memories can be many things. Pictures in our mind . . .*

The throne room disappeared, replaced by a cascade of images, from the tranquil scene of a mother and child strolling along the sand near placid water to the chaos of a thousand men and horses smashing into an enemy line upon a rocky field already littered with corpses.

Memories can be sounds . . .

Screams filled the air: soldiers dying, steel clashing against steel, hammering into bone, cutting into flesh—

Don't, I pleaded. *Don't make me listen to th—*

But Corbier wasn't done. *And then, of course, there are those memories within the body itself . . .*

Suddenly my fingers ached to feel once again the familiar smoothness of a rapier in my hand, not squeezing with the trembling rigidity of a rank amateur, but the sure, confident grip of a true swordsman, one for whom the blade was an extension of his own arm.

My feet shifted of their own accord, sliding a few inches wider apart, letting my weight settle evenly on the balls of my feet. My thigh muscles quivered, longing for the sensation of a single perfect lunge, the kind that would send the tip of my blade flying like an arrow past my opponent's guard.

The Vixen's polite cough returned my attention to the throne room. She had slipped off her boots and stripped out the laces, using them to quickly and efficiently fasten the length of her gown around her legs, turning the skirts into a pair of bulbous trousers loose enough to enable a full lunge.

'Any last words, my rabbit?' she asked, swiping her rapier viciously through the air. With her other hand, she gestured lazily to Rhyleis. 'After all, we have our very own Troubadour here to capture all this for posterity.'

Might I have the pleasure of a verbal riposte this time? Corbier asked.

Before I could answer, the words began tumbling from my mouth, spoken with a nobleman's elegance and a soldier's brutality combined. 'Lady Ferica di Traizo, I declare to all present in this hallowed chamber, before the good Gods of War and Coin themselves, that you, worthless daughter of a worthless House, are a craven, feckless creature. Your existence is an abhorrence against the grace of the saints and the dignity of the gods. That you should ascend to the title of margravina is an affront to the very aspiration of nobility. Your heart is a ruined, empty vessel. You are without honour and without courtesy. For these, and for your many, many other sins' – my fingers wrapped around the hilt of the rapier, and drew the first four inches of steel from the scabbard as Corbier said with a smile – 'I am for you.'

Elation spread throughout my entire body, as if a man could become drunk on undeserved hope.

We can do this! I thought, marvelling at the possibility that Corbier's skill with a blade might allow me to survive the night. *The two of us can beat the Vixen at her own game—*

No, Corbier said, and the word sounded like a death knell.

But I thought—

A new memory assaulted me, this one rooted even deeper than the others: the feeling of my body pivoting, just slightly, as my arm reaches full extension. The tip of the sword evades the enemy's parry, piercing cloth, then skin, the feeble resistance of muscle and sinew quickly overcome until, sliding between the ribs, at last it buries itself deep into a still-beating heart. This would be no mere win; there would be no ending at first blood.

My right hand drew the rapier from its scabbard in a motion so fluid it was like water flowing down a river. Memories of a hundred past duels flooded my thoughts, a torrential river that dragged me below the surface.

We aren't going to defeat the Vixen, Corbier said, taking his first steps towards the noblewoman whose arrogance exceeded even his own, and whose callous cruelty the Red-Eyed Raven would not tolerate.

We're going to kill her once and for all.

CHAPTER 41

THE RAVEN'S BLADE

With a rapier in her hand, Ferica di Traizo, the Vixen of Jereste, was a marvel to behold. I could still remember the first time I'd stood among the cheering crowds of a packed courtroom, holding my breath as she glided around the duelling circle with preternatural grace, always smiling. Lean and broad-shouldered, she looked more feminine in her fencer's blouse, waistcoat and trousers than when draped in the gaudy finery of a noblewoman. Professional duellists often claimed that the hardest part of fighting the Vixen was to stop oneself from falling in love long enough to remember to parry.

'Are you going to cavort about like an overexcited puppy all night, my Lady Fox?' I asked.

My voice, but Corbier's words. Far more unnerving, I was holding my rapier too loosely, allowing the point to drag along the floor as I sauntered around the circle with no more finesse than a man on a midday promenade.

The Vixen pivoted on her back foot and launched herself into a devastating lunge, moving almost too quickly for the eye to follow. Even as reflexes not my own kicked in and my guard came up in a diagonal sweep to knock her blade away, her tip dipped under mine and caught me on the forearm. Before I could so much as attempt a counter-attack, she'd returned to her previous position and resumed walking the circle.

I stared down at the trickle of blood from the shallow cut. 'Are you sure you're a vixen?' I heard myself ask. 'You prance like one of those show ponies ridden on parades by soldiers too old to fight.' My knee came up in a preposterously high step and then stomped on the ground once, twice, thrice. 'Can you do sums as well?'

'First blood has been shed,' Beretto shouted from the corner of the room where he and Rhyleis were forced to sit like idle spectators, surrounded by six of the palace guards. 'Honour has been satisfied!'

'The actor is correct,' Captain Terine said. 'The matter is now settled. The combatants will withdraw.'

I laughed, a deeper, crueller sound than had ever before emerged from my throat. 'You ought to know your own duchy's duelling laws better than that, Captain. While it's true that the presiding magistrate has the right to call *primada sanguida* to halt any duel at first blood, the principle only applies after *both* fighters have made their initial attack.'

The Vixen's eyes narrowed as she at last understood why her opponent had made no move to strike.

Clever plan, I thought. *Except you've just let it slip and now she has the advantage over us!*

Corbier was untroubled. *Whatever paltry benefit she gains from knowing our intent is vastly outweighed by the overconfidence that knowledge will instil in her. You said it yourself: our Lady Fox likes to play with her food before she eats. Her style is to launch feints and half-thrusts here and there, gradually ensnaring her opponent until it's too late for them to regain their own tempo. She'll be more cautious now.*

The Vixen and I continued to circle each other. She launched a flurry of slashes and low thrusts, but Corbier refused to let me even attempt a parry; he simply had me give ground, a small step at a time. The cost was a nick to my left cheek and another shallow cut on my sword arm.

Your strategy doesn't appear to be working, I pointed out, feeling the blood trickling down my face. *Perhaps if you moved our fucking arse a little more?*

Again Corbier ignored my fear. *You pretend at ignorance, Damelas Chademantaigne, but I can sense your instincts as easily as you perceive mine. Your grandmother trained you from childhood – that learning is deep inside you even now. Why do you refuse to let it out?*

Because you're wrong, you lunatic. I'm no swordsman, and I'll be even less of one if you let the Vixen take my legs out from under me!

Almost as if she'd heard me, she ducked down low and placed her left hand on the floor to hold herself steady as she swept her sword three inches above the ground, threatening to sever my ankle. I lifted my forward foot at the last instant without a trace of gracefulness, looking more like an old man trying to step over a puddle.

What a fool she is, Corbier said, again not bothering to counter-attack.

She's the deadliest fencer in Jereste.

Fencer, perhaps, but a fencer isn't a duellist. Have you forgotten your Errera Bottio already?

One of the principal things I'd taken from *For You Are Sure to Die* was that Bottio must have become terribly pessimistic in his old age.

He was the only master of his day who understood the true essence of the duel, Corbier insisted.

Which is?

Once again the Vixen came at me, opening with a false lunge that she promptly turned into a leap to my right side. At the last instant, she pirouetted to slash at my neck, leaving me no time to get my own blade up to block. I was forced to protect myself with nothing but an open hand. The Vixen smiled as she returned to the opposite side of the circle. I looked down and saw blood flowing freely from the sliced skin on the palm of my left hand.

Excellent, Corbier said. *Now, where was I?*

Explaining how the fact that we've been wounded four times works in our favour.

I felt the corner of my mouth rise in a smirk. *To be honest, the first three weren't all that helpful, but this last one will be sufficient.*

Sufficient for what? A terrible thought occurred to me: when Corbier had left Pierzi's fortress, he'd just witnessed the deaths of the woman he loved and the children he'd never known were his. He'd fled only because Ajelaine had begged him to, but in his heart, his dearest wish had been to end his own life.

Is that what this is? I asked the muddled collection of memories that were now controlling my limbs like a mad puppeteer. *You've a death wish?*

Every duel ends in death, Damelas; that is what Errera Bottio teaches us. Those who care too much whose death it is will always lose. That is the gift I give you now. It is the gift your grandmother was born with, the gift your grandfather only partially understood and one that you have run from your entire life.

'You're bleeding a great deal, my rabbit,' the Vixen said. Her forehead glistened with a faint sheen of sweat from her exertions, but she moved with no less speed and grace.

'What, this?' I asked, holding up my bleeding palm. 'I've had worse paper cuts.' My own words this time. The banter I could handle without Corbier's help. It was the sword fighting that was the problem.

She laughed, a light *glissando* on a silver flute. 'Come now, you've shown us all what a fine actor you are, but the performance grows wearisome. Set down your blade and I pledge to grant you time to finish your prayers before I send you to the gods.'

Corbier barked his own laugh, deep, like the rumble of a war drum. 'Can all these fools really fear *you*, my Lady Fox? Can it truly be *your* face that faint-hearted fencers conjure in their nightmares? What use is all your skill, all your training, when, with every move you make, it becomes more and more apparent that you have never learned the first rule of the sword?'

'A great many men before you thought the same thing,' she countered. 'Out of courtesy, I will see to it your grave is dug next to theirs.'

Corbier drew my smirk wider. 'Yours is a dull sort of evil, isn't it, little foxling? Banal, pedestrian. The blunt brutality of one who has spent so long pretending to be merciless that you have forgotten you have never experienced true cruelty yourself.'

'And yet you haven't had the courage to thrust even once. Will you not demonstrate this devastating savagery you keep promising me? Come now, my rabbit, how much longer must I wait?'

Corbier stopped me from moving and let my point drop low again as he squeezed my left hand into a fist. 'You need wait no longer, Lady Fox. Listen you to the ticks of the clock. Count down from three and you will meet the good God Death for the first and last time.'

She stared at me in disbelief. To announce the time of an attack was surely to guarantee its failure. 'Three,' she said.

I nodded approvingly. 'Go on.'

'Two.'

'Almost there. Remember the faces of all those lesser men and women you have killed in the duelling circle with your bravado and your tricks, for you'll be reunited with them soon.'

The Vixen brought her sword into guard, standing light on the balls of her feet. 'One.'

Nothing happened.

What are you doing? I asked.

But Corbier was silent.

Everyone in the room – the guards, Captain Terine, Beretto, Rhyleis – were all held frozen by the spell of this moment. And still I didn't attack. I felt something strange happening in my sword hand and glanced down to see that it was trembling.

Corbier?

There was no answer.

The confusion and sudden panic must've shown on my face because Ferica di Traizo began to laugh. 'Oh, my darling rabbit, what a performance you ga—'

Without warning, without so much as a hint of preparation, the shaking was gone, and though everything that followed took place within the same tick of the clock Corbier had promised, to me it all felt slow, almost languorous.

First the tip of my sword came up high, but I knew that was only a distraction. Corbier had positioned us so the light of one of the hanging lanterns would reflect off my blade at this precise angle. Ferica blinked, but she was already getting her guard up to defend against the coming thrust. I watched in confused awe as my left hand flung out, spraying blood from the wound she'd given me moments ago into her eyes, blinding her. Reflex overpowered all her years of training and she swung her sword wide to keep me at bay, but Corbier merely had me lean back, letting the point barely scratch the tip of my nose. Before the Vixen could bring her weapon back into line, I stepped inside her guard, so close that I was able to grab hold of her shoulder even as Corbier delivered the thrust no one witnessing the fight had believed would come.

The sound was . . . *wet*.

Ferica di Traizo's eyes tried to blink away the blood, staring at me, unseeing. With my hand still gripping her shoulder, I eased her down to the marble floor. She opened her mouth as if to thank me for the courtesy.

'Don't try to speak,' Corbier whispered. 'The blade has missed your heart. I said I'd kill you in one thrust, but I lied. Two is better. The first is to disable you, the second is to be savoured.'

Stop, I cried, *she's beaten! It's enough—*

Corbier was laughing at me now. *You think the Vixen will thank you for sparing her life? On the contrary, the moment she can fight again, she'll come after the big oaf you adore so much, your beloved grandfather, and everyone else you've dared to love. She'll kill them one after another until she can draw you back in the circle to finish what she started.*

Ferica di Traizo tried to scream, turning her head towards the guards as if they might come to save her, but my hand clamped over her mouth.

'Have no fear, Lady Fox. Your money and influence will have them rushing to your aid momentarily. Alas, the instant the first clod's boot hits the floor will mark the moment of your death.'

Don't do this, I begged. *I'm not a murderer.*

Not yet, no, Corbier agreed even as he drew the blade from her in preparation for the death blow, *but you're about to become one.*

Suddenly the crash of a door slamming open echoed throughout the throne room, followed by two pairs of footsteps and a voice bellowing with imperious outrage. 'What madness is this?' demanded Duke Firan Monsegino. 'Lay down your arms this instant, both of you!'

Lady Shariza was at his side and when her eyes searched out for mine, I felt sick knowing that what she saw was the steady, unfeeling, cold-blooded stare of a trained killer ready to take a life.

Enough now! I shouted in impotent silence at Corbier. *His Grace has commanded an end to the duel.*

But Corbier wasn't listening to me any more. My gaze shifted fractionally as it moved to Monsegino, no longer seeing the Violet Duke, but in his place a golden prince.

'Pierzi,' I heard myself say.

No! It's not him, you fool! It's—

Before I could implore Corbier to stop, Duke Monsegino, who I'd always assumed to be a clever man, but now proved himself an utter fool, raced across the throne room, drawing his own bejewelled court sword from its scabbard.

Glee rose up like bile in my throat.

No, I begged, *no, you mustn't – NO! Don't do this—*

But Corbier's mad, euphoric rage had sent me stepping right over the now forgotten Vixen so that I could drive my rapier into the Duke of Pertine's heart.

The penalty for interfering in a lawful duel is as old and violent as this country, Corbier informed me over my failing struggle to regain control. *You'd think a monarch would know better.*

My legs took me from a run to a leap in the air; my arm extended the tip of my rapier in an elegant and deadly arc. In that split second, I knew there was no possibility of Duke Monsegino parrying the thrust.

A flash of sparks from steel crossing steel blinded me. As I hit the floor, Corbier's reflexes sent me into a roll under the sword's second cut that would've taken my head off – a blade not wielded by the duke. I came back up to my knees and pivoted around to find the tip of that blade touching the ball of my throat.

When I looked up, Shariza was standing over me.

There was a moment – barely a fraction of a second – in which I thought I was suddenly seeing two worlds again, just as I had when I'd been both with Shariza in the present and Ajelaine in the past. It was different this time, though. Now I saw two versions of the same woman: one hesitant, held back by an unexpected kinship and attraction that longed to grow into something deeper, overlaid with a second image which all too quickly replaced the other. The flat, cold-hearted expression left no doubt that with the tiniest pressure of her blade, she was ready to kill me.

'His Grace requests that you desist now,' said the Black Amaranth.

CHAPTER 42

THE SHARPEST BLADE

Beretto and Rhyleis tried to run to my side, but Shariza's curved dagger revealed itself in her other hand and held them at bay. 'Put down your rapier, Damelas,' she said to me. 'It's over.'

She moves well, Corbier observed, forcing me to rise. *No false flourishes, no wasted tension in the shoulders, not like the fox at all.*

I'll be sure to tell her you approve, I told him. *Now, without wanting to sound ungrateful, it would be a big help if you'd leave me so I can try to keep us from getting killed.*

Corbier gave no sign of hearing me and I felt excitement beginning to build up in me anew. *In all my years of duelling, I never faced a Dashini before. This will be most diverting.*

No – you can't—

'Damelas . . .' The anguish in Shariza's tone gave voice to the danger I faced. Whatever attraction there might be between the two of us wouldn't stop her from fulfilling her duke's command. 'Put down your rapier. *Now*.'

'Yes, of course,' I said, but my hand didn't move.

I see the flaw in her. She keeps watching your eyes. A mistake.

I'm begging you, don't do this—

Is this affection for you that afflicts her? Whoever heard of a Dashini being lovestruck?

Shariza's not our enemy, you idiot!

She will be and you know it. Whatever attachment she may feel for you, she is loyal to Pierzi who wi—

Pierzi is dead, you fool!

There was a moment where Corbier's confusion made him hesitate, but just as quickly it was gone, buried beneath the Red-Eyed Raven's bloodlust. *They're all the same,* he raged. *One day soon you'll be no use to this duke and when next you meet his Dashini, you'll find her eyes devoid of any sentiment for you.*

'Damelas, please,' Shariza said. The tip of her blade was trembling at my throat. 'Don't make me do this.'

'Brother, look around you!' Beretto called out, trying in vain to intervene. 'The guards are aiming crossbows at you.'

But Corbier was determined to get revenge on everyone he could for the pain that burned inside him. He would use me to spill as much blood as it took to wash away the memory of Ajelaine's murder. Combat was the only pleasure left to him, and the duel with the Vixen had aroused a mad desire for vengeance too powerful for me to contain.

Unless . . .

I forced my eyes to focus on Shariza – *only* Shariza, and sent my thoughts back to the moment on stage when our lips had met for the first time. The kiss had come and gone all too quickly, but like Beretto always says, *'A true player can fall in love seven days a week and twice for matinees.'* I drew those sensations back to me, allowed myself to experience both desire and hope for a love I knew could never be mine.

What are you doing? Corbier demanded.

Now it was my turn to refuse an answer; instead, I pushed further into the memory, feeling my arms around Shariza's waist and hers around mine, going deeper still until now he could see both her *and* Ajelaine at once.

No! Ajelaine is dead – murdered by Pierzi! Don't make me—

I replayed that kiss, that embrace, the promise of a future together over and over again, even as Corbier resisted with all his hate and sorrow.

'Hold him a moment longer,' Rhyleis called out.

Corbier turned to see the Bardatti standing next to him, rising up on her toes to whisper into his ear.

What is that tune she sings? he demanded of me. *Why does it sound so familiar, like a melody from my childhood. Soothing, like . . . a lullaby?*

I felt a tightness in my forearm and saw my left hand was now wrapped around Rhyleis' throat as Corbier forced my fingers to squeeze her into silence. A moment later, my hand fell away, my knees buckled and darkness overtook me, its embrace so warm and gentle that I wondered if this was what death felt like.

PART THE FIFTH

The Duellist

When BARGAINS *are made,*

BETWEEN

ACTOR *and* SPIRIT,

A PRICE MUST ALWAYS BE PAID

CHAPTER 43

THE STRANGER

He woke inside a stranger's home and a stranger's life. A foreign landscape of shabby furnishings bordered by stained walls suggested a leaking roof, all fogged with the stench excreted by the dregs of humanity doubtless housed on the floors below. Unmerited poverty festered in slums, this he had always understood, but not why any sane, able-bodied man or woman would choose to live in confined misery rather than chance the streets where at least one wouldn't feel so . . . *entombed*. He examined the bandage wrapping his left hand. A wonder they'd found cloth clean enough for the purpose in a hovel like this.

'He's waking up.'

A beguiling timbre, melodious and sweet, rich in devious subtlety. The light-haired one, then: the Bardatti who'd bewitched him. Through the dim haze of candle smoke, he sought out the sharp features of her face and found her watching him. The conceited smirk badly needed wiping from her lips.

'Look at his eyes,' she announced. 'Corbier still has his hooks in him.'

Her companion loomed over him: a great, red-bearded mother hen with a warrior's build, squandered on one who looked as if he were one stern word away from weeping himself to sleep. A waste of a strong arm if ever there was one.

But a truer friend than you've ever known, came an unruly thought. *He'd trade his life for ours even now.*

The unexpected surge of affection cracked the armour of Corbier's disdain and brought down his guard long enough for me to retake the reins of my own mind and body. My first act of rebellion was to roll over on the sofa and vomit all over the floor.

'Saints!' Beretto swore, leaping out of the way. 'Is he ill? Should I find a physician?' He was ignoring the fact that neither of us could afford one.

'This is no wound, nor disease,' said a third person, emerging from the dark corner at the far end of the squalid living room, where even Corbier's acute senses had failed to notice her. Shariza came to me, the allure of those dark eyes and the unbound curls falling to her shoulders a sharp contrast to the rapier she still held in her hand. 'It is shame that plagues him.'

Shame.

That wretched word unleashed great racking sobs as I recalled the blood I'd so gleefully spilled, the hunger I'd felt to paint the pale marble floor crimson. Tears dripped from my eyes like rain through the holes in the roof and down onto the mess I'd made on the floor as my body tried to expel this sickness inside me.

'Oh, gods, I'm sorry!' I cried incoherently. 'I almost . . . I would have . . .'

Even as I wept, Corbier's enraged sneer tried to force its way onto my lips. *The Dashini was ready to kill you, you mewling babe – you think she won't do so again when the time is right? And next time she will surely succeed.*

Once again I set my will against that of the Red-Eyed Raven. *Enough. No more of your blind bloodthirst and butchery. Whatever vengeance you failed to secure for Ajelaine and the children in your own time will not be found in mine.*

After a brief battle inside me, the fist clenching around my heart released and Corbier went silent.

'It's getting harder, isn't it?' Shariza asked.

I gazed up at her, surprised to find the slender thread of attraction that bound the two of us was still there, even after my bout of madness. I longed to feel the calluses on her fingertips where our hands had touched during the play, the unexpected coolness of her lips when we'd kissed . . .

'And what of my apology?' asked Duke Firan Monsegino, stepping into the living room from the adjoining kitchen. His blue brocade silk coat and magnificent jewellery were no less out of place in this decrepit apartment than violets blooming on a dung heap.

'Your Grace,' Shariza said, 'I instructed you to wait until—'

Monsegino waved her warning away as he came to stand before me. 'My reputation is bad enough without actors spreading gossip about how the Violet Duke cowers in kitchens waiting for permission to be admitted into their presence.'

'Forgive me, your Grace, I—' My apology faltered when my tear-blurred vision showed me not the slender Monsegino in his finery, but the towering figure of Pierzi in his gold-inlaid armour. I blinked twice and the golden prince was banished, leaving only the Violet Duke behind.

'You're getting that look in your eyes again,' Monsegino observed. 'Perhaps you'll be so kind as to warn me before Corbier next tries to assassinate me?'

I stared down at my hands, still clenched into fists. 'Saints! How did I become this monster?'

'There now,' Beretto said, kneeling to slop a rag over the mess on the floor, grinning apologetically at the duke whose polished black boot he had to wipe after sloshing vomit on it. '"Monster" is a bit harsh, isn't it? I've thrown up worse than this many a night, and who was it cleaned it up for me?'

It was a trite attempt at levity, but I went along with it anyway. 'Your fool of a roommate, I imagine.'

Beretto sniffed back his own tears. 'My fool of a friend.'

'Ugh,' Rhyleis groaned, throwing her hands up in the air. 'Must I write a love song about this great friendship of yours? Two failed actors living in a shithole of an apartment, wiping up one another's puke and telling each other, "Tomorrow, my friend – tomorrow we'll show the world that two such players as we cannot long be held down."'

'Actually,' Beretto said, dropping the filthy cloth into a bucket and walking into the kitchen to dispose of it, 'that's not bad.'

'I'd pay to hear it,' I added, sitting up and almost instantly regretting it when my head began to swim. When I felt myself falling back, Duke Monsegino surprised me by putting a hand behind my shoulders, steadying me before gently setting me down on the sofa. 'Are the three of them always like this?' he asked Shariza. 'I'm finding it difficult to know when they're not acting.'

The Black Amaranth cracked an uncharacteristic smile as her eyes caught mine. 'Forgive me, your Grace, but I find it rather endearing.'

'Terrific,' Rhyleis said, her derision aimed towards the heavens. 'Now the Dashini is turning into a sentimental milksop. Saint Ebron-who-steals-breath, will someone please bring back Corbier? At least he was unpredictable.'

Beretto returned from the kitchen and settled himself into one of our rickety chairs. 'Unpredictable? *He's* the fucking monster here. I'd just begun to find him sympathetic – heroic, even – but now? I think I'm glad Pierzi kills him in the final act.'

Monsegino reached down a gloved hand to flick a questing cockroach from the toe of his boot. 'I'm inclined to agree with Master—?'

'Beretto,' the big man said enthusiastically, and went to shake Monsegino's hand before the duke could snatch it away. 'Beretto Bravi of South Lankavir. Actor. Playwright. Professional lovemaker and, should the gods grant any justice in this poor country of ours, a future Cantor of the Greatcoats!'

'That's . . . rather a lot of aspirations, Master Bravi,' Monsegino said, attempting without success to retrieve his fingers from the huge paw.

What the duke didn't see – what I saw only because I knew my friend so well – was that beneath Beretto's genial smile was an implicit threat of what might happen next if Monsegino had come intending retribution for my actions.

What Beretto wasn't seeing was the way Shariza was moving slowly towards him.

'Let him go, Beretto,' I said.

Beretto smiled congenially and released the duke's hand.

Monsegino wiped his liberated palm on his coat. 'I'm here because Lady Shariza suggested – somewhat forcefully, I might add – that we needed to get you out of the palace quickly before word spread of your . . . lapse in judgement.' With a glower that made it clear that all was *not* forgiven, he withdrew a folded note from his pocket. 'Besides, as I understand it, unless I submit to your questioning, your uncouth Bardatti friend will begin smearing my name with this little . . . ditty she's composed.'

'It's called a congretto, your Grace,' Rhyleis clarified sweetly. 'And while I consider being called uncouth by a nobleman of your stature high praise indeed, you should know that I've ruined better men than you for daring to refer to one of my compositions as a "ditty".'

'Shariza?' Monsegino asked.

'Yes, your Grace?'

'The next time she opens her mouth to threaten me, put something sharp in it, would you?'

You see? Corbier asked, returning with even more force than before. *He's no different than Pierzi. Another would-be tyrant waiting for his moment to—*

'Enough!' I shouted, rising to my feet. 'You wage war like children while our enemy overtakes the field!'

Every head in the room spun in my direction. My voice had sounded as if it belonged to another – not Corbier, precisely, but a steadier, more commanding presence.

Saints! That was like something Ajelaine would say, I realised with a start. *If this keeps up, I'm going to lose any sense of who I am – or at least, who I was before this Veristor madness overwhelmed my life.*

I turned the momentary confusion to my advantage. 'We can't continue this way,' I told them. 'The Orchids are roaming the streets, spreading terror and leaving bodies behind. Half the city's convinced these "Orchid Laws" of theirs are as binding as your own, your Grace.' I locked eyes with Monsegino. 'You might dislike Rhyleis' impudence, but I don't enjoy being ambushed by the fucking Vixen of Jereste, only to discover you've forged an alliance with her. Nor do I appreciate being pressed into service as a pawn in whatever game you're playing.'

Monsegino's glare was almost enough to make me sit back down again.

'Unlike those in your profession, Damelas, I am not privileged to "play" at anything. I suffer such allies as the circumstances of my reign demand, for the results of my mistakes are measured not in jeers from my audience, but in lives ruined.'

'I—'

Like a dam holding back a flooding river, Monsegino's composure broke at last. 'You come at me with *songs?*' He crumpled the piece of paper and threw it to the floor. 'When a poorly negotiated trade agreement signed by my hand sends a thousand farmers into poverty? When I'm forced to grant permits for the increased importation of pleasure drugs and over-strong liquor, watching death and misery multiply throughout my duchy – but should I dare prohibit their sale, even to the slightest degree, black marketeers take over? When thugs who set up shop behind legitimate businesses go breaking limbs of any who try to refuse their demands? The price of a single wrong move on my part will lead me to the emptying of my own treasury within weeks as I try – and fail – to compete with the bribes paid to my own personal guards. Within months . . . within *months* I'll be facing a rebellion led by an army I can't even see! You think I *want* to ally myself with a psychotic killer like Ferica di Traizo? Without the support of her family's soldiers, I'll lose the entire duchy to the damned Iron Orchids before the year is out. My life is no *game*, Master Veristor – and I do *not* appreciate any implication to the contrary!'

The Violet Duke strode to the window, the thud of his boots on the uneven floor drawing thumps on the ceiling and angry shouts from those in the apartment below.

I was about to walk over to him, but Shariza's hand on my arm stayed me.

An anxious silence filled the enormous space left behind by the loss of the comforting belief that people like Monsegino wielded all the power and could therefore be held responsible for the lives of their citizens.

'Well, there's something new,' Beretto muttered, returning from the dumbwaiter with a tray of mismatched mugs containing wine of dubious origin. Mother had outdone herself. 'A duke just made me feel guilty.'

'I do not—' Still staring out the window, Monsegino's shoulders rose and fell in surrender. 'Forgive me. I've no business burdening any of you with such matters.' He rested his head against his forearm, which was pressed against the shutters. 'So let us instead speak of the business in which our respective fates intersect.'

A wave of genuine sympathy for this overwhelmed young nobleman passed through me, but it was outweighed by the duty I owed the cast and crew of the Belleza, who'd already paid a heavy price for my sins.

'Your Grace,' I began formally, 'what is the Court of Flowers?'

'A ghost story – a tale to terrify new dukes just beginning their reign. A secret cabal of nobles, working in the shadows, pulling the strings of those like me who might otherwise confuse a throne with power and a crown with greatness.'

'But who rules them?' Beretto asked, proffering a mug.

'No one,' Monsegino replied, waving away the drink. 'They do not exist.'

'Forgive me, your Grace,' I began, 'but how is that possible? We've seen the Iron Orchids – seen the things th—'

The duke held up a hand to stop me. He walked over to the crumpled congretto, picked it up and turned to the candle on the small table. Without a word, he lit the verse Rhyleis had composed, then returned to the window and tossed it out. It floated away into the night like a flaming butterfly.

'The note is gone, yet the threat remains,' he said.

At last I began to piece together the events that had dominated my life ever since I'd first flubbed the herald's lines on stage. 'You've exhausted your efforts to find the Court of Flowers,' I said. 'Neither your agents nor your allies,' – I could see Shariza's troubled expression from the corner of my eye – 'not even the Black Amaranth, can find them.'

'Not at present, no,' Monsegino agreed.

Oh, such a cleverly deceptive turn of phrase, your Grace.

'What you mean is that you can't find them *in* the present,' I said, feeling the heat rising in me, even without the Red-Eyed Raven's influence. 'You said you don't play games a moment ago, but that was a lie, wasn't it?'

'What do you mean, brother?' Beretto asked.

'That damned play – the one that's turned our lives upside down and got Roz killed! The duke doesn't care about what happened to Corbier and Ajelaine, but he believes the Court of Flowers was formed in *their* time, a hundred years in the past, so he's using me to flush them out!'

'But how?' Beretto pressed. 'Even if the Court of Flowers did begin back then, how would that—?'

'*Because he's bluffing!*' I shouted.

'Of course,' Rhyleis said, her eyes alight with comprehension. 'Brilliant!

Whoever rules the Court of Flowers today has no way of knowing the limits of the Veristor's gift. They can't be sure Damelas won't uncover their origins in Corbier's memories, so the closer he appears to get, the more likely they are to make a mistake and reveal themselves in the here and now.'

Monsegino's sombre violet eyes were filled with equal parts shame and grim determination. 'If Damelas *can* uncover their origins in the past, we can put an end to their machinations in the present. If not . . .'

'If not, we must force them into overplaying their hand,' Shariza said.

Perhaps you should learn from her example, Corbier whispered to me. *How far will you go to protect those you love?* The now familiar itch returned to my bandaged left hand, together with the urge to curl my fingers around the leather grip of a sword. *Devotion is not the weeping of a broken heart. It is the long, hard edge of a rapier, wielded without hesitation, without mercy.*

'Brother?' Beretto asked.

'I'm fine,' I said, but I could see the concern in their expressions, and I noticed that Shariza had moved to discreetly put herself between me and the duke.

'It's getting easier to see when the Red-Eyed Raven takes you,' she said.

Despite that, Monsegino stepped closer. 'Is Corbier truly so filled with hate for me, so thirsty for my blood?'

I shook my head. 'I don't think so. He's changing, though. When I first started hearing his voice, he was only mildly interested in my affairs. When I encountered the Vixen and her rent-boy in the alley, he wanted to duel her on the spot, but not to kill her; he just wanted to demonstrate that he was better than her – that he could defeat anyone he had to—'

'To show Ajelaine that he could keep her safe,' Shariza finished for me. 'I felt that in your performance last night – as if Corbier needed to prove to himself that the violence that ran so hot in his veins was a gift that could protect those he loved. But after she died, vengeance was all that was left to him.'

Beretto was nodding his head. He clapped a hand on my shoulder. 'Yes – yes, it makes perfect sense! The Corbier inside you is whoever he was at the moment we stopped the performance.'

'But if I'm truly a Veristor, why does it matter at what point we were in the play? Why can't I just summon his memories right now and ask all the questions I want about his life – about what he did after Ajelaine's death?'

It was Duke Monsegino who answered, and he did so with a kind of amused disbelief. 'You know, Damelas, for an actor, you appear to be unconscionably oblivious to the magic of the theatre.'

'That's exactly what *I've* been telling him!' Beretto said happily, reaching out his other arm to thump the duke boisterously on the shoulder.

'The big idiot's right,' Rhyleis said, looking down at her worn leather boots. 'I've travelled more of this country than any of you can imagine. I've journeyed across oceans to other lands. I've traded tales with witches and warlocks, mages and sorcerers. I've watched esoteric ceremonies and religious sacraments, witnessed outcomes both horrific and wondrous.'

'So? What's any of that got to do with the theatre?' I asked.

'Imagine a play in your mind,' she replied. She walked over to me and put a hand over my eyes. 'See it through the gaze of a stranger from a far-off land, one who's never heard of the theatre, or even seen an actor.'

'So they don't have plays in these exotic foreign lands?'

'Stop interrupting. Picture the players in their costumes, the props they wield, the candelabra illuminating the strange sets. Visualise the audience, sitting there in hushed silence.'

I removed her hand from my face. 'You're talking as if a play were some kind of spell.'

'Of *course* it is,' Beretto boomed, wringing his hands together excitedly. 'What we do isn't merely *performance*; it's *ritual* – and just like with any ceremonial spell, the magic only works when all the right elements are in the right place.'

I returned to the sofa and slumped down, suddenly burdened with the dread certainty that Beretto, for all his foolish fancies about the sacred nature of the actor's art, was absolutely right. 'Saint Zaghev-who-sings-for-tears,' I swore, 'so our only hope of uncovering the Court of Flowers before they kill us all is to go ahead and put on the final act of the play?'

Rhyleis and Beretto grinned at the same time, proving irrational optimism to be as contagious as any disease. Even Shariza and the duke were nodding in agreement.

'Cheer up, Veristor,' Rhyleis said, slapping me playfully on the cheek. 'Nobles across this city are paying in gold and gems for a ticket to the final act. I've a suspicion that for once in their miserable, privileged lives, they're going to witness a performance worth the price of admission.'

CHAPTER 44

THE PERCUSSIONIST

Less than a day had passed since last I'd been at the Operato Belleza, but returning with Beretto and Rhyleis that afternoon, I felt like a stranger. Outside the stage door, life in the alley had returned to its normal, dreary ways. Roslyn's body had at last been pulled down from the lantern-post and her blood had been cleaned off the flagstones. All that remained was a broken piece of the sign that had hung from her neck: *Let actors give us merry tales.*

A few drops of Corbier's fury must have still been flowing through my veins, because I found myself badly wanting to meet the men who'd inscribed those words. *You haven't yet learned the meaning of melancholy, you bastards – but I'll teach you soon enough.*

'Gonna be a good one tonight?' asked Grey Mags, sitting in her usual spot, knitting her scavenged lengths of wool.

'Nothing of particular note,' I replied, swallowing my anger so I wouldn't take it out on her. Mags was so thin these days, more rags than flesh. If we had a cold winter this year . . .

'Might see if I can buy meself a ticket,' she said. 'Our Zina got herself a starring role yet?'

The clatter of Vadris the drug-pedlar's cart rolling along the cobblestones preceded his guttural laughter. 'You can't afford a ticket, you poxy old sewer frog!'

'Got meself a pair of copper tears yesterday,' Mags protested. 'Fixed a rip in a proper Lord's coat – he said as how I sewed better'n his own tailor, he did.'

'Bet you those two copper that Lord can't get a ticket hisself, you old sow.' Vadris jerked a thumb at me. 'His Lordship set the city on fire with his little scam.' He turned to offer up a sarcastic grin. 'Come on, then, Damelas, let us in on the game, eh? Don't leave yer old friends out in the cold with nuthin' but stray coppers while you fill yer purse with noble silver.'

'Old friends', I thought, my eyes drawn to the brooch pinned to the drug-pedlar's collar. *Was it you, Vadris? Were you the one to tell the Iron Orchids how to find Roslyn? Did you help them torture and murder her?*

I wondered, just for a moment, how it might feel to drive the point of the rapier I'd held hours before through the bastard's heart – but I couldn't allow myself to be taken by Corbier's rage again, not when there were so many other lives inside the Operato Belleza at risk of the Orchids' vengeance.

I forced my breathing to slow, my hands to relax. 'I'm sorry, Mags,' I said at last. 'The show really is sold out.'

'Oh,' she said, as if it meant nothing at all, but in the cracks of her fading smile, I saw the hurt of ten thousand nights in the damp and cold, of being mocked and kicked and spat on by even the lowest of men.

'Really, Mags, if I could—'

'Hah,' Vadris roared, 'don't waste yer sympathies on 'er, Damelas. She'd only stink up the place – ain't 'ad a bath since the last duke's reign.'

'Shut your mouth, Vadris.'

'Or wot? Gonna stick me with one o' them wooden swords of yours, "Archduke Corbier"?' Vadris pulled a butcher's cleaver from his cart. The edge was pitted, but it looked plenty sharp.

You see, you fool? Corbier whispered, the promise of violence waking him like a church bell. *You could have crushed his throat with your bare hands a moment ago, but you hesitated and now you'll need to take a few cuts from that cleaver before you end him. Next time, let me—*

Rhyleis and Beretto had kept silent until then, but now, ignoring Vadris' leer, Rhyleis squatted down next to Mags and pulled two metal discs from her pocket. They looked like large bronze coins, only with loops of cord attached to the backs. She slipped one loop over her thumb and the other over her forefinger, then began clapping them together in a simple rhythm. 'Are those knitting fingers of yours deft enough to keep time with these?' she asked.

Mags looked at her suspiciously. 'Why?'

Rhyleis handed her the discs and showed her how to attach them to her fingers, then clapped out a rhythm.

Mags followed along. She wasn't perfect at first, but soon got the hang of it. The old woman grinned. '*Clinkety-clink, clackety-clack,*' she sang along.

Rhyleis rose to her feet and reached out a hand. Mags tried to give her back the discs, but Rhyleis took hold of her arm instead and raised her up. 'I'm short a percussionist in this half-arsed company. You'll watch me for cues, follow the rhythm I set and muffle the discs the instant I shake my head. Understand?'

Mags looked at her wide-eyed. 'I'm to be a player, then?'

'A musician – a percussionist, to be more specific,' Rhyleis corrected. 'It's like an actor, only much more important.'

Mags grinned foolishly, delightedly, magnificently. She turned to Vadris. 'I'm a *percussionist*, me,' she declared.

There was a pause as Vadris stared back at the old woman, who was so full of fragile joy that not even he was arsehole enough to take that smile away from her. 'Aye, Mags. That you are.'

Beretto walked over to Rhyleis. Towering over her, he asked, 'I was wondering, how many men fall in love with you on any given day?'

'Not many. Only two or three, usually.'

He nodded sagely at that. 'Glad I'm not the only one, then.'

As the four of us headed up the steps and through the stage door, Mags asked, 'Wait – how much do I get paid?'

CHAPTER 45

STAGING THE BATTLE

The entire company of the Knights of the Curtain – actors, supernumeraries, costumers, carpenters, musicians and stagehands – waited anxiously to find out what was going to happen next in this bizarre play that had taken over their lives. Only Shariza was absent, though few minded; half of them were afraid she might kill them, the other half that she might steal their roles.

And what fear does she stir in you?

It would have been reassuring to dismiss the taunting voice as Corbier's, but I was learning to distinguish where the Raven's mocking ended and my own began.

Why was it so easy to conjure up the sight of Shariza sitting on the bed, the unexpected warmth of her skin through the thin fabric of Ajelaine's gown, the subtle taste of salt on her lips? And why was it so hard to remind myself of all the plays in which a naïve young hero falls in love with a mysterious stranger, only to be betrayed by her during the final act?

'Ah, our Veristor returns,' Shoville said, smiling confidently as he sauntered over to greet us.

'Uh oh,' Beretto murmured. 'This looks bad.'

'Bad?' Grey Mags asked. 'He looks loose as a goose to me.'

'That's the problem,' Beretto explained. 'Theatre directors are *never* relaxed. Panic is their natural disposition. To pretend otherwise can only mean the situation is more dire than any of us imagined. He hasn't even complained about Rhyleis hiring a new percussionist for the band.'

'My star – my *saviour*,' Shoville announced brightly as he clapped me on both cheeks. 'Now we can begin our rehearsal in earnest.'

'Rehearsal?' Teo asked, brandishing a sheet of paper. He unfolded it and read it out loud, '*Act 3 – Battle of Mount Cruxia. Damelas cues actors through the battle. Satisfies both Duke M + audience. Ensures this fucking nightmare is over with no more dead actors.*'

He crumpled the paper into a ball and threw it against the wall. 'Tomorrow night we're supposed to stage the entire fucking war scene – which also happens to be the fucking climax of the play. So how the fuck are we supposed to fucking choreograph a fucking war scene if we've no proper fucking script?'

'Maybe you could just insert the word "fucking" into the story whenever you get confused,' Rhyleis suggested.

'Don't fuc— Keep to your own business, minstrel.'

'*Musician*,' Grey Mags corrected, clacking her percussion discs for emphasis. 'It's like an actor, only more important.'

I could hear variations of Teo's complaint bubbling among the rest of the cast; even the stagehands were muttering angrily. Sounded like no one was happy with our esteemed Directore Principale's master plan.

'Friends, compatriots, Bellezans,' Shoville called out, holding out his hands, palms up, like a man begging for spare change, 'let us not bog ourselves down in mindless minutiae and detail.'

'Well, we must do something,' Beretto said to the complainers. 'Perhaps if we were to start with the old script and see where that takes us?'

'Exactly my plan!' Shoville declared gratefully, wiping away beads of sweat from his forehead.

The last thing I wanted to do was pile more trouble onto the harried director's shoulders, but there was no getting around the obvious flaw in his plan. 'Um . . . Corbier doesn't show up until halfway through the scene. It begins with Abastrini delivering a four-page speech.'

'Ah, no,' Shoville said, 'we can't have that, not now.' His sweaty palm thumped my chest. 'This new historia demands that we open with our star.'

'You mean *the duke* demands it,' Abastrini said. He was leaning against the windowsill in the far corner of the room, polishing the broad blade of his sword – a steel blade, I noted, rather than painted wood.

'Now Ellias,' Shoville began, trying to placate the man, 'let's not quarrel over petty—'

'*Petty?*' Abastrini interrupted. With his broadsword clutched tightly in his fingers as if he were about to charge into battle, he strode up to the director, his belly practically bowling the man over. 'You think I care about the billing? Roslyn *died* – and still you prattle on about trivialities. You pretend all is going according to plan, when I and every member of this once-noble company are forced to betray every principle on which the Knights of the Curtain were founded. We are *actors*, not court jesters! When the Belleza was first given over to us, you spouted a grand speech about how we would never prostitute ourselves to the whims of the mob. We would bring the historias to life on stage with dignity and integrity. You promised we would show the people of this city a deeper truth than the Lords of Laughter or the Grim Jesters would ever dare. Yet now you've allowed this damned Violet Duke – this *foreigner* – to treat the Belleza as his game board, with us the pieces he moves here and there, laughing all the while as we dance to his tune—'

'Enough!' Shoville bellowed, so entirely out of character that it brought the room to silence – if only for a moment.

'You ought not raise your voice against us, *Lord Director*,' Abastrini warned. 'Have you forgotten? You may rule us while the play is on, but this run will soon be completed and then it's up to *the company* whether to renew your contract' – he looked around, milking the dramatic pause – 'or to seek direction elsewhere.'

'Then do so,' Shoville said, his scowl for once as dark and threatening as Abastrini's. 'Take the Belleza from me if you think you've the votes.' It was his turn to press a finger into Abastrini's shoulder. 'But as you so rightly point out, Ellias, this play *is* still running, which means *I* command the Knights of the Curtain as surely as any general in the field – and believe me, I will take just as dim a view of desertion or mutiny.' He gave Abastrini a surprisingly forceful shove, causing the actor to stumble backwards. 'So get to your damned position or I'll see to it the entire duchy knows you for a faithless half-penny player!'

Even the great Ellias Abastrini went pale at that threat. He returned to his perch by the window, but couldn't resist the final word. 'Tonight we do as you say, Shoville, but tomorrow – and my oath on this – tomorrow will be the last time you walk through the doors of this hallowed hall whose honour and dignity you have sold so cheaply.'

The first skirmish might have been over but the tension wasn't dissipating. Sides were being drawn and the Knights of the Curtain were as divided as Pierzi's and Corbier's forces had been all those years ago. Almost half the company supported Shoville, but as many were behind Abastrini. I was beginning to wonder if we might end up staging an *actual* battle before the day was out.

'Saint Iphilia-who-cuts-her-own-heart,' Grey Mags swore, elbowing me in the ribs, 'you actors really are prone to melodrama, aren't you?'

'Positions, everyone,' Shoville called out. 'Pierzi's troops on the left, Corbier's on the right. Stagger the lines to fill out the space. Foggers, have you the smoke braziers ready?'

The crew on either side of the hall nodded their assent and began measuring greyburn powder.

'And now, Master Veristor,' Shoville announced, 'take command.'

Take command? I don't have a clue what Corbier did at the Battle of Mount Cruxia, even less how to command an army . . .

'What am I to say?' I asked. 'Should I give some of Pierzi's lines from the first—?'

'Forget the lines, lad,' Shoville said. 'They mean nothing.'

Teo snorted. 'So speaks our noble director and playwright.'

Shoville ignored him and squeezed my shoulder. 'This is war!' He gestured around at the actors. 'Men and women are fighting – *dying*. Chaos and fire spreads all around you; smoke chokes your lungs and blinds you. What you say next could determine whether those who have entrusted their lives to you will survive, or perish at the hands of the man who killed your wife and sons. *That* is where our tale begins.'

I gazed out at the wide rehearsal hall, squinting as I tried to observe not the dusty floor and idle actors gazing back at me in bored irritation, but hardened warriors, eyes wide with both terror and rage. I pictured blood spilling all around me, desperate men staring at me, awaiting my commands, knowing death was coming for all of us.

Saint Zaghev-who-sings-for-tears . . . a man would have to be mad to accept such a burden.

'Yes, yes!' Shoville cried, peering up at me despite the fact I hadn't said anything yet. 'You're there, in the shit and mud, boy, I can feel it! Now, lead your army—'

I focused my thoughts inwards, seeking out Corbier's voice, but the Archduke remained silent.

Come on, damn you, give me something. You're the one so Hells-bent on revenging yourself against the prince – although why you would've cared about the battle itself when all you wanted was to find Pierzi—

Wait . . . is that where the scene really begins? Not at the beginning of the battle, but at the end, when it's just Corbier and Pierzi facing off against each other?

That first night, when I'd blacked out on stage after the climax of the play had gone to the seven Hells, I hadn't even been able to recall what I'd said that had got the audience so up in arms. Beretto had filled me in afterwards – something about calling Pierzi a . . .

'Foul deceiver!' I cried, drawing my sword from its scabbard and pointing it at Abastrini across the hall. 'You have lied to your people, murdered your enemy's lover, butchered his children – and now you would slay their father with that same poisoned blade? You called for a herald, you dog? Here stands your messenger. I will travel these lands and see to it that the entire world learns the truth: that you who would make yourself sovereign are naught but the vilest malefactor in all of history!'

The whole cast was staring at me, wide-eyed in confusion, but I could tell they felt it, too. Something was shivering inside them, vibrating, like a hammer striking against stone . . .

'Yes,' Shoville murmured, 'yes, that's it, *that's* where our final act begins.'

Abastrini strode forward to meet me in the centre of the hall, and in the gleam of his feral smile, I saw he was ready to follow this dark thread as far as it led.

Despite the confidence both he and Shoville were showing in me, I wasn't at all certain I'd got this right. There was no tell-tale feverishness as there had been the other times Corbier had taken me over. But I *was* feeling *something*: a tension in my muscles, a rushing in my blood – the physical reactions my grandparents always spoke of as presaging a fight to the death. I didn't have to squint my eyes any more to imagine the fog creeping up over the rocky field in front of me.

'It's working,' Teo said, amazed. 'I can smell the smoke, feel the heat of the fires – I can hear the thump of boot heels, as if an army were marching towards us even now.' He glanced around at the rest of us in awe. 'Does that mean I'm a Veristor as well?'

The haze was becoming a bit excessive, but when I looked over at Hiraj and Caleth, the company's foggers, they were staring at each other in confusion; neither had fed their greyburn powder into the braziers yet.

It was Grey Mags who was first to work out what was happening. 'Yer fools! Yer ain't witnessin' the Battle of Mount Cruxia – that's *real* smoke – someone's setting the theatre on fire!'

CHAPTER 46

THE BARRICADES

Patrons entering through the Operato Belleza's main arch for the first time would chuckle when, above their heads, they would note the bronze plaque.

Home to
the Knights of the Curtain

It was, after all, a funny name for a group of actors.

Lazy theatre critics, competing companies of players, and even the paupers and pickpockets plying their trade in the stage-door alley had found endless ways to mock the company's ostentatious sobriquet.

But as the entire cast and crew stood in that rehearsal hall, the smoke rising all around us, the doors barred to keep us from fleeing, nobody was laughing any more.

'They've jammed a steel bar across the bolt slides on the other side of the door!' Teo shouted, yanking on the handle with such desperate determination that it came off in his hands.

The smoke was growing thicker with each passing second, making it increasingly hard to breathe. Several actors ran to join Teo in bashing at the doors with assorted stage props, although most of them shattered at the first strike.

'Not the stage weapons, you fools,' Beretto bellowed as he raced for the props cupboard at the back end of the hall, 'we need the old metal ones—'

He grabbed a rusted axe from one of the shelves and went charging back to the barred double doors. With a mighty roar, he swung at the wooden panels. The axe head survived three blows before coming off the haft, but by then the top panels had been smashed through.

More smoke poured inside, but with Teo's and my assistance, Beretto was able to reach through the gap to lift the heavy steel bar holding the doors in place. It fell to the floor with a crash, but even with the three of us shoving, something outside was still keeping the doors from budging.

Beretto poked his head through the gap. 'There're bundles of kindling right und—'

Teo must've spotted something Beretto had missed because he suddenly screamed, 'Look out—!'

'What?'

I grabbed Beretto by the back of his collar and hauled him out of the way just as a gleaming blade sliced downwards on the other side of the door. Now we could all see the armoured men forming a blockade to keep us from escaping.

'What the Hells are those symbols on their breastplates?' Teo asked, blinking tears from his stinging eyes.

'Orchids,' I replied.

'Somebody's supplying these fuckers with armour now?' Beretto groaned.

Your war begins, actor, Corbier's voice whispered to me. *Best prepare for battle.*

Battle? I'm not a warrior – I don't know how to—

Perhaps not a battle then, the spirit said contemptuously. *A slaughter.*

The Orchids had lengths of damp silk wrapped around their mouths and noses, but I could still make out the feral grins beneath.

'These unconscionable cankers want to see us burned alive,' Abastrini shouted, running towards us with both his own broadsword and another axe for Beretto. Shoville was at his heels.

'What about the doors at the back of the hall?' Teo asked.

'They've set up fires all over,' Ornella coughed. 'The smoke is coming up from the basement below as well. They've kept the outer hall clear so they can watch us die from the smoke . . .' She started coughing, but turned to help Rhyleis, who in turn was trying to prop up Grey Mags.

'We can't fight them off alone,' Abastrini shouted out as he and Beretto employed their blades in increasingly vain attempts to push the Iron Orchids back from the doors.

There wasn't much Teo and I could do but jab our own rusty swords through the broken panels in hope of distracting the soldiers long enough for Beretto or Abastrini to deliver a deadlier strike.

'We need to mount a counter-attack,' I said helplessly, but when I turned, I saw the rest of the terrified company crowded together at the back of the rehearsal hall, staring blankly at the calamity unfolding before them as if they were merely the audience. The broken old weapons they'd found in the props cupboard hung limply in their hands as they wailed to the gods for mercy.

I turned back to help Beretto and Abastrini just as the larger wooden panels in the doors came apart completely, revealing the Orchid soldiers on the other side, fanning the smoke into the hall from the fire they'd set in front of the main doors and laughing uproariously at the sight of their cowering prey.

Damn their laughter, I cursed silently. How were a band of players with no training and no real weapons supposed to fight back against fire and steel?

They can't, Corbier said, without sympathy. *A band of players without training or weapons can only suffer and die. You need an army to fight an army, and soldiers need a leader.*

He was right. *Someone* needed to lead the Knights of the Curtain into battle.

'I—'

'Right then,' a tremulous voice declared before I could finish my sentence.

I heard a great many contrary emotions in those two words: fear, horror, shame, guilt – and woven among them, something entirely unexpected.

That was the moment when Hujo Shoville, Lord Director of the Operato Belleza – a slight, pot-bellied man with a receding hairline, a man who'd never known much more respect within the theatre's walls than without, seized the hour. With a look of grim determination, he marched to the back of the rehearsal hall to face his terrified colleagues.

'Actors,' he began, his tone growing steadier and louder with each word he spoke, 'stagehands, costumers, carpenters, musicians – cast and crew, one and all: *form up!*'

The lot of them stared at him in utter confusion.

Shoville spoke again, and this time his voice nearly shook the walls around him. 'FORM. UP.'

The confused members of the Knights of the Curtain shuffled clumsily into the same positions they'd adopted for the battle scene of Mount Cruxia.

The director began striding along the front of their line like a general inspecting his troops, but instead of berating their poor posture or the ungainly way they were holding their weapons, he praised them.

'Good. *Good!* I see no *players* here – no, the actors are gone. The stagehands have disappeared. Carpenters and costumers, ushers and ticket-takers, all vanished. Before me stand warriors brave and true: brother and sister knights of the most sacred temple this city has ever known.' He jerked a thumb back at the doors and the masked Iron Orchids in their enamelled steel breastplates. 'Those fools out there? They consider you naught but players. Well, I say let's give them a performance they'll never forget! The play? That of a black, bloody war the likes of which has never before been seen in this city: a tale of battle-hardened men and women who broke their enemies' line – who smashed through the barricades and chased the cowards into the night, pursuing every man-jack of them with such ferocity that from this day onwards, no soldier, no guardsman, no duellist will ever walk by a member of this company without tipping their hat and saying, "Well met, Sir Knight".'

'Damn,' Beretto muttered next to me, awkwardly swinging his axe through the gap in the broken door panel. He shattered links on the chainmail shirt protecting one of their attacker's arms, but didn't manage to break through to the flesh underneath. 'Good speech.'

'We'll need more than speeches,' Teo muttered, throwing bits of broken door panel at the Orchids in a bid to distract them while Abastrini harried them with his broadsword.

From somewhere at the back of the hall, a drum began to pound. Rhyleis was beating out a cavalry rhythm, fast and steady. Next to her, Grey Mags, coughing so hard she was barely able to stand, was clacking her percussion discs in perfect time.

Somewhere deep inside me, deeper even than the depths where Corbier's stolen memories dwelled, I felt a stirring – an *awakening*. The stories my grandparents had told me of the valour, grace and dignity that had earned the Greatcoats their legends . . . I saw that now in the faces of the men and women in this smoke-filled hall, and with it, I caught a glimpse of what this city could be – what our people could be: the kind of person that, for the first time in my life, I badly wished to become.

At Shoville's orders, a group of hands pulled down a pair of painted wooden columns. They might be bits of set, but they were heavy enough that each one took three men to lift. The director himself grabbed hold of the front of one before turning back to his ragtag little army.

'Knights of the Curtain: my brothers and sisters, our audience awaits.' He raised his arm on high and drove his fist through the air towards the barricaded doors. '*Charge!*'

The roar that erupted from the cast and crew was like thunder hurled down by the gods themselves. Beretto, Teo, Abastrini and I had to jump out of the way before the two columns came at us like battering rams, the stagehands screaming like wild men as they charged the enemy. What remained of the double doors burst into kindling. Three of the soldiers on the other side went tumbling to the ground, steel breastplates caved in from the force of the blow. The rest of the cast and crew, armed with anything hard or sharp they could lay their hands on, ran into the breach.

Beretto watched them for a moment, coughing madly, a bloodthirsty grin splitting his bearded face. 'Magnificent bastards!' he shouted hoarsely, and launched himself into the fray.

CHAPTER 47

THE BATTLE OF THE BELLEZA

The armoured attackers clearly hadn't expected much resistance from a pathetic band of actors, and they went down hard beneath the press of players, stagehands and musicians rallying to the call of our director, as desperation and outrage took the place of training and skill. Extravagant steel breastplates with their enamelled grey orchids on fields of black were crushed underfoot by worn boots. Shiny new helms were battered by rusted stage weapons, broken table and chair legs, even the occasional musical instrument. The Knights of the Curtain might not be soldiers – but neither were the brutes and bravos who'd come to burn down our home.

By luck as much as sheer force of numbers, we broke the enemy's line.

Even in the familiar confines of the Belleza, however, the smoke and chaos made it difficult for us to get our bearings. When I glanced back at my fellow actors, I could have sworn hardened soldiers from Corbier's time had taken their place. Then I'd blink back the smoke-induced tears and see only my fellow Knights of the Curtain, battling for their lives.

What's happening to me? I asked silently.

Perhaps your Veristor's gift has summoned memories other than mine, Corbier suggested drily. *A pity your comrades will soon end up just as dead as my own warriors.*

He was right. Our only hope of survival was to break through the main hallway, rush past the backstage wings and into the auditorium, from where we could make for one of the street exits or the back alley. But everywhere we turned, there were more Orchids, swarming over us while setting fire to oil-soaked floors and walls.

'How many of these steel-carapaced cockroaches have infested our home?' Abastrini demanded, reeling back from the press of three armoured men almost as big as him, each wielding short-hafted axes.

Ornella, armed with a spear, ran to help him, Beretto and I close behind. I choked a moment, stepping over the body of an usher who'd died with his cleaning cloth in hand. His only crime had been his diligence in polishing the oak chairs in the theatre.

How many others have already perished? I wondered, but Corbier's warning shout clanged inside of my skull.

There'll be one more if you don't watch yourself, you fool!

A pair of Orchids had been hiding in the alcove to our right. The first man came out with his longsword ready to decapitate me.

Drop down low when the first man swings, Corbier advised. *Then use the strength of your legs to shove him into his comrade as you come back up under the blade.*

The Raven's instructions worked surprisingly well. One swordsman stumbled back into the other and both crashed to the ground. Ornella slipped past me and used the butt end of her spear to bash first one then the other in the face with surprising precision and no hesitation whatsoever.

Pity it wasn't she who possessed the Veristor's gift, Corbier observed. *Her, I could have worked with.*

Well, I'm all you've got. I pushed forward through the passage behind Beretto and Abastrini. *And if I die tonight, no one will ever hear the end of your tale, so best you and I deal, your Grace.*

'Which way?' Beretto called out as he smashed the pommel of the broadsword he'd commandeered from a downed Orchid on the head of the last of the militants blocking our way. 'Front exits or the alley?'

Whichever is narrower, Corbier advised. *It will be harder to get so many through, but easier to defend.*

'The alley!' I replied.

Beretto nodded and led us through the smoke-filled maze of halls.

The fire was beginning to rage now that some of the walls were fully alight, orange-red flames licking up the sides. The muffled thud of feet and shouts of encouragement from those behind who were hauling the battering rams propelled us onwards.

You'll have five minutes, no more, Corbier warned, *and after that, your battalion will suffocate from the smoke even before the flames reach them.*

I swung my blunted iron sword at the enemy, managing to force them back just long enough for Ornella to thrust her spear forward. With that look of grim determination on her face, I would have sworn she was playing Penzira the Lionesse.

'Sainted Hells,' Teo swore as the tip of Ornella's spear drove up beneath the gorget protecting the Orchid's throat.

'Forward!' Ornella roared as blood came gushing from the man's mouth.

Beretto cheered and we all rushed through the gap she'd made and into the last passage, which brought us within fifteen feet of the stage door. All that separated us from freedom were the eight armoured Orchids guarding the exit.

'Too many for us, damn it,' Abastrini growled.

'Turn back! We have to turn ba—' But Teo's shout faded into the smoke as another dozen Orchids emerged from behind us, boxing us in.

My heart sank as I saw our way out, in plain view and yet beyond our reach. Beretto and Abastrini at the front were trying to force the Orchids away from the door, but for all their prodigious strength and ferocity, the two of them were actors, not soldiers, and already exhausted. Beretto had a bleeding gash across his right shoulder and a crimson trail was winding its way down his face from a cut high on his brow. He kept shaking his head to keep the blood out of his eyes. One of the Orchids started taunting him, trying to unbalance him in preparation for the death blow.

I pressed through the crowd to get to my friends. I was holding a rapier now, though I had no recollection where it had come from – one of the downed attackers, maybe? Or perhaps one of the crew had handed it to me . . . still, none of that mattered. I stabbed at the man harrying Beretto, but my tip just snagged on the chainmail links protecting the

Orchid's neck above the top of his steel breastplate without breaking through.

A rapier is a duelling weapon, Corbier reminded me. *War is butchery. The heavier the cleaver, the deeper the blow.*

'Broadsword,' I shouted behind me, throwing my rapier to a costumer, who stared at it as if it were some kind of exotic animal. 'Someone pass me a broadsword—'

Teo was clutching just such a weapon, but he gave me a cockeyed look. 'What fucking good will it do you? You can't fight any better than the rest of us.'

'I've got to try, damn you!'

But Teo clung to the sword, holding it close to his chest as if it might somehow protect him from fire and militants alike.

Beretto and Abastrini were both staggering now, swinging widely to block the enemy from getting past them to begin the mass slaughter. The smoke was getting worse. The men and women of the Belleza were fighting with courage worthy of the poets, but they would soon be overwhelmed by the well-armed thugs who'd been sent to murder every last one of us.

Injustice set its own blaze deep inside my belly with the burning need to punish these bully-boys who'd set on innocents. Fear twisted into anger, which became an unquenchable desire for violence that turned the world red.

If I might assist? came Corbier's cold, cruel voice inside me. I could feel that strange tingling in my arms and legs, as if two different sets of instincts were trying to command my limbs.

I won't become your puppet again, I said, knowing that once the Red-Eyed Raven's bloodlust was loosed, there would be no stopping him. *I won't murder indiscriminately. I just want to get my friends out of here alive.*

Then what do you propose?

Can you . . . ? I don't know . . . lend me some of your knowledge, your memories, without taking control of me?

You would water down my practised skills with scruples and second-guessing? You'll be disoriented, forced to reconcile contrary sets of experiences at the same time. At best you'll be half the swordsman I was. There was a hesitation, then that became a kind of curiosity. *Then again, I'm dead, so apparently my talents weren't enough to save me in my own time. Say the word, then, Veristor, and I'll provide what you ask, but be warned: such recollections as I offer will be most . . . disturbing.*

I whispered, 'Raise the curtain.'

Memories not my own flooded every fibre of my body, and what seconds before had been a terrifying calamity was suddenly little more than banality: yes, there was fire – there often was. There were enemies – there were always enemies. The sheer familiarity of it all caused my breathing to slow and my shoulders to relax. I tore the sleeve from my shirt and tied it around my mouth and nose to keep out a little of the smoke. All I needed now was the right weapon for the job that awaited me.

'Teo, behind you,' I shouted.

The slender young man spun, raising the broadsword high, searching for an opponent who wasn't there. I reached out, grabbed the quillons and yanked the weapon towards me. Teo's wrists bent backwards and with a yelp, he relinquished the weapon.

I didn't even look back as I took the sword in both hands and shouldered my way forward to reach the line of Orchids blocking the stage door.

Vertical cuts only, Corbier's voice advised. *The hall is too narrow to be swinging wide and smashing into the walls like the rest of these fools. Up and down, as if you were chopping wood.*

Somehow I doubted that Corbier had spent much of his privileged life outdoors cutting firewood, but I did as I was told. My movements, so relaxed in comparison to the chaos all around me, were smooth, precise, clean: *up and down, up and down.* Memories of the thousands of times Corbier had practised were all there for me to draw on – and so too were the recollections of every time those skills had been used against human flesh.

Go for weapon hands, when they offer them, Corbier advised. *They'll instinctively protect their faces, so first you must draw their attention to something else – a smashed knee will bring their guard down and expose their heads for a killing blow.*

I'd like to avoid those if I can—

A snort. *Did you not notice your dead colleagues? Your first 'Ajelaine'? And have you forgotten your Errera Bottio? 'Every enemy heart which beats is an ally's which does not.'*

I'd memorised every saints-damned word Errera Bottio ever wrote, which was how I knew the legendary duelling master had never said anything of the kind.

Really? Perhaps it was me who said it, then. No matter, I suppose, since you're apparently determined to ignore the fellow coming up on your flank.

I spun a quarter-turn to my left just before a sword came crashing down at my skull. My own instinct was to jump out of the way, but Corbier's took over and instead I leaned back just far enough to watch the blade swoosh down a few inches from my nose. Unfortunately, that left me now facing the wall of the hallway with too little room to raise my own weapon up for a counter-cut.

The quillons are as much a part of the weapon as the blade, Corbier scolded, and almost without thinking, I reversed my grip on the hilt, leaving the point aimed straight down, and thrust one end of the steel quillon into my opponent's face. The sound of bone crunching and blood erupting from the man's nose was perversely pleasurable.

Now the leg, Corbier advised and this time I didn't hesitate before plunging the sharpened tip of the blade straight down into the exposed flesh just above the knee. The prize this time was a scream of agony. To his credit, even as the Iron Orchid was sliding to the floor, he tried a last-ditch thrust with his own sword, but a simple pivot knocked the enemy blade out of the way.

Don't become enamoured of one technique, Corbier warned. *And stop staring at the man's bleeding face, you fool!*

Sorry, I just—

The Red-Eyed Raven's memories and experiences mingled awkwardly with my own feelings, for the deep satisfaction I was experiencing at the sight of a downed opponent was overwhelmed by my own nausea.

Perhaps you'll feel less conflicted after one of his comrades sticks a blade through your belly? Take one down, move on. The instant you commit to one attack, let your eyes find the next.

A groan from my left turned out to be Ornella. Her long silver hair was matted with blood, her face filthy from the soot, and she was clinging to the remains of her broken spear, reduced to using it as a club. 'I'm all right,' she said, wiping filthy sweat from her eyes. 'Help Beretto and Abastrini – the gods-bedamned Orchids are going after them more than the rest of us.'

'What about those behind us?' I asked.

'Already fled,' she replied with a hacking cough. 'Just before their fires made the other hallways impassable. We can't turn back now, or we'll be burned to cinders.'

Trapped between the blaze and the blade, Corbier said. *Still sure you don't want me to take over?*

I ignored him and continued methodically working my way to the front of the line, Corbier's reflexes ducking me beneath one blade even as I buried my own into the shoulder joint of another Orchid. I found myself grinning when the steel rings of the fellow's surcoat, unprotected by the breastplate, shattered from the impact even as the tip continued its journey. My blade came away bloody, which widened Corbier's smile.

The hallway was littered with bodies now, both defenders and attackers. The wounded, dying and dead had become a barricade of wasted flesh blocking the way to the door, now only a few feet away.

'Damelas?' Beretto asked, coming up on my right and pausing to bring his axe crashing down on an enemy's helmeted head. 'Is that you in there?'

'Aye,' I replied, although I'd never said 'aye' in my life unless it was a line in a script. 'Well, mostly,' I conceded, thrusting my sword at a looming face. The man jumped back and bashed himself on the stage door – but it held, which meant it was barred from the outside.

'The faithless bastards really left their own brethren to burn with us?' Beretto spat.

'Bring those battering rams,' I shouted.

'You mean the wooden columns?' some idiot asked.

'No, I meant run out and find a supplier of siege-engines and see if he'll give you a good deal on a used one. *Of course I mean the fucking columns!*'

Don't let minuscule victories go to your head, Corbier warned. *And never give speeches in the middle of a battle unless you're about to die, and then only when there's a Bardatti nearby to add it to your eulogy.*

I smashed the pommel of my sword into the back of the head of a man trying to drive Abastrini to the ground, then reversed the motion and slashed Beretto's opponent.

I'm doing just fine, in case you hadn't noticed.

You're becoming battle-drunk, Corbier warned. *You aren't feeling it right now, but the smoke is damaging your lungs. Every breath you take is another gift to the enemy.*

You have a lot of axioms, has anyone ever told you that? I asked, but this time I kept my mouth closed.

There were just two Iron Orchids left guarding the door, and they looked like they'd quite happily have fled long ago, had there been anywhere to flee to. Evidently, no one had bothered to tell them they were to be martyrs to their cause, trapped inside the burning theatre along with their intended victims.

'Out of the way,' someone called out and I barely had time to flatten myself against the wall as one of the columns came charging at the stage door. The two Orchids weren't so lucky: it caught them both and smashed them into the barred door. They slumped down to the ground, dead or dying – but the door held.

'Again—' Abastrini croaked and the grim-faced stagehands, all hacking and coughing, backed up a few feet and struck again. This time the door buckled on its hinges – but the column shattered.

'Make way,' the second group said, backing up further this time. We were all conscious that this was our last chance. With a roar, they charged.

Please, I begged, *whichever of you gods and saints care for the petty lives of mortals, let the courage of these brave souls be—*

The battering ram exploded into a thousand pieces. Despair rose up in me – until I saw the door had shattered as well. Lethal slivers of wood had shot everywhere, embedding in the walls and piercing the flesh of those caught too close, but even they didn't care, because at last freedom beckoned.

In the alley, sweet, blessed rain was falling from a merciful night sky.

'Out, everyone, quick now,' Beretto gasped, and actors and crew, bloody, weary, and all grinning like the condemned offered a last-minute reprieve, poured out into the wet alleyway.

Drop the broadsword, Corbier's voice advised me. *You'll want that rapier now.*

What—? Why?

Because this part of the fight is done.

I looked around for the rapier I'd discarded earlier and found it lying on the floor just within reach. As I followed the others outside, I saw more than two dozen Orchids, some in that same enamelled plate armour and others in the grimy clothes of labourers, waiting for us with swords and spears in hand. The fire was raging up to the very top of the Belleza, lighting up the night sky. Some of the alley's usual denizens were trying to fight back, but like us, they were outnumbered and out-weaponed.

'Let's teach these blackguards the first rule of the sword,' Beretto cried, running into the fray, ignoring the wounds he'd already suffered.

Corbier's usually cold and calculating voice asked with interest, *The first rule of the sword?*

An old Greatcoats saying, I informed him as I raced after Beretto. *'Put the pointy end in the other guy first.'*

For once the Red-Eyed Raven sounded amused. *As duelling maxims go, I suppose that's as sound as any old Errera Bottio ever wrote.*

CHAPTER 48

THE FIRE IN THE ALLEY

I had barely a second to get my bearings before my path was barred by a slim, broad-shouldered figure whose features were entirely hidden behind a black silk mask with a painted grey orchid over the mouth.

At last, Corbier exulted. *A worthy opponent!*

What the Hells are you talking about? Who is—?

The masked figure stalked towards me, the plain but perfectly made swept-hilt rapier in her hand marking her as a professional duellist. Worse still, her movements were instantly familiar.

The Vixen of Jereste.

How the Hells is she even standing? I asked silently. *We stabbed her through the chest last night!*

I missed her heart, Corbier replied. *I wanted to see her eyes when . . . well, never mind that. I suspect she's been dosed with a fortune's worth of prodigialis magni – a useful concoction, by the way. Given how many people want you dead, you might consider acquiring some. But apparently given a choice between a nice new castle and killing you, our Lady Fox prefers the latter.*

'Why bother with the mask?' I asked, my hand already trembling on the grip of my own far heavier and clumsier rapier. 'Did you think I wouldn't recognise you, Lady di Traizo?'

Don't be a fool, Corbier told me. *The mask isn't to hide her identity; it serves merely to afford the magistrates doubt over her presence here, should evidence of this massacre ever come to court.*

The Vixen wagged a reproving finger at me. 'It's *Margravina* di Traizo now, remember?' That same hand rose up to pinch the black silk covering her face. As she laughed brightly, the grey orchid over her mouth twisted eerily. 'The Masked Margravina, the minstrels will call me. Has a nice ring to it, don't you think? Like a heroine from one of the old sword romances.'

'Speaking as an actor myself,' I began, keeping my point towards her even as Corbier was shouting at me to take up a more aggressive posture, 'I fear the role of heroine might lie outside your natural disposition.'

My voice sounded hoarse, anxious and overcautious. It was all I could do to keep my concentration on the Vixen while my friends were screaming and dying in the light of the flames consuming the Belleza.

Try feinting to her open line, Corbier suggested. *Follow with an attack on the outside. The prodigialis will affect her balance, and the mask is an encumbrance to which she won't be accustomed. Even the slightest check to her peripheral vision will throw off her game.*

I tried to follow his instructions, but the Vixen wasn't so easily fooled; her steps traced a narrow circle in the alley's confines, avoiding every broken cobblestone and piece of debris.

She's been waiting out here, mapping her terrain, I realised, *which means the Orchids must have more armoured bastards out the front, ready to herd us back here if we'd managed to escape that way.*

'Fascinating,' she said, watching my movements. 'I expected to meet either my rabbit or the Red-Eyed Raven, but here I see something in between.'

Following Corbier's earlier advice, I kept silent as I feinted with the tip of my rapier at the grey orchid on the Vixen's masked face, only to then drop low and extend myself into a lunge for the forward leg. She was too quick, though, pulling her foot back even as she dropped her own point to thrust at my right shoulder. Only by slapping the attacking blade away with my left hand was I able to save my sword arm from being skewered. My palm was still covered in bandages from the night before, but the razor-sharp blade separated the cloth as cleanly as the flesh, leaving fresh blood seeping from the wound.

Stop fretting over paper cuts, Corbier advised. *She's prepared for either of us. You must confound her expectations.*

Drawing on Corbier's memories of fencing bouts against true masters of the blade, I attempted a series of staccato manoeuvres, blending deception into genuine attack and back again, but the Vixen parried them all handily, and within seconds I had collected several more shallow cuts on my arms and cheeks.

'Good,' she said, as if urging me on, 'you're better than I'd believed, my rabbit – but still not good enough.'

I glanced around, hoping for assistance, but the Knights of the Curtain were barely holding their own against the armoured Orchids. And I was winded now. Fusing Corbier's experience with my grandparents' training made me a better fencer than I'd ever been before, but nothing could alter the fundamental mechanics of my own body. The archduke had been taller, with a longer reach, so I kept having to stretch out at the last instant to reach targets that would have been well within Corbier's range. I was quick enough, but I lacked the muscle endurance of a hardened soldier. I was already exhausted.

Worse still, the Masked Margravina knew it.

'Really wonderful technique,' she remarked after my last volley. 'Do you know, Damelas, I think you might have had a promising future as a duellist – well, if you had any future at all.'

I remained silent, but this time Corbier had other ideas.

'I thank you for the compliment, my Lady Fox. Allow me to offer one of my own: rarely have I encountered a woman blessed with the privileges of birth, wealth and training, who nonetheless overcame the qualms of civility and dignity to hide her coward's face behind a mask while devoting herself to the midnight butchery of barely armed civilians.'

Weren't you the one advising me not to waste my breath? I asked.

Words are like any other weapon – to be used when the time is right and your opponent is vulnerable to their sting.

The Margravina di Traizo's shoulders tensed for the first time. 'I will cut your tongue from your mouth for that remark, Rabbit.'

You see? Corbier remarked smugly.

I do. Allow me to follow your example.

I stuck out my tongue and mumbled, 'Here it is, my Lady.'

For some reason, a child's taunt – the kind of thing Zina might do – infuriated the Vixen far more than Corbier's elegant quip.

'Shut your mouth, Rabbit. I won't let you ruin this moment. Seventeen years ago, Virany Chademantaigne stole from me the only person I loved, and who loved me. Your grandmother didn't just defame and convict the woman who gave birth to me, she put her down like a dog! Let Virany's spirit roil in the seven Hells as I slip my blade first through the heart of her grandson and next through her husband's!'

She whipped the flexible end of her slender rapier out like a snake in an attempt to slice my still-exposed tongue, but for all her speed, the target was obvious, allowing me to duck beneath the blade and extend my own rapier up in a diagonal line so the Margravina sliced the underside of her own arm on the tip.

A crude gambit, but effective, Corbier noted approvingly.

She tried to recover her composure with a more tentative riposte, but her mask contorted when she grunted in pain.

What fragile flowers the nobility have become in your time, Corbier observed. *Easily goaded, full of arrogance for their skill with a blade, yet fearful of earning the scars they should be proud to wear. They think themselves masters of the sword while slaughtering untrained innocents, never testing themselves against an equal. Shall we remedy this deficiency in our Lady Fox's education?*

Despite my fatigue, the thought of finally ending this damnable vendetta brought a grim smile to my face. *This once, your Grace, you and I are of one mind.*

For the first time, two sets of contrary instincts found common ground as I weathered Ferica di Traizo's onslaught with increasing confidence: thrust, parry, counter-attack, lunge . . . The noblewoman's precision and skill were daunting, but I found within Corbier's experiences and my grandmother's training a style to match her. Where the Vixen's sword sought out targets with exquisite form and lethal accuracy, I met her with a combination of Corbier's calm, Virany Chademantaigne's daring and my own outlandish theatrical training. I darted high and low, exposing my chest to her lunge only to then beat her blade aside, following up with a shout of 'Huzzah!' as I leaped high off the ground, dropping my point low in a devastating thrust that forced the margravina to retreat.

The fight went on for an eternity, blade-to-blade, with no awareness of the mayhem surrounding us. From the corner of my eye, I caught the dream-like shadows that my opponent and I cast upon the alley wall, lit by the flames devouring the Operato Belleza. It was like being an audience member, watching two players, equal in skill but contrasting in style, performing a larger-than-life fight scene. Elongated as it was, my own silhouette was almost a stranger to me: I looked taller, longer-limbed, broader of shoulder – almost as if I were witnessing the legendary Corbier himself, duelling in the streets of Jereste for the first time in a hundred years.

How poetic, the archduke noted sarcastically. *But since it's your hide that'll be skewered by this fool and not mine, perhaps you could spend less time admiring your shadow and more on actually winning the fight?*

Fair point, I thought, retreating under a flurry of strokes. But I had the advantage now. Weary as I was, the Vixen was faring even worse, forced to focus as much on trying to make sense of my fencing style as delivering her own attacks. Trepidation was creeping in, her thrusts and lunges becoming ever more cautious. If this *were* a scene in a play, now was the time when the margravina would either die or drop to her knees and beg for surrender – unless, that is, the playwright has decided to throw in a last-minute and entirely contrived rescue.

'Orchids, to me!' the Margravina di Traizo shouted.

Oh, fuck all the saints! I swore as the Vixen was instantly surrounded by half a dozen of her armoured bully-boys. I glanced around for help, but those on my side were barely holding their own against the arsonists, and we'd have lost that fight long before if the alley-rats had not taken up rocks and broken bottles in defence of our home and theirs.

Suddenly two of the Orchids encircling Margravina di Traizo parted and her blade swooped out in a magnificent lunge that cost me a bleeding cut just above my left eye. Immediately afterwards, the Orchids swept back in front of her, shielding her from counter-attack.

Even through the mask, I could see the margravina's manic grin. She beckoned to me from within her armoured ring of protectors. 'You see, Rabbit, you're not the only one with tricks up your sleeve.'

Corbier took offence and I gave voice to his outrage. 'Have you no honour at all, Margravina di Traizo? Do I truly find you cowering behind your subjects as they fight your battles for you?'

She laughed at that. 'Should the carpenter apologise for using a hammer to drive a nail rather than her fists? Does the warrior shuffle in embarrassment over skilfully wielding a shield?'

Despite the bloodlust I could feel coming from Corbier – and from me too, now – the archduke made me retreat from the line of Iron Orchids now stalking towards us.

We won't win like this, Corbier warned. *You must make them chase you.*

Chase me where? There's no space to manoeuvre.

Ah, yes. That does seem to be a problem.

The Orchids who'd come to the margravina's aid began laughing as they advanced. 'Rabbit, Rabbit,' some of them began to chant, and only then did I realise these might be the very same bravos who'd harried me through the city a year ago.

With what looked suspiciously like practised efficiency, they slid out of the Vixen's way whenever she attacked, reforming silently around her as she retreated.

There was no way for me to win this fight.

Why bother with this sham? I wondered as I was forced to back up further into the alley. *Why not just have them rush me at once and kill me?*

You really don't understand how the nobility see the world, do you? Corbier asked. *It is a play in which they must always be the stars, and they will do whatever is required to ensure the story told will suit their own high opinions of themselves.*

'*Rabbit, Rabbit!*' the Orchids surrounding the Vixen called out merrily.

'Careful, my doves,' she warned. 'Don't kill him – I want his sword hand severed from his wrist and his tongue removed. I want him with a collar around his neck, kneeling by my side when I kill his grandfather and end this at last.'

My gaze flashed around the alley, searching for a more advantageous position, but both ends were now blocked by the Orchids, who had regained control and were pressing the cast and crew backwards towards the flames raging within the Operato Belleza, offering them a choice of death by steel or by fire.

I could use a little help here, I told Corbier.

But the archduke's reply was distant, fragmented. I could hear the misery – the sudden, unquenchable sorrow – in his voice. *Forgive me, Player. I have failed you, just as I failed Ajelaine. I . . . I cannot bear witness to tyranny winning the day yet again.*

Corbier's memories began to fade and the instincts honed from a lifetime of duelling and warfare fled my limbs.

You coward! Don't leave me like this—

The rapier felt heavy in my hand now, and worse, I felt clumsy, stiff. My fingers couldn't find their grip any more and my arm couldn't keep the point in a decent guard position.

I'm done for, I realised as the margravina and her protectors closed on me. *My friends will die. If she does leave me alive, I'll be maimed, left to beg for copper tears until cold or starvation takes me. She'll murder my grandfather, and the Iron Orchids will rule this city – and whoever commands them will have won without ever having to show their true face.*

I tightened my grip on my sword and took a step towards her. *The Hells for that. Let them try and capture me while I'm stabbing the living shit out of them. If I die today, at least I'll die like a gods-damned Greatcoat!*

'Look at that,' the Vixen chuckled. 'My rabbit still has some fight left in him.'

As bitter frustration filled me, fury rose from deep in my belly and my mouth opened wide to give voice to that rage. The roar that ensued was as deafening as an ocean rising up to crash down upon this unjust, undeserving world, as if the alley itself were screaming its outrage at this desecration.

It took me a second to realise the sound hadn't come from me.

I saw it first in the wide-eyed expressions on the faces of the Iron Orchids in front of me, then in the eyes of the Masked Margravina. I spun round to see a massive figure charging the enemy, leading a troop of soldiers in Duke Monsegino's pertine-blue livery. After a moment, I recognised Captain Terine, and alongside her was Lady Shariza, dressed head to toe in black and moving like a devil's shadow through the alley. I wasn't sure which was the more terrifying sight.

The Iron Orchids decided to call the outcome a draw and ran from them both. The Vixen followed, but not before calling out to me, 'One last night of freedom then, dear Rabbit. We have yet to have our final encounter . . .'

My whole body was shaking, not from fear this time, or even anger, just utter disgust.

Even now, with all this blood spilled and fire and mayhem spreading everywhere, it's all just a game to her.

A deeper and more troubling thought occurred to me as I suddenly recalled one of Sigurdis Macha's lines from *The Garden of Majesty*: *How often we find those in power and those who seek it grasping like children at each other's toys.* The nobles of this city were capable of intrigues and schemes, but not this slow, patient strategy that appeared to be unfolding all over the duchy. Someone had to be orchestrating all of this – someone who wasn't a child.

But who? How do you have a conspiracy with no conspirators?

Then Captain Terine called out, 'The gods love things in threes!' Her expression left no doubt as to just how badly she wanted to massacre the Orchids. 'In their honour, leave me three of the varlets alive for questioning. Wash these streets clean with the blood of the rest!'

Another roar of approval rose up from her troops as they rushed past me like a hurricane, leaving a single, tall blade of grass untouched.

'Are you hurt?' Shariza asked, pausing in front of me, her eyes tracing every cut on my face and arms.

'I'm fine,' I said, summoning a grin to reassure her. 'If you're not otherwise occupied, there's a masked margravina back there who could do with a bit of smiting.'

Shariza tilted her head, watching me like a cat. 'I can never quite tell if you're a timid person who pretends at times to be brave, or a brave one who's been trying to convince himself for far too long that he's a coward.'

Exhaustion and one too many brushes with death made me reckless. 'Which one stands a chance of winning your heart, my Lady?'

'Both, it appears,' she replied, and surprised me with a kiss on the cheek. Then, just like that, she was gone.

I sought her through the madding crowd as the ducal forces easily overwhelmed the Iron Orchids, catching glimpses here and there.

Wielding a pair of foot-long stiletto blades, she went sneaking in and out of the mass of armoured bodies, leaving a sliced leg here, a slit throat there. This was neither duelling nor warfare: it was more like watching a plague of locusts ravaging a field of wheat.

Dashini, I thought dumbly. Most of us knew little about the ancient order of unstoppable assassins. The only thing I could say for certain was that Lady Shariza, the Black Amaranth, was unquestionably one of them.

'By the blood of every saint,' Beretto swore, limping over to stand beside me, 'I must advise you in the strongest possible terms never to disappoint that woman.'

I looked over my friend as intently as Shariza had examined me. 'You're bleeding everywhere,' I said.

Beretto brushed my hand away. 'It's mostly their blood, not mine. We've done remarkably well for a bunch of untrained actors facing off against armoured militants.' He looked down at the battered axe in his hand. 'For a minute there, when you and I were fighting back to back, I felt something rising within me, almost as if I had become . . .'

'Become what?'

He shook his head. 'Nothing. The fog of battle has addled my senses.' He gave a chuckle that ended in a hoarse cough. 'Who would have thought that Shoville might have made an outstanding general had he not chosen to become a mediocre theatre director?'

Despite my own injuries, despite the sight of the Operato Belleza still blazing, I couldn't help but laugh at the thought of General Shoville leading real troops into battle, pausing every few feet as they charged up the hill to adjust a soldier's helmet or tabard. 'Just because we're fighting a war doesn't mean we have to look like ruffians,' he'd have said.

A cheer went up as the last of the Iron Orchids fled, the duke's soldiers in pursuit. I doubted they'd get far.

But looking around, my grin faded. Bodies littered the alley, far too many of them Knights of the Curtain – but even more were wearing armour adorned with the orchid symbol. Actors, crew and alley-rats alike hugged and shouted of their victory while the massive torch that was all that remained of the Belleza shot sparks into the night sky, a signal fire to the Gods of Love and Craft that one of their greatest temples was no more.

'What's the matter, brother?' Beretto asked. 'Are your wounds . . . ?'

I shook my head, only then noticing the dampness of tears on my cheeks. I tried to cover them up with a joke. 'Just imagining how much of a bonus Zina will be expecting from poor Shoville now. As if the little swindler wasn't already a bane on our poor director's pur—' I stopped abruptly, feeling the blood drain from my face. I grabbed Beretto. 'Zina wasn't in the hall when this started. Did she—?'

I turned to the crowded alleyway and began shouting her name over and over, screaming at the others to shut up so I could hear her answer, but no answer came.

I found Tolsi huddled against a wall and had to shake him from a confused trance. 'Where's Zina?' I demanded urgently. 'Was she with you?'

The boy gave no reply, just scrunched himself as small as he could, as if trying to hide from the world.

I shook him harder. 'When did you see her? Was she inside? Talk to me, Tolsi!'

'The boy's in shock,' Teo said, trying to pull me away, then someone else grabbed my elbow and yanked me around.

'I saw her,' Ornella said. Her long silver hair was black with smoke and grit and dirt, her wrinkled skin covered in cuts and bruises. She was still clutching her makeshift club. 'I saw her this morning. Shoville had her mending costumes . . .' She started coughing again, then managed to croak out, 'Saint Ethalia-who-shares-all-sorrows . . . she was in the basement—'

But by then I was already running towards the fire-ravaged stage door, ignoring the smoke billowing from it and pushing my way into the ruins of the Operato Belleza.

CHAPTER 49

AFFAIRS OF HONOUR

Someone, probably Beretto, tried to stop me, but I still had enough of Corbier's memories to strike just the right spot on my best friend's wrist to free me from his grip. I made my escape, shoving past Teo, who tried to bar my path next, and ignoring Beretto shouting, 'Damelas, *stop!* You'll light up like a candle wick!'

Blinded by the smoke, I tried to call out Zina's name, but instantly fell to coughing as I stumbled through the smouldering hallway. The overwhelming heat was already singeing my clothes, and at every step I felt sure I would break through the disintegrating floorboards.

'Zina,' I croaked again, pressing forward into the hellish heat and smothering walls of smoke, but still there was no answer.

You're going to die, I thought I heard Corbier say, but it was my own voice this time. I tried to ignore it, desperate to believe that I could make it through the smoke and fire by sheer force of will. I pleaded silently with any saint who might be listening, praying they would keep Zina safe until I got to her . . .

Whoever it was who'd answered my prayer was surely no saint, but a demon: a monster looming out of the smoky gloom. The shadowy, misshapen silhouette was the colour of blood, its limbs too many in number, some thick as tree-trunks, others emaciated, dangling limp from its torso. The creature spoke no words but growled as it came stomping towards me as if intending to crush me underfoot.

As a boy, I'd laughed at my grandfather's tales of devils and demons lurking under the bed, waiting for badly behaved children to go to sleep so they could feast on their entrails. Now I wasn't so sure. I reached for my rapier, forgetting I'd abandoned it in the alley when I'd run back into the theatre.

Suddenly the demon charged me – and as it did, it croaked, 'Get out of the way, you artless, boil-brained codpiece!'

Ellias Abastrini's bulk was enveloped in one of the Belleza's crimson curtains, which he must have soaked in water, judging by the vast quantities of steam pouring off him. He was carrying Zina's limp form in his arms. Stumbling backwards, I caught my footing just in time, then turned and raced ahead, kicking aside burning debris to clear a path.

The moment we emerged into the alley, Grey Mags ignored her own numerous burns and cuts and took charge of Zina. 'She's alive!' Mags cried in disbelief, 'and there's barely a scratch or a burn on her!'

The same could not be said for Abastrini, whose hair was a tangle of charred ends framing his soot-covered face. His eyes were haunted, like those of a man who'd escaped from the deepest Hells, only to leave his soul behind.

'Saint Laina's blessed bosom,' Beretto shouted, trying to hold Abastrini up, 'I'll never call you anything less than a hero from now on—'

But Abastrini had collapsed, sobbing, to the ground.

'There, there, man,' Beretto murmured, 'no shame in it, mate, not after what you've—'

'I did nothing,' Abastrini wept.

'You saved the girl—'

He shook his head wildly, sending the freely flowing tears flying. 'It was Hujo – all Hujo.'

'Shoville?' I asked, only now realising that I hadn't seen the director since we'd breached the Orchids' line. All the strength drained from me and I sank down next to Abastrini, who was gulping his words like a sobbing child.

'He . . . I-I saw Hujo r-run back into the b-building – I th-thought he'd lost his m-mind, but he was g-going for the girl. I told him . . . I told h-him he was mad, it was t-too late to save her, but he wouldn't listen. He *never* fucking listened. Something fell on me – a beam, I think – and I couldn't get up, but Shoville . . . The damn thing was on fire, but he got it off me anyway – his hands must've been burned through to the bone. I tried to pull him out with me, but he – he p-pushed me away. He swore the smoke wouldn't be so bad in the basement, so the girl would surely be alive. Clever bastard, Shoville, he always was. He soaked one of the old curtains with the bucket for cleaning the stage – he g-got her out of there, but then . . . then he . . .' His words trailed off and he hung his head, still weeping.

'It's all right,' I said, knowing it wasn't and it wouldn't ever be again. 'Just . . . . just breathe, Ellias.'

Around us people were shouting orders, organising the soldiers, residents and onlookers alike into a bucket brigade to douse the flames, but Abastrini was determined to finish his confession.

'One of the Orchids had taken refuge down there when the fire got bad. He followed Shoville up, tried to grab the curtain from him. Saint Zaghev knows, we could all have survived if he'd just . . .'

He broke down again, but after a moment, he snarled, 'That bastard Orchid stabbed Hujo in the back.'

He struggled to his feet, awkwardly grabbing at Beretto's shoulder to steady himself. 'Are there any of those fuckers left?' he demanded. 'Someone get me a damned sword—'

'It's done,' I told him, rising to press a hand against Abastrini's broad chest. 'Vengeance doesn't . . . We can't bring back the dead, not with blades any more than with tears.'

Abastrini's rage sagged and crumbled, leaving behind only misery. 'The last thing I said to Hujo . . .' His words were almost a plea. 'I swore that I would see him voted out as Directore Principale – even though he and I started the company together, even though he always tried to make things right with me. I called him craven to his face a hundred times and every time he'd bow and scrape and try to calm me down. I thought him a coward, but he . . .' Abastrini stared at me pitifully, desperate for some sort of reassurance. 'He was so very brave, wasn't he?'

'Brave as any knight,' I agreed. 'A true Knight of the Curtain.'

A cheer rose up from the soldiers – not for my declaration, but for the fire they'd finally got under control. No doubt they would return to the palace and tell anyone who'd listen how they'd heroically saved the lives of a group of poor, pathetic players caught up in a battle they could never have won. Their recounting would never mention how Beretto, armed only with a blunt, rusty axe, had taken down a half a dozen armoured bully-boys, nor would anyone hear of the crew who'd made battering rams of a stage set and smashed through the barricaded doors meant to ensure the entire company burned to death. And no one would ever know that an unassuming, middle-aged, pot-bellied director named Hujo Shoville had rallied a ragtag company of players to charge dozens of armoured warriors, then walked calmly back into the conflagration to rescue a street girl he'd known less than a week.

The soldiers began to sing out of tune, a song about honour and glory, and I found I despised them almost as much as the men who'd destroyed the Operato Belleza and stolen the dreams of everyone who'd ever stood upon its stage.

Violet Dukes and Iron Orchids. May they all be wedded in the fires of the seven Hells.

'Damelas,' Lady Ajelaine called to me softly, 'you must come to me.'

Not, not Ajelaine, you idiot. Shariza. What's wrong with you?

I turned and saw the Black Amaranth was standing not two feet away, studying me even as she held a hand out to me. I supposed my anger must be written as plainly on my face as the Belleza's sorrow was now for ever inscribed upon the scarred remains of her once mighty walls.

Whatever emotions Shariza was feeling were impossible to discern. No doubt spies learned early on to mask such things. Still, I thought I sensed concern, perhaps even affection between us, and so I steeled myself to hear her tell me how sorry she was for the losses we had suffered this night.

'We have to go,' she said.

'Go? Go where?'

She looked away for the briefest instant – just long enough for me to see right through her.

'Duke Monsegino,' I said. 'He dispatched you here to retrieve me, didn't he?'

'As soon as word came of the attack, he allowed me to bring his guardsmen. In return, yes, he commanded that I bring you back with me.'

The smile that came over me was bitter, but genuine. I felt almost grateful now, for I had been certain I would never be able to convey the full depths of my displeasure to Monsegino and all the other dukes of this world.

I turned and began walking down the alley.

'Damelas?' she called out to me.

I turned back briefly and gave her a terse bow of farewell. 'Tell his Grace I decline his invitation.'

CHAPTER 50

THE SUMMONS

I had no destination in mind, only a determination that, for once, I would defy the natural order of the universe that said men like Monsegino and Corbier set the course of history, and the rest of us had no choice but to play the parts assigned to us.

Player. Such an odd word, really, implying not simply a participant in a game, but one who made choices and had a stake in winning, who set out a strategy and followed it, clasping hands together excitedly to see if, in the end, they would triumph. But an actor does not *play* the game; our destiny is already determined by lines writ on paper, our final words chosen by others long before we're given the chance to utter them.

We're not players at all, I thought bitterly. *We're just pieces for others to move as they will.*

Jereste itself, this city whose citizens were raised to venerate art as a gift from the gods, was itself a game board. Children were born, raised and buried in the same neighbourhoods as their parents and *their* parents before them, never rising from poverty, never sinking from privilege. Burglars and pickpockets plied their trades not from the purses of the wealthy but off the backs of their fellow paupers. The rich who rode inside opulent carriages, fancying they could go wherever they pleased, returned night after night to the same mansions inherited from their parents, rarely seeing beyond their own walls. The city was a prison for all its inhabitants.

And you, Duke Monsegino, do you feel any freer than the rest of us, sitting in that grand throne room of yours, forced to send others out to do your dirty work?

Are you not as much a captive as I am, surrounded by those noble families who call you their liege and to whom you must pander or risk not just the crown being taken from your head but your head from your neck?

'Damelas!'

I'd never heard Shariza shout before. I decided her voice was better suited to subtle, threatening whispers.

'Have you come to stroll the streets of this glorious city arm-in-arm with me, my Lady?'

The sound of her footsteps picked up. In the short time we'd known each other, I'd grown accustomed to not hearing her movements, which made me wonder if she was deliberately making her heels clack against the cobblestones so as not to make me uncomfortable.

Her hand grabbed onto my arm in a grip that quickly disabused me of that notion. 'Damelas, the duke commands your presence.'

'Alas, as you can see, I'm headed in the opposite direction.'

The deceptively strong fingers wrapped around my forearm squeezed tighter, forcing me to stop. 'You're headed where?'

'To wherever a person can live free of the encumbrance of dukes, past or present. Would you like to join me?'

'No such place exists, Damelas. You know that.'

I turned and caught her gaze. I loved the deep black of her eyes; I supposed I was coming to love a great many things about her. But I was beyond romantic self-delusion now. 'No such place exists precisely because men like Duke Monsegino always have people like you hunt us down when we dare to go in search of it.'

'Please,' she said, 'you're in shock. You've seen terrible things this night, and the grief inside you feels too much to bear, but bear it you must, because—'

I reached out and let my fingers slide through her dark curls, impertinently allowing the palm of my hand touch her cheek. 'Because very soon you're going to decide that words won't be enough to persuade me, because the Black Amaranth is the sort of name that can only belong to a spy, an assassin and, above all else, the personal servant to the Duke of Pertine. You warned me, didn't you? I kept calling you Shariza but you said I should think of you as the Black Amaranth. Do all the Dashini take names like that? I suppose it doesn't matter now. The only thing that matters about the Dashini is that they never fail to complete their missions.'

'Damelas, don't do this. Don't make me—'

I put a finger to her lips. 'So in a moment you're going to knock me unconscious – a toxin hidden in a fingernail, perhaps? A precise strike to some minor muscle that causes a man to pass out instantly? Then you'll catch me as I fall and those guards who, out of politeness for my *grief*, as you so gently put it, are staying out of view until summoned, will come running. The next time I open my eyes, those same guards will be propping me up in Duke Monsegino's throne room, where he will tell me *the way things are*. And when he is done giving me *my* orders, those guards will force me to my knees to bow before his Grace.'

She looked stricken. 'If you know all this, why must you play the belligerent child?'

'Because when I dared to play the hero, people I cared about *died*!'

I hadn't meant to shout at her. Shariza wasn't to blame for the burning of the Belleza or the death of its director, or the usher, or any of the dozen or more who fell beneath the Orchids' blades. Her actions were driven by duty, tempered by what mercy she could afford, but always in keeping with the promises she'd made. In a city overrun with corruption, at a time when no one was who they claimed to be, the Black Amaranth was that rarest of blooms: a person of honour who always told me the truth.

'People die for reasons far beyond your intervention, Damelas,' she said gently.

I shook my head. 'You're wrong, don't you see? All my life, I have run from fights. You think the Vixen was the first person to call me Rabbit? People have been calling me worse than that since I was ten years old. My own grandmother hated my cowardice. But you know what she never understood? Nobody got hurt because of me. Nobody *died* because of me.' I tore the silver Veristor's mark from my collar. 'Had I run from this, had I fled the city and ignored Corbier's voice in my head, Roz would be alive. Shoville would be alive.' I hurled the silver brooch to the ground. 'Tell me I'm wrong and I'll come with you,

Shariza. I'll bow before the duke and do his bidding – only tell me that doing so will prevent more of my friends from dying.'

She held my gaze, not turning away as others might when forced to confess an ugly truth. Even now her eyes weren't soft, not even with the faint glimpse of tears there. 'You know I can't, Damelas.'

I nodded, determined to hold my tongue to keep from saying something that would for ever break whatever tenuous thread bound us together. But my skin was still blistered from the fire and my lungs still ached from the smoke. Corbier's mocking voice was drowned by the roars and screams of men and women killing and dying for no reason I could see, save that they, just like Shariza, were doing what they believed was their duty.

'Then do what you came to do, my Lady,' I said. 'Follow the script without restraint or remorse. Play your part.'

Her lips tightened and I saw tiny wrinkles at the corners of her eyes that I'd never noticed before. 'You speak to me as if I had no heart, as if I were a wind-up toy that goes in whatever direction it is pushed. But you're wrong, Damelas: I do have a heart, and if ever I questioned that before, you've removed all my doubts, because these cold, cruel words that slip so easily off your tongue are breaking it!'

Stop now, I told myself. *Drop to your knees, kiss her hand and beg forgiveness. How hard must it be for someone who's lived a life like hers to confess such vulnerability? If Beretto were here, he'd shout at you to admit to her – and yourself – that you love her, that the distinctions between you don't matter. If Grandfather were here, he'd remind you that the difference between a boy and a man is grace.*

But I wasn't Beretto, nor was I Paedar Chademantaigne. A fire had brought down the Operato Belleza tonight and somewhere under its ruins, the body of Hujo Shoville still smouldered.

So I said, 'I fear, my Lady, that a heart is a terribly inconvenient organ for one in your profession. You should thank me for ridding you of it, as I thank your master for ridding me of mine.'

I never saw her reaction, or if tears had come to her eyes; instead I closed my own and spread my arms wide. 'I'm ready,' I said.

I barely felt the blow that rendered me unconscious.

CHAPTER 51

THE DUKE AND THE DULLARD

I awoke, slumped in the embrace of an unexpectedly comfortable chair, to a blurry vision of alabaster and gold splendour. Despite being seated, I felt oddly tall, until a glance down at my feet revealed the three marble steps elevating me above the floor. I squeezed the arms of the chair, my fingers luxuriating in the soft padded covering. Closer inspection revealed a lustrous silvery velvet embroidered with blue flowers. Pertines, in fact.

Well, that makes sense, doesn't it?

I couldn't quiet my wheezy laugh. Burned by fire, beaten by Iron Orchids, knocked unconscious by the Black Amaranth herself, and now I found myself lounging upon the Violet Duke's own throne.

And for my first act as ruler of this misbegotten duchy, I thought drunkenly, *I hereby decree that everyone must stop naming themselves after flowers.*

'Damelas?'

My bleary-eyed gaze followed the voice until I located the first supplicant in what would no doubt be a long and illustrious reign.

'Ah, Firan, old chum, here at last,' I bellowed enthusiastically. 'Now, I'm sure you're wondering why I summoned you . . .'

Duke Monsegino stepped into the moonlight shining through the magnificent curved panes of the throne room's domed ceiling. His Grace appeared to be covered head-to-toe in blood and ashes – that, or he was wearing a scarlet silk shirt beneath a long coat of rich black brocade. Possibly the latter made more sense.

'Are you all right?' the duke asked. 'You were . . . giggling.'

'Merely the unfortunate consequence of having gone mad some time ago, your Grace. Why, even now, as you visit me here in what I am certain must be a suitably dank and dispiriting dungeon, my shattered mind conjures up elaborate delusions in which I find myself – and do, I beg you, forgive the disrespectful nature of these hallucinations – seated upon a rather magnificent throne.'

'Less than a day ago I came to your dwelling and found the experience . . . enlightening,' the duke said without sarcasm. 'I hoped this conversation might be more constructive if you saw the world from my perspective.'

'And a fine perspective it is,' I said, patting the luxuriously upholstered arm of the throne. 'A perfect stage for what I assume is meant to be a bold new production of *The Duke and the Dullard*.'

'Excuse me?'

'Come now, Firan, your delightful aunt Kareija was at pains to tell me you were a lover of the theatre – surely you know the play?' I leaned back against the throne and stretched out my legs, crossing one ankle over the other and gazing dreamily up at the night sky through the glass dome. 'We begin with a melancholy monarch, new to his crown and yet already weary of its many demands. Desperate for distraction, he offers his chamberlain . . .' – I gestured absently at Monsegino – 'a bold wager: "Half my treasury will I stake upon my contention that so little is the regard given a duke in this benighted country that any dullard"' – I jerked a thumb at myself – '"could sit this throne a full year and not a single member of my court prove the wiser."'

Monsegino's lips pressed together, suggesting there were limits to even a duke's patience.

I was of a mind to test those limits further. 'Now, our chamberlain, exasperated by his liege's contemptuous regard for the crown, decides to teach him a lesson. While the duke is away, finalising his marriage to a foreign princess, the chamberlain scours the land until he finds the most gullible man in the entire country – one who just happens to look exactly like the duke – and seats him on the throne.'

'Damelas, in deference to your losses, I've humoured this long eno—'

'Humour?' I pointed to the duke with one hand while touching the tip of my nose with the forefinger of the other. 'Exactly so, your Grace, because you recall what happens next, don't you?'

'That is *enough*. Your rendition of the Clever Jester routine is no doubt highly entertaining, but I brought you here t—'

I stamped my foot down on the throne's marble pedestal and gave a roar of royal outrage worthy of Abastrini. 'You dare speak to your liege this way? I asked you a question, impudent lout: what happens in the final act of *The Duke and the Dullard*?'

The seconds ticked away in silence until finally Monsegino yielded. 'The duke returns to find the dullard's haphazard rule far more auspicious than his own, with the land now prosperous and its people joyous.'

I clapped my hands together. 'Just so.'

The muscles of Monsegino's jaw tightened visibly. When he spoke next, it was through clenched teeth. 'Are you trying to provoke me into imprisoning you, Damelas?'

I'll admit I was dimly aware that exhaustion and heartache were a poor defence against a duke's wrath. But the Belleza's embers still burned in my throat.

I rose from the throne, carefully descended the three steps to the marble floor and bowed as deeply as my aching bones would allow. 'Imprison me, your Grace?' I asked. 'What the fuck do you think you've been doing up till now?'

Monsegino's fist clenched, his hand rose and I waited for a blow that never came. Allowing his arm to sag at his side, the duke asked, 'Is it the foolish, broken heart of Damelas Chademantaigne who mocks me thus, or the reckless spirit of the Red-Eyed Raven?'

'A distinction without a difference at this stage, wouldn't you agree?'

The two of us watched each other in silence, then the duke sighed. 'Insolence from an actor calls for swift punishment. If, however, it is Archduke Corbier who compels your words . . .' The barest hint of a smile crossed the duke's lips. 'Well, technically, he outranks me.'

I couldn't tell if this was meant to be a joke – if it was, it wasn't very funny – but for some reason, I laughed anyway, and soon we were both chortling like schoolboys.

'Your Grace is wasted on the throne,' I said, trying to catch my breath. 'A great future awaits you in the comedias.'

Monsegino, barely able to get the words out, giggled in a most unducal fashion. 'What, and trade the crown of iron spikes my enemies have planned for me for a mere jester's cap? A man of my rank must maintain his dignity, you know!'

At first, the sense of release was overwhelming, unexpected, undeserved and unimaginably welcome, but I couldn't seem to stop laughing, until deep-bellied glee became uncontrollable sobbing. My legs went out from under me and I fell to my knees, prostrated on the marble floor like a grovelling courtier. Shame overwhelmed me as I wept before the man whose political machinations, however well intended, had contributed to the death of bold, ribald Roslyn and gentle, earnest Shoville, and so many others besides.

A tentative hand patted my shoulder, then pulled away, as if ordinary comfort was a foreign language. Retreating to the safer ceremonial dignity of his office, Monsegino said, 'You have the condolences of the Duchy of . . .' He hesitated. 'Hells, Damelas – I never meant for *any* of this to happen, not to you or to your friends. I wish . . .'

A long silence elapsed until at last the duke's more formal, commanding tone returned. 'You have to finish the play, Damelas – you must dive one last time into Corbier's past and return with the secret of the Court of Flowers.'

'And what do the dead get for their trouble?' I asked, my words quick and sharp, delivered like a slap to the duke's dignity.

'Excuse me?'

'You said I had your condolences, your Grace. A generous gift indeed, but what do the dead get? Free funerals? Spouses and children spared the high cost incurred even for the meagre death rites merited by common players?'

The duke rose to his feet. 'If they wish it.'

'A pension, perhaps? Can't have the households of patriotic artists go hungry when winter comes, can we?'

Monsegino walked to a table near the wall by the great windows opening onto the courtyard below. He poured wine from a painted ceramic flagon into a simple bronze goblet. 'Are we negotiating now, Master Chademantaigne? Are you expecting promises of wealth? A position at court, perhaps? Maybe the arrest and execution of the Margravina di Traizo before she finally kills either you or your grandfather? Tell me, what will it cost me to have you perform your duty to your sovereign and your city?'

I considered the question. There was a certain pleasure to be had in envisioning the gratitude of the most powerful person in all of Pertine. Unfortunately, I'd yet to make that person's acquaintance. I scratched at an itch at the back of my neck which turned out to be dried blood. It wasn't my own, but whether it belonged to friend or foe, I would never know. Staring back at the duke, I said, 'Corbier would've liked that coat.'

'What?'

'Your coat. Corbier would've liked it. You have similar tastes in clothing.'

Monsegino plucked at his lapel. 'I don't understand. You want my coat?'

'No, your Grace, I merely suggest you consider the role of the Red-Eyed Raven for yourself; find a nice stage somewhere – alas, the Belleza's is no longer available – and reveal whatever "truth" pleases you.'

The duke swirled the wine in his goblet before draining it in one swig. 'I shouldn't have stopped you playing the Clever Jester, Damelas. Your portrayal of the Hapless Naïf lacks conviction.'

'I'll drop my mask when you drop yours, your Grace.'

Monsegino turned back to refill his goblet. 'I am willing to negotiate, but I will not be made to beg.' He drank this one as quickly as the first, then poured a third. With his free hand, he gestured to the throne. 'A line of nobles a mile long come to me *every* day, offering their counsel – their *advice* – and each one leaves convinced they've wound me around their little finger.' He lifted the goblet to his lips, then stopped. 'Behind my back they call me "the Violet Duke" and mock me as a foreigner, but all they accomplish by that is to remind me that I am both an outsider *and* the lawful ruler of Pertine.'

He drained his goblet, and reached for the decanter before finishing, 'You *will* perform the final act and you *will* use your Veristor's gift to unearth the secrets I need to unmask the Court of Flowers. I will not allow the Iron Orchids to pose as rebels when we both know they are something far more devious and dangerous. The truth lies somewhere in Corbier's past and I *must* know the answer. Mock me all you want, Damelas, but I am still the damned Duke of Pertine and so long as I reign, that which I command *will* come to pass.'

The duke might have intended to convey strength, but his words betrayed only weakness. Perhaps Shariza was right and he was a decent man underneath it all, but it didn't matter. I was done risking the lives of those I loved, especially on someone whose golden crown would soon be replaced with iron spikes.

'Thank you for allowing me to sit on your throne, your Grace,' I said, 'but I'm done playing *The Duke and the Dullard* with you.'

'Damn your arrogance! Can't you see I'm trying to save this cursed duchy before it's too late?'

I looked up in time to see the goblet come flying through the air, a trail of ruby-red drops splattering in its wake. The duke's aim was remarkably accurate. The bronze rim struck me square on the forehead. As the goblet clattered to the marble floor, my fingers went to my brow. They came away smeared with blood – my own this time.

'A blow well struck, your Grace.'

'Saints, man – On my honour, I didn't mean to . . .'

The apology trailed away. Monsegino's face hardened and at last he retook his throne. I didn't hear him shout for his guards or ring a bell, but he must have given some signal, because the doors burst open, a dozen armed soldiers poured in, and within seconds I was wrapped in chains and on my knees before the throne.

'Neither of us chose our roles, Damelas, but we must both play them until the final curtain falls.'

At his gesture, the guards lifted me into the air, not even granting me the dignity of walking myself to whichever cell they had ready for me. I relaxed in their grip, imagining myself borne aloft on a luxurious palanquin.

'A piece of advice then, your Grace, from one player to another: beware of getting too comfortable in your role. That's always when another actor comes to take it away from you.'

CHAPTER 52

THE BARS

Crouched in a suitably dank cell, my back pressed against the cold iron bars, I passed the time scratching with my fingernails at the blood and muck that was threatening to become a permanent part of my skin. The guards had left behind a jug of water for the second night in a row, an unusual kindness, given the point of locking up a man for refusing to obey a ducal order was, presumably, to change his mind. I'd drunk half the water, but kept the rest to scrub as much of myself as possible.

Lacking both light and a mirror, I stopped every few minutes to run my fingertips over my skin, trying to tell if it felt clean, or if I needed to keep exhuming more of the man I'd been before the battle of the Belleza – before all of this madness had started.

'The flaying of prisoners is typically the job of a trained torturer. Shouldn't you leave such abuses to the professionals?'

The whisper came so close to my ear that only the grace of a generous saint prevented me leaping away from the bars like a panicked rabbit.

I guess she really was being polite two nights ago when she allowed me to hear her walking up to me.

'Just an itch,' I said. 'Possibly fleas.'

'Over every square inch of your body?'

I leaned back nonchalantly against the bars, still refusing to look at her. 'Has no one ever told you it's impolite to spy on a condemned man? How long have you been hiding there?'

'Not so long,' she replied, but I caught the defensiveness in her tone. 'I didn't want to . . . it seemed important to you, this obsessive cleansing.'

'It's a ritual my grandmother did when she returned from a mission. She wanted to make sure she brought none of the violence and despair of her travels into our lives.' A troubling thought occurred to me. 'My Lady, are you here for my execution?'

The heavy silence that had me holding my breath was broken by the rasping sound of an amberlight match being struck. A brief flash of light reflected on the back wall of my cell, followed by the flickering of a torch that floated in mid-air until it came to a stop in what I guessed was an iron holder.

With my back still to the bars, I watched the play of light against the rough stone of the cell wall, imagining myself sitting in the alley outside the Belleza with Grey Mags and Zina, boasting that I couldn't stay long, for the vital role of the herald awaited me upon that sacred stage. I stayed like that a while, waiting for whatever came next. If Shariza had been sent to kill me, well, it was just a shame it would happen so far from the Belleza and my friends.

The Black Amaranth finally answered my question with one of her own. 'Were I here to execute you, would I tell you?'

The words were glib, the tone light, but something lurked underneath. Hurt? Resentment? I couldn't tell. Maybe I'd never been able to tell and all those conflicted emotions I'd allowed myself to believe were at play within her had been nothing but a tale I'd been telling myself to lessen the ache of my own longing.

'I suppose not,' I replied, 'although I must confess, I've little experience with Dashini assassins.'

She sighed, and I felt her shoulders press against mine as she sat back to back with me on the other side of the bars. Her dark curls tickled my neck.

'I'm done apologising, Damelas Chademantaigne.'

'I hadn't realised you'd begun.'

'I never hid from you what I am, nor what I do. We all have our roles to play and I have played mine with as much dignity and decency as my profession allows. I would think you of all people would understand that.'

Guilt made my skin itch. Or maybe it really was fleas. 'That's the thing, my Lady – when it comes down to it, I've never been a particularly good actor.'

Her shoulders shifted and then her fingers reached back to touch my cheek. 'I cannot speak for the rest of your audiences, but I have often found your performances unexpectedly charming.'

My first instinct was to pull away. The fire that had left the Operato Belleza in ruins was still smouldering inside me; people I cared about had died. But I had no way to punish the Iron Orchids and whoever led them, nor even Duke Monsegino, and I found I lacked the will for pettiness.

'Shoville once told me that no actor could come to grips with their character until he appreciated all their . . . *incongruities*.'

'What did he mean?'

'I didn't really understand at the time – all the herald had to do was to walk to the middle of the stage and deliver a handful of words. Who in all the Hells cares about the damned herald anyway? I thought he was just . . . you know, being Shoville.'

'And now?'

'Now I understand what he was talking about – how someone can be two opposing things at once. That's what makes us human.'

Feeling her callused fingertips on the soft skin of my neck, I found myself enjoying the . . . *contradictions*. Shariza was as deadly as the God Death himself, yet often almost needlessly gentle with me. She'd allowed me so many chances to peer through the cracks of her mask, offering a look or a smile that felt like a doorway to the hidden part of her, inviting me inside.

My grandfather always said, 'Love is an onion, my boy. Leave it too long and the heart of it will rot. So you've got to carefully peel back the layers until you find beneath something so beautiful it brings you to tears.'

I could almost hear my grandmother groaning at his misty-eyed sentimentality.

'Damelas?'

Hearing her say my name made me realise I'd been mumbling. It also made me realise how much better I liked my name when she was the one saying it, which brought to mind a question I'd been pondering for some time. 'Is Shariza your real name?' I asked.

'No.'

'Too bad,' I said. 'I rather like it.'

The ensuing silence cooled the air between us. I wondered if perhaps I'd offended her. It would be typical if my grandfather's advice got me into trouble with a Dashini assassin. But then I felt her shoulders settle against mine once more. Were it not for the iron bars between us, I might have imagined the two of us an old married couple sitting together in front of the fire recounting the petty trials of our day.

I couldn't see her smile, but I heard it in her voice when she said, 'Then Shariza I will be.'

All I wanted was to sit here, pretending for a while we really were those people, but I couldn't.

Leave it too long and the heart of it will rot. So you've got to carefully peel back the layers.

I forced myself to my feet, hurting as much from where I'd scrubbed my skin too fiercely as from my injuries. I turned to face her through the bars. She had risen too, considerably more gracefully.

'There's something I've been wondering,' I said.

In the dim light I couldn't quite make out the subtle changes to her face. I hoped it was a smile and not a look of profound dread over what stupid thing I might say next.

She spoke first. 'You're wondering if what happened between us on stage belonged to Corbier and Ajelaine, or whether some part of it was ours.'

I nodded.

'Damelas, the Dashini are forged as weapons. Our hearts are trained to be still, our passions unfelt. Questions of love and desire belong to a life I've never known.'

'Oh.'

She reached out and stroked my jaw, then her thumb and forefinger pinched my chin and she shifted my head a little. 'So I'm afraid we'll have to find our answers the hard way.'

She pulled me closer until our lips met between the bars. The dungeon's dry air caused a spark between us and I almost pulled away, but Shariza's hand was at the back of my neck now and she held me close, her mouth still on mine, giving, but not soft. I liked that about her. She wasn't pliant, the way most women assumed men expected them to be, nor demanding, as Roslyn had been during our stage kiss. Shariza didn't moan or whisper to me; there was no performance to it, only breath and desire and playfulness. The intimacy of a thousand, thousand words passed between us in those short moments . . . but all too soon, I felt her pull away.

Only as I was searching her eyes for some sign of what I'd done wrong did I hear two sets of footsteps echoing down the passageway.

'I have to leave you now,' she said. 'The duke has many enemies and I must visit a few of them tonight.'

I grabbed her hand. 'I need a favour.'

'Ask it.'

'Monsegino will be looking for ways to force me to finish the play. I'm not asking you to betray him, but if he . . . Shariza, if he ever asks you to pay one of your "visits" to Paedar Chademantaigne, I beg you, refuse him.'

She held my gaze a moment, then leaned her forehead against mine. 'Oh Damelas, I do wish you hadn't waited until now to ask this of me.'

'What? Shariza, please, tell me you didn't . . . He's an old man! He neve—'

The footsteps were getting closer and I realised I'd misheard them earlier: it wasn't two people, but one, with the addition of a metal-shod cane striking a regular beat against the uneven stone floor. I didn't need to see the figure rounding the corner to recognise that familiar gait.

'Grandfather?'

CHAPTER 53

THE KING'S COURTESY

'Well, my boy,' the old man on the other side of the bars started, leaning on his cane. His lined face split into a grin. 'See what comes of ignoring your grandfather's warnings about the perils of the stage?'

'You never warned me of any such thing! In fact, wasn't it you who sent me to drama school? Grandmother was dead set against it.'

'Really? I remember it differently.'

I banged my forehead against the iron bars separating us. 'You remember *everything* differently! That's why no one ever believes your stories.'

My grandfather chuckled. He had a reedy, wheezing voice, but when he laughed, the rich, resonant baritone could fill a canyon.

'What's so funny?' I asked.

The old man clanged the metal ferrule of his cane against the bars. 'Seems to me that the problem here is far too many people believing *your* stories.'

Shariza placed a hand on the sleeve of his worn leather greatcoat. 'I'll leave the two of you to catch up.'

'What nonsense is this?' Paedar demanded, covering her hand with his. 'Abandoning me to my felonious grandson's slanders before you've heard even one of my righteous tales? I am relying on you, fair maiden, to judge whether man or boy is the more charming storyteller.'

'I fear, Master Chademantaigne, that your grandson is no boy, I am no maiden, and that my duties await.'

His grin reappeared as he winked at her. 'And I daresay this would be a bad time to leave the duke without his finest protector.'

She gave him a wry smile in return. 'Indeed, I'm informed he's already been challenged to a duel he'd prefer not to fight.'

'Then until we meet again, my dear.' He released her hand at last, then offered her a bow so deep it belied his need for a stick. They hadn't called him the King's Courtesy for nothing.

After Shariza had left, Grandfather dragged over a stool and settled himself close to the bars. 'I like that girl. Do tell me there's a wedding in the offing.'

'I've known her barely a week.'

He shrugged. 'So what? I'm an old man, in case you hadn't noticed, and your grandmother's been gone a long time now. If I'm to meet a new wife before I meet my undertaker, I'll need to seduce a large number of women to select the right one. Weddings are excellent occasions for such noble endeavours.'

'So I'm to believe this concern for my own marital status *isn't* about my failure to provide you with a permanently captive audience for your stories in the form of a brood of great-grandchildren?'

The old man waved the suggestion away. 'Why would I care about that? Your decrepit grandfather just wants to get laid before he croaks.'

Despite the dire circumstances and the dim prospects for my future, my grandfather never failed to make me smile. I reached through the bars to clasp his hand. 'I'm sorry it's been so long since I came home, and even sorrier you had to find me in this place.'

'Don't be silly,' he said, shaking my hand loose. 'What man *doesn't* want his grandson's mysterious paramour – by the way, that girl's a delight, and utterly mad for you, but I suspect she might be a Dashini – where was I? Oh yes, to have her show up at his humble dwelling to inform him his grandson sits rotting in a dungeon beneath the Ducal Palace of Pertine?'

'I really am sorr—'

'Pah! Enough with your apologies, boy. Incarceration by the local duke is a badge of honour in our family. Lords and viscounts, margraves, margravinas and daminas – sooner or later they all want to lock us up for getting in their way. Why, if I told you how often I'd found your grandmother chained inside some Hellish cell awaiting a noose around her neck, you'd call me a liar.'

'I call you that anyway, you old reprobate.' I glanced at the sturdy iron bars between us. 'But now that you mention it, how did you get Grandmother out so many times?'

'Well, that's the job, isn't it? Sometimes I negotiated a deal, sometimes I bribed the guards. This one time, when she was stuck up north, I recruited a band of Avarean mercenaries and we blew up the prison. Ah, fun times.' He reached into one of the greatcoat's capacious pockets. 'Most jailbreaks, though, simply involved one of these.' He held up a polished iron key on a scarlet ribbon.

'You have a key to the palace dungeon?'

He grinned. 'Boy, I have keys to half the gaols in Tristia. Sometimes your grandmother and I would get arrested just so we could sneak in greenwax to make a mould of the locking mechanism. After all, you never know when you might need to make a speedy exit.' He held the key up to the light. 'But this one I got from his Grace upstairs.'

'Duke Monsegino *gave* you a key? He only just had me imprisoned two days ago! Why would he—?' I shuddered to a halt as Shariza's words a few minutes before resurfaced. 'Grandfather, tell me you didn't—'

He made a show of pursing his lips. 'Well, you know, I'd begged an audience that I might plead your case, but the man was paying me barely any attention and his lackwit advisors kept droning on and on, some nonsense about "legal impediments" and "precedence" and all that rot. Can you imagine? Some needle-necked bureaucrat instructing *me* on the law?'

'So you challenged the Duke of Pertine to an honour duel? Grandfather, Monsegino's hanging onto power by the barest thread. He might've had you killed on the spot. Besides, even I know there's no legal requirement for a nobleman to accept the challenge of a commoner.'

The recalcitrant old rogue rose from the stool and asked haughtily, 'Oh? You think these dukes and viscounts and margravinas don't know what happens when you mess with a Greatcoat?' He turned sideways to the bars, extended his stick as if it were a rapier and made a few shallow thrusts. 'Why, I'd have his Grace running like a chicken from a wolf around the duelling circle.' He took a step forward – and losing his balance, quickly brought the stick back down to catch himself. 'Truth be told, I think the duke just didn't want the publicity that would've come from skewering a retired magistrate in front of half his court. In fact, I have my suspicions that he may have acted in haste earlier and sent that lovely Dashini of his to get me so he'd have an excuse to free you.'

'You'd better hope that's true. Virany Chademantaigne would have had your hide for using your rank as a former Greatcoat to wheedle your grandson out of a cell.'

His expression turned solemn, his tone firm. 'Your grandmother would've torn the bars off this place to free you, boy.'

I stared down at the cracks in the floor of my cell. 'Only because she wouldn't have believed for a second that I might get myself out.'

'Because she loved you.'

I let it go. That particular subject could only bring us both pain. Instead, I forced a smile and asked, 'So, are you going to let me out of here, or did you just come to brag about your days as a Greatcoat?'

But my grandfather was notoriously hard to fool and refused the bait. His eyes, usually so full of mischief and good humour, took on the steady, steely glare he got before a duel began, when he was examining his opponent, separating the mask from the man.

'Grandfather?'

'Your grandmother *loved* you, Damelas,' he repeated. 'More than you can imagine.'

'I'm not—'

'But she never understood you.'

And there it was. He always did know how to goad me into losing my temper. 'My grandmother thought I was craven – a coward, a disgrace to the name of our ancestors. And you know what? She was right! She saw it in me from the moment she pulled me from my dying mother's womb. She tried to talk the cowardice out of me, train it out of me, even beat it out of me, but she always knew *exactly* what I was, Grandfather. It was you who never understood.'

The mark of a skilled fencer is how they react to their opponent's thrusts and counter-attacks. The mark of a duellist, however, is in the way they ignore the enemy's feints. My grandfather didn't show the slightest sign that I'd even spoken.

'Do you remember when you were six and we enrolled you in that school at the Monastery of Saint Anlas?'

'Another of your stories?' I slammed my palms against the bars. 'Has your addled old mind forgotten that you're standing in a dungeon and I'm imprisoned in a cell?'

'Then maybe you'll listen for once.' He sat back down on the stool, rested his chin on his cane and closed his eyes, lost in remembrances of times past. 'One of those little monkling bastards – smallest of the lot, as I recall – jumped you outside in the cloister.'

'They thought I had money because only nobles sent their children to study at the monastery, so the other boys figured I must have something worth taking.'

'Got to love the spiritually minded, eh? Anyway, the ugly pup – what was his name?'

'I don't remember.'

'Tintus Salaco.'

'Why did you ask if—?'

He dismissed the question. 'We never told you this, but your grandmother and I spied on you those first few weeks at the school. Couldn't help ourselves.' He pinched his leather collar. 'Wear one of these long enough and people look for ways to get at you through those you love. Anyway, we watched those boys jeering at you and little Tintus in the middle of the circle. Pissant little brat sucker-punched you before anyone had even called the fight to begin.'

'Schoolyard brawls are woefully lax in their adherence to proper duelling etiquette.'

Paying no attention to my sarcasm, he continued, 'Exactly. Anyway, there you were, what? A foot taller than Tintus? The grandson of two Greatcoats – and by then your grandmother had taught you a few of the dirty tricks she was famous for. But you—'

'—ran away,' I finished for him. 'Yes, I ran away to cry in my room.'

'Exactly,' he repeated.

My head sagged against the bars. 'And you and Grandmother saw it all? No wonder she kept forcing those damned lessons on me.'

The iron ferrule scraped on the ground and I felt the warmth of my grandfather's hands enclosing my own fingers. 'She saw how frightened you were and she didn't want you to be scared. She didn't understand the real reason you ran. But I knew. I always knew.'

'Grandfather, please . . .'

The old man's hands squeezed around mine. 'You were afraid – but not of that little wretch's blows. Even as he laughed and spat on you, calling you every dirty name in the book, that sensitive nature of yours told you he was terrified, practically wetting himself. You've always had that talent, Damelas – to see deeper into people, to hear the meanings buried under their words. You knew that if you punched the boy back, the others wouldn't let you stop until you'd beaten him bloody; that's just the way children are. So you ran away, Tintus Salaco got to be a hero to his friends and no one else got hurt.'

'You're remembering it wrong, Grandfather. You always remember things wrong.'

'All these years you've been telling yourself – and anyone else who would listen – what a coward you are, how feeble, how pathetic with a blade. And why not? As long as Damelas Chademantaigne is a proper coward, no one will ever expect him to become a Greatcoat like his grandmother. No one will ever expect him to fight duels. No one will ever expect him to *hurt* people.'

'*No one will expect him to protect the ones he loves,*' I heard myself say aloud, my voice so thick with Corbier's guttural disdain it shocked me. 'Forgive me, Grandfather. I didn't mean t—'

'Is this the great Archduke Corbier? The Red-Eyed Raven come to take credit for deeds not his own?' His eyes pierced through mine.

'*I saved your craven grandson's life, you old fool – I lent him the skill and nerve he lacked. I gave him—*'

Paedar reached through the bars and smacked me across the forehead. 'Oh, do shut up, you preening crow.'

With an effort of will, I forced back the Archduke's ire. 'Grandfather, please don't antagonise him.'

He laughed. 'Or what? You think some ancient spirit will overtake you, make you reach through those bars and throttle me?'

'He almost made me kill once before. And besides, he's right. Corbier's saved my life a dozen times now. The Vixen, the Iron Orchids who burned the Belleza – any one of them would've killed me but for Corbier—'

The old man spat on the floor. 'That for your great archduke.' He spat again. 'And that for Prince Pierzi – for all of them. Just like noblemen to believe that even in death they can take credit for the achievements of others!'

'Grandfather, honestly, you didn't see the way I fought. I actually beat the gods-damned Vixen in a duel!'

He shrugged as if the feat were insignificant. 'So what? Your grandmother had you fencing from the age of six. She taught you her tricks – the disarms, the distractions – and you were always clever, and quick, too. I imagine you've kept up with your rapier work?'

'Well . . . a little,' I admitted, thinking back to the countless practice bouts with Beretto. 'But to face the Vix—'

He waved the objection away. 'Oh, I've no doubt the Red-Eyed Raven was as devilish a master with the blade as the history books claim, and no doubt his memories helped here and there, but my boy' – the old man slid the key into the lock on the iron door – 'I think the only thing Corbier really gave you was an excuse.'

'An excuse?'

'He let you believe that perhaps it was someone else holding that sword – someone else doing the lunging and thrusting. *Someone else hurting people.*'

What morbid sentimentality, Corbier said silently. *An old man's dream of finding his dead wife's daring in the eyes of his grandson.*

Is he wrong, then? Was it your bloodlust I felt, or was it me all along?

But the Red-Eyed Raven gave no answer.

The lock gave up with a clank and he pulled open the door. 'Let's get out of here, boy. This place is making me nostalgic for the old days.'

I picked up my filthy shirt from the floor and gingerly pulled it over my battered torso. 'What happens now?'

'Now? We leave the city. I know a smuggler or two who owe me favours. They'll sneak us out in a caravan before anyone's the wiser.'

He smirked. 'Think of it, boy, you and me, on the road, breaking hearts and kicking arses.'

I looked past my grandfather's cavalier good looks, undiminished by wrinkles or the age spots on his leathery skin, to the mischief in his upturned mouth and twinkling eyes. Even now, well into his seventh decade, the King's Courtesy could fool just about anyone.

But not his grandson.

I started laughing.

'One night in a cell and already you've turned into a raving lunatic?'

'Grandfather, did you really expect me to believe that you came all the way here, fed me all that nonsense about how I was never really a coward, just so incomparably noble that I didn't want to hurt anyone – all so that you and I would then abandon the city that you and Grandmother fought so long and hard to protect?'

He looked more serious than I had ever seen him. 'That was different. When you're ready to take up the fight – really and truly ready to give it your all – you must know deep inside what it is you're fighting for.'

'What did you and Grandmother fight for?'

'Virany fought for the truth.' He reached up and took the torch from the holder in the wall and handed it to me. 'A worthy enough reason, I suppose. But me? I only ever fight for love.' With his cane clacking on the stones, the old man started down the passageway. He paused then, waiting for me to catch up. 'Maybe it's time someone in this family found a way to fight for both.'

CHAPTER 54

GAOL BREAK

I followed my grandfather from the cells beneath the palace, through heavy, iron-banded doors, up increasingly wide staircases and along ever more gleaming halls until at last we reached the ground level and made for the gates to the courtyard and a semblance of freedom. The guards we passed glared, smirked or pretended to spit to mark our passing, all keeping their hands on the hilts of their weapons as if at any moment they might decide to execute the impudent commoners who dared leave the dungeon while still breathing.

My grandfather loved it. 'Feels just like the old days,' he murmured happily as he gave a polite nod to the retainer flanked by two spearmen who had reminded us – *twice* – that I hadn't been freed, only paroled on the duke's goodwill – and that I could be arrested again at any time without cause.

'How is that different from everyone else in this city?' I'd asked before my grandfather had shushed me and then gone about puffing up the retainer.

'Don't bother the gentleman with your silly questions, boy,' he had said, patting the fellow's chest repeatedly. 'He's a very important man, with a lot to do, yes? And we are fortunate for his generous nature.' He actually stopped to shake the retainer's hand, several times. 'Very important fellow. Our thanks, sir. Many, *many* thanks.'

After we'd gone, I couldn't help but give my grandfather a withering look. 'What was all that about? I thought they called you the King's Courtesy, not the King's Lickspittle.'

The old man had a veritable spring in his step now. 'Ah, I do miss it, my boy. The dirty looks, the whispers of "Trattari" or "tatter-cloak" from primping thugs with precious little brains and even less honour. The subtle hint that, at a moment's notice, they might draw their blades on you and then, well, anything could happen. Positively enriching!' He opened his left hand and showed me the three coins and two keys on his palm.

'You *pickpocketed* a ducal official?'

'He was rude,' my grandfather replied, as if that explained everything.

'Some magistrate,' I said, laughing despite my concerns for the potential cost of such brazenness. 'When next they need to replenish the Order of the Greatcoats, I know a few thieving alley-rats who would be more than qualified, if that's the standard.'

The old man huffed at that. 'Well, now, it's true that there are some . . . um . . . *regrettable* parallels in the skillsets required of both burglars and travelling magistrates, but if you knew the law at all, you'd have realised that fellow lied to us. All that nonsense about him having the ability to have us arrested and executed on his own remand? That's a crime, you know – "abuse of delegated authority" is the legal term in Pertine. Now, I *could* have taken him to court for it, proved my case, got a judgement against him for damages due to "infliction of undue distress or discomfort", but the lower courts are so backed up these days, I thought I'd just handle the matter myself.'

'By pickpocketing him?'

'Call it a fine. I believe a nice breakfast will remove all traces of my undue distress.'

As we passed beneath an arched passageway to the high-ceilinged foyer and the double doors that would lead out of the palace, I asked, 'What about the keys? Those looked like they were for the fellow's house and gate. How do they figure into your "undue distress"?'

'Ah, those. Well, if for any reason that fine gentleman should choose to use his authority to have my grandson arrested, detained or so much as jostled in the street, I'd be *extremely* distressed. I might even have to resort to using those same keys to pay him a visit and mete out a great deal of discomfort.'

I stopped and took a moment to identify the source of the unexpected lightness in my chest. 'You really are an excellent grandfather, you know that?'

The old man gave a little cough to mask the break in his voice as he adjusted his coat. 'I do have a certain patriarchal flair, don't I? Even when my fool of a grandson neglects to ask for my help.'

I grinned. 'Especially then, thank every saint dead and living.' I stood there, marvelling that after being condemned by a duke, I was about to walk out of the front gates a free man. 'I still can't believe you bluffed Monsegino into letting me go.'

My grandfather's smile was unusually sheepish. 'Well, my boy, truth be told, I did have a little help.' He walked on a few feet, then paused to balance the hook of his stick on his right wrist before shoving the ornately carved oak double doors until they swung open.

Outside, more than two dozen grim, determined faces were staring at us: ragtag players and beaten-down crew, every one of them bearing the marks of their ordeal during the fatal attack on the Belleza two nights ago. Despite the cuts, bruises, burns and broken limbs, each stood firm as stone, defiantly facing off the far more heavily armed guardsmen who were watching them warily.

Shoville was right all along, I thought. *They really are Knights of the Curtain.*

The dignity of the moment was shattered by the boisterous shouting of a certain red-bearded lunatic who pushed past our comrades, batting aside the pair of crossed spears barring his way as he raced up the stone steps.

A second later the breath was being squeezed out of me.

'Brother!' Beretto cheered, hugging me relentlessly. 'You're free – the doors of your prison thrown open, the shackles binding you unleashed—'

'Yes,' I wheezed, trying to escape from the iron grip long enough to take in a lungful of air. 'Though it doesn't feel that way at this precise moment.'

Rhyleis came up behind Beretto, a guitar slung across her back, looking mildly disappointed to find me free already.

Beretto finally put me down, only to start prodding at my chest in search of newly inflicted wounds to go with those already there. 'You don't look tortured. Did they torture you?'

'Not as much as you're apparently intent on doing.'

I looked out at the others: Ornella, her silver hair now tied in a warrior's topknot, a quarterstaff in hand; Abastrini, looking faintly drunk, keeping one hand on the hilt of his broadsword as he stared menacingly at the duke's guards, apparently oblivious to the dirty, bloodstained sling supporting his injured left arm; Colm and Cileila, the carpenters, holding their largest hammers at the ready; Bida and Dalca, who used to spend all their time bickering over which of them should understudy for Roslyn's parts, now standing shoulder to shoulder with daggers drawn. Even tall, gangly Teo, perpetually sullen, loomed there, prepared to do battle alongside his comrades to help free me. Every one of them bore twin charcoal stripes down their cheeks.

'What have they got on their faces?' I asked, only now noticing Beretto had them too.

He took out a small brown cloth bag and opened the drawstrings before holding it out to me. 'Ashes,' he replied with grim determination. 'From the Belleza.'

'The Orchids took her from us,' Ornella said, steel in her voice, 'and they took our Hujo.'

'Nearly took all of us,' Teo added.

'Aye,' Abastrini grunted, coming to the front. 'And what answer do we give, Lord Director?'

My feet were edging backwards. My grandfather's hand pressed against my back to keep me from retreating further.

'*Me?*' I asked incredulously. 'I'm no director – I'm not even much of an actor!'

'That much we knew,' Teo muttered.

That sparked uproarious laughter.

'Listen!' I shouted, fearful that their desperate mirth was blinding them to the danger they proposed. 'I can't lead you all into some grand battle. We haven't the numbers, and even if we did, the Orchids are just puppets; they're nothing but a symptom of the disease. The true enemy tearing our city apart is this damned "Court of Flowers" – and they've been hiding in the shadows for generations! I can't . . . There's no way to—'

How could I make them understand? It was all too big, the secrets too long buried. What hope did a troupe of actors have fighting shadows from the past? But as I stood there in front of them, it became painfully clear to me that nothing could deter the Knights of the Curtain from this holy mission they were on.

Abastrini pumped his fist in the air. 'Then history itself is our battlefield, and on such hallowed and haunted ground must a Veristor lead the charge!'

Beretto joined in with rising enthusiasm. 'The enemies of our city think they can hide their origins in its past? Then from the past shall we flush them out!'

Saint Zaghev-who-sings-for-tears, I thought. *Through death and misery they've trodden, a band of lowly actors, unbroken, unbowed.*

I turned to my grandfather. 'Was it like this with the Greatcoats?'

The old man shrugged. 'The speeches weren't usually so flowery – well, except for Falcio, the First Cantor, of course. But you're dealing with actors, so I suppose you've got to expect a little melodrama.'

For once I disagreed with my grandfather's blasé assessment. There was a stirring inside me, not only for the passion of my fellow cast and crew, but for what Abastrini had so keenly perceived: history *was* the battlefield. The truth lay buried there, and who but a Veristor could unearth it so that a company of actors who loved their art more than their own skins could bring the past back to life in front of the entire city?

Truth and love, I thought. *The only two things worth fighting for.*

Truth and love, Corbier unexpectedly agreed.

Will you help me? I asked.

The Red-Eyed Raven chuckled, for once without mockery. *It looks to me you have all the help you need, Veristor. A most unusual band of warriors, yet warriors as true as any who came before them.*

Damn right.

'Knights of the Curtain,' I cried out to them, 'we left our audience without an end to our play the other night – tell me, is this not cause for outrage?'

'Aye!' the others shouted.

'When our critics tell us, through fire and blood, that ours is a story not worth the telling, should we not give answer to that charge?'

'Aye!'

'When they burn down our home and murder our director to keep us from staging our play – and that for an audience of but a paltry few hundred inside a rickety old theatre – shall we not instead share that truth before the entire city?'

'Aye!' they roared. '*Aye! Aye! AYE!*'

The guards inched away, apparently no longer quite so determined to strike a threatening pose before this bristling crew. I stuck two fingers inside the bag of ashes Beretto was holding out to me and very deliberately drew my own charcoal lines down one cheek and then the other.

'I am Damelas Chademantaigne,' I said, and for the first time in my life, that name meant something – to me, to my friends, and soon, to my enemies as well. 'The foes of this city demand a duel? They have made a grievous error, for a duellist they have found.'

'Bloody right you are!' Ornella shouted.

'They want a war? Then by their own desires have they summoned their doom, for we will show them an army.'

'The noblest ever assembled!' Abastrini declared.

'They seek to hide in the shadows?'

I paused, and the others waited, watching me with bated breath. So too did the guards, who had moved to the sides in what might almost be interpreted as respect.

'Well then,' I said, dropping from my voice any further bombast, for none is needed when speaking the plain truth, 'they've made the worst mistake of all: for we are *actors*, and bringing the past to life is the very nature of our art. We see deeper than others, we look upon the truth without fear – and nothing – *nothing* – can long hide from our gaze.'

Holding my ashy fingers out to my fellow Knights of the Curtain, I declared, 'We will spread the word to every corner of every street, to the highborn and the low, the wealthy and the destitute. Tonight at last will the truth of Corbier, Pierzi and Ajelaine be told. And the secret that bound them – the mask concealing those who conspire against this city – will be revealed!'

Their cheers could have shattered glass windows. Within seconds they were dividing the city's districts between each other, while Rhyleis had started scribbling something in that notebook of hers, no doubt composing a suitably rousing congretto for the purpose.

'Alas, brother, there is one tiny problem,' Beretto said quietly to me. 'With the Belleza in ruins and every other company debasing themselves to the Iron Orchids, where are we supposed to stage a play that can house an audience of half the city?'

I turned to my grandfather. 'Approximately how discomfited was Duke Monsegino when you bullied him into freeing me?'

'Hard to say,' he replied after a thoughtful pause. 'Would you describe his usual skin colour as a sort of livid purple? He appeared to be distressed that his court might think he was being too indulgent towards an impertinent and quite possibly treasonous actor.'

I grinned, and turned to motion for the guards behind us to let me back into the palace. 'If he thought that was bad, he's really going to hate what comes next.'

PART THE SIXTH

The Veristor

In which our

DARING HERO,

uncovers at last the

MACHINATIONS OF HIS FOES,

alas, somewhat TOO LATE . . .

CHAPTER 55

SUITS OF ARMOUR

The duke kept me waiting three hours before a stiff-necked steward in a ruffled collar and violet coat announced, 'His Grace commands your presence within the Hall of Eminence upstairs.'

'The hall of what now?'

The lackey shot me a thin-lipped smirk that suggested my ignorance was entirely expected, then turned on his heels. 'This way, if you please,' he said, striding like a peacock towards the stairs.

The Hall of Eminence turned out not to be a hall at all, but a gallery on the topmost floor of the palace. On one side, two dozen gleaming suits of polished armour, each distinguished by its own distinctive gilded, enamelled and engraved ornamentation, stood like sentries upon marble pedestals. Names were inscribed on shining brass plaques beneath, and opposite was a row of stained-glass windows depicting battles in which each duke had clearly won the day. Single-handedly, judging by the tableaux.

I'd rather an actor or an alley-rat at my side than any of you lot, your Graces.

'I should have you thrown back in your cell,' Duke Monsegino said, staring out of one of the stained-glass windows.

He was more plainly dressed than I'd ever seen him, in a collarless black shirt over black trousers. No cloak. No crown, although he was still wearing the heavy silver bracelet around his left wrist I'd first noticed when he'd played the role of a carriage driver the first night we'd met. As he'd done then, he removed a tiny blue-glass vial from one of the silver cylinders and drank from it, wincing. He rubbed at his eyes afterwards as if they were stinging.

'Your grandfather's challenge took me by surprise,' he went on, bending to peer through one of the lighter panes at the crowds growing below. Merchants and labourers, artisans and artists, even the duke's less savoury subjects – small herds of nobles and their richly dressed families – were all shuffling into the courtyard of the Ducal Palace. 'But if you keep pushing me like this, Damelas, I swear I'll duel the pair of you myself.'

'You commanded a play, your Grace. We require a stage.'

'Not in my . . . *fucking* . . . courtyard,' Duke Monsegino swore awkwardly, pausing before and after the obscenity as if uttering that word represented an unconscionable but necessary sacrifice of his own dignity. 'Your request is denied. I command you to find some other theatre.'

I joined the duke at the window and tapped on the glass. The crowds were already more than enough to fill the largest of the city's operatos several times over. Word had spread quickly that the final act of the play everyone had been talking about was to be performed in the courtyard of the Ducal Palace itself – and was open to all-comers.

'I'm afraid it's too late to secure a different venue, your Grace. And I wasn't asking for permission.'

The singing that had begun an hour ago had been growing in volume and now, even up here, we could make out the song, something sad and majestic that spoke of love and loss in the past, and of a brave but troubled sovereign in the present, wrestling with the most difficult decision of his reign.

'Let me guess,' Monsegino said, scowling as the chorus came yet again. 'That wretched Bardatti Troubadour of yours is rousing them all with another of her bloody congrettos.' He paused, then asked, 'Or is it congretti? *Whatever*. Am I to be *for ever* cursed by that heinous woman's compositions?'

'Only if you speak to me in that tone again,' Rhyleis said pleasantly.

Monsegino and I spun in unison.

The Troubadour was leaning casually against one of the suits of armour. 'Oh, and the plural is indeed "congrettos", your Grace.'

'How in the name of Saint Forza-who-strikes-a-blow did you sneak in past my guards?' Monsegino demanded.

'Ah. I might have helped with that.' My grandfather emerged from the shadows opposite and brandished an oddly shaped triangular key. 'Did old Meillard not show you the secret tunnels before he died? Excellent way to get in and out of the palace unnoticed. Every duke should have them. Especially the unpopular ones.'

'Why are the gods themselves so plaguing me with actors, Troubadours and bloody-minded Greatcoats?' Monsegino complained. 'Are you really so blind, Damelas? Can you not see my rule is hanging by the frayed threads of those few paltry accords Kareija has been able to negotiate with the great Houses to keep them from siding with whoever's running the Court of Flowers and their Iron Orchids? Now you're asking me to humiliate myself before those very families – who already see me as an illegitimate foreigner – by stuffing my courtyard with hoodlums and drunkards?'

'Strictly speaking, your Grace, the lad doesn't require your permission to use the Great Courtyard. Players of the grand operatos may stage performances in any public square where there is an urgent and earnest—'

'"—urgent and earnest importance to the public good", yes, Master Greatcoat, I'm well aware of this duchy's archaic traditions.' He gestured at the rapier hanging at the old man's side. 'Have you come to challenge me to another duel?'

The old man winked at Rhyleis as he replied, 'Only if you speak to me in that tone again, your Grace.'

After a few moments of uneasy silence, Duke Monsegino sighed in defeat. 'I doubt killing an old man in a duel would do much to win me the hearts of my people.'

'Losing to an old man would do even less for your reputation,' the King's Courtesy pointed out graciously.

The duke began pacing up and down the gallery, stopping to stare now and then at the suits of armour, as if hoping his ancestors would step off of the pedestal and rid him of his tormentors. 'Very well,' he said at last, coming to a stop in front of one breastplate so heavily gilded it might have been fashioned of gold instead of steel. 'I grant you permission to stage the final act of the play inside the Great Courtyard. However, I have a request of my own – and by "request", I mean something which you will do for me whether you like it or not.'

Here it comes, I thought. 'Your Grace, of course I would be delighted to honour any favour you might ask of me.'

'That fat fool Abastrini? He looks, talks and acts *nothing* like Prince Pierzi.'

'You mean, based on the historias?' I asked pointedly.

'What? Yes, of course, based on the historias – what else? It's an embarrassment, watching him waddle about with that great belly of his barely fitting inside his armour. Ellias Abastrini will not perform the role of the prince.'

I gave my grandfather a small shake of my head to keep him from intervening. This had been coming since that very first carriage ride, when the duke had used Shariza to find out why I'd botched the herald's line.

I played the game anyway. I joined him beside the suit of armour with the lion embossed on the breastplate. 'Your Grace, the performance is set to begin at nightfall. It is rather late for us to be casting another actor.'

'Oh, you won't need to search far.' Firan Monsegino began removing, piece by piece, his great-great-great grandfather's ceremonial armour from its mounting. 'I'll be playing the part of the prince myself.'

CHAPTER 56

THE STAGE

Five thousand people could comfortably fit within the Great Courtyard of Pertine's Ducal Palace. Fully twice that number were jammed inside the gates now, the heat from the press of bodies banishing the twilight chill. The stage, built for the duchy's ceremonial events, was carved from oak, with marble columns and ornate wings sweeping out on either side. A massive curved overhang not only protected the stage from the elements, but also projected the voices of those performing beyond the crowds and into the city streets.

'Makes the Belleza look like a shithole, doesn't it?' Teo asked, gazing around in awe as they waited in the wings.

Beretto favoured the young actor with an unpleasant smile. 'Say that again and I'll knock your teeth out, Teo.'

Like stagehands lifting the curtain, the clouds above began drifting away, revealing the first glimmers of a full moon and promising a sky full of stars to illuminate the performance.

I looked through the audience, trying to count those soldiers in the liveries of the great Houses, standing in squadrons – not so much scattered as positioned around the courtyard.

What secrets are you so worried about being revealed, my Lords and Ladies? Do any of you even know, or are you all unwittingly serving the Court of Flowers?

Captain Terine had her squad arranged in a semicircle in front of the stage, four rows of twenty grim-faced soldiers facing an uncountable horde who could overwhelm them in seconds, should the occasion arise. She was looking rather nervous about that possibility.

When a new figure strode up the stairs and into the wings, Beretto gasped and tugged my arm.

Duke Monsegino certainly did look the part of Pierzi, resplendent in shining, perfectly fitted armour. A heavy crimson cloak swung from gold cords threaded through metal loops welded to the pauldrons over his shoulders. The golden lion with ruby eyes embossed in the centre of his breastplate gleamed in the torchlight.

'Is that Prince Pierzi's *original* armour?' Beretto asked.

I nodded, wondering how many weeks it had taken the armourers to modify the pieces to fit him, for Monsegino was slighter than his ancestor.

You knew all along it would come down to the two of us at the end, didn't you, your Grace?

The crowds, catching sight of their gleaming duke, gasped in awe.

Abastrini sniffed. 'Well, of course, if *I'd* walked on stage wearing all that frippery, people would've taken me for the real Prince Pierzi, too.'

Beretto patted the actor's belly. 'If you came on stage in Pierzi's armour, Master Abastrini, that lion on the breastplate would be so stretched out it would look like a giant ruby-eyed frog.'

The two fell silent, watching the duke approaching us.

'Are you and your fellow actors ready, Master Veristor?' Monsegino asked.

I didn't answer, but instead led the duke away from the others so that no one would overhear us. 'When it begins, your Grace, you *must* remain in control. See what he sees, hear his words, but do *not* let him overwhelm you, else you'll lose yourself and be trapped inside his memories.'

Monsegino's eyes betrayed his shock. '*You know?* But—'

'Viscountess Kareija told me you adored the theatre as a child, and how you were driven to become an actor yourself, but were prevented by your aristocratic rank. Then, of course, there's the incongruity of Prince Pierzi's many-times-great-grandson obsessively pressuring us to present what's looking to be a pretty grim truth about the duchy's greatest hero. You hear his voice, don't you?'

The duke's shoulders slumped. 'Ever since I was a boy. I didn't understand what it was, not at first, but I loved the historias and sometimes

I'd get this . . . pounding in my head, as if . . . well, as if something – some*one* – was trying to break free. I didn't know who he was, only that when I saw the great plays of my family's history, I'd become nauseous and a great anger would come over me. It was always the same: I'd feel as if Pierzi was trapped in a single moment in time. Over the years, as I grew to understand my proper role as a nobleman of Pertine and gave up any thoughts of becoming an actor, it faded.'

He straightened. 'Until one night, when I happened to be sitting in the back of the upper gallery of the Operato Belleza. I was pleased – if surprised – to discover that *The Battle of Mount Cruxia* no longer afflicted me. But then a minor player came onto the stage to blurt out the same dull line I'd heard a dozen times before—'

'Only I screwed it up.'

'The moment you said those words, it was as if someone had awakened a long-sleeping bear in my skull, one who promptly went about smashing into the walls of his cave trying to escape. All the pain and fears and sickness I'd experienced as a boy returned a hundredfold.' He gripped me by the shoulder. 'This time I *have* to know the truth. Pierzi himself wants it revealed.'

I glanced at the crowds outside. Everyone was waiting to see the final part of the play – and what orders their masters would then give. 'You might have to pay a very high price to find out.' I looked pointedly at the soldiers.

The duke's laugh was bitter and brittle. 'Families like the di Traizos are the real rulers of this duchy. They always have been, despite the great lie that the duke sitting the throne is glorified by the gods and by the great deeds of his family.' Monsegino clutched his head as if to stop it splitting apart. 'Whatever secret is locked up inside my skull, the price of keeping it there is too high for me now. It's too high even for Prince Pierzi.'

Twilight gave way, and as full darkness cloaked the courtyard, the moon and stars above brightened, as if celestial stagehands had lifted the shades. I held up my hands, expecting to see them shake as usual before a performance, but tonight they were as steady as the foundations of the earth itself. When I glanced over at Monsegino, his own trembling fingers were fumbling with his cape.

It was hard not to feel sympathy for this inexperienced, violet-eyed ruler of a troubled duchy; neither of us had asked for this 'blessing' inflicted by the saints. Here in the Great Courtyard, before the entire city, we were about to unleash the memories of two men who'd despised each other with a fury that had lasted long past their deaths.

I checked the rapier at my side, wondering how well I'd fare against the duke should things go awry. Neither of us would come out of this final act unscathed, of that I was certain.

Love and truth. I had promised my grandfather I would fight for them both, but as I couldn't imagine that love would have any part in what came next, truth would have to suffice.

'The hour has come, your Grace,' I said, taking my first step onto the stage. I reached deep down for whatever shred of my grandmother's daring I had in me before turning back to flash a smile at the man who might soon kill me.

'Time we let Corbier and Pierzi have their reunion at last.'

CHAPTER 57

THE BATTLEFIELD

By tradition, the first show after the death of a theatre's Directore Principale opens with the entire company taking the stage to sing a dirge. No higher honour could be given to a director that's gone to the embrace of the gods than the dedication of those left behind to keep the show alive, and during the most poignant scenes of the play, to deliver a line here or there skywards, as if addressing one particular member of the divine audience.

I hoped to do Shoville's memory justice, though I'd never been much of a singer. 'The Player's Lament' is a simple enough tune, though. It begins and ends with the same intentionally ambiguous line, *Still, the dead sing.*

I managed to get as far as the first chorus before I slipped into the past, to find hundreds of soldiers charging at me from all directions. Blades rose and fell as warriors in Pierzi's gold livery and Corbier's black fought with a fury I'd never seen before. Swords slashed and spears thrust, their manic rhythms an endless refrain of blood and death surrounding me.

A scream erupted from my throat, shattering the sombre moment on the stage that I could barely see beneath the bloodier vista before me. The rest of the cast scattered to take their positions, while the nearest audience members, just faint apparitions now, threw themselves backwards in panic. The ripple of their hapless attempt to flee became a wave that spread through the thousands of bodies packed into the courtyard.

I struggled to master myself. Never before had the visions been so clear so quickly. Was my hold on the present weakening from too much use of the Veristor's gift, or was the strange ritual magic Rhyleis had spoken of amplified by the largest audience ever assembled in the city of Jereste?

'*Gods and saints alike*,' I swore, watching the spectral soldiers swarming all around me, fighting, killing . . . *dying* . . . Bile rose up in my throat.

I'd never been to war, and no one had warned me that those who knew death was upon them emitted a stench, magnified by numbers, overpowering in its effect and bloody in its result. There were no orderly lines of soldiers marching to their doom, their faces grim yet brave; no rousing war songs were being sung. Here, only madness reigned.

I drew my rapier – and instantly realised I'd picked the wrong weapon. This was *war* – why hadn't I brought a longsword? – but there was nothing I could do about it now.

As my fellow players began miming the great Battle of Mount Cruxia, I allowed my sight to shift back to the unfolding chaos of a hundred years ago.

Was this where the Court of Flowers achieved their first victory? I wondered in horror as half-mad, filthy men and women dripped mud and blood and worse. With broken armour hanging off wounded torsos and shattered limbs, they swung their weapons in wide, desperate arcs as likely to decapitate their comrades as their enemies. The noise – oh, Saint Birgid-who-weeps-rivers, *that noise:* a constant scream of terror and rage and worst of all, the deranged, gleeful cackling at the death of an enemy who falls at last, sinking into the soggy ground until mud fills their mouths and at last puts an end to their shrieking agony . . .

What did you think war looked like? Corbier asked. *An endless series of elegant duels, each politely awaiting the magistrate's bell to begin, followed by masterful displays of fencing, and all peppered with clever witticisms?*

I don't know. I thought . . .

You didn't think at all, Player. That is the gift soldiers give to those they defend – not merely protection from the enemy but protection from the truth of what their safety costs.

Somehow, between the howling battle cries and wet, gasping death rattles, I began to hear complaints among the audience, wondering why the Raven wasn't yet taking part in the action.

You need only watch and follow, Corbier told me. *The end of my tale awaits us.*

I found myself walking in Corbier's shadow, stalking the field in search of the man he'd come here to kill. *Wait!* I called out, resisting the pull, *we can't just run headlong into a duel with Pierzi!*

The Red-Eyed Raven's laugh was brittle, almost feverish. *What do you suppose happens when two men despise one another so greatly that they send five thousand soldiers to the slaughter, all for the chance to kill each other?*

The Court of Flowers, I stammered, *they must be here, somewhere in your memories. Help me find them befo—*

My destiny is already written! Corbier roared at me. *My doom is incontestable. You are here to witness my death, Veristor, nothing more!*

I struggled against the Red-Eyed Raven's indomitable will. *Listen, you fool! We may not be able to change what happened a hundred years ago, but if there's evidence that the Iron Orchids began in your time – that they aren't some recent patriotic citizen uprising – then I can discredit them in the present. Please, Corbier, reliving your vengeance against Pierzi won't save Ajelaine, but the truth could save my city!*

But Corbier was no longer listening to me. He yanked me along like a puppy on a leash, forcing me to follow in his footsteps as he sought his final release from pain.

Everything I saw was tinted red.

CHAPTER 58

THE VENDETTA

'Where are you hiding, Pierzi?' I heard myself roar across two worlds.

Up and down the bloody slopes of Mount Cruxia, the Red-Eyed Raven searched for his nemesis, and on the stage, Duke Monsegino, barely ten feet away from me, appeared equally lost in a trance as he scoured the field for his enemy.

In the present and the past, the two of us weaved in and out of the crowd in a bizarre dance: one moment we'd meet and our blades would cross, the next, we'd be swept apart by the chaos of battle or by actors cleverly ploughing between us, sending the two of us spinning away to separate parts of the stage. The audience gasped each time Monsegino and I passed each other as though blind.

'He's right there!' someone would shout, only to be clouted in the head and hissed into silence by an aggravated neighbour.

Drawn by those voices, I took a moment to look out into the audience. Flashes of soldiers fighting in the past appeared among them, but they never overlapped with the onlookers as they did with the actors on the stage.

They have no part of this tale, Corbier informed me.

It's their lives at stake – their city!

Then someone should have taught them how to fight for it.

Before I could counter that cruel, cynical assessment, my gaze was drawn to the other watchers among the crowds, those whose fine clothes and noble bearing set them apart. As my awareness flitted back and forth between past and present, the distance of a few feet stretched out in the Red-Eyed Raven's gaze all the way to a distant hill, where a group of equally elegantly garbed men and women on horseback were watching the battle. Behind each was a spear flying their House colours, held high by attendants dressed in liveries of the same colours. Glittering armour peeked out from beneath their raiments, but instead of fighting, these rival nobles were sipping tea poured from a single gleaming kettle. Although there was no way for Corbier to hear over the din of battle, I was convinced these 'enemy Houses' happily exchanging pleasantries were gambling on the outcome of one part of the battle or another.

What role do you seek to play in this tragedy, my Lords and Ladies? A sour taste came to my mouth as the battle swirled all around me. *Is it just a game to you, spinning the rest of us like tops while you wager on which will fall first?*

In that instant, my own smouldering rage overwhelmed Corbier's control and in the present, I broke that sacred barrier between actor and audience to yell, 'You who would make yourself sovereign are naught but the vilest malefactor in all of history!'

You chide me for seeking vengeance, Corbier mocked, *yet here you are, weeping and wailing at enemies barely aware of your existence. You do no more than shout into a hurricane.*

Normally I would have agreed, except ... hadn't those words I'd used been the exact ones I'd spoken on stage the night I'd fumbled the herald's line? Why had I repeated them now?

You're saying you never spoke those words yourself? I asked Corbier.

A bark of laughter erupted from my lips. *A trifle too melodramatic for my tastes.*

But if the line hadn't come from Corbier, then whose memories had caused me to shout it from the stage?

'Damelas, what the Hells are you doing?' Beretto whispered furiously as he and Teo cut in front of me so that their apparent duel would hide the fact that I wasn't moving.

Stop delaying us, Corbier growled to me, trying to force my legs to carry me to the other side of the stage where Monsegino and the climax of the inevitable tragedy awaited us. *Let his entrails warm my blade, or mine his, then at last I'll be reunited with my Ajelaine!*

Hearing her name shook me from my paralysis. Ajelaine, the supposedly innocent maiden for whom all this blood was being shed, never a player in this game of dukes and princes, yet always at the very centre of the board.

A now familiar itch came to me – that vexing conviction that even now our performance was just a repetition of the same lie being told over and over across an entire century. I closed my eyes and shook my head to force away the chaos all around me so that I could find a moment's clarity.

'What's wrong with him?' I heard Teo ask between grunts as Beretto's wooden sword battered down on his wooden shield.

'I need time,' I told them. 'Cover for me.'

'*Cover for you?*' Teo asked incredulously.

'Shut up and pretend to be an actor for once, Teo,' Beretto replied, adding a flurry of glancing blows to distract the audience. 'Whatever you're trying to do, brother, I'd hurry the Hells up!'

Speak to me, I begged Corbier. *Tell me the truth, for once. Spurned love might start wars in books and plays, but not in real life.*

You doubt the depth of my anguish? Corbier's voice was like a cold wind in my chest, but I was done being cowed by spirits.

Of course not. No one could doubt what an aggrieved lunatic you are.

Across the stage, Monsegino was making a show of searching for his enemy, just as Pierzi was doing in the past, yet both quests felt . . . staged, somehow.

What kind of man was Pierzi? I asked Corbier abruptly.

You think this is the time to—?

Was he reckless, like you? So driven by his passions that he would risk an all-out war over a woman he must have known never truly loved him? Was he truly so petty?

There was a slight hesitation before Corbier reluctantly answered, *No. No, he wasn't. Nevino was always the more reasonable of us. Even after our friendship ended, I'd never seen him act rashly – not until that night.*

That accorded with the biographies of Pierzi's life. The prince had been logical, almost calculating: methodical on the battlefield, cautious on the throne. Yet even now, in both the past and present, Nevino Pierzi appeared to be rushing to a confrontation with his nemesis, with the end result – who would live and who would die – no more certain than a flip of the coin.

My fists and teeth clenched. *Think, then, damn you!* I shouted at him. *What could have driven Pierzi to murder and mayhem?*

I don't know! Ajelaine always understood him better than I did – and better than your farcical plays and history books. You were there with me, Veristor. You heard her warn me that Pierzi had gone mad with jealousy.

That much was true, but it was precisely what confused me the most. Why had Ajelaine spoken of Pierzi's envy to the man she *knew* would respond with a foolhardy attempt to steal her away?

The answer was as simple as it had been elusive: *because she was lying.*

Corbier's spirit erupted with outrage. *Ajelaine* loved *me! She would never—*

I ignored the pounding in my skull, just as I ignored the action unfolding on the stage, where the Knights of the Curtain were now taking turns to improvise scenes of the battle, using made-up dialogue to make it look as if my standing there like a statue was all part of the performance. They were doing a surprisingly good job of it.

Not the first time they've all had to hide my incompetence, I thought wryly.

Traitor! Corbier raged, still trying to force me to where Monsegino waited. *Will you not grant me even the pretence of that vengeance that was denied me in my own time?*

Not yet.

The others would have to hold this mad play together a while longer, for the answers weren't here any more than on the field of Mount Cruxia.

Then where? Corbier asked.

Two nights ago, as the Belleza burned and the Iron Orchids fled the scene, there had been a moment where I thought I'd heard her voice, but I'd assumed it had been Shariza calling to me. It had never occurred to me that the memories of another might be haunting me.

Damelas, you must come to me, she'd said.

We have to go further back, I told Corbier. *I think Ajelaine's waiting for us.*

CHAPTER 59

THE RETURN

Pushing myself backwards through time was like walking along an endless hall filled with theatre sets, the images painted on them appearing and disappearing too fast for me to see. People and events rushed past like dancers on a stage, spinning in and out of view. Corbier's memories were like a book; I could flip the pages, but never stop at one long enough to read the words written there.

The Bardatti warned you, Corbier reminded me. *Your gift requires the ritual of the theatre to guide you.*

And he was right, of course. A Veristor wasn't some back-alley medium conducting séances for a few coppers. This was *ceremonial* magic, so key elements had to be in place for me to have any control over where it took me. A stage was one piece of the puzzle, but far more vital were the other actors.

'Damelas?' Beretto asked again, blocking me from the view of the audience. Centre stage, Teo appeared to be delivering an extended monologue about how ordinary soldiers are forgotten by time, even when they're the ones who truly win wars. 'We can't keep this up forever.'

I allowed myself a grin, for at last I understood how to use this gift – or curse, whichever it was. For the first time since this nightmare had begun, I was eager to pursue it.

'It's okay,' I said, and pushed past Beretto to make my way towards Teo. Ornella noticed my approach and wisely put an end to the youth's interminable speech by pretending – rather forcefully – to drive a sword into his back. Monsegino, standing on the other side in his golden armour, began to slowly stride towards me, assuming the two of us would bring the play to its bloody climax at last.

When the duke spoke, his rich, almost playful tone belonged to Prince Pierzi. 'How many times have we crossed blades on this very battlefield, you bloody-eyed bastard?'

Corbier's grim satisfaction contorted the muscles of my face, bringing forth a cruel smile that matched the Prince's own. 'A dozen times – perhaps a hundred? A thousand?'

Monsegino dropped the broadsword he'd been carrying and unslung the scabbard of a duelling rapier from his belt. 'Then, by all the gods, let this time be the—'

'Not yet,' I said.

The duke froze. The audience gasped. The other actors stared in confusion, still miming their own fights. In the past, Corbier and Pierzi were already circling each other, readying themselves for the duel that would end one of their lives. But I resisted, and by will alone, slowed the passing of those moments down to a crawl.

'Before belligerent blood drenches sacred soil,' I began, filling the stage with my voice and drawing all eyes to me, 'let first the cause of our enmity be known, for it was not hate which tore two friends apart, but love.'

Monsegino wasn't much of an actor, but he was clever, and he recovered admirably. 'You would speak to me of *her*?' he demanded. 'Now, when blades are drawn and our doom is fast upon us?'

It was a good enough line, but it wasn't Monsegino I needed right now. Fortunately, the one I *did* need understood immediately. She surreptitiously shed the soldier's breastplate and helm she'd put on so she could stay close to the duke and came to stand between us.

'When better to summon a ghost,' Shariza said, assuming the role of Ajelaine's spectre, 'than when the sword is drawn but the fatal blow has not yet been struck?'

Hujo Shoville couldn't have scripted it better, I thought. Once again, I focused my Veristor's ability to set the scene in motion.

What are you doing? Corbier asked, his thirst for vengeance losing its hold now that he saw his Ajelaine standing there before him. *This isn't how it happened!*

I know, but while this may be your life, it's my damned play, so we're going to start doing things my way.

I brought my rapier up into guard, but walked with unnatural slowness, matching the timing of my movements to those of Corbier's memories unfolding a hundred years in the past. In the present, I spoke a hastily composed stanza.

'With each bitter blow given,
Let the truth be made plain –
No tragic tale of friends riven,
But the secret quest of Lady Ajelaine.'

Like the last syllable of a spell, that simple rhyme sent me hurtling back to a different time and place . . .

. . . to her.

CHAPTER 60

THE RIDER

Wave after wave of Corbier's memories slammed into me, one after another, drowning me in unfamiliar sights and sounds, then flashing past before I could make sense of any of them.

You're going too far back, Veristor, the Red-Eyed Raven warned. *The stage is not set for where you seek to travel, and no script guides you to your destination.*

I'm done with scripts, I replied, concentrating on seeking out Ajelaine among the multitude of Corbier's experiences, but every time I caught a flash of her, or the fleeting scent of her hair wafting on the air, she was gone again, as if the memory was being snatched away from me. I had no trouble finding the culprit: Corbier was holding me back.

She's not some pretty picture or a few lines from a play, he said bitterly. *You seek to stomp through my most precious memories—*

Then relive them with me – bring me to Ajelaine—

No! Do you still not understand, Player? The hardest memories to endure aren't those of pain and suffering, but of love itself – I cannot see her as she was in happier days without tarnishing those moments, forever staining them with her blood.

I shivered at my own remembrance of Ajelaine's death. The sprays of scarlet from her children's throats, the gush of crimson erupting from her belly. Corbier's ocular condition lent a red tinge to everything he saw, making the blood spilled that night look unnatural, almost theatrical, a horrifying image imprinted onto his eyes.

I'm sorry, I said, aware of the cruelty I was inflicting, *but we must see her again.* And at last I grabbed hold of a passing memory.

The gusting winds halted, but my feet couldn't find the ground; instead, I was being jostled up and down on aching buttocks.

On the stage, I heard Beretto whisper anxiously, 'Saint Laina's tits, brother, you look like you're humping a wild pig. Tell us what's going on! We can't cover for you if you don't give us anything to work with—'

'I'm ... I'm riding a horse,' I said aloud, looking down to see my black-gloved hands clutching at leather reins. My boots had slipped out of the stirrups and I was bouncing in the saddle. Branches dancing with red, gold and orange autumn leaves stroked my face as we flew past.

'Just barely,' said the young woman laughing next to me, but when I turned, all I could make out was golden-brown hair whipping about her face, and a wide grin as the slender figure in brown riding gear raced into the rushing wind.

'Ajelaine,' I said aloud for the audience, 'merry and mischievous, a girl of perhaps thirteen, who flirts recklessly with both danger and love.'

Fourteen, Corbier corrected me. *I was a year younger, as she never failed to remind me.*

'Right, we can work with that,' Beretto said.

I returned my awareness to the tree-lined path on which my bay horse was galloping far too fast for comfort. I felt like an oversized straw doll strapped to the back of a pony.

'You're not a very good rider, are you, Raphan Corbier?' Ajelaine asked, letting go of her reins to wag a disapproving finger at me. Her massive black charger dwarfed my own mount.

'I'll get better,' Corbier replied, promising himself he would, too, no matter how hard he had to practise. 'Besides, this beast you've given me is ill-tempered. What is this foul hellion's name again? Storm's Teeth? Bloodbath? Hellmount?'

Ajelaine laughed. 'Buttercup.'

Distantly, I heard myself recount the joke on stage, and peals of laughter from the audience. It was a struggle to keep track of both worlds, but the players were adding to my halting explanations, improvising outrageously to keep the crowds entertained.

The young Corbier wasn't laughing, but marvelling at how calm he felt despite Ajelaine's teasing. She was the only person who could mock him with—

Stop, Corbier begged me, *please. This was the moment I first fell in love with her. Don't make me—*

'You're a bit early, I'm afraid,' Ajelaine said.

I gaped, seeing the way she was staring at me from atop her horse. 'My Lady? Did you—'

The girlish smile turned serious. 'Careful, Veristor. You may converse with me here, but keep silent in your own time.'

I'm not just witnessing Corbier's memories any more! I marvelled, simultaneously exhilarated and terrified. *I'm speaking to her – to Ajelaine!*

With her instruction, I found I could speak through Corbier, while keeping my mouth shut in my own time as my fellow actors covered for me.

'How is this possible, my Lady?' I asked Ajelaine, but she was shaking her head.

'Alas, we've no time for frivolous musings, Veristor. You've come too far back. We must meet elsewhen, you and I.'

'*Elsewhen* . . .'

What's going on? Corbier demanded. *She never said any of these things—*

'Off with you now,' she commanded, dismissing me with a wave. 'Seek me in the orchard after the ball three years hence, when I am seventeen. Raphan ought to remember it clearly enough; he made a terrible fool of himself that night.'

Still reeling, I tried to push myself forward in time, but with the damned horse jouncing me up and down, my concentration couldn't hold.

Every other time I'd ventured into Corbier's recollections, there had been some sort of physical jolt that had shaken me back to my own time. I must have spoken aloud, for Ajelaine had an impish grin on her face.

'Oh, worry not about such trivialities, Veristor. As I recall, there's a jolt coming Raphan's way momentarily.'

What is she talking about? I asked Corbier.

How am I supposed to know? My recollections of this moment are of an idle afternoon's flirtation, the two of us riding through Ajelaine's favourite haunts until . . . oh, Hells . . . now I remember!

What—?

'See you in a few years, Veristor,' Ajelaine said, winking at me just as Corbier's horse ran me right into a low-hanging tree branch that smashed into my forehead and sent me tumbling to the ground.

CHAPTER 61

THE RUFFIAN

I landed on the rocky path so hard I thought I'd cracked every one of my ribs, but at least Corbier found amusement in my discomfort.

I'd forgotten how badly that hurt.

'You couldn't have warned me?' I asked aloud.

The sky had turned dark, with the moon barely a sliver, but the stars cast glittering reflections upon the apple trees surrounding me.

'Warned you?' a woman's voice demanded as she strode out from the shadows. 'I warned you a thousand times, you reckless idiot!'

A slender hand reached down and I looked up to see Ajelaine in an extravagant ball gown, sun-streaked chestnut hair draped over her face. She bent down, grabbed my wrist and hauled me to my feet.

'You're heavy for a boy,' she groaned.

'I'm sixteen,' Corbier protested, 'and barely a year younger than you.'

While Beretto returned to shielding me, I cued the actors with a flurry of hissed whispers. I caught a glimpse of Teo donning a courtier's jacket to take up his role in the encounter as Shariza made a show of upbraiding him, and the two of them spun a comedic interlude pulled from any number of romantic farces, allowing me to return to the starlit orchard.

Ajelaine's methodical hands dusted off Corbier's indigo coat. He'd lost one of the big silver buttons now gleaming in the soft light of the intricate lanterns hung from posts along the flagstone path where they stood. It had been ripped off during the scuffle in the ballroom. He weighed up the risks of retrieving it.

'Don't you *dare* even think it,' Ajelaine warned, as if she were reading my mind.

'I didn't say anything,' the youthful Corbier said indignantly.

'You didn't have to! You wear your clumsy intention like an ill-considered moustache upon your lip!'

Laughter drifted into the misty air between us. Corbier's reflexes had me reaching for the hilt at my side, but of course the fashionable court sword had been left in the palace. Fortunately, the laughter had come from a hundred years hence, from the audience watching Teo and Shariza.

'Boys!' she and Ajelaine exclaimed with feigned surrender at the same moment.

Instead of withering under the embarrassment, I found myself grinning, filled with Corbier's pride. He usually preferred the sword to fisticuffs, but he'd wiped the smirk off that overstuffed peacock's face well enough during the scuffle.

Twice my size, he was, Corbier boasted. *Wrestling a bear would've been easier, but I took him down all the same.* Damn, but my jaw ached.

Ajelaine rolled her eyes at me. 'A boy I named you, and a boy you are, Raphan, fighting a schoolyard brawl in the duke's own palace.'

Needing to provide enough fodder for the cast to buy more time, I chose to present Corbier's side of the story rather than Ajelaine's, declaring loudly, 'A matter of honour, a test of mettle – an intolerable insult that only fists could settle.'

Not my best rhyme, but even here, a hundred years in the past, I could hear the oohs and aahs from the audience in my own time; the people of Jereste loved any story that began with 'A matter of honour.'

Ajelaine was unimpressed. 'How quickly history's facts are twisted for the convenience of the storyteller.'

I continued anyway, drawing on Corbier's recollection of the duel. 'Our villain? The wretched offspring of privilege and vice who dared claim carnal knowledge of the virtuous Ajelaine, his foul jest made before the entire court. His insidious purpose? To demean the good name of she who would one day rule over his nefarious House.'

Yes! Corbier said enthusiastically. *For once you're getting the story righ—*

Ajelaine slapped me across the cheek. Hard.

'Ow! Damn it!' I shouted in both the past and present.

Now that part I don't remember, Corbier informed me.

I prayed the audience wouldn't notice my outburst over Teo's outrageous rendition of young Corbier challenging Beretto to a boxing match.

'You idiot!' Ajelaine yelled, pulling me back to the romantic ambiance of the palace orchard and this distinctly un-romantic encounter with her. 'That big oaf in the mustard silk coat played you for a fool, Raphan. He'd been ordered to goad *Pierzi* into a duel, not you. They were trying to trick him into a public brawl that would embarrass him before the generals to prove he couldn't be trusted with a battalion when he leaves for the borders next month. I'd finally convinced Pierzi to ignore him when *you* had to swoop in like a near-sighted seagull and crash into everything!'

In the dim fog behind her, Teo and Beretto put on a comical fight, which had the audience cheering and jeering their favourites – but I was more confused than ever. Nothing like this had been mentioned in any of the histories.

Forcing my words to be spoken only through Corbier's lips, I asked, 'My Lady, why would—'

'Their intent is to sow doubts about Pierzi as future prince of the duchy,' Ajelaine said, cutting me off again. She did that a lot, I realised.

On this point we are in agreement, Corbier said silently.

Ajelaine continued berating us, pacing in a circle as she explained, 'This is what I've been trying to make you understand, Raphan: Pierzi's enemies don't think like you or I do. They're not concerned with tonight or tomorrow; their schemes are planned years – even decades – in advance. All the while you two idiots are playing with swords, they play their vile games with our people, with our laws, with the very fabric of our society.'

I couldn't help but gaze at her in wonder. Seventeen years old and she was already uncovering conspiracies that had eluded every historian in Pertine.

Did she really say these things to you all these years ago? I asked Corbier.

I'm not sure . . . but yes, now I remember. She used to go on and on about these little intrigues she was piecing together from conversations gleaned here and there, oddities in various records and manifests. I wasn't paying attention at the time because—

'He never listened to me,' Ajelaine said.

I stumbled back against a tree trunk. She was talking to *me* again, not the sixteen-year-old boy trying to court her. Before I could ask her how this was even possible, she entwined her fingers with mine and led me through the orchard.

'Raphan loved me with a fire brighter than the sun itself.' She sighed, the wistful tone of a much older woman. 'But he never listened to me, not really. He wanted so badly to prove himself the heroic figure that no one believed someone possessed of those disturbing red eyes could ever be. Pierzi was no better, convinced his golden hair and handsome features marked him for some grand destiny. This is how the Court of Flowers set the two of them against each other.'

I briefly turned from her to my own time to toss in a feeble joke, enough for Teo and Shariza's improvised comedic wooing to keep going, then returned to the far stranger courtship in the past.

'My Lady, how can you be aware of me, and of events that happened many years after those taking place here tonight?'

She leaned against my arm as we walked and I found the warmth of her body intoxicating. No wonder sixteen-year-old Corbier had struggled to pay attention to her warnings at the time.

'You expect me to explain your own gift to you, Veristor?' she asked, laughing. Soft brown hair tickled my cheek. 'I'm not even sure if *I'm* really here. Perhaps I'm long dead, buried deep beneath the ground of my mother's estate, and all this is a dream to you and dust to me.'

She squeezed my arm tighter. 'I can tell you this much, though, Damelas Chademantaigne: memories aren't simply a sequence of events in time, nor do they belong to one person only. Our thoughts and experiences echo long after we are gone. This is your true gift, Veristor: you give voice to the dead.'

'Are you Ajelaine's spirit, then?' I asked aloud, 'come to guide me to the truth?'

She stopped and turned to face me. For an instant, her features wavered and I saw Shariza standing before me on stage.

Damn me, I cursed silently. *I said that in front of the audience, didn't I? The others must be wondering what the Hells I'm doing.*

But Shariza was taking it in perfect stride. On the stage she took my hands in hers and said, 'Seek not your answers in spirits, my love, for it is the truth itself that haunts us this night.'

In the past, the young Ajelaine chuckled. 'Oh, I like that. She's got quite a flair for the dramatic, that one.'

When she smiled that way, she took Corbier's breath away, and it was his voice murmuring, 'Ajelaine . . .'

A longing overcame me – Corbier's deep, desperate urge to feel Ajelaine's lips once more against his. His need threatened to overwhelm my own volition, but I forced the compulsion aside.

No, I told him firmly, *this is why you failed to pay attention to her warnings the first time, you love-struck idiot. This time we* must *listen.*

'The Court of Flowers,' I said to her, praying Beretto, Teo and Shariza could keep covering for me a while longer. 'Who are they?'

Ajelaine shook her head, the cascade of chestnut tresses interweaving with Shariza's darker curls in the present. 'I was too young here, my suspicions not yet proven. I knew only that someone was manipulating the affairs of the duchy, seeking to destabilise our city.'

'But who's behind it all? Why are they doing this? In my time, the Iron Orchids are killing people, forcing unconscionable laws—'

'Orchids?' she asked, tapping a finger to her lips. 'How odd. Orchids are my favourite flower, but they're not native to Pertine, nor to anywhere else in the country.'

'What? Of course they are – there are orchid shops all over the city.'

She stopped. 'How can that be? Unless someone starts importing them sometime between my century and yours – but to what purpose? You speak of these Iron Orchids as if they're some sort of military force. Perhaps the symbolism is important to them. Ah, but yes . . . that would fit what I've observed in their actions.'

She began dragging me along again, ducking under low-hanging branches and swerving to avoid protruding roots, walking and talking so quickly I had trouble keeping up with either her feet or her words.

'There's a deviousness to those plotting against Nevino and Raphan, an almost mathematical precision to their moves, but I have noticed an arrogance as well – a need to leave traces and tracks as if this were a game and they have bound themselves to a set of rules of their own devising.'

I stopped her beneath a white stone arch adorned with a carved dove carrying what looked to be a heart in its beak. 'My Lady, forgive me, but have you evidence to support these speculations?'

'Oh, I acknowledge it's little more than an intuition right now.' She poked my chest. 'Come and find me later, Veristor. Seek me out nine years hence, in the field by Pierzi's fortress where first you saw me.'

'But my Lady . . .'

Somewhere a hundred years from here, ten thousand people were watching two dozen actors playing for time.

It's a bit late to be picking and choosing what you believe, Veristor, Corbier observed drily.

Fair point.

'All right,' I said to her, 'but I'm going to need a way to shake loose from *this* moment and I'd prefer it not involve braining myself on a tree.'

'Oh, no need for anything so dramatic,' Ajelaine said. She pointed to the arch above them. 'You see, this is a legendarily romantic monument, and around now is when Raphan says something truly stupid to me.'

Corbier cut me off. His recollection of this moment, standing in the warm, misty night air beside the only girl he would ever love, conspired with his irritation at her inability to recognise the necessity of the duel he'd just fought in her honour. And so, repeated his stupidity.

'If you desire me to be your husband one day,' the sixteen-year-old Corbier began, still obstinately convinced he was right to throw the first punch against the man who'd insulted her, 'then you must accept that it is my duty and privilege to defend you in my own fashion against those from whom you cannot protect yourself.'

Oh saints, I swore silently, *you didn't really say that to her, did you?*

What? I thought I was being roman—

I barely had time to notice Ajelaine balling her fingers before the blow struck me like a mallet on the temple. My grandmother would have approved of her using the side of her clenched fist rather than the more fragile knuckles. As Corbier stumbled back, dazed, I felt myself once again falling out of his memories.

Nine years later, I reminded myself, *on the grassy field outside the fortress where I saw her that first night in the Belleza . . . when poor Roz still played the part.*

But as my vision cleared, there was no fortress awaiting me, no grassy field. I was back on the massive stage outside the Ducal Palace where the panicked screams of the audience had drawn me back into the present.

CHAPTER 62

THE MOB

The quiet orchard was whisked away like the colourful cloth backdrop of a comedia, leaving me disoriented as I went stumbled across the ducal stage like a blind man. My senses returned to me one at a time. First came the frenzied shrieking from the audience, and the methodical clomping of boots and clanging of swords against shields. I slammed my hands against my ears to drown out the cacophony, yet still the rhythmic bellowing shook me, the thumping and clanging in perfect time with shouts of '*Juridas Orchida! Regidas Orchida!*'

The Orchid Laws! The Orchid Reign!

Through blurred eyes, I squinted at the hordes, noting the dull swathe of common folk in their common dress broken up by islands of nobles in gaudy finery. This motley conglomeration of Jereste society was being sliced in half by the menacing blades of a grey-clad militia marching in clumsy formation towards the stage.

My sense of smell returned next, assailing my nostrils with the stench of too many bodies packed too close together, sending me reeling back. Malodorous humanity is a constant companion to those whose living is measured by arses in seats, but mere moments ago I'd been breathing in the sweet scent of apple trees, caressed by the fresh breeze dancing through the orchard. Now the air tasted foul, slithering inside my mouth and throat, choking me with a nausea tempered only by the sudden sharp pain in my knees that suggested I'd fallen to the polished oak boards.

Saint Ebron-who-steals-breath, I swore, unable to get to my feet again, *why won't my head stop spinning?*

You pushed your gift too far, Veristor, Corbier warned me. *You delved into memories of Ajelaine beyond the boundaries of my own.*

But I failed – I still don't know who rules the Iron Orchids, and now they're here, threatening to—

Corbier's tone was grim. *Your enemy does not make threats, Damelas Chademantaigne. This is the endgame. This city and all that you love hangs upon a knife's edge. Witness how the enemy are positioning themselves.*

My vision sharpened as if I were seeing the world through the Red-Eyed Raven's crimson gaze. The frantic beating of my heart slowed as confusion turned to cold calculation.

The courtyard looked like a giant game board, set with ten thousand pieces. The main column of Orchids wasn't as big as I'd first estimated; there were perhaps three hundred of them in total. That was still more than four times the size of Monsegino's personal guard assembled at the front of the stage, but the latter were surely better trained and better led. They could hold off a direct assault.

You watch the bow, but you fail to see the arrows, Corbier warned, and only then did I notice that half again as many Iron Orchids were stationed around the inner gates, surrounding the audience, and each was armed with an eight-foot-long spear. If they turned their weapons on the crowd, they'd be able to drive them like a herd of wild boar onto the stage itself. Duke Monsegino would be trampled to death by his own subjects – along with me and the Knights of the Curtain.

'Up, brother,' said Beretto, hauling me to my feet. 'I fear our audience is captivated by the performance, but not in the way we might have hoped.'

I shrugged off his grip and raced to the front of the stage. Five feet below, Captain Terine and her guards were barring the main column of Orchids from approaching the stage, but doing no more than that in order to prevent what would surely be a catastrophic slaughter of innocents.

'Why aren't you arresting the damned Orchids?' I shouted down at her.

Captain Terine turned and growled back at me, 'We're outnumbered, in case you hadn't noticed. The damned city guards have abandoned the courtyard, and my duty is to protect the duke. Until his Grace orders me otherwise, neither I, nor those under my command, will leave our post.'

I went to seek out Duke Monsegino, who was on the other side of the stage, lost in his role as Pierzi. He was still searching the battlefield of Mount Cruxia for his enemy, awaiting the inevitable end to this miserable tale.

Inevitable, perhaps, Corbier said silently, *but what if Pierzi and I never witnessed the true ending? What if the real story happened elsewhere?*

What do you mean? You showed me Ajelaine and the children being killed.

Unbidden, the sickening scene in the tower bedroom that had set all this tragedy in motion played again in my mind. I saw Pierzi's curved blade slicing through the necks of Ajelaine's two boys, and the sharpened point burying itself in her belly . . . and again, I found myself confounded by the speed with which it had all transpired, the flawless execution, the almost sublime brutality. Corbier had lost the woman he loved and the sons he'd only just discovered were his – and Pertine had lost its only hope of uncovering the secrets of the Iron Orchids and their shadowy masters.

Was that the real reason Pierzi killed her? To keep her from further antagonising the Court of Flowers?

But Corbier gave no reply.

'I need to go back,' I shouted aloud. '*I need more time!*'

On the stage, my fellow actors, their courage proven a dozen times over already, rallied to me. Even amidst this chaos, they tried to hide their fear that I had led them to their doom.

'What do you want us to do, brother?' Beretto asked, a spark of hope lighting his eyes.

In the courtyard, the Orchids keeping the perimeter were readying their weapons, ready to spur the crowds into a mad rush for the stage – while their duke, still lost in the role of Pierzi, was waiting for me to begin the duel that would mean death for one of us. His guards, paralysed by their duty to protect their lord, were too few to mount an attack against the invaders in any case, even if he did come out of his fugue long enough to order a counter-attack.

Swords, I thought bitterly, staring at the naked blades of the Orchids in the central column, *why is it the fate of the many is always decided by those few who command the most swords?*

You fail to see them as I do, Player, Corbier said. *The enemy is too small in number to win the day by force of arms. Panic is the blade you must now blunt.*

How are a handful of actors supposed to convince ten thousand terrified men and women to ignore the armed thugs all around them?

I felt his shrug coming to my own shoulders. Alas, that is beyond a warrior's talents.

But not beyond ours . . .

The idea was implausible, preposterous – and yet fitting, in a way. If it worked, it would surely give credence to Shoville's claim weeks ago that actors were the gods' most inspired creation.

'Any chance we have lies in the past,' I told the others. 'I have to return to Ajelaine, but to do that, I need a distraction.'

'Distraction?' Abastrini demanded. The blustering actor, his costume armour straining to encompass his broad shoulders and abundant belly, stomped across the stage to me, eyes wide with that subtle hint of madness that always made sharing a scene with him simultaneously terrifying and somehow comical.

'You sodden-witted fustilarian!' he hissed. 'You addle-brained walking cataclysm – how, I ask you, are we supposed to distract the fucking Iron Orchids? Do you expect me to yank down my trousers and wave my cock at the enemy in hopes they fall on their swords in astonishment and despair at beholding such a kingly sceptre?'

Despite the danger looming all around me – not least from Abastrini himself – a reckless laugh slipped past my lips. 'As it happens, that's *exactly* what I need.' I bent at the waist to give the ranting melodramatist a deep bow. 'Master Abastrini, I believe our audience would be eternally appreciative if, during this brief intermission, you might regale them with a performance of . . . "*The Rampant Paramour*".'

Abastrini stared at me, mouth agape. 'You want . . . *what*? You want me to . . .' He glanced over at the petrified crowds huddling back from the Iron Orchids. 'All by myself?'

For so long I had despised this pugnacious boaster for his arrogance, his smug self-importance and above all else, his criminally overrated acting abilities. Now I was about to bet all our lives on those very talents.

'Master Abastrini, in the history of the theatre, no actor has been tasked with a more challenging role than the one I beg of you now. So I ask you, can you name for me any player in this city – or any other – more capable of delivering the necessary performance than the man standing before me?'

Ellias Abastrini swallowed. Everyone knew he was past his prime, debased by drink and self-pity until his very existence was a parody of the actor he'd once been. Yet now the steel inside him, long-buried beneath bluster and indulgence, shook itself free. His shoulders squared and his chest swelled as his belly admirably attempted the opposite. A fire long dimmed by languor, lust and lethargy gleamed anew as his lips parted in a feral smile.

'For Hujo Shoville,' he said.

Then Ellias Abastrini shoved his way through our fellow actors, stormed his way to centre stage and, like a mythical warrior conjured out of legend, faced off against the tide of panicking innocents and bloodthirsty thugs.

And told a dirty joke.

CHAPTER 63

THE RAMPANT PARAMOUR

'The Rampant Paramour' is widely acknowledged among actors to be the most lascivious, perverse and corrupting soliloquy ever written. The vulgar monologue is rumoured to have been composed decades ago by a trio of players confined in a gaol cell together, awaiting trial for criminal bawdiness. Being massively drunk at the time and deeming the charges against them entirely unfounded, they decided to prove their innocence by concocting a performance so depraved that once presented to the court, the magistrate would have to agree that, by comparison, their previous crime had been negligible.

The first actor recited 'The Rampant Paramour' before the court, and all in attendance did indeed gape in horror at this unearthly degradation of common decency. The other two then demanded their own opportunities to best his performance. The magistrate, a fair jurist by all accounts, duly allowed them their turns.

After the trial, their bodies were left hanging from the courthouse awning for a full seventy-seven days – a week longer than that mandated for any other known crime. And even now, should a player appear at risk of becoming dangerously bawdy, their fellow actors will surreptitiously signal them, holding one hand down with the three middle fingers wriggling like dangling corpses.

For this reason, 'The Rampant Paramour' is only performed backstage, long after the last audience member has left, when reckless players vie for the dubious honour of exceeding in lewdness and offensiveness all those who have gone before.

And here was Ellias Abastrini, performing 'The Rampant Paramour' for the largest audience ever assembled in Pertine.

He swore. He bragged. He pranced about the stage, gesturing incessantly at his groin, claiming to list – without pausing for breath – a full three dozen titles granted to his member by kings, queens and religious mystics who came from far across the sea, his manhood to acclaim. He described sexual feats both physically and – so we all devoutly hoped – spiritually impossible. He was not even halfway through before every face was flaming crimson – even before he presented his own blushing cheeks to them while describing one of the titles granted his vaunted staff – in farts.

It was *shocking*, *hideous*.

It was *glorious*.

The sheer shock of the performance first paralysed, then captivated the audience, some convulsing with laughter, others roaring their disapproval. By the ninth verse, a remarkable number of noblemen had fainted. The Iron Orchids, who had stopped their advance, now stared at the stage in baffled stupor. Tonight, with the fate of the city, the duchy and possibly the entire country at stake, Ellias Abastrini held an army at bay with nothing but his foul mouth and his prodigious phallus.

'Genius,' Rhyleis breathed, her face aglow with an unfeigned awe I would never have believed of the cynical Bardatti.

Alas, my own efforts were less formidable.

Why can't I get back to Ajelaine? I asked Corbier again, but the Red-Eyed Raven remained silent, leaving me helpless, with no idea why my Veristor's gift had abandoned me.

'Pull yourself together, brother,' Beretto said, shaking me by the shoulders. 'Not even Abastrini can keep this up for ever!'

'I'm *trying*! But I don't know how to get back to that exact moment outside the fortress. The Veristor magic won't work properly unless we first set the scene—'

'What do you need?' Beretto asked.

I started to answer, but was cut off by a quiet voice next to me. 'He needs someone to be his Ajelaine,' Shariza said. Her long dark curls fell over the shoulders of a gauzy indigo gown. 'This is the nearest match I could find to the dress Roslyn wore that night . . .'

My eyes drank in the sight of her while I prayed her presence could light the magic to send me back to the dewy-wet grass outside Pierzi's fortress a hundred years earlier. My breathing slowed as my senses shut out everything happening around me, all save for her . . .

Nothing happened.

'Focus, brother,' Beretto urged.

I shook my head. 'Something's wrong . . . It's as if I'm trying to play a song on an instrument that's not properly tuned. I can't—'

Shariza looked at me as if she understood, although I couldn't imagine how. 'I think . . . I think I'm not meant to be a prop for you to gaze at, Damelas. Tell me of Ajelaine. What was she—?' She stopped suddenly and gazed off into the distance for a moment.

'No,' she said then, 'not Ajelaine. Tell me about *Roslyn*. What was she doing during the performance? What was going on in her head that night? Something that might have united her with Ajelaine in the past?'

'Ajelaine and *Roslyn*?' I was aghast. 'You couldn't find two people with less in common. Ajelaine was sitting outside Pierzi's fortress, playing a lute and periodically stopping to write in a leather-bound book. She was waiting for Corbier, hoping for just a brief moment with him, a single kiss to— Oh, saints, that's it!'

'What is?' Beretto asked.

'*Roslyn.* She was obsessed with this idea that we should rile up the audience that night by going off-script. She wanted to add a stonking great kiss to our scene.'

The big man grinned. 'Ah, a magical kiss! I suppose that makes for a more suitable miracle than Abastrini parading his genitals for the audience.'

'No,' Shariza said firmly, 'we mustn't kiss.'

I was taken aback by her vehemence. What had made her suddenly so averse to kissing me that she'd risk losing everything to the Iron Orchids?

Shariza took my hands in hers. 'It wasn't the kiss that united Ajelaine and Roslyn that night.' Her dark eyes rose to meet mine, enthralling me, binding me to her. 'It was the *longing*.'

Of course, I thought, *the feeling, not the act.*

'I can be *that* Ajelaine,' Shariza said, smiling, and with that smile, ensorcelling me all over again. 'I know something of what it is to crave the kiss of a man I know I cannot have.'

This was the closest either of us had come to giving voice to our feelings – that strange, unexpected and undeserved desire to be loved by someone so different, yet so . . . familiar. I tried to pull her closer, to say her name, but the sweltering, stinking air around me had begun to cool. My cheeks and hair were dampened by the mist as the world quieted, and the name I spoke was . . .

'. . . Ajelaine.'

CHAPTER 64

AJELAINE

She was waiting for me outside the fortress, as she'd been the first time I'd slipped into this strange world of memories and spirits. A woman of twenty-six now, her hair had darkened since our walk in the orchard, blonder strands giving way to a deeper chestnut shade all the more enticing to Corbier's eyes.

My entire city is under siege, I reminded him. *Do you suppose we could focus your recollections on something other than her looks?*

Still the torn soul trapped in those brief seconds after he'd fled her bedroom, with the spray of her blood on his cheeks and the desperate need to avenge her murder a drumbeat in his heart, he relented.

You are right, Player. Ajelaine is dead, and if history is correct, then retribution was denied me. My vengeance is irrelevant now. Only her legacy matters.

Pierzi's two lieutenants loomed over her, the disdain and mockery more transparent now than when first I'd come to this place. Their words struck a far more troubling chord this time.

'. . . for even the loveliest pertine bows before the Court of Flowers.'

The taller of the two men gave a curtsey so shallow it was an insult, serving only as a means for him to flaunt the ornate iron emblem at his collar. He pinched it between thumb and forefinger, smirking, as he and his confederate walked away from her.

I very badly wanted to chase after them and wipe the grins from their faces with the tip of Corbier's rapier, but this time, it was Corbier who restrained me.

A sword makes a poor weapon with which to fight the tide of history. You taught me that, Player. Truth must be our blade now. Truth, and love.

'Raphan?' Ajelaine asked, seeing me step out of the shadows. She set her lute aside and rose from the carved oak bench, glancing nervously back the way the two men had come. 'You should have waited until—'

'I come for you,' I said, my voice hoarse with Corbier's grief, and my own. 'And none shall stay my hand.'

She turned to me. Pale blue eyes narrowed as she once again recognised me through Corbier's visage. Her smile warmed me. 'Ah, Veristor, you've returned.'

'My Lady, those two men – are they members of the Court of Flowers?'

'That pair of sycophants?' She snorted. 'Servants of servants, lackeys to other lackeys who themselves couldn't name a single one of the miscreants who command them.'

'And your investigations?' I pressed her. 'Nine years past you told me to meet you here. Have you uncovered the identities of those who rule the Iron Orchids?'

'No.'

That simple denial crushed the last hope I'd brought with me, this one chance paid for by the daring of my fellow actors and the sacrifice of decent men and women in the ruins of the Belleza.

'It's all been for nothing,' I said, turning away from her, unable to countenance Corbier's love and admiration for this woman, whose optimism was in its own way as reckless and damaging as his propensity for violence. The two of them truly were a pair, their rash idealism as destructive as the sentimental historias used to propagate the lies of the past.

'Veristor . . .' she began.

'Please don't call me that, my Lady. Everyone's been trying to convince me that becoming a Bardatti Veristor was a gift. I thought it a curse, but I was wrong; it's nothing so grand. Actors aren't beloved of the gods any more than we are condemned by them. The gods are jesters, mocking those who dare attempt to rise above their proper station. This ability inside me is simply their latest joke.'

At last a twilight breeze rustled through the leaves, breaking the silence between us.

'Are you done yet?' Ajelaine asked.

'Done what?'

'Feeling sorry for yourself.'

'My Lady, you misjudge me. I am an actor. We never tire of feeling sorry for ourselves.'

I heard a different rustling then, the shuffling of leather against canvas. When I turned, I saw she'd removed the leather-covered book I'd seen when first I'd come to this time.

'I suppose you'll have no use for this, then?' she asked, holding it out to me.

It was a plain thing really, the emerald-green leather not yet worn by time or misuse. Something about it tugged at me – a memory, but not of the distant past. The Grand Library . . . a hand-written journal filled with somewhat perverse poems and faintly obscene illustrations . . . A book entitled *The Court of the Flowers* by one Sigurdis Macha.

'You're him,' I breathed. 'You're . . . And this – this is the second book, the one Duke Meillard stole from the Grand Library . . .'

She grinned wickedly. 'Perhaps you're aware that *Sigurdis Macha* means "Cutter of Weeds".' She pushed the slender tome against my chest. 'This book will be my scythe.'

I took it from her, fearing it would disappear in my hands or that I wouldn't be able to read the text, but when I opened it, I recognised the handwriting, and when my eyes travelled across the handful of filled pages, I saw the culmination of Ajelaine's investigations and the cause of her exuberant pride.

And my heart broke.

'These are the Orchid Laws,' I said. 'The ones they're trying to force the duke to enact in my own time.'

She sounded oblivious to my despair. 'Exactly. Step by step I've traced their actions, the bribes and blackmails, the political manipulations and targeted killings.' She tapped a finger on the page. 'This is their true aim: this is what the Court of Flowers seeks to bring about, in my time if they can, in yours if they fail.'

'But it's just . . . it's nothing but a list of proposed edicts.'

'Precisely.' Her fingernail ran down the scrawled lines on the page. 'But see how *odd* they are? Demands for the removal of bans on pleasure drugs? Mass imprisonment of the homeless? Eviction of foreign artisans? I need only uncover who benefits most from this particular combination of decrees and I will have found our enemy.'

But I already knew who benefited from the enactment of these laws – or believed they could, at any rate. Someone so desperate to bind the Iron Orchids to the ducal throne that, on learning of the banned book's existence, they'd used a tiny brooch of ebony with a diamond eye at its centre to steal the only existing copy from the Grand Library.

You thought you were protecting Pertine's future. Instead, you've doomed us all.

Ajelaine snatched the book from my hands and snapped the emerald-green leather cover closed.

'A year or two, no more,' she went on, stuffing it back in her canvas bag. 'Come and find me hence and I'll be able to give you the identity of our enemy.'

'But you won't even be—'

My jaws clamped shut, clenched by the will of another.

No, Corbier said. *Don't take away her final days of optimism. Allow her this one dream before endless night falls.*

She turned back to me. 'Raphan?' she asked. 'I thought I heard him speak, but I couldn't make out the words.'

'Nothing,' I said. 'It is nothing, my Lady.' With Corbier's assistance, I forced a smile to my lips. 'On my oath, the Court of Flowers will rue the day they caught the attention of the notorious Sigurdis Macha.'

She laughed at that. 'When next we meet, Veristor.' She wagged a finger at me. 'Not too soon, though. I must proceed carefully, methodically, else it's I who will attract the attention of the court and their foul Orchids.' She reached out and smoothed the front of the travelling coat Corbier had worn on his journey here. 'Now, can you get back by yourself, or must I punch you in the face again?'

'I fear you must,' I said, keeping my smile in place even as my eyes stung from the coming tears. 'Perhaps a trifle gentler this time, my Lady.'

But I was wrong. I needed no assistance to return to my own life, for in that moment I saw a ghostly blade slice the misty air between us. I stumbled backwards, the heels of my boots no longer digging into the soft grass, but slipping against the hard oak boards of the stage.

Ajelaine called out to me, but I never heard her words, for it was another's voice shouting at me now.

'I have you, Corbier, you red-eyed bastard! No more will the raven herald the death of princes, for now it is the prince who hunts the raven!'

I looked up to see Firan Monsegino looming over me, Pierzi's mad rage in his gaze and a sword in his hands. There was no trace of the gentle, self-doubting Violet Duke. Monsegino had lost himself to the Veristor's gift.

And now he was going to kill me.

CHAPTER 65

THE LONG-AWAITED DUEL

My right arm rose up by instinct, the forte of my rapier shivering beneath the blow of Monsegino's heavier blade. The duke raised his sword and for a fraction of an instant, I wondered whether I should bother parrying the next cut.

The Belleza lay in rubble, its valiant director buried beneath, just steps away from where Roz had been vilely murdered. The palace was under siege by throngs of well-armed Iron Orchids, grinning as they watched the Violet Duke about to slay the very actors he'd brought here to perform this blasphemous, unpatriotic play. Soon the entire duchy would belong to the Court of Flowers, and purchased far more cheaply than they could have dreamed. And the one woman who'd stood a chance of uncovering their identities had been slaughtered a hundred years ago by her husband before the truth could be found.

What was there left to fight for?

Unexpectedly, it was Corbier who answered. *The truth has failed us both, Veristor. Let it be for love that we fight on.*

It's a little late for the notorious Red-Eyed Raven to be getting sentimental, don't you think?

Later still for you to embrace cynicism. Witness now your own memories for once . . .

In the instant between the rise of Monsegino's blade and the fall, my own past unfolded before me: a stern-faced, middle-aged woman in a long black leather coat, checking each of the dozens of hidden pockets, filling them with tricks and traps and tools, before at last belting the rapier to her side and walking out the door, leaving behind a boy who struggles to understand how his grandmother could love him and yet be so unloving. A fine-haired, stoop-backed man, old even then, but with a grin that could have seduced the Saint of Chastity herself, tells the boy stories – all lies, of course – to make him forget his fears and loneliness. His ageing grandfather is a man driven by a love so deep that only recently has the boy, now a man himself, begun to fathom its depths.

The Vixen will have Paedar Chademantaigne in the duelling circle the moment you're no longer alive to stop her, Corbier reminded me with cold certainty. *Is that not cause enough to resist?*

More than enough, I agreed, rolling into an awkward backwards somersault. I found my footing with reflexes that belonged not to Corbier but myself. Had my grandfather been right about me all along?

I'd seen what violence had done to my grandmother, how each time she'd come back a little more hardened, her soul worn a little more, like leather being stretched too thin.

I guess that's why I learned to run.

But I was done running.

I ducked low just as Monsegino's blade slashed for my throat. The duke, his violet eyes darkened by the all-consuming memories of Prince Pierzi, smiled as he repeated the words he'd uttered once already. 'How many times have we crossed blades on this very battlefield, you bloody-eyed bastard?'

He's trapped in the moment, still waiting for the final duel with his nemesis . . .

I took up a low defensive guard, my rapier at the ready. 'A dozen times – perhaps a hundred? A thousand?'

Monsegino levelled his own blade, the point in line with my throat. 'Then by all the gods, let this time be the last!'

With those words, my world vanished. My fellow actors, the crowds, the palace itself were gone, and in their place was the bloody battlefield of Mount Cruxia once more.

'Let no man interfere!' Prince Pierzi called out. For the first time I realised his voice was deeper than Monsegino's, his jaw wider, his bearing more terrifying. 'On pain of death and such accursed verdicts as the gods decree for those who betray the sanctity of the duel, let no blood be shed save ours, until the soil be consecrated by vengeance too long delayed.'

Corbier echoed the instruction to his own men, and the two armies, visibly shocked by this strange command, backed off, leaving the archduke and the prince facing each other in a circle some fifteen feet wide, the perimeter formed by the thousands of armoured soldiers.

'You're a fool to face me alone, Pierzi,' I heard myself say. The taste of coppery blood filled my mouth where I'd bitten the inside of my cheek.

Corbier rebuked me for my fool's eagerness. Pierzi was no amateur – for him to openly issue the challenge when he had so much more to lose than Corbier meant he was certain he could win.

The prince's blade darted out, again and again, in mock feints as we circled each other. 'There was a time when I won as many matches as you, Raphan.'

Corbier's mother had named him Raphan, which meant 'gentle spirit', but that was before his eyes had changed colour and she'd forsaken him. No one but Ajelaine had been allowed to call him that ever since.

'That was a long time ago, *Nevino*. We were only boys.' I brought my rapier into line. 'Although I recall warning you even then that fencing and duelling were entirely different pursuits.'

And with that, Corbier sent me leaping across the distance separating us from Pierzi. Such bold manoeuvres were dangerous – it was perilously easy to lose one's footing – but Corbier had aimed carefully and the heels of his boots were finding purchase on the muddy ground even as the tip of his rapier drove for Pierzi's heart.

'Fast,' the prince said as he stumbled back, barely batting the attacking blade out of the way. 'You always were damned fast, Raphan.'

'Stop calling me that!' I shouted, fighting to contain Corbier's rage. 'Raphan is a boy's name. It's the name one friend calls another. And we, Pierzi, are bloodsworn enemies!' I tried a feint, aiming low before flipping the tip of my rapier up high as I lunged, making another try for his heart.

'Your one great flaw betrays you again, *Raphan*,' Pierzi said as he caught the thrust on the forte of his rapier and turned it down in a semicircle. Bringing Corbier's blade out of line allowed him to press forward, shoving me backwards. 'For all your speed, you are predictable, always going for the same target.'

I could no longer hold back Corbier's fury. 'Would that I'd been faster and my aim truer, you black-hearted bastard, that I might have killed you before you slew those two sweet boys and the woman I loved!'

Pierzi drew back, creating distance between us again. '*Me?* But have you not heard the story circulating all across the city? My nobles claim it was *you* who crept into my castle like a Dashini assassin, you who murdered those two innocents and the helpless woman who spurned your advances. The tale is spreading already, through every malodorous tavern and sumptuous salon, the gossips repeating it far and wide, while minstrels sing this truth far beyond our fair duchy.'

'A lie—'

'Indeed,' Pierzi admitted, 'and one of many! Lies are the grease that keeps the wheels of state turning, Raphan – that's what you never understood, even when the shifting allegiances of our Houses first began tearing our friendship apart. This world is built upon lies. You and I, we stand upon pedestals raised for us by those same noble Houses who then set us against each other, while the poor souls beneath us bow and scrape and offer up whatever meagre wealth they might have – indeed, too often their very lives – for our comforts, and all because they believe the very same lies we have always been told: that some men are born to rule and others to serve. We may all be equal before the gods, but some of us are, shall we say, more equal than others.'

'Don't you *ever* speak to me of the lives of common folk,' I broke through. 'You never cared for them any more than Corbier did!'

The prince eyed me quizzically. 'You speak of yourself in the third person now, Raphan? Is it another's spirit who guides your hand? Shall we call this ghost the Red-Eyed Raven, then?'

I ignored the jibe and began moving again, each circle fractionally smaller – slowly, almost imperceptibly, drawing closer to my opponent. It was a trick my grandmother had taught me, one easy for even experienced duellists to miss.

'You could have ruled unfettered, Pierzi. You could have had Corbier's lands, his titles, whatever your foul greed demanded. All he wanted was Ajelaine.'

'It wasn't *my* greed demanding anything,' Pierzi said, dropping his voice almost as if he didn't want anyone else to hear Corbier's words.

He said something else then, so quietly that I reflexively leaned in closer to hear, and in so doing fell into a trap the rankest amateur would have seen coming. Pierzi leaped upon me, his sword arm high with the point aimed low so the force of his weight would drive it right through Corbier's chest.

I twisted out of the way, but the price of survival was losing my balance on the muddy ground. Unable to parry, I could only knock the thrust aside with the knuckle-bow of my rapier's guard. Pierzi, anticipating the move, caught hold of my wrist, preventing me from regaining control of my weapon, which left me with no choice but to grab Pierzi's forearm in turn, and suddenly the two of us were caught in a *corpa-té-corza*, each sword hand trapped in the other's grip.

'Listen to me, you fool!' Pierzi whispered, his face just inches away. '*Nothing* is what you believe.'

I was so taken aback I nearly lost control of Pierzi's sword arm. 'Tricks and deceptions – that was always what you were about, wasn't it, o Prince?'

'Aye, you blistering idiot: tricks and deception – that's *exactly* what I'm trying to tell you!'

Suddenly I found myself looking not through Corbier's blood-red eyes, but my own, and not at Pierzi but into the face of Duke Monsegino. From the shock on the duke's face, he too had no idea what was happening.

'Where are we?' Pierzi whispered.

It was Corbier who replied, 'Another place, Nevino – another time, inside minds and bodies not our own. We are but memories here.'

I was about to take advantage of Pierzi's inexperience at finding himself in a different, weaker body, but Corbier held me back.

Listen to him, you fool! Something happened back then, in my time – something Pierzi tried to reveal during the battle, but in my rage and madness, I failed to hear him.

Duke Monsegino broke through Pierzi's control and said through gritted teeth, 'Damelas, we must go back. This is our one chance to finally learn what happened to them.' He let go of my wrist and shoved me away – and just as quickly as the ducal courtyard had reappeared, it faded again, hurling us back to Mount Çruxia and leaving me with a stinging cut on Corbier's arm.

The Prince's troops were cheering; the archduke's supporters were crying out in dismay.

'You see, I've learned a few tricks since we last fought,' the prince said, giving a mocking bow. 'Some of them from you, Raphan.'

Why does he keep calling us by the name only Ajelaine knew you by? I asked silently. *Is it a clumsy ruse to anger you, or a message?*

With the soldiers baying for blood, I was forced back into the fray, and now I was in control of the duel, pressing Pierzi back almost to the edge of his own troops. The prince's technique was good, but he couldn't match Corbier's natural ferocity, and soon was stumbling from a vicious cut to his thigh where part of his armour had come off during the fight. He fell to one knee.

I could kill him, I thought absently. *One thrust and the vengeance that history denied Corbier could be won.*

No, the Raven said. *The victory was Nevino's, not mine, and nothing we do can change that. The truth is the prize for which we fight.*

'Well, well,' Pierzi said, grimacing from the painful, bleeding slash, 'I suppose there's something to be said for animal instinct and blind rage.'

Unsure what was happening, but determined to keep up the act, I played the role required of me. 'Save your last words for something other than mockery, Nevino. Beg Ajelaine's spirit for her forgiveness. Beg the dead to give you mercy when next you see them.'

'Oh, I would, believe me,' Pierzi said. 'I would pray to the ghosts of those two innocent boys and the spirit of that shining, brilliant woman, of whom neither of us were worthy.' Suddenly his left hand came up from the ground and as he flung mud into Corbier's eyes, he leaped to his feet and weaved the point of his rapier in a deadly pattern of thrusts and cuts.

Blinded by the mud in my eyes, I frantically batted the blade out of the way as I stumbled backwards.

The prince's attacks were slowing, however, and soon the two of us were once again caught up together, each struggling for control of the other's weapon.

'Alas, I'm afraid it's entirely too early for me to be making apologies to the dead,' Pierzi said, almost merrily.

I kicked out at Pierzi's knee, a less than honourable manoeuvre, perhaps, but one that might gain Corbier the advantage. 'Only because my blade hasn't yet found your heart.'

'No,' Pierzi said, and in avoiding the kick, he pulled me so close we were almost nose-to-nose over our crossed rapiers. He whispered something – something Corbier, maddened by rage and loss, deafened by the drumbeat of his heart, hadn't heard on that bloody mound a hundred years ago.

But I heard Pierzi's words now, though I almost couldn't believe my own ears.

What Pierzi had said was, 'Because Ajelaine and the children aren't dead.'

CHAPTER 66

MERCY

Ajelaine and the children aren't dead.

Those words pierced Corbier's defences swifter than any arrow. From the moment he'd watched the blood spilling from her belly and the throats of the two boys, his entire being had been suffused by those memories, witnessing their deaths played out over and over again.

But if she were truly alive . . .

I jolted back to awareness and found my heels sliding back on the smooth wooden stage as Duke Monsegino shoved me away. The crowds were cheering wildly again, half of them roaring for Damelas-as-Corbier, the others for Monsegino-as-Pierzi, as if this were nothing more than a fencing match. They applauded madly as first one of us gained the advantage, then groaned in despair when our fortunes reversed, barely taking notice of the Iron Orchids among them. The uniformed militants now appeared to be content to stand idly by, resting their spears on the ground, looking more like costumed supernumeraries than a genuine threat to the people of Jereste.

My attention was brought back to the fight when the duke closed the gap between us – inadvertently opening himself up to the killing thrust that I was within a hair's-breadth of delivering. I narrowly avoided committing murder in front of ten thousand witnesses by swinging my point aside and grabbing at Pierzi's arm to bring us into the exact same *corpa-té-corza* in which we'd left Corbier and Pierzi a moment – or a hundred years – ago.

'Damelas, listen to me,' Monsegino whispered fiercely, spinning us both around so that the duke was facing away from the audience and could convey his message unseen. 'We must devise a plan.'

'*Now?*' I asked incredulously.

The two of us fought each other into another half-turn, allowing me to ask, 'Is it true? Did Ajelaine and the children survive? How long have you known?'

Monsegino whispered as we pivoted a third time again, 'I only learned of this during tonight's performance, when Pierzi's memories turned to that moment in which he hoped to reveal the truth to Corbier. But the Raven's wrath made him deaf to Pierzi's pleas to listen. Damelas, the killings were staged – it was all a trick, a piece of theatre, even down to the fake blood in sheep's bladders . . .'

Saints, I thought, *the very technique we've used in a hundred different plays at the Operato Belleza. I should have recognised it at the time, but Corbier's eyes tinged everything in crimson, so I couldn't spot the deception.*

'But why?' I murmured.

Just then, I caught sight of Beretto and Teo, garbed in Pierzi's colours as they had been when playing his lieutenants in the previous acts, and at last I understood. 'Pierzi's retainers – the ones with the orchid emblems on their collars. They were spies for the Court of Flowers?'

Pretending to lose his footing, bending beneath my pressure on his blade, Monsegino gave the hint of a nod. 'Ajelaine had attracted too much attention with her investigations into the noble Houses. Pierzi began to hear rumblings of a plot against her, and when she refused to back down, he instead conceived an elaborate piece of stagecraft to deceive those engineering murder and mayhem between Pierzi and Corbier. It is this play within a play that you and I must now continue . . .'

Monsegino's right foot hooked the back of my leg and sent me crashing down to the hard oak. My rapier fell from my hand, coming to rest a few inches out of reach. The duke stood over me, the tip of his all-too-real blade resting against my throat.

'Yield, Corbier. Yield, and I may yet show you mercy.'

But before I could even think how to respond, Monsegino was shaking his head. 'Nay, waste not your venom on me, you snake. Wriggle there on the ground and consider before you speak.' The duke turned and gave a wide smile to the audience. 'We have all night, after all!'

A surge of laughter rose from the crowds, even those who'd been cheering for me earlier. There was even greater delight from the Iron Orchids, who started jeering for the Violet Duke to prove himself at last.

'We must go back one last time,' Monsegino whispered through gritted teeth. 'There is still a final secret left to unearth: what really happened to Ajelaine and the children?' With a sudden bark of laughter, he shouted, 'Was that a cough I heard, you red-eyed raven? Are you choking on your own feathers now?'

'Mercy!' I shouted, even as I made a show of surreptitiously reaching a hand out to the side for my rapier, signalling my intent to commit crass betrayal and earning me loud hisses from the crowds.

'Good,' Monsegino whispered, pretending not to notice. 'Now, listen close: the moment the play is ended, the Orchids will attack. Your actors must make use of the chaos and confusion to give one of us the chance to make the truth known to all. Do you understand what I'm asking of you?'

I spared a glance for my fellow Knights of the Curtain. They'd sacrificed so much already in this mad cause. How could I ask them to now give their lives?

You won't need to, Corbier informed me. *They won't wait for you to ask.*

Holding back tears, I whispered, 'Gods protect them, you're right.'

The duke roared with laughter. 'Really, Corbier? You? Praying to the gods? I doubt they will even notice your false prattling.' Suddenly, Monsegino's foot swung up as if I'd kicked it out from under him. I grabbed my rapier and, jumping to my feet, stabbed downwards, only just missing the duke's heart before he rolled out of the way to shouts of excitement from the audience.

The stage now set, I relinquished control of my mind back to Corbier. As the courtyard filled with screaming crowds gave way to the muddy battlefield littered with blood-soaked soldiers, I realised that, no matter what followed, this would be the last time I visited Corbier's past . . .

. . . for here was where the Red-Eyed Raven was destined to die.

CHAPTER 67

THE SACRIFICE

There was a moment, come and gone faster than the beat of a hummingbird's wings, when the intricate machinations of this century-long plot to bring ruin to the Duchy of Pertine began to make sense to me. The complicated thrusts and parries, the bizarre demands for seemingly unrelated laws, the two rivals manipulated into a doomed and fatal duel and, most pernicious of all, the historical transformation of the daring and inquisitive Ajelaine into a demure object for them to fight over . . . Each became the movement of a game piece upon a board larger than this entire city. In another second, perhaps two, I might have found the answer to the ever-elusive question: who rules the Court of Flowers?

But time, which had been so malleable of late, now ticked inexorably down with the rhythmic thumping of the executioner's boot heels upon the boards of the gallows as he approaches the soon-to-be-hanged man.

In the past, my jaw ached where Pierzi's rapier hilt had struck Corbier. The two of us broke apart once again, sending the soldiers into a howling frenzy. Like the Iron Orchids in the present, they screamed for the inevitable conclusion: one man standing, the other dead.

Corbier and I had rarely agreed about much during our brief and bizarre relationship, but we both knew it had to be him.

Pierzi's lieutenants, he said silently as he circled our opponent on the muddy ground. *The smirking ones with the orchid emblems on their collars that I failed to notice in my own time. They must have learned of the boys' eyes turning red and realised they were my offspring. It would have been a small matter to put pressure on Pierzi to prove his resolve by ending their lives.*

Agreed. So Ajelaine persuaded Pierzi to go along with her plan of staging the deaths. She just needed to accelerate your conflict with Pierzi faster than the Court of Flowers had intended. Fortunately, by the time you arrived at her bedroom window, your sense of righteous outrage was already burning so hot that you were easily deceived.

But why? Corbier cried silently as he exchanged thrust and counter-thrust with Pierzi to the roars of the soldiers on either side. *Why didn't she tell me her plan? Why didn't Pierzi tell me he was being blackmailed by his patrons?*

I knew the answer, though I wasn't sure about inflicting the truth on him.

What is it? he demanded. *What are you holding back?*

Ajelaine and the children's deaths needed to be so convincing that Pierzi's lieutenants would be worrying about your escape rather than examining the bodies. The prince needed them to go after you, which meant they had to believe you were in a mad fury. I'm afraid you're just not that good an actor.

I caught Corbier's silent chuckle. *We must both pray that's no longer true, then.*

'Well, you bloody-eyed raven?' Pierzi demanded, making a fine show of stumbling and trying to regain his balance. 'Shall we make an end of our feud once and for all?'

Our eyes met, and for an instant, I could feel the bond between him and Corbier reawakening. Years of mistrust and enmity began to fade, leaving behind a thousand memories of boyhood, of dangers shared and victories won together – of rivalry, yes, but not resentment. They'd loved each other as brothers, these two, almost since birth. They should have been fighting side by side to make the duchy whole. Instead, someone had decided it was better if one disposed of the other, ensuring that whoever survived would never be strong enough to rule without the wealth and military might of the noble Houses, who themselves were being controlled by the Court of Flowers. The crowned prince and his offspring would for ever be puppets dancing to the tunes of their shadowy masters.

'It has to be this way,' Pierzi said, and for an instant the arrogant mask fell and his true self shone through. 'One of us lives. One of us dies.' More quietly he whispered something which at the time Corbier had mistook for a final insult, but now heard differently. 'I was never worthy of her, Raphan. Let this be my gift to you both.'

With a shock, I realised what was about to unfold.

Pierzi means to sacrifice himself!

Then he's a fool, Corbier said. *For a man so gifted at politics, Nevino was always ignorant of intrigue. Even had I lived, the moment those sycophants surrounding him discovered Ajelaine had survived, they'd be after us, for they feared the prospect of her reign far more than Pierzi's or mine.*

'Have you ever wondered about the Afterlife?' Corbier asked aloud, moving unsteadily to buy a little more time for them both.

'I prefer to contemplate a long and happy rule,' Pierzi said with a wry chuckle, raising the point of his weapon as if preparing to launch into the next attack.

'I think about death all the time,' Corbier went on. 'Perhaps it's because I was so sickly as a child. These red eyes of mine, you know.'

'And what do you envision when you ponder the Afterlife, Raphan? Do you see yourself sitting a throne with hordes of beautiful women begging you to attend them in the bedchamber?'

The prince's soldiers laughed then, noting that their man looked steadier on his feet than the archduke.

Corbier gave a tentative beat with the tip of his rapier against Pierzi's, knocking it out of line for just a moment, and said, 'I confess I do not see myself at all. Instead, I imagine her, Ajelaine, living on a little island. You know the one? It belonged to my family years ago, though I suppose if you are prince, it's yours now. But still, I see her walking the shore, holding the hands of those two boys. She smiles down at them, then looks up at the sun warming her lovely face as she remembers someone she once knew, a foolish young man with raven-black hair and the red eyes she tried to convince him looked more like rubies than blood.'

Pierzi nodded, signalling he understood. 'I too imagine her that way.'

Corbier smiled. 'Then let one of us have the spoils of this world and the other with his blood bring that perfect dream into reality!'

He beat Pierzi's blade a second time – a common enough tactic, and one he'd used often in their innumerable fencing matches when they were boys. Nevino couldn't help but reflexively counter the obvious attack. I felt the muscles of Corbier's back leg tense as he readied himself, then lunged straight for his best friend's chest—

No! I shouted in lonely silence, no one listening to me now. *No – it can't end like this! There has to be another—*

The tip of Pierzi's rapier glided along Corbier's, pressing it out of line. An instant later, the tip pierced leather, then flesh, slipping between two ribs to skewer the heart of a man who'd wanted nothing more from life than love, and from this moment forth would be remembered as the Red-Eyed Raven: the most despicable and bloodthirsty murderer in the duchy's noble history.

The sorrow of Corbier's unjust end was soon overcome by the agony of the rapier blade buried in his chest and the scream it drew from me.

I had played the role of a corpse any number of times upon the stage.

I'd never understood what it was to die.

CHAPTER 68

THE ARREST

The sky above was filled with stars and I thought I heard the hush of the ocean gently spilling its waves upon a shore. I imagined the sound of footsteps on the sand, getting closer. A smile came to my lips and an ease stole into my heart that almost made it possible for me to ignore the sword in my chest.

Almost.

The knowledge of what had taken place a hundred years ago returned in a rush. Everything Duke Monsegino and I had learned in the past, we'd played out on the stage. Beretto, Teo, Ornella, Abastrini – all of them – had improvised from the subtle cues I'd given them and revealed to the ten thousand citizens crowded inside the courtyard of the Ducal Palace of Pertine the devastating truth of Archduke Corbier and Prince Pierzi: that neither had been a sainted hero or cursed malefactor, just two men consumed with their own sense of destiny and the strength of their sword arms. These would-be heroes had failed to notice the strings attached to their limbs being tugged here and there by unknowns who never took the stage, yet determined the course of their lives.

Only in the end, there on that muddy, blood-soaked battlefield, had the frayed threads of friendship enabled them to conspire together to save the life of the woman they'd both adored, and her two children.

All of which would have gone significantly better for me had I not been stabbed in the process.

Duke Monsegino, it turned out, was an able fencer, even a decent duellist. What he *wasn't*, alas, was skilled at the equally complex but subtly different art of stage combat, and specifically, the part where you *don't* skewer your fellow actors.

The thrust that had pierced Corbier's heart in the past had missed my own in the present, but only because after slicing effortlessly through shirt and skin, the tip of the blade had struck a rib and slid down the side. The amount of blood seeping from the wound was more than enough to make up for the lack of any stage trickery.

I certainly feel dead enough, I thought miserably.

A sudden gasp from the audience drew my gaze to the other side of the stage. Lady Shariza, barefooted, clad in a plain dress of dull white linen and lovely beyond words, was walking towards me. Zina held her left hand, Tolsi her right – and when I blinked, I saw two boys, laughing at something their mother had just said, happy and innocent despite the bright red of their eyes.

I was about to signal Shariza away: why give the audience the satisfaction of this illusory happy ending? Corbier's memories ended with his death, and there was no reason to believe this scene ever took place.

Please, he begged, *let me have this moment – let me see it unfold as it might have been . . .*

Acquiescing to his plea, I pretended to feel no pain as I rose to my feet, my rapier clattering to the stage. Her appearance shifted between Ajelaine and Shariza with every step and I was overcome with love for both of them, as I was filled with grief for Corbier.

The sound of a throat being cleared drew my attention to the side of the stage where Duke Monsegino, still in his golden armour, was looking on, weeping like some silent saint forced by the gods to bear witness. Without needing a nudge from me, he shed the guise of Pierzi and took on that most ancient of roles, the eulogist.

'Let us imagine them together,' he began, his rich tenor carrying over the near-silent crowds. 'Let us allow ourselves this one moment of beautiful delusion, a small gift in exchange for the terrible truths we have had to face. Let us believe that somewhere, somehow, a different Archduke Corbier, one not caught in the web of deceit woven for him by the same men who ensnared Prince Pierzi, walks upon the shore of a small island not far from here, where a young woman fleeing for her life took refuge with her sons. And let us imagine one small, perfect moment . . .'

Shariza let go of Zina and Tolsi's hands and ran to me. She had tears in her eyes and though it should have been impossible, I saw reflected in them a taller man, lean but broad of shoulder, with raven-black hair and ruby-red eyes.

And Raphan Corbier was smiling.

Thank you, he said, and the spirit or memory or whatever it was that had inhabited me these past weeks drifted back into the past where he belonged.

Duke Monsegino was finishing his soliloquy. 'There has only ever been one redemption for any of us: the one which led Nevino Pierzi to take pity on the woman who had come to their marriage already pregnant with the children of his nemesis; the same spirit of valour which guided Raphan Corbier, the Red-Eyed Raven, to sacrifice himself, so that those he loved best should know peace.'

In the stillness Monsegino left behind, a whisper came from the crowd, then another and another, until they grew in volume like the rising tide upon the shore. 'Let them kiss,' the audience pleaded. 'One kiss—!'

A small request: one tiny lie to ease the pain brought on by so many uneasy truths. How could it harm anyone to imagine Ajelaine and Corbier together in the afterlife?

But the Iron Orchids were on the move. The column that had split the crowd in two was advancing on Monsegino's personal guard, while those ringing the massive courtyard had turned their spears on the crowd and started driving them towards the stage. They would soon overwhelm us.

'Firan Monsegino,' one of the Orchids called out, 'you have committed treason most foul against the decent folk of Pertine.' The sneering thug held out a rolled sheet of parchment as if it were a sword. 'By the demand of tradition and soon of law, your tyrannical oppression of this duchy is at an end. Yield yourself for judgement before the Court of Flowers!'

Below the stage, Captain Terine was struggling to keep her paltry troop formed up against the steadily growing onslaught of the Orchids and the panicked crowds they were funnelling towards the stage.

'Damelas, what should we do?' Beretto asked.

I almost laughed. What should they do? Become Veristors and travel back a year, so when a cowardly messenger fleeing a duel invades their sacred operato, they can hand him over to the bully-boys to drag him back to the duelling court and let the Vixen do her worst? But I had discovered the hard way that the Veristor's gift didn't work that way. It could no more alter the past than it could save the present.

The Knights of the Curtain, the bravest, the best men and women I'd ever known, were about to die, and along with them, the Duke of Pertine and any hope this duchy had of being free.

I was surprised to find Shariza still with me; I had expected her to have made her way to the duke's side. Instead, I caught a trace of a wry smile – only . . . I was absolutely positive that smile belonged to someone else.

'What did you say?' I asked, unable to hear her quiet words over the chaos being unleashed in the courtyard.

As she opened her mouth, the cacophony was replaced by the soft rustle of waves upon a distant shore.

'What's happening—?'

She reached out, placed her hands on my cheeks and leaned closer, and I thought Shariza was about to kiss me, but instead she spoke a third time, and at last I heard her.

'Alas, we've no time for tragic romance, my dashing Veristor,' Ajelaine said as the night sky was banished by a blazing sun overhead and two boys ran from her side to play on the beach. 'You and I have a duchy to save.'

CHAPTER 69

THE NEVER QUEEN

Ajelaine was older now, with strands of silver in her chestnut hair. The iron in her gaze reminded me more of Ornella than the vivacious young hellion who'd teased me on horseback in Corbier's early memories. But while the years might show on her face and hands, still her eyes shone with mischief and inquisitiveness. She was as beautiful as the dawn.

The elaborate curtsey with which she greeted me sent the rough hem of her faded blue linen dress flapping in the breeze. 'You look surprised to see me, Veristor. Did I not promise we would meet one last time?'

'You did, but—' I had to struggle for a moment to hold onto the vision of Ajelaine, superimposed over my own world, although the stage was covered in sand and the screaming crowds in the courtyard had merged into the cries of seagulls flying overhead. This felt more tenuous than my previous ventures into the past.

'How is this possible, my Lady?' I asked. 'Corbier's memories have always carried me to you, but his tale has ended and his voice is lost to me.'

Ajelaine rolled her eyes at me. Apparently, age hadn't muted her propensity for mockery. 'For a Veristor, you suffer from an awfully short memory, Damelas Chademantaigne. Did I not explain to you many years ago in the orchard that your talent reaches beyond the recollections of a single individual? That yours is the gift to hear those echoes of our thoughts and experiences, and your duty to—'

'—to give voice to the dead,' I finished for her. 'Forgive me, my Lady, but what was years ago for you was mere minutes for me and I've hardly had time to master my art.'

'A pity,' she said, kneeling to pick up a fistful of sand, then holding it up so that I could see it slowly slip through her fingers. 'Time, like memory, is as limitless as the grains of sand on this beach, yet to each of us is given precious little, and none of us have the means to hang onto it. Have you not learned the lesson at last, Veristor? Your talent must be more than some self-serving means to journey into the past. Yours is a gift meant to be shared, Damelas.' Her eyes met mine. 'So long as you're willing to pay the price.'

'What price? What must I do?' I asked. 'The Iron Orchids are taking the city. The duke's guards will soon be overwhelmed by their—'

'Lies and loathing.'

'My Lady?'

She wiped the sand from her hands and set off down the beach. 'Lies and loathing, Damelas. These are the weapons of our enemy.'

Panic and irritation made me forget myself and I seized her arm to stop her. 'They have rather a lot of swords and spears, too!'

She stared down at my hand as if it belonged to someone else.

My grandparents would have argued vociferously over which of them got to knock some sense into me for grabbing a woman's arm without her consent. I went to withdraw, but Ajelaine placed her own hand over mine and held it there.

'Fear,' she said. 'Remarkable, isn't it?'

'Forgive me, my Lady, I didn't mean—'

She dismissed the apology with a shake of her head. 'You fear for your friends, for the lives of the people you love – and yet fear makes us so much smaller than we ought to be. Do you suppose it can do likewise to an entire city? A duchy? A nation?'

'I . . . Yes, I believe it can.'

She slipped her arm into mine and resumed her stroll along the shoreline. 'Fear prevents us from listening to one another. Raphan loved me so much, but his adoration turned to fear for my safety, and that kept him from listening to me. I am rather done with men who cannot listen, Damelas.'

I was sweating now, and not only from the heat of the sun, for she was right: I *was* afraid, and that was making it hard for me to hear what she was trying to tell me.

'Listening, my boy,' Shoville would have reminded me, *'is an actor's most valuable tool.'*

Mastering myself, breathing in slowly to still my pounding heart and forcing the frustration and panic from my voice, I said, 'I attend you, my Lady.'

'Good. What brief moments remain to us are a gift too precious to be squandered. Lies and loathing are the weapons of the enemy, which means truth and love must be ours. Let us begin with truth.'

Hope sparked inside me. 'Then you did it? You discovered the secret of the Court of Flowers? You can tell me their names?'

The corner of her mouth rose in a smirk that was now utterly familiar to me. 'I have indeed uncovered their secret.'

She stopped and reached into the pocket of her dress. She held out her closed hand to me as she'd done before, but this time, she turned it palm up. Her fingers unfurled to reveal the desiccated grey petals of a flower that should have turned to dust long ago.

'An orchid?' I asked. 'That's not a name, my Lady. It doesn't tell me who's behind all of this.'

'It is a symbol,' she replied. 'A flower, foreign to our shores in my time, yet in yours it blooms throughout the duchy, perhaps even the entire nation of Tristia.' She held it out as if it were some grand revelation.

'My Lady, the Orchid Laws you uncovered are nothing but a jumble of asinine demands for the removal of restrictions on liquor, drugs, the lowering of the legal age of prostitution, these bizarre prohibitions against unpatriotic art, and bigoted punishments against refugees and the poor. There's no—'

'Exactly!' she declared excitedly, closing her fist around the dried petals, crushing them with a vengeance. 'I wasted *years* investigating the nobility and the criminal underclass alike, looking for those who might benefit from that precise assortment of laws. And in your time, not even the duke's Dashini spy has uncovered the Iron Orchids' leaders?'

'No, but that doesn't mean they don't exist—'

'It means *precisely* that, Damelas.'

I stared at her clenched hand. 'The orchid,' I whispered, catching her meaning at last. 'A flower that has spread across Tristia and yet isn't native. You're saying the only people who would benefit from the Orchid Laws . . .'

'. . . would be those *not* from our shores,' she finished my words. 'Conquerors who desire to see us weakened, defeated not through force of arms, but by twisting our own society against itself.'

'Lies and loathing,' I repeated.

Ajelaine began counting off on her fingers. 'Decrees demanding the imprisonment of the homeless breed resentment and distrust. The brutal targeting of immigrants prevents the growth of shared knowledge and understanding. The spread of imported liquors and pleasure drugs sows addiction and despair. Allowing girls and boys to be forced into prostitution changes the way we view all our children. Banning heretical art—'

'—stops us from questioning what we're doing to ourselves,' I finished. Anger was rising, a rage that would have made Corbier himself pale.

Ajelaine opened her hand with a flourish, as if completing a magic trick, revealing a small pile of grey dust like the ashes of one long dead.

'Saints save us,' I breathed. 'There is no Court of Flowers, is there? That's why we've never been able to find them in my time. They've been gone for decades . . .'

Ajelaine blew on the little pile in her hand, sending the dust into the breeze like the ashes of the dead.

When she looked back at me, I saw the tears of frustration in her eyes. 'This is the genius of our enemy, Damelas. They didn't invade us – they didn't need to. Instead, they designed a scheme so finely crafted that they needed to send only a few agents to our shores to set it in motion. What we call the Court of Flowers isn't a cabal of men and women, it's a machine with springs and gears forged from our own venal ways: a masterpiece of hidden hierarchies and endless intrigues perfectly aligned to the weaknesses already present in our society. Damelas, our own nobles are unwittingly financing the war that is destroying us from within. The Court is like . . . like an enemy army in which *we* are the foot soldiers, armed with weapons we turn against ourselves: rumour, gossip, prejudice, blackmail, brutality – and above all else, *secrecy*. The clockwork of conspiracies begun in my time continues into your own, because new members recruit themselves, never realising the cruel, destructive, elegant truth at the centre of it all . . .'

The image of Ajelaine began to shift and shimmer . . . Beretto was shaking me, calling me to return, yelling that everything was going to the seven Hells. I could hear more shouting, from Captain Terine and her guards, trying to hold back the flood of Iron Orchids, and terrified citizens about to swarm the stage. My city was about to fall, but not to the outside enemy we'd been searching for all this time.

I felt chilled to the bone as I whispered, '*We* are the Court of Flowers.'

CHAPTER 70

SURRENDER

I returned to the stage to find myself staring at the backs of my fellow Knights of the Curtain, who had massed around me in a final valiant attempt to protect me, this time from the panicking crowds rushing towards the stage. I kept expecting to hear Corbier's sardonic whisper deriding the futile valour of players and stagehands who didn't know when they were beaten, but the Red-Eyed Raven was gone, leaving me without his counsel – or his skills.

Out in the courtyard, Captain Terine and her soldiers were fighting a losing battle, fending off the central column of three times as many Iron Orchids, even as another large party of armed thugs herded the confused and terrified citizens of Jereste like cattle towards us.

'Madness,' Abastrini said.

Ornella, standing at his side, brandishing a shield from the battlefield scene, disagreed. 'Not madness, chaos. *Controlled* chaos. It's to ensure the duke can't escape.'

When I looked around for the duke, I found him lying in a heap next to me, mumbling incoherently as he struggled to rise.

'What's wrong with him?' Shariza asked, kneeling beside us.

I smoothed Monsegino's sweat-soaked hair from his forehead. 'He ventured too deeply into Pierzi's memories. This was his first time and he wasn't ready for the repercussions.'

'Rally the army,' Monsegino commanded, wild, unfocused eyes turning to me suddenly. 'My people cannot fight alone – we must have warriors, trained soldiers—'

'Dukes don't have their own armies, you fucking moron,' Teo spat, wiping away the blood oozing from a cut on his forehead where a rock had struck him. Ignoring Shariza's warning glare, he jabbed a finger out at the courtyard where soldiers owing fealty to the great Houses had assembled to protect their lords, leaving their sovereign to his own devices. 'Should've kissed a few more noble arses before you sat yours on the throne, I reckon.'

Under normal circumstances, Teo would have just earned himself a beating, followed by a month in the cell I'd only recently vacated. But the duke's mind was still stumbling between our world and the past.

'We must have warriors,' he repeated in a daze. 'Mount Cruxia – they are gathered at Mount Cruxia.'

I reached down to help him to his feet. 'Your Grace, Mount Cruxia has been a graveyard for a hundred years. You have to let go of Pierzi's past. Focus on where you are now, here in the courtyard, bef—'

I was cut off by the crash of another charge. The rampaging column of Iron Orchids had nearly breached Captain Terine's more disciplined shield wall, driving dozens of innocents onto the swords of the ducal guards, losing their lives for no better purpose than to wear down the defenders.

'Don't suppose you learned something wonderfully useful in the past?' Rhyleis asked as she and Beretto lifted painted wooden kite shields over the duke's head to protect him. 'Perhaps the identity of whichever bastard among that rabble the duke's favourite Dashini needs to kill to induce the rest to lay down arms and surrender?'

I could hear the thread of hopefulness in the Troubadour's cynical question, which only made the truth more heartbreaking.

'They have no leader,' I said sadly. 'The Court of Flowers is nothing more than . . .'

Saint Ebron-who-steals-breath – how am I supposed to explain in moments what took Ajelaine two decades to uncover?

'The Court of Flowers is like a play with no director,' I said at last. 'The parts have been so cleverly written that each actor thinks their lines make them the hero, and they go on repeating the same scenes of intrigue and revenge over and over, believing this to be their time, even though the script they follow was composed by a playwright long dead.'

Beretto's eyes widened as he made sense of my words. His thick red beard was glistening with sweat. 'Well, that makes this a fucking depressing end to our own play, then.'

The company kept glancing back at me, all those furtive expressions betraying both their fear of impending death and their determination to face it bravely.

Duke Monsegino, clinging to my arm to keep his balance, saw it, too. 'Knights . . . when I gaze upon them, I see knights.'

'That's because they *are* knights, your Grace.' I jabbed a thumb at the clusters of noble House soldiers in their gleaming armour and bright livery. 'And possessed of more honour and dignity than any of those who claim that title.'

'Yes,' Monsegino agreed, bobbing his head like a drunk. 'Knights. We need more – dozens more. Hundreds. *Thousands*. A general must have his army. Bring my knights to me!'

The flash of a silver braid whipped by as Ornella spun on her heel. She strode over and backhanded the Duke of Pertine.

'Back away, sister,' Shariza warned her.

Ignoring the chilling threat in the Black Amaranth's tone, Ornella said, 'A general must *lead*!' She grabbed Monsegino's golden breastplate. 'Instead of moaning about your lack of an army, perhaps you could learn from your time on stage and *pretend* to be a leader for your people in their hour of need!'

'Ornella, that's not going to—'

But I was cut off by Monsegino squeezing my shoulder. His wits must have returned to him, for his expression was as sombre and despairing as the moment demanded. He swallowed, dusted himself off, then bowed to Ornella. 'My Lady, by your command, I will.'

Firan Monsegino, Duke of Pertine, stepped to the front of the stage, in easy crossbow range of those who'd come to take his crown, and spread wide his arms. At first it looked as if he was committing suicide, awaiting the shot that would end his brief reign. But the duke knew what he was doing, for he had positioned himself at the voci forte, and when he spoke, his words were projected far and wide.

'Nobles of Pertine!' he roared, and even in the chaos, everyone turned to look at him. 'Margraves and margravinas, viscounts and viscountesses, lords and daminas, hear me now, for though I might not be the ruler of your choice, still am I duke by law, by blood and, damn you all, by the will of the gods. Beneath their watching eyes, I command you thus: send forth your troops to protect the innocents trapped inside this courtyard. These machinations of power and deceit may be but a day's amusement for you, but the lives of those we are charged to protect are as precious as yours, as vital to this city and this duchy as my own. Stand for your brethren, here and now. Assemble your troops before me, and in return . . .'

There was a moment's hesitation in the duke's oration, as if he were about to trade away something that he wasn't quite sure was his to give.

'In return, I will abdicate. To you I will render the power to choose who sits the throne of Pertine and wears the crown I never asked for and will be well rid of.'

A tense silence followed the duke's appeal. Shariza tried to interpose herself between him and the crowds, but then something unexpected happened: the bright pennants of the noble Houses began to cut through the crowds with smooth efficiency, the soldiers heeding the curt orders of their commanders.

'Those *bastards*,' Beretto muttered. 'The nobles must have planned this all along – they've just been waiting for Monsegino to abdicate!'

The Iron Orchids apparently shared his outrage, and although they tried to resist, their column was soon forced back, their lines cut once, twice, thrice, as contingents of armoured knights shoved them aside.

'I can't believe it,' Teo said, aghast. 'They're actually . . . those soulless rich bastards are actually going to save us?'

Had Teo been watching the duke's face as I was, he would have seen that this was no heroic rescue.

Barely a dozen breaths later, an embassy made up of a dozen nobles strode through the protective lines of their private armies to ascend the stairs onto the stage, claiming it as their own.

At their centre was Viscountess Kareija.

CHAPTER 71

THE CORONATION

Viscountess Kareija walked unhurriedly across the oak stage, her lustrous coral tresses bound in a simple golden circlet, a stately Pertine-blue gown elegantly fitted to her voluptuous figure sparkling beneath the stars. Richly clad nobles in House colours followed behind her like a gaudy bridal train.

'*She's* our surprise villain?' Beretto grumbled. 'And people tell me *my* scripts are predictable.' He clapped me on the back. 'At least we're not going to get massacred, eh? I was never that enamoured of Monsegino anyway, and I imagine her Ladyship will prove herself an only fractionally shittier ruler.'

'What makes you think that?'

'She would've been duchess anyway, had old Meillard not decided at the last minute to alter the line of succession for her nephew. Maybe this is as just an outcome as we deserve.'

I desperately wished I could share his sanguine prediction that the madness overtaking our city would end with nothing worse than another in a long series of mundane power struggles among the noble Houses. But though Corbier's voice was gone, the Red-Eyed Raven's instincts were ingrained in me now.

And those instincts were telling me the real devastation was about to begin.

Duke Monsegino waved the Knights of the Curtain aside as his aunt approached. Shariza held her ground.

'It might be hard to fit you for a proper crown,' the Black Amaranth warned the new Duchess of Pertine in a voice devoid of hesitation or humanity, 'without a head upon which to set one.'

'Shariza, enough,' Duke Monsegino said.

She scowled at him, but he smiled in return, placing his hand on her shoulder tenderly. I had never seen him touch her before.

'My pitiful reign has known only one consolation,' Monsegino said, so quietly I felt like an intruder eavesdropping on an intensely private moment. 'Your counsel, your loyalty and above all else, your friendship. Now your service to me ends, most gracious Lady, and I would see you live a long and happy life elsewhere. I am your liege no longer.'

Shariza's dark eyes never left the viscountess. 'Then you're in no position to be giving me orders, your Grace. My service to you will end when *I* choose. You have little say in the matter.'

Out in the courtyard, a stillness had fallen over the crowds. The Iron Orchids, perhaps only now discovering that they were mere bit players in someone else's production, shuffled anxiously as they watched not the stage, but the weapons of the armed soldiers surrounding them.

'Oh, Firan,' Viscountess Kareija said, looking amused by his exchange with Shariza, 'if only you aroused such loyalty in your own subjects.'

'Or at least in his family,' Ornella said, taking up position next to Shariza. The two women gave each other an almost imperceptible nod, a silent pact made between them.

'Fuck the nobility and their armoured thugs,' Beretto whispered to me. 'What this city really needs is an army of Ornellas.'

Kareija, however, stepped between the two women and extended her bejewelled hand to Monsegino. 'Your admirers question my loyalties, Firan.'

The duke bent down to kiss the proffered hand. 'They do not know you as I do, Aunt.'

The viscountess turned to me. 'I didn't lie when I told you I never aspired to the throne, Damelas. When my father brought Firan to our city and displaced me to name him heir, I made no move against him even though I knew he was doomed from the start. The Iron Orchids were bound to grow in power and influence. I needed to bring them to my nephew's side.'

'So you stole your father's diamond pass to remove the second Sigurdis Macha volume from the Grand Library,' I said, unable to keep the fury from my voice. 'You thought the edicts described within would be the key to securing the Orchids' support.'

Whatever righteous indignation she saw in my eyes, she returned tenfold. 'I was prepared to give up *everything*! I encouraged others to bend the knee to my nephew, even punishing my most ardent supporters when they tried to mint currency in my image.' She shook her head, the confusion and sorrow in her voice sounding entirely genuine. 'Yet still Firan engaged in reckless and futile reforms, ignoring my counsel and turning his own nobles *and* the Iron Orchids against us.'

Monsegino kissed her hand a second time, as if accustoming himself to inevitable subservience. 'You were most generous in your restraint, Aunt.'

As he rose, she slapped him across the face with the hand he'd kissed, as if he were a child who'd made one too many flippant remarks. Shariza would have killed her then and there, had not the duke clamped a hand on her arm.

'Look where you've brought us, Firan!' Kareija cried, gesturing to the frantic crowds awaiting the next cataclysm that would surely befall them. 'You have turned this city against itself – and you have undermined the traditional rights owed to the great Houses!'

Some trace of the man that Monsegino had been – or perhaps he had hoped to become – reasserted itself. 'Of which "rights" do you speak, Kareija? The right to keep the populace drugged and insensate? The right to embezzle funds meant for the maintenance of sewers and streets until the entire city is crumbling underfoot?'

He paused a moment, as if suddenly embarrassed to realise they were airing family grievances in front of thousands of commoners, then chuckled at the irony.

'Kareija, you never asked why your father chose me, a foreigner – the "Violet Duke" – to take his throne. Perhaps it was because he knew that having lived your entire life benefiting from such corruption, you could never conceive of foregoing its privileges.'

She weathered her nephew's defiance without malice, apparently unaware that the twelve nobles who'd accompanied her to the stage were looking on in amused patience as she played at the role of monarch. One of them, a heavyset man in an expensive burgundy silk coat, approached to whisper in her ear.

Kareija nodded, and when she turned back to face her nephew, her posture and bearing had changed, making her more regal and less human.

'Firan Monsegino,' she began, her commanding tone that of the heroine princess at the end of the play whose spell will compel the vile dragon to submit to justice, 'for treason against the Duchy of Pertine, you are by unanimous decree of the noble Houses of Pertine deposed from the throne. I have been named duchess in your stead. For the love I bear you, the sentence demanded for your crimes will be commuted to banishment. By morning you will be gone from this city, by week's end from the duchy, never to return on pain of death. Submit to this sentence willingly, binding those supporters you have to peace, and we can put an end to any further bloodshed.' Without so much as taking a breath, she added, 'Do you accept these terms?'

Beneath the stern, almost placid mask he tried to keep in place was a tortured soul at war with itself. He had dreamed of being the hero in this tale. Now, like Corbier, he would be for ever consigned to the role of the villain.

'Promise me one thing, Aunt,' Monsegino said at last.

'I've already offered you more—' She stopped and sighed. 'Ask what you will, Nephew.'

'Promise me you'll investigate those who secretly command the Iron Orchids. Your new duchy has enemies, and they have a name.' His fists clenched with a barely restrained outrage that was now familiar to me. 'You must unmask the Court of Flowers before it is too late.'

'Oh, Firan.' She placed her hands over her mouth for a moment, as if witnessing a loved one succumbing to madness. 'As you will,' she said at last. 'On my oath as Duchess of Pertine, I will poke my nose into every nook and cranny of this duchy in search of these phantoms that so trouble your fevered imaginings.'

Without another word, Duke Firan Monsegino knelt before his aunt and bowed his head. 'I hereby confess my guilt and accept my sentence. With my last act as duke, do I urge those few in this city who love me to keep the peace and to serve Duchess Kareija as your true and lawful monarch, in any way she requires. Long may she reign.'

A cheer rose up, first from the paltry assemblage of nobles on the stage who'd helped orchestrate the coup, then a louder one from their troops. Even the Iron Orchids shouted their approval. I experienced my first moment of patriotic pride when the rest of the folk in the courtyard – the merchants and craftspeople, the artisans and alley-rats – remained silent as ghosts.

They long to fight for their city, I thought suddenly. *They lack only the means.*

Monsegino rose and held out his wrists, awaiting the shackles.

I doubt I'd ever seen anyone look quite so relieved as the new Duchess of Pertine did then. She hadn't been lying about her devotion to her nephew; she truly believed that taking Monsegino's crown was the only way to save his life. There might have been something noble about that, were this not a world infested by the Court of Flowers.

'Knights of Pertine,' she commanded, 'escort the prisoner to the city's boundary. Give him a good horse and a full purse and let him bring four companions to keep him safe as he journeys out of Pertine to wherever the gods wish him to go.'

To Monsegino she added, 'I suggest you take Captain Terine with you. She, at least, appears to be loyal.'

At his nod, she said, 'Captain?'

The ducal guards standing below the stage were flanked by the brightly coloured knights of the noble Houses. Captain Terine began to select from among her meagre troops an honour guard for the duke.

She never finished.

At a cue from the nobles assembled on the stage, the knights below turned on the captain and her guards. Before she could even cry out, a hundred swords had risen up high, the steel catching the light from the stars above before they came down in a rain of blows.

Monsegino screamed and tried to run to Captain Terine's side, but she was already beyond saving. I grabbed one arm, Shariza the other, to stop him from throwing himself at the murderers.

The heavy-bellied nobleman in burgundy silk who'd been whispering what had surely been lies in Kareija's ears moments before now stepped forward, at last bringing the game to a close. 'Firan Monsegino, for violation of the Orchid Laws, you are sentenced to suffer the fate of all tyrants.' He turned to the grey-clad thugs in the courtyard, but whatever he said next was lost in the thunderous cheers when they saw the nobleman turn up the collar of his coat, revealing a brooch made of iron in the shape of an orchid.

'Traitor!' Kareija screamed, her outrage paired with a backhand that sent the man reeling. 'Seize him at once,' she demanded of the knights climbing the stairs to the stage.

Instead, gauntleted hands pulled her away from her nephew and formed a protective guard around both her and the arrogant fools who believed they had conceived and executed this coup. When she tried to push her way past, the other nobles held onto her.

'Duchess, you must not interfere,' said a foppish young courtier sporting large emeralds in his ears. 'The safety of the sovereign is paramount. You have a duty to your people.'

'Are you mad? Our soldiers outnumber the Iron Orchids ten to one—'

'With respect,' said the nobleman holding her against her will, in his grin a gleeful anticipation no longer restrained, 'both the Orchids and the soldiers are *ours* now, *your Grace*, united by our noble cause. The Court of Flowers sees no reason to risk their lives to rescue a traitor from the justice of his people.'

A conspiracy that recruits its own conspirators, I thought, watching the end unfold just as Ajelaine feared it would. Then her earlier admonition came suddenly to my mind: '*The Veristor's gift is meant to be shared.*'

I tried, I thought bitterly, *but what good is revealing the truth when those with the power to fight for their city have no love in their hearts for it?*

A contingent of Iron Orchids strode onto the stage and took hold of Monsegino's arms and legs. The duke's earlier courage fled him when he saw six of their comrades wheeling forward a wooden gibbet, and a fifth standing by with a hammer and seven iron spikes. He struggled frantically, like a rabbit caught in a snare.

'Fucking Hells!' Abastrini swore with an uncustomary brevity. 'They're going to crown the duke – right here in front of the whole city!'

Shariza was trying to find a way to get to him, but the knights had a trio of crossbows trained on her.

'We've got to run,' Teo said between gritted teeth. 'We can't save the duke, but we can take advantage of all this chaos, disappear into the crowds and—'

'No,' I said.

I hadn't spoken loudly, but the coldness in my voice had sliced through all the noise around us, even as it cut through my own doubts.

This rabbit doesn't run any more.

'What do we do?' Ornella asked, nearing sixty years of age yet still brandishing her shield and spear like a warrior woman of legend.

I wished her bravery could wash over me, over this entire city, and cleanse our streets of doubt and fear. Beretto had been right: what the people of Jereste needed wasn't more soldiers in pretty liveries and shiny armour. They needed spirits like Ornella's.

'Oh, saints,' Teo groaned, staring at me as all the others were doing now. 'He's losing it again. He's drifting into that Veristor nonsense of his.'

As it happened, Teo was right.

One last time, I thought, feeling a pressure in my skull worse than any I'd experienced in all my trips into Corbier's memories before.

'Damelas?' Beretto asked. 'Now's not the time to leave us, brother.'

'I'm not going anywhere,' I said, gritting my teeth from the pain. 'I'm staying right here. Get ready, all of you.'

'Ready for what?' Teo asked.

'Damelas, you can't,' Rhyleis cried, as if she'd worked out what I was going to attempt. 'The Veristor's gift isn't meant for this—'

But I had already closed my eyes and was pushing my awareness past the unbearable agony and into the echoes of a thousand memories of the dead, even as I forced my consciousness to stay rooted in the present.

A gift meant to be shared, Ajelaine had told me. I'd thought she'd meant that it was my duty to uncover the truth of past events and make them known to all. But I finally understood what she'd been trying to tell me. A Veristor could do so much more . . . *as long as you're willing to pay the price.*

In the aching quiet of my mind, I laughed. *Pay the price? For these lunatic actors I adore? For this city? My Lady Ajelaine, I hope some remnant of your spirit is watching . . .*

'Places, everyone,' I said aloud. 'The final act's about to begin.'

CHAPTER 72

THE VERISTOR'S GIFT

The hardest part was keeping myself from being swept back into the past, into those memories of battles won and lost; the thrills of sword thrusts brilliantly parried, of those last, terrible instants of terror when a cold blade buried itself in a chest or belly. Undaunted, I forced my mind to wade deeper into the ocean of their lost recollections, drawing them into myself.

I will give the dead voice, I swore, the copper taste of blood filling my mouth where I'd bitten my lip to distract myself from the pain. *Even if it kills me.*

'What's happening?' Beretto asked, taking my arm over his shoulder to keep me upright. 'Make him stop – we're losing him!'

'Hysterics won't help him,' Rhyleis snapped, and grabbed my jaw. 'Listen to me, Veristor. You've bound yourself to too many memories. Whatever happens, you must not let go of the present, do you understand? Damelas, can you hear m—?'

Screams arose from the courtyard where the Iron Orchids had erected their gibbet and were lashing Monsegino's limbs to it. Seven men were brandishing iron spikes, relishing the cheers of their fellows even as they ignored the cries of the new Duchess of Pertine. Kareija was screaming for someone to save her nephew even as her own nobles restrained her. No one was listening to her, nor to those in the crowd who recognised injustice when they saw it, but lacked the means to fight back against swords and spears.

'By all the gods,' Ornella swore, 'they're really going to do it! They're going to commit this . . . this atrocity in front of the entire city!'

The heat of her smouldering fury was shared by all our fellow Knights of the Curtain. Fists clenched, jaws tightened to breaking point. Despair was a palpable thing now; it felt to me as if a thousand necromancers from the old tales were summoning devils to overrun the world.

Saints give me the strength to conjure a few spirits of our own, I prayed, as my mind began slipping helplessly into the past. *I'm not strong enough – I can't—*

A familiar shoulder slid under my other arm to share my weight. I'd begged him to stay away tonight, yet some part of me had counted on him coming. Through the cacophony raging in the courtyard and the even louder noise in my skull, I heard the voice which had always been there when I needed it, from the day my mother died giving birth to me, through all the loneliness and fears of my childhood.

'I'm here, my boy,' my grandfather said. 'With you to the end.'

'And me,' Beretto said, with what might have been a sentimental sob.

More love than any two souls could possibly contain, I thought, relinquishing the responsibility of keeping myself upright to my grandfather and my best friend. *That must be why they share it so freely.*

'Take me down to them,' I said, my voice gravelly from the pain. 'I need to be among them.'

'Are you mad?' Abastrini demanded, putting his bulk between us and the steps to the courtyard. 'You'll be killed!'

I tried to conjure a smile out of the throbbing in my skull. 'I'm not one for suicide, Master Abastrini. I merely go to fulfil the duke's last request of me before he gave up his crown.'

The other Knights of the Curtain stared back at me, confused, but after a moment, Abastrini, who perhaps understood the ways of the Veristor more than he realised, breathed, 'Saints, can such a thing be possible?'

'I don't know,' I replied. 'Let's go and find out.'

Abastrini shoved the others into position around me as Beretto and my grandfather helped me down the steps and into the panicked crowds of Jereste's citizenry who were trying and failing to evade the Orchids' goading weapons.

'This had better be one Hell of a speech,' Beretto muttered as they reached the bottom.

'It's not a speech,' I said, thinking it was unlikely anyone could hear me over the racket. *It's a play.*

I allowed my mind's eye to drift back to the battlefield of Mount Cruxia, searching for a particular warrior there even as my gaze sought out the nearest of my fellow citizens here in the courtyard. I nearly laughed out loud when I saw it was Vadris. The drug-pedlar was crouching in front of me, no sign now of the orchid emblem of which he'd been so proud.

Apparently even sleazy pleasure-pepper merchants can have souls.

Letting go of Beretto and my grandfather, I reached out a hand and grabbed Vadris' collar. The man spun to face us, dread filling his wide eyes.

'Damelas? Saints, Damelas, have you come to rescue your old friend Vadris? Please, I can't—'

I slapped him across the face, then proclaimed, 'Your name is' – I reached back to Mount Cruxia – 'Seriva Denor. You are a spearwoman in the army of Archduke Corbier. Stand with your feet wider and—'

'Are you mad?' Vadris demanded, cutting me off. 'You want me to pretend to be a woman? I'm not some petty player in one of your—'

'I'd do what he asks,' my grandfather interrupted, gesturing to the Iron Orchids pressing ever closer, 'and I'd pray my grandson is about to do something this sorry world has never before seen but badly needs, because the alternative isn't going to be pleasant.'

Only overwhelming terror of impending death could have persuaded him, but that was in plentiful supply. Vadris widened his stance, held up his hands into fists and shouted at the top of his lungs, 'I am Seriva Denor, spearwoman for Archduke Corbier, and I—'

Now, I thought, placing my hand on the back of the pedlar's head, willing a single one of the thousands of memories pounding inside my skull to take up residence in Vadris.

Nothing happened at first. Vadris stood there, his features slack, almost disinterested – then the corners of his mouth rose into a smile far different from the leers and smirks I'd seen on his face before.

'Oh,' Vadris said, 'this is going to be rather amusing.'

Suddenly he ducked down low, broke through the panicking folk in front of him and grabbed the end of an Orchid's spear. With a deftness and precision entirely at odds with his own inexperience, he brought his right foot up and slid it along the shaft of the spear until his heel smashed into the Orchid's hand and broke the man's fingers. Vadris snatched the spear, held it up over his head and spun it gracefully before driving the sharpened steel tip into the enemy's throat.

'By all the gods,' Beretto breathed. 'How is this possible?'

'The old songs said Veristors could inspire armies,' Rhyleis said, her voice filled with awe. She looked as if she badly wanted to drop the sword she was holding so she could take out her notebook and start composing herself. 'We always assumed it was through the secrets they revealed, delivered through grand speeches. But this – *this* – is what they meant!'

I'd already grabbed hold of a woman in blacksmith's leathers, dodging her punch as I reached inside my mind and drew on another set of memories. 'Luzanne of Gamrock,' I said. 'Swordswoman of—'

It happened faster this time, and before I'd even finished, she'd pushed me aside.

'I'll take this, if you don't mind.' The blacksmith snatched the sword from Rhyleis and examined the blade. 'Shit craftsmanship,' she said, before rushing past the crowd and taking the head of another of the Iron Orchids.

'Krev Medan,' I said, taking the hand of a shopkeeper.

The memories slid from me smooth as silk, and were instantly taken up by the stoop-backed fellow. 'One more battle, eh?' the shopkeeper asked with a grin before running into the fight. Within moments he was tearing the shield away from one of the knights assisting the Orchids and bashing his helm off with it.

'You're doing it, boy,' my grandfather said proudly, keeping a firm arm around me to keep me on my feet.

Faster and faster they came, the recollections of dead soldiers, hazy phantoms offering their experiences to farmhands, merchants, artisans and alley-rats alike. Soon I couldn't keep up. The pressure was becoming too great for me to contain.

'What's wrong?' Beretto shouted. 'He's bleeding from his eyes and ears—'

'Grandson, are you sure—?'

I couldn't answer, but I knew I had pushed the Veristor's gift too far.

Rhyleis grabbed my arm. 'You can't do this one by one, Damelas. You've got to open yourself up and let the memories out – let them all out!'

Now, just as I could feel my mind coming apart, I found the answer to the question plaguing me since this had all began: who saves a city from an enemy who can never be caught, whose deeds can never be punished?

Clinging to my grandfather and my best friend, I threw my head back and *screamed*, each word smashing through the din like a hammer shattering long-rusted iron.

'*Jereste!*' I cried out first, because Jereste, like any city, was an expression of *hope* – of the mad and unfounded belief that by coming together, men and women could shape a society that was greater than the meagre sums of their own lives.

The crowd of artisans and merchants, the beggars and alley-rats, even the maddening memories breaking my mind apart, all became silent for a single moment. Thousands of eyes stared back at me, blurry through tears, pleading to know what was expected of them.

Inside that silence, I spoke the second word.

'Arise.'

There was no great clap of thunder at first, no hue and cry . . . then a rumbling ignited within the crowds as people started *remembering*: stories of daring and decency, myths of heroism and compassion, heard at the knees of parents and grandparents, or played out on the stages of operatos across the city, or told by children in alleys miming sword fights with sticks. The memories I'd borrowed from a thousand battlefield dead spilled forth into the waiting crowds – the knowledge, instincts and experience of trained warriors finding a home inside the brave and determined people of my city.

A roar suddenly erupted from ten thousand throats as the citizens of Jereste turned on their would-be conquerors, fighting at first with fists, then their enemies' own weapons, untrained hands wielding them with astonishing skill.

'You've done it, brother!' Beretto cried, his face alight with wonder. 'Saint Laina's tits, that I should live to witness—'

Then he too heard the calling of one long dead and gave a war cry full of furious joy, swiftly followed by Rhyleis – and with Ornella and Abastrini on either side, the four of them led the Knights of the Curtain into the fray – leaving my grandfather and me the sole audience.

Wiping blood from my eyes, I leaned heavily on my grandfather's shoulder, the only thing keeping me upright, and the two of us bore witness to the unfolding war against the Iron Orchids.

Even as the last of my strength – maybe my very life – seeped out of me, I grinned, spotting two small figures perched on the top of the great arch above the main gate, skinny legs dangling as if they were paddling in a lake. Zina was firing a crossbow balanced on her lap into the mass of Orchids, while Tolsi handed her the bolts. It took both of them to wind the crossbow each time, but Zina's aim was true and the pair of them were wreaking havoc. I suspected they had had no need of the battle memories of soldiers from the past.

I turned to look back to the stage, where nobles who'd thought themselves so very clever, even as they'd mindlessly followed the carefully laid plots of schemers long dead, stared around in confusion at the discovery that this city – this duchy, this *world* – was not theirs to play with as they willed, after all.

Let actors give us merry tales, lest we make them melancholy, said the words inscribed on the wooden sign the Orchids had hung around Roslyn's neck after they'd crowned her in the alley.

You thought to mock us, my Lords, but we have given you our tale now. And should you ever again hunt and murder those we love, we actors will make of all the world a stage.

I felt my grandfather shudder, and turned to find the old man weeping. 'Grandfather?'

He shook his head. 'Don't mind me, my boy. I just wish she were here, that's all.'

'Grandmother would have loved to have been in the midst of that brawl, wouldn't she?'

My grandfather gazed at me solemnly. 'What Virany would have loved was to see her grandson come into his own and accomplish what a thousand duels could never achieve.'

I knew his words should fill me with pride and reconcile me to my conflicted memories of my grandmother, but I wasn't ready yet. I still had too many other memories crowded inside me.

'You should put me down,' I said. 'No doubt you'll be taking on the recollections of some great general and leading the others in battle any second now.'

'I don't need orders from long-dead spear-carriers,' Paedar Chademantaigne said as he guided me back up the steps to the stage and set me down beside one of the massive marble columns. 'I'm a Greatcoat, boy, and my sword arm serves neither kings nor spirits.'

I caught sight of a figure moving on the other side of the stage and only then understood what my grandfather was about to do. I tried to grab the old man's arm, to keep him safe, but was shaken off.

'Your grandmother fought for truth, but I've only ever had one cause,' the old man said, smiling.

'Grandfather, no!'

But the old Greatcoat had turned to face the threat from which I'd tried so hard to keep him all this time.

'How pleasing,' said the Vixen of Jereste. She wore no orchid veil this time, and her theatrical "Masked Margravina" garb from the fight outside the Belleza had been replaced by a traditional white leather duelling vest and trousers, '. . . to know that avenging my mother's degradation at the hands of Virany Chademantaigne will also put an end to her wretched grandson's interference in the affairs of this duchy.' She raised her slender rapier in a mock salute. The blade was already dripping blood from whoever she'd killed on her way to get us. 'Tonight, at last, I fight to reclaim my mother's reputation, my city's right and proper rule, and the world's natural order.'

I tried to find the strength to rise, to summon up Corbier's talents, or even my own, and finally bring the Vixen's vendetta to an end, but I was spent. I slumped there, forced to watch as a brave man with ageing hands and an unsteady grip drew his rapier from its scabbard.

'That all sounds terribly complicated,' said Paedar Chademantaigne, coming into a stiff, almost antiquated guard. 'I prefer to fight for love.'

CHAPTER 73

THE CODGER'S DUEL

I had never actually seen my grandfather fight a duel. After my grandmother had died, he'd insisted on fencing with me now and then, to keep up our skills, but it was little more than routine exercises before he launched into another tale of his adventures as a Greatcoat. As I grew older, I became increasingly concerned that my grandfather was speaking of those days as if they'd never really come to an end.

They would be coming to an end now.

When I had faced Ferica di Traizo two days ago, Corbier had mocked the Vixen of Jereste for being a fencer rather than a true duellist. The Red-Eyed Raven's influence was lost to me now, but I could see that criticism was doubly true of my grandfather, who moved with shaky sluggishness, an almost pathetic figure in a long, heavy, leather greatcoat. His light rapier trembled in the air as if the weight were too much for his arm.

The Vixen was suitably amused. 'Does that trick work often?' she asked, as her quick thrust was neatly parried. She responded with a disengage, followed by a slash to his face, this one evaded by a shuffling step to the right as he ducked beneath the blade.

'Mercy, most esteemed Lady,' he rasped plaintively. 'Take pity on these old bones.' His free hand plucked at his neck. 'Naught but loose skin left of me. Surely too little meat to satisfy so voracious a vixen.'

Ferica waved at the courtyard, where the battle for Jereste was being fought by hundreds of Iron Orchids wielding spears and swords against commoners armed with nothing but courage and the memories of long-dead warriors. 'Come, Master Chademantaigne,' she urged, 'neither of us have ever had so grand an audience to bear witness to our skills. Let's not play idle games with each other.'

'You have me all wrong, Mistress.' He came into a more elegant guard this time, his sword arm straight and true, back arm arched in a graceful curve. 'Damelas is the actor in the family. Virany was the duellist. Myself, I care for neither audiences nor sword fights. I came here for one thing only.'

'And what might that be, old man?'

He raised his point a fraction higher. 'To put you down once and for all, you savage lunatic.'

Margravina Ferica di Traizo's good humour vanished instantly. It wasn't like my grandfather to hurl insults; that he did so now was surely a tactic – but it was entirely the wrong one to use on the Vixen of Jereste.

'Look at yourself,' she hissed, circling him, forcing him to keep adjusting his footing on the polished oak stage. 'Your flesh is weak, your eyesight fading.' She wiggled the tip of her sword in the air mockingly. 'Can those milky cataracts even follow the movements of my blade?'

He whipped his own point out and nearly – so nearly! – knocked her weapon aside. But the Vixen's speed was rightly legendary, and she disengaged easily.

'You're too slow, old man. Too weak, too blind, too frail. What have you left?'

He winked at her. 'Naught but my charm, Margravina.'

He spread his arms briefly – as if he, the mad old dodderer, were about to bow to her. I prayed she'd wait, allow him this final bit of mischief, but of course she didn't. Without warning, she burst into a long, graceful, heart-rending lunge.

I screamed even before the tip of her rapier had struck home, knowing her aim would be true and my grandfather too slow to get out of the way in time.

The old Greatcoat looked down at the steel blade piercing the leather of his coat right over his heart.

And he smiled.

He rapped his knuckles against his chest, and even over the din of the fighting in the courtyard, I heard the clacking.

'Oh, and the bone plates of my coat,' he said, grinning at the Vixen. 'Sometimes those work even better than charm.'

Before she could withdraw her rapier for a second attack, he flung out his hand, his fingers splayed open. A fine yellow powder billowed into the air between them. The Vixen backed away, but she was too late. Howling with rage, she rubbed furiously at her eyes.

'And ocharis powder,' he said, stepping first left, then right, as if he meant to run past her. 'Did I mention that? Nasty stuff,' he added, waving at her with his free hand. 'Makes everything blurry.'

Still blinking madly through her tears, the Vixen gave a defiant shout as she lunged again. 'Too bad for you I can follow your wheezing cackling with my ears just as easily, you old—'

She froze when she saw her blade had missed by almost a foot.

'Alas, the hallucinogens in the ocharis mess with one's hearing, too.'

They were so close now that even with his considerably shorter lunge, the tip of my grandfather's rapier buried itself deep in her thigh. When he withdrew it, she screeched with pain.

He stepped back and waited for her to recover. 'Now, where were we, my dear?' He rapped at his chest. 'You mentioned my enfeebled flesh?' Next he pointed at her still-tearing eyes. 'My lousy vision, you now share, and of course' – he put on a show of languidly thrusting at empty air with his rapier – 'my being far too slow to defeat you. How's that leg doing?'

The Vixen was unable to put her full weight on her right leg and she was struggling to recover her balance.

For the first time, I thought I saw something akin to respect in her expression when she gazed at my grandfather – respect, and maybe even fear.

'The paradox of the old,' he said, suddenly launching into the fight, driving her back with a series of quick thrusts and feints, 'is that we have precious few years left, and yet still too much time on our hands.'

She tried to encircle his blade and disarm him, but he drove his tip straight for her and she was forced to disengage.

'It's more than a year since the day you were meant to duel my grandson.' He continued harrying her with a flurry of attacks which, while slow, still took all her efforts to deflect now that she was wounded and confounded by the ocharis powder. 'Would you like to know how I idled away the hours, my dear?'

'You're an old man!' she shouted, swinging her blade wide. 'You'll never defea—'

He ducked underneath and came up with a fully extended arm. Had he been even a fraction faster or his reach an inch longer, he might have skewered her throat, but he sounded entirely untroubled by his near miss. 'I spent all that time conceiving just how a feeble, half-blind old man might defeat the great Vixen of Jereste.'

The lunge he demonstrated might have belonged to a much younger man. It was clean, smooth, a thing of wonder to behold – but it was still too slow, and the Vixen's eyes were clearing even as she got used to compensating for the wound in her thigh.

But my grandfather wasn't letting up; he recovered from his lunge and attacked again and again, and even though any sane duellist would have saved what little breath he had to spare, still he spoke. There was a fury I had never before heard in the old man's voice, a burning rage born of the primal, untamed instinct to protect those he loved.

'He's my *grandson*!' he shouted, slashing in a downwards, diagonal arc that the Vixen was barely able to evade, only for his rapier to then deliver a rising cut on the other side that forced her to stumble back. She tripped over some abandoned stage swords and fell over backwards, and he yelled again, '*My grandson!*'

To watch a man near seventy fight with such sublime skill and ferocity was a wonder beyond all those I had witnessed, both in the past and now in the present, as the people of Jereste fought armed thugs for their city.

But it wouldn't last – it couldn't. Paedar Chademantaigne's best days had passed him by decades ago, and no matter what clever ploys remained to him, he was no match for the Vixen of Jereste.

She rolled gracefully onto her feet, leaped over his slash at her legs and knocked his blade aside with her own, then hooked up a wooden stage sword with the toe of her left boot and kicked it into my grandfather's face. The wooden crossguard struck him on the nose and he stumbled as he backed away from her.

Now the Vixen's pursuit began in earnest. With a brutal beat of the forte of her rapier against his, she weakened his grip, then, moving like lightning, she brought her tip around his blade and jerked it upwards.

His sword flipped up into the air, spinning end over end, and when it came back down, it appeared in the Vixen's left hand, just like a magic trick. The old Greatcoat was left standing there, wheezing, his empty hand open, like a beggar waiting for a coin that would never find his palm.

I expected Ferica di Traizo to smile with pleasure at the flawless elegance of her victory, but there was no joy left in her, only an unquenchable thirst for blood and a transcendent need to watch the life ebb from an old man's eyes.

Drawing on every ounce of my remaining strength, I rose to my feet – only to crash to the ground, utterly drained. Desperate to be closer to my grandfather before he met his end, I forced myself to my hands and knees and began crawling towards them, begging all the while, 'Please, take me – *please*, take me instead.'

But the Vixen wasn't listening to me. Whatever ire she bore me was nothing compared to the seething hatred my grandfather had ignited in her.

'Did you *really* believe,' she began, and her voice was devoid of any trace of her customary pretence at courtly wit and elegance. She stopped for a moment, as if even she couldn't comprehend the arrogance of her enemy. 'In your wildest, most senile imaginings, old man, did you truly believe that *you* could beat *me*?'

His breath coming in great gulps, the old man knelt down and placed his hands under my arms to help me up.

'Well, I hoped . . .'

He stopped then, the two of us leaning against each other like toppling trees suspended in precarious balance. 'I wanted to believe it was possible,' he confessed, still panting. He glanced up at the sky, but the stars were fading as the dawn light chased them away. 'I wanted her to see me save our grandson's life with nothing but a rapier in my hand

and the love we shared for him in my heart.' He shook his head, as if only now realising how foolish – how *old* – he sounded.

But neither love nor courage were substitutes for strength.

'Grandfather . . .'

Ferica di Traizo placed the tip of her sword at the old man's throat, resting it there as if waiting for him to acknowledge it.

He nodded, just a fraction, enough for the point of the sword to yield the first drop of his blood.

'I had to try. You understand, don't you?' he asked her. There was an old man's weary smile on his face. 'It would have been such a fine story.'

'It would have,' she acknowledged, then she looked out into the courtyard where the battle was coming to an end. Against all odds, the Iron Orchids had been routed. Some had fought to their deaths, more fled, but most of those still alive had laid down their arms and were begging for mercy. 'But even on this night of wonders, the gods do not grant miracles to romantic old fools.'

He chuckled. 'You know, you sound just like her.'

With the point of her sword pressed at his throat, knowing this might be some final attempt at a ruse, the Vixen asked, 'Who?'

'My wife, Virany. She never made room for love in the violence of a duel. Love, she always said, was a hindrance in battle, something to be set aside once the sword had been drawn, lest it weaken one's resolve.' The old man's gaze drifted skywards, as if his long-dead wife were looking down at him now. 'You never believed me, dearest heart. You thought I was a silly romantic whenever I told you that love is the sharpest blade of all.'

The Vixen's lips had curled into a snarl at the first mention of my grandmother's name and her arm tensed as she prepared to thrust the blade through my grandfather's throat. 'When you meet your wife in the seven Hells, tell her she was righ—'

Slowly, as if not to frighten her away, my grandfather raised a hand to his neck, just below where the tip was preparing to bury itself in his flesh. One finger traced a line across his sagging skin, and then, as if by some dark and terrible magic, an echoing red smile appeared on the Vixen's throat.

'How did you—?'

Blood seeped from the wound, then began to spill, faster and faster, down the front of the ivory ruffled shirt beneath her duelling vest. My grandfather grabbed the rapier as her legs buckled, then the Vixen collapsed to the stage floor, revealing the figure standing behind her.

'You took your time,' my grandfather observed calmly.

The Black Amaranth shook her curved dagger, sending drops of blood flying from its edge onto the stage. 'I had to make sure the duke got inside safely. Besides, you appeared to be making a speech. Something about love conquering all? I thought it might be rude to cut you off.' She stepped closer, looked down at the Vixen's body splayed on the floor, then up to meet my grandfather's gaze. 'Twice, as I slipped through the crowds towards the stage, I saw a moment when you had the advantage of her. Why didn't you kill the Vixen yourself? Why did you wait for me?'

My grandfather huffed, then his face split into a grin and his eyes briefly flickered back up to the sky. 'It's not often a man gets to win an argument with his wife.'

Shariza looked so confounded by my grandfather that I broke into a wheezy laugh. She might well be one of the deadliest assassins to ever stalk the earth, but nothing in her Dashini training could have prepared her for Paedar Chademantaigne.

My grandfather and Shariza dragged me to the back of the stage, where we sat gazing out as the sun rose and sanity slowly began to settle over the courtyard.

'I can't believe it,' I said faintly, feeling the exhaustion deep in my bones. My eyes kept flickering shut, but I badly wanted to see what wonders the Knights of the Curtain had wrought upon our beleaguered city.

I smiled as I caught a blurry glimpse of Beretto out among the crowds, fist in the air, fighting to be heard over Abastrini; no doubt the two were arguing over who got to give the victory speech. Closer at hand, I noted my grandfather with a rather too familiar arm around Shariza's shoulders; he was obviously regaling her with the many schemes he'd devised to defeat the Vixen, should she not have arrived in time to save him.

In the courtyard, there was even more confusion, for the fight had ended and the common folk found themselves brandishing weapons they scarcely knew how to hold, while around them lay the results of their hard-won victories and sacrifices. The voices of those long-dead warriors whose own battles had ended upon the bloody slopes of Mount Cruxia were dissipating now, returning first to me, and then back into the past where they belonged. Artisans and merchant lords, alley-rats and even those few nobles who'd chosen to fight against the Orchids were turning to each other, sharing first shock, then grim nods of acknowledgment. Some even shook hands.

Not a bad end to my first play, I thought.

'Damelas?'

I looked up to find Shariza standing over me. She looked unexpectedly confused and awkward. I was about to comment on it, but couldn't quite compose a response that was both witty and comforting at the same time. Only then did I recognise that look: Shariza was afraid.

I heard her say, 'Damelas, you're bleeding from your eyes and ears again. Whatever you're doing, you've got to stop.'

She was shaking me now, which was also strange, as I couldn't feel her hands on my shoulders. A breeze – that's what I was feeling, like all those memories drifting through me were caught in a rising wind. The sensation grew stronger, and soon I couldn't hear her or my grandfather, even though the two of them looked like they were shouting at me.

A chill began in my fingertips and toes, then slid up my limbs. As I looked out at the victory celebrations beginning in the courtyard, the sense of elation and pride at the part I'd played in these grand events fled me. It was as if I didn't belong to this place and time at all – as if I'd been an actor performing a role and now the curtain was falling and it was time for me to leave the stage.

The wind really was awfully strong now. If I'd not been leaning against the back in this enormous amphitheatre with its massive marble columns, I'd surely have been blown away like a leaf. It was raining now, too, for my cheeks and upper lip were wet. My grandfather's trembling hand wiped the rain from my face, but his fingers came away slick with blood.

Oh. I felt the memories of all those dead at Mount Cruxia grasping at me, pulling me back with them to their own place of burial.

I understand now.

CHAPTER 74

THE BURIAL MOUND

There was a terrible pain in the left side of my chest. I tried to rub it away, but the broken end of a rapier blade embedded there kept getting in my way. All around me lay the dead and dying, some moaning or weeping, though most were silent.

I'm sorry, Corbier said.

I was less surprised by the Raven's voice than I was at my pleasure in hearing it.

I can't believe I'm saying this, but I think I missed you.

Let's not get too sentimental, Corbier warned. *We have larger affairs with which to concern ourselves.*

I coughed hard, choking on the blood in my throat. A second later it shifted enough that I could breathe again. In my own time, I'd suffered a minor wound where Monsegino's blade had scraped against one of my ribs. Here, however, Pierzi's tip had slid effortlessly between the bones to reach a far deadlier target. Why wasn't Corbier dead by now?

As always, you descend into melodrama, Player. Only on the stage does every duel end with a rapier blade through the heart. Do you have any idea how difficult it is to hit such a precise target? Pierzi wasn't even trying to attack; I had to trick him into stabbing me.

We're going to live?

Oh, no, we're definitely going to die. The tip nicked the heart before it buried itself in my lung. It's just a slower and considerably more painful death.

I considered the grim prognosis. My chest *did* hurt a great deal, but

I wasn't overly troubled by the sensation. Pain, I discovered, turns out to be far less frightening when you know it's fatal.

I'm glad you're here, Corbier said. *I wasn't sure I'd be able to draw you back to me.*

I'm here. You're not alone.

The Raven chuckled. *Again, you assume sentimentality, Veristor. You think I brought you here to hold my hand as I bleed out in the mud?*

Then wh—?

Before I could finish the question, the answer became apparent. Across the battlefield, those remnants of the archduke's troops who hadn't surrendered were fleeing, pursued by Pierzi's soldiers. The wounded were being carried away, while enemy soldiers not quite dead were being dispatched. A figure in physician's blacks was walking towards me, but Corbier had lost so much blood that my eyes could make out little more than a faint silhouette. Something about how the man moved, his unhurried, *dispassionate* gait, chilled me to the bone.

Who is that? I asked.

How should I know? Corbier replied. *There's something not right about him, though, something . . . troubling . . . and maybe . . . familiar.*

The physician knelt down by my side. The sun was behind him, rendering his features nothing more than indiscernible shadow.

'You lost,' the man said. There wasn't a trace of anger in his voice, nor compassion, nor anything else, really. His words were merely an expression of fact, although I thought I could hear the faintest hint of curiosity.

'You were not meant to lose. Pierzi is your inferior with a blade, especially when you are angry. You let him kill you. Why?'

Corbier replied in two gasping exhalations, 'Ill. Luck.'

The man posing as a physician didn't laugh. 'Giving Prince Pierzi this easy victory means his own army is not depleted as we intended. He will be too strong a ruler now. Our plans must be delayed.'

As one of Pierzi's lieutenants approached, the strange man examined Corbier's wound.

'Can he be saved?' the soldier asked. 'The prince would—'

'Alas, no,' the imposter said, and his voice was deeper now, filled with weariness and sorrow. He would have made *such* an actor. 'The wound is too deep for my meagre skills. May the gods curse me, I've not the talents to—'

The lieutenant patted him on the shoulder. 'The prince will understand that you did all you could.'

After he left, the stranger resumed his earlier taciturn demeanour. 'We will have to begin again,' he said, 'and as generations come and go, still our plans will unfold as they must.' He grabbed Corbier's jaw, not hard, but firm, and demanded, 'How did you know? How could a fool like you cause us this setback?'

Corbier coughed as he tried to summon enough breath to utter some final insult, but it was me who spoke.

'Can you see me?' I asked with Corbier's voice.

The man posing as a physician looked genuinely startled.

'Because I see you,' I told him.

'What are you?' the spy demanded, squeezing Corbier's jaw harder.

I forced a smile onto Corbier's lips. 'No one of consequence. An insignificant rabbit, too small to factor into the intrigues you assemble from the fecklessness of your victims.'

'Then you cannot stop—'

'You will never think to look for me. That will be your mistake, for I will haunt your every step – and I am not alone. Look behind your back from time to time, Schemer, Intriguer. I am coming for you, Manipulator.'

If you keep soliloquising, he'll figure out you're an actor, Corbier warned, *and an overly melodramatic one at that.*

The man in black considered my words. 'We are the Court of Flowers,' he said at last, and glanced around before placing his hands around Corbier's neck. He began to squeeze. 'We reign in secret, naught but shadows to the once and future slaves of this land. Even your legendary Greatcoats cannot stop us.'

With the last dregs of Corbier's fading strength, I defied the slender fingers crushing my throat. 'Then I will form a new court,' I whispered, 'and we will put the shadows themselves on trial.'

EPILOGUE:

THE TROUPE

Where secrets are revealed,
and prices paid,
a stranger arrives,
and wounds are healed.

CHAPTER 75

ALWAYS IN THE EYES

Over the days that followed, consciousness became an elusive, unreliable companion. Every time I woke, faces were looming over me, mouths opening and closing, their words faint and distant. Their eyes told me I might yet die. Sometimes I'd try to rasp reassurances, but before my dry lips could utter a word, I fell back into the abyss, which was growing ever more familiar, and ever more comforting.

But my body clung obstinately to life, and after a time, the fraught expressions I saw whenever I woke showed me their new fears: *Why wasn't I speaking? Why was I sleeping all through the days and nights? Had I pushed my Veristor's gift so far past its limits that I'd irreparably shattered my mind?*

For my part, I was fascinated by the myriad variations in those ever-present eyes watching over me: big, round eyes beneath thick red brows that surely belonged to some barbarian warlord out of myth rather than the kindest, most gentle soul ever to bring grace to my life. Narrower, darker eyes, filled with a thousand dangers, whose uncharacteristic anxiousness tugged at the corners of my mouth, making me smile.

Other sets of eyes suggested irritation as much as concern; I assumed they must be physicians.

The eyes that finally brought me out of my slumber were of a particular blue so rich they might almost have been called violet; they drew from me the first words I'd spoken in many days – which was unfortunate, because one would expect an actor's first utterance to have a little poetry in it.

'*Observations Of Ocular Maladies*,' I muttered.

'Damelas?' His Grace, Duke Firan Monsegino, leaned over me and offered a pewter goblet. 'Do you need to drink something?'

I did, but now that I could see a bit more clearly, I felt it prudent to examine my surroundings. That's when I saw the scarlet curtain and my heart began to race.

Saint Zaghev-who-sings-for-tears! I'm back on stage and I haven't memorised my lines – I can't even remember which part I'm supposed to play—

'It's all right,' the duke said, pressing a hand gently down on my shoulder. 'There's nothing to fear.'

Nothing to fear? Has this half-witted nobleman never faced an enraged audience after a botched performance at the legendary Operato Belleza before?

I turned my head towards the wings, praying that the director would be there to mouth my lines at me . . .

. . . and remembered that Hujo Shoville was dead, his remains entombed beneath the ruins of the Belleza. Tears blurred my vision.

I wiped them away, and only then noticed that the curtains weren't just in front of me, but on either side as well.

A bed, I realised. *I'm in a bed hung with red velvet curtains.*

My free hand was lying on something equally sumptuous. I stretched my fingers to stroke the coverlet. This was the most luxurious bedchamber I'd ever slept in before. I lifted my head an inch, then pressed it back down again, allowing the remarkably soft pillows to envelop me once again. Above me, a mahogany canopy was adorned with painted blue pertines beneath golden crowns.

At last I figured out where I must be, which brought on a fit of wheezing laughter. Damelas Chademantaigne, a pauper from Cheapside, had not only sat upon the ducal throne of Pertine, but had spent the last several days or weeks lounging around in the duke's own bed.

'Damelas,' Monsegino asked, 'what were you saying – is there something you need? Shall I go and find Beretto or Shariza?'

'Nothing of conse— No, wait, I remember now. *Observations Of Ocular Maladies, Being An Account Of Certain Peculiar Conditions Of The Eyes Such As Those Of Prelate Urdius, Archduke Corbier, And Other Notables.*'

Monsegino's unnaturally captivating eyes widened in confusion. 'A book? Do you want me to send for it?'

I managed to prop myself up on my elbows before nodding at the pewter goblet, and the duke held it to my lips so I could drink. I raised a shaking hand to wipe away the water dribbling from my mouth and noticed my sleeve, which made me suspect I was wearing a monstrously expensive embroidered silk sleeping robe. I feared it, too, probably belonged to the duke.

'When I was researching the part of Corbier,' I croaked at last, 'I wound up in the Grand Library, thanks to Viscountess Kareija.' I coughed for a bit, then asked, 'How is she, by the way?'

'Imprisoned,' Monsegino replied. 'Awaiting sentencing.'

'Rude accommodation for one's relatives,' I observed, and waved tremulously at the opulence all around me.

Monsegino sighed. 'I'll set my aunt free soon enough. I just need to lure a few of her co-conspirators out of hiding. I've put it round that anyone who turns on her will be granted clemency. It's damned complicated tracking down traitors when almost none of them know who the others are.'

'What happened after I . . . ?' My voice trailed off. *After I what? Died? Allowed the memories of a thousand dead soldiers to possess my fellow citizens without their consent?*

Monsegino gave a wry smile. 'The instant the battle ended, those same nobles who'd stood by as I was about to be crowned with iron spikes gave very moving and patriotic speeches demanding that I retake the throne. Should you ever lack for particularly melodramatic actors, I can offer a number of recommendations.' His momentary good humour dissipated. 'Alas, those outbursts of feigned loyalty are making it all the more difficult for me to identify the truly dangerous ones.'

I gestured for more water to soothe my parched throat, then said, 'I've every faith that you'll unmask the deceivers, your Grace, given your own expertise in hiding your identity.'

A flicker of anger crossed Monsegino's face, but he was a decent sort, as rulers went, and the outrage faded quickly. '*Observations Of Ocular Maladies*,' he repeated. 'Was that how you figured it out? Or was it my great-great-great grandmother who informed on me?'

'We were rather busy trying to stop a hundred-year-old conspiracy, your Grace. I'm afraid the subject of your disreputable parentage never came up.' I peered deeper into the duke's eyes. 'How do you manage it, anyway? The book suggested there might be a way to repair the condition, but warned that it would be—'

The duke removed his heavy silver bracelet and held it up so that I could see the tiny blue glass vials inside the silver tubes decorating it. When I'd first seen Monsegino drink from one of them, I'd assumed he'd been imbibing a narcotic.

'Bloody unpleasant,' he said, staring at it as if he would rather grind the vial beneath his boot heel. 'It burns the throat before giving you a blistering headache for hours afterwards.' He slid the tiny bottle back into the bracelet. 'But it kept me alive, and it kept her secret.'

Her secret. Ajelaine's.

'So you knew all along that Pierzi had allowed her sons to marry into his line after she died? That you are, in fact, a descendant of Corbier as well as Pierzi?'

He shook his head. ''Only once you and I were on stage and I finally took hold of Pierzi's memories. When I was seven, I thought the red appearing in my eyes was some devilish curse. The effect wasn't nearly so pronounced as the histories claim Corbier's was, but it was enough that my parents were forced to pay outrageous sums to keep my nannies from exposing me as some sort of demon-spawn. Later, I understood the underlying illness to be relatively benign.' He held up his hand. 'I get tremors sometimes, and of course everything I see is tinged with red.'

'I'm sorry,' I said.

The duke smiled. 'Oh, it's not so bad. What I see reminds me that the world can be a dangerous place. Perhaps it's a gift, in a way; I don't think you can be a good ruler if you don't understand what it is to suffer, at least a little – and to have to hide who you are.'

'But surely that's over now? Now the people know the truth about Corbier, I'd think they would accept you as Ajelaine's heir, wouldn't they?'

Monsegino refilled the goblet and handed it to me. It was a dismissal, of sorts, although it was the duke who rose and went to the door. 'I'll go and find your friends,' he said. 'Perhaps you would be so kind as to convince them to return to their own homes now? Hosting two dozen endlessly drunk and eternally ravenous actors for an entire week might have been marginally better than having our city's heroes camped outside my walls day and night, but I'd really like my palace back now.'

I stared at the pewter goblet in my hand. The sight of the mottled grey metal so like iron brought a bitter taste to my tongue. 'It's not over,' I said. 'The Court of Flowers – the Iron Orchids – those who set this in motion aren't done with us.'

Monsegino stopped at the door. 'No doubt you're correct,' he said, opening it wide to let the light from the outer hall banish the shadows inside the bedchamber. 'So for the sake of our people, I hope you're not done with them, either.'

CHAPTER 76

THE ARCHER

Three days later, my recovery had progressed enough that I was able to slump in a chair in the corner of a tavern, annoyed beyond words that Rhyleis – the person who had insisted I meet her here on a matter of *vital* importance – was late. *Two hours* late.

The last time I'd been in the Busted Scales, I'd been a boy, accompanying my grandmother, at her insistence. Back then, before the dukes had beheaded King Paelis for the capital crime of insisting his travelling magistrates be allowed to bring some semblance of justice to their lands, there had been taverns like this in just about every city in Tristia. The Busted Scales was named and modelled after the legendary Greatcoats tavern in Aramor, where members of that ill-fated order would meet, drink and share tales of their trials and tribulations. It was a place to celebrate when justice had prevailed, and – no doubt more often – commiserate when ignominy and venality once again won the day.

I wasn't in the mood for either.

The duke had rooted out a number of the conspirators among his court, trials were beginning and the common folk of Jereste were rejoicing at this new piece of theatre in which the rich were being held to account for their crimes. The entertainment was almost – *almost* – enough for them to forgive the Violet Duke's ban on a number of pleasurable but peculiarly addictive drugs. They were still deciding how they felt about the prohibition on underage prostitution.

Cynicism is its own sort of vice and I tried to take heart in the proposed new housing for the homeless and refugees in Pertine. It probably wouldn't make much of a dent in the suffering of the poor, but it was a statement of intent. The duke had also decreed the Belleza would be rebuilt, with no expense spared to restore it to its former magnificence.

I hoped they would at least fix the leaks.

All this promise of renewed vitality was perceived as a great victory by the people of Jereste – a veritable *triumph*, Beretto would have said . . . except that it hadn't been long before the body of a foreigner was found hanging from a lantern-post in the tanners' district. Iron spikes had been driven into his skull to form a crown around his head. Those who discovered the body wept at his death and raged against those who had committed the atrocity.

At least the Iron Orchids no longer openly paraded the streets; no emblems adorned the collars of bully-boys and bravos. They would operate in the shadows for now, as no doubt they had done before, waiting until the day when the good citizens of Jereste tired of all this civility and decency, until the sight of their victims drew gleeful scorn instead of tears.

How do you disassemble a conspiracy so ingenious that it requires no leaders to keep itself running?

'That's a long face for an actor,' said a voice, rousing me from my bitter thoughts.

The man seated at the next table was hidden in the shadows. Balanced on the chair opposite him was a wooden case some two feet by three feet and perhaps six inches high. Resting on his lap was a well-worn shortbow and quiver.

I had seen enough lately to recognise those versed in the arts of violence.

'Go to Hells,' I said politely.

The soldier or mercenary or assassin or whatever he was chuckled and took another sip from his mug. 'Aren't actors supposed to be charming?'

I leaned forward until I could make out the man's reddish-blond hair and features. He'd have been devilishly handsome, if not for the self-satisfied grin, which confirmed this was no chance encounter.

'Hear me now,' I said, conjuring as much of Corbier's aristocratic smugness as I could muster. 'If you're one of the Iron Orchids or some secret leader of the Court of Flowers come here to kill me, then kindly get on with it or fuck off. I'm unimpressed by thugs and murderers who amuse themselves by chatting up their prospective victims.'

I drew from its scabbard the first two inches of the rapier Shariza had insisted I begin wearing. 'In case no one warned you, I've had the memories of a hundred-year-old duellist who's an even bigger arsehole than you running around my head, and they tell me a bow is a shitty weapon to bring to a bar fight.'

The man sighed. 'Why do swordsmen always obsess about the bloody bow?'

I would have sworn his hand never moved, but when next I looked down, the tip of an arrow was pressed firmly at my crotch.

'After all, it's the arrow that kills you,' the archer informed me.

'Sorry I'm late,' Rhyleis said cheerfully, setting down a pitcher of ale and three mugs on the table. 'I see introductions have already been made.'

I let go of the hilt of my rapier and buried my head in my hands. 'Saint Zaghev-who-sings-for-tears, Rhyleis, must you *always* be a pain in my arse?'

'Zaghev is one of the dead ones,' said the man at the other table, placing his arrow back in its quiver and sliding over on the bench to join me. 'He's been replaced by Eloria-whose-screams-draw-blood. I'm told she's worse than Zaghev ever was, though in all fairness, neither can hold a candle to Rhyleis, who is, in fact, a pain in *everyone's* arse.'

'You don't know the half of it,' I muttered, taking a swig from the mug she'd put in front of me – only to spit half of it out when I finally noticed what the archer was wearing.

'You're a Greatcoat!' I sputtered.

'Well, after a fashion.' The fellow pulled down the collar of his leather coat to reveal a fur lining. 'I'm a Rangieri now. It's kind of like a Greatcoat, only . . . well, actually, I haven't figured out the difference yet.'

Rhyleis leaned over and whispered conspiratorially – assuming conspiratorially meant *as loudly as humanly possible* – 'Brasti's not exactly the sharpest arrow in the quiver, if you get my meaning.'

'Brasti *Goodbow*?' I carefully set the mug down to keep from spilling the rest onto my lap. 'Brasti-the-King's-Arrow? Brasti who took down a thousand armoured knights with a hundred half-trained archers? Brasti who slew the new god who'd come to enslave Tristia with nothing but a stone tied to an arrow?'

The bearded man's grin grew so wide that I'd swear every one of his very white teeth was gleaming in the candlelight. 'Yes!' he bellowed aloud, slamming a fist on the table and sending spilled beer everywhere. 'At long fucking last!' He threw an arm around my shoulder. 'Oh, you and I are going to be great friends indeed!'

Rhyleis rolled her eyes. 'For the love of all the saints dead and alive, Damelas, *why* did you have to say those things?'

'He's *famous* – haven't you heard the stories? The songs?'

'*Songs?*' Brasti asked, wide-eyed. 'There are *songs* about me?' He removed his arm and clasped his hands together in prayer to Rhyleis. 'Sing me one, I beg you!'

The suffering on her face was palpable. 'Have you any idea, Veristor, how much work the Bardatti have had to do to suppress those damned nursery rhymes?'

'Aha – I *knew* it.' Brasti jabbed a finger at the Troubadour. 'All this time, you and fucking Falcio and Kest and everyone else has been making out as if nobody's ever heard of me, when in fact *I'm* the most beloved hero in all of Tristia – admit it.'

'I never said "most beloved",' I muttered.

'If we could get to the business at hand?' Rhyleis interjected, ignoring the Greatcoat's prodding. 'You know, dark forces at work, enemies hiding in the shadows and so forth?'

Brasti snorted. 'What else is new? This is Tristia. Things are always going to shit.' He reached over and grabbed the wooden case from the chair, shoved the pitcher and mugs aside and set it on the table. 'Nonetheless, the last thing I need is the new First Cantor of the Greatcoats up my arse, so I'd best give you this, then I can be on my way.'

'What is it?' I asked.

Rhyleis shocked me by reaching over and taking my hand. 'An invitation, Veristor. A call to honour your family's past and help us protect our nation's future.'

Brasti carefully flipped open the three polished brass clasps and slowly opened the lid, as if this was part of some ancient ritual. When I leaned closer to look inside the case, I shared the archer's reverence.

The dark brown leather was enthralling to behold – the perfect smoothness of it, the glint of the oils making it supple and waterproof, even the faint impressions where the bone plates had been sewn inside to protect against an enemy's blade. The coat was folded so that only the top three buttons were visible. The buttons were covered in black leather, but I knew each one concealed a gold juror coin, meant to pay those who were recruited to uphold a magistrate's verdict.

Neither of my grandparents had allowed me to examine their coats – it had been something of a superstition with them – but I knew there were dozens of pockets inside, containing the tricks and traps the wearer needed to defend their own life and to enforce their judicial verdicts.

'It's . . . exquisite,' I breathed, my fingertips itching to stroke the leather.

Brasti smiled, evidently pleased by my reaction, and shared a look with Rhyleis. 'Damelas Chademantaigne,' he began formally, 'on the instruction of Chalmers, First Cantor of the Order of Travelling Magistrates, and on behalf of King Filian the First, I hereby name you to the Greatco—'

'No—' a voice shouted.

I was more than a little surprised to discover it was mine.

'That's . . . not the usual response,' Brasti said.

I pushed down the lid of the case. 'I'm sorry. I'm . . . I'm honoured – more than you could ever guess. But this . . . this was my grandmother's calling, and my grandfather's, not mine. Even after everything that's happened, I'm no Greatcoat. I'm a Bardatti, I suppose – a Veristor, if I ever figure out what that really means. But mostly, in my heart, I'm an actor.'

Brasti Goodbow watched me in silence. A solid minute passed before he nodded at last. 'Considering the shit plays I've seen in the past few years, I suppose we need good actors more than mediocre magistrates.' He turned to Rhyleis, his expression vastly less sanguine. 'And you, you lousy, scheming Troubadour. You had Chalmers send me all this way for *nothing*? When I first got word, I just naturally assumed you wanted to bed me at last – which I would have refused, by the way – but no, I ride all the way to fucking Jereste just to deliver a greatcoat to a guy who refuses it because he wants to be *an actor*?'

Rhyleis looked not the least bit guilty. 'Well, obviously I hadn't expected him to refuse.'

Brasti gave a barking laugh. He turned to me and said, 'You know how she goes around pretending to know everything about everyone, droning on about the mystical genius of the Bardatti?'

'She . . . may have mentioned something along those lines.'

'Ha!' Brasti said, slapping the table again. 'Well, she's rubbish at it, so take it from me – never, *ever* follow her advice. Half the time she's so busy mooning over Falcio, who couldn't care le—'

'Falcio val Mond?' I asked. 'The former First Cantor who . . . who isn't nearly as famous as you?'

'Nice recovery,' Rhyleis said, furiously scribbling in her notebook.

'What are you writing?' Brasti asked her suspiciously.

'A song,' she replied. 'About you. Do go on about what rubbish my counsel is and how I constantly embarrass myself.'

'Now, Rhyleis,' Brasti said anxiously, putting his hands up in surrender. 'Let's not do anything hasty. We're friends, remember? I'm even willing to reconsider my reluctance to sleep with you.'

'Keep talking,' the Troubadour said, still scribbling in her notebook. 'You want to be famous, Brasti Goodbow? Oh, I'll make you famous . . .'

I had the strange sense I'd wandered into someone else's story, but amusing as it was, frivolity wasn't for me right now. I reached over and flipped the brass clasps on the case closed. 'I'm sorry you came all this way for nothing. I'm surprised, actually, because usually Rhyleis is uncannily adept at figuring out what people are going to do . . .'

I turned and stared into those inscrutable blue eyes of hers. 'In fact, why would you have sent a request to the new First Cantor on my behalf at all? You're the one who keeps telling me how much more important the Bardatti are than the Greatcoats – would you even have allowed me to become a Greatcoat if I'd wanted?'

There wasn't a trace of guilt in her smirk. 'Trade the first real Veristor in a generation for a thick-witted magistrate? Don't be ridiculous.'

Brasti threw up his hands. 'Then why in the name of Saint Laina's glorious left tit did you send word demanding that the Tailor come out of retirement to make a new greatcoat? What am I supposed to tell the First Cantor now? I can't just go back to Aramor, drop the coat in her lap and say, "Sorry, he decided he'd rather be an actor." The other Greatcoats will laugh me out of the castle!'

Rhyleis appeared distinctly untroubled by that prospect, but in her gaze I saw something else. . .

'You really are impossible not to love, aren't you?' I asked her, and turned back to look at the case.

'What?' Brasti asked. '*What?* Did you miss the part where she made me ride all the way here and now I have to carry this stupid case back and—'

'Perhaps you don't need to take the coat back to Aramor,' I said. 'In fact, if you think your First Cantor might be willing to bend the rules a little, I believe I have a solution that will satisfy everyone.'

Brasti Goodbow looked suspicious, which was only fair given Rhyleis' smug grin.

'I'm listening . . .'

CHAPTER 77

THE TROUPE

The Knights of the Curtain assembled one last time among the ruins of the Operato Belleza, standing in the ashes of our former home, with scorched props and charred pieces of set still lying among the cracked stone and burned timbers. Actors and crew alike, we all wore the bruises, cuts, and scars of our battles here and at the palace. Several were leaning on crutches or each other, broken bones and lacerated skin yet to heal.

We were all grinning like fools.

'I still can't believe we did it,' Beretto marvelled, one hand stroking his red beard as if he were playing the Affable Inquisitor from *Between Two Midnight Murders*, come here to investigate the inexplicable mystery of how a troupe of players had overcome impossible tribulations.

'I'm still not sure *what* we did,' Teo admitted.

I felt as if I should explain, but I couldn't think where to begin. Abastrini saved me by kneeling down to pick up a handful of cinders, then squeezing them in his hand as if by sheer force of will he could crush the ashes into something better – something brighter. Something living.

Then he stood, straightened his back and said, 'We made Hujo Shoville proud. That's what we did.'

Ornella came to his side. 'We gave the people of this city reason for hope. Hujo would've liked that.'

'Nah,' Grey Mags said, clacking the brass percussion discs that never left her fingers any more. 'What we did is, we gave them feckin' Orchids cause to fear us.'

A few among the crew gave her sidelong glances as if she, an alley-rat only recently elevated into their company, had no business speaking so boldly on this hallowed ground, and Mags, like most folk who knew what it was to be ignored, went silent and stared down at her patched and ragged shoes.

How brittle we are, I thought, witnessing this woman, who'd shown herself as brave as any soldier in defending her city, now collapsed in on herself. *It's as if the gods, caring so little for their creation, fashioned humanity from glass so fragile we can shatter each other with a single dirty look.*

The gods, however, hadn't counted on the heart of Beretto Bravi, which was so big it could encompass half the world and keep safe the spirits of all those he embraced.

'Rightly said, Mags,' he chuckled. 'Nothing would've made Hujo Shoville shit himself with joy more than the knowledge that all of us here, his Knights of the Curtain, had taught the thugs and bully-boys of this city to scurry away when players come calling!'

Cheers rose from all assembled and they nodded at each other – and at Mags too. Grinning, she clacked her percussion discs alongside the clapping of hands and stomping of feet.

That's my best friend, I thought, watching in wonder as Beretto took Mags by the arm and led her into a whirling dance. *My brother.*

When the impromptu celebration stopped for breath, they turned once again to me, no doubt wondering why I hadn't joined in. They wanted something from me – a grand speech, a closing soliloquy; anything that would give them an excuse to cheer once more and then go home, to dream of putting on ever-more-fabulous productions for what would surely be adoring throngs of theatregoers awaiting our next play.

'I'm leaving,' I said.

The clamour and the smiles died down.

'You're *what*?' Teo demanded. 'Tell me I didn't just hear you sa—'

'I'm leaving the company. I'm leaving Jereste.'

The others started shouting questions, but Teo refused to be denied his moment of outrage. 'Now? You're leaving us *now*? When the Orchids have been beaten, the Vixen is dead and we *literally* saved the life of the Duke of Pertine? He's promised to rebuild the Belleza – every noble I encounter is practically *begging* to empty his pockets for a front-row seat at our first production—' He shook his fists at the sky as if threatening the gods themselves. 'How could even you be so damnably inconsider—?'

His final indictment was cut off when Abastrini's thick hand clamped over his mouth.

'You see what happens when you allow one of these scurrilous bit players even one monologue? Can't shut them up after that.' Abastrini waved at me. 'Go on, then, explain yourself, Veristor.'

Ever since I'd awakened in the duke's chamber and discovered I hadn't died from pushing my unwanted gift further than my body could withstand, I'd been searching for the right words to say goodbye to this family of mine. I'd tried convincing myself that the vow I'd made a hundred years in the past to that shadowy figure looming over Corbier's dying body had been spurious, not something Fate could hold me to. But despite all the things I didn't know, as I'd told my grandfather this morning, of this one thing I was certain: my path led away from Jereste.

'You're going hunting, aren't you?' Shariza asked.

These past few days, she had taken to holding my hand when it trembled from exhaustion, or when I remembered too keenly the moment Corbier's heart had stopped. Her closeness was a constant reminder that I was still alive, and that there were things to live for.

'Hunting?' Beretto asked. 'What is she talking about, brother?' He swung an arm out to the city street beyond the ruins. 'We won, didn't we?'

'We won,' I acknowledged. 'And that's how it always works in the best stories, isn't it?' I asked the others. 'Brave heroes overcome impossible odds to rescue the prince in his tower or to slay the serpent in its lair. The villains flee, the innocent rejoice.'

'Sounds awful,' Teo groaned, yanking Abastrini's hand from his mouth. 'I can see why you're insisting that we all be properly depressed about our victory.'

'Tell me what happens *after* the victory, Teo?'

'Simple. The heroes get fucking drunk and sleep with every rich, beautiful man and woman in the city – which some of us would very much like to get to, if you could manage not to ruin everyth—'

Teo stumbled, his eyes unfocused. Abastrini had clubbed him on the side of the head with a meaty fist. The blow hadn't been enough to knock him out, but it did shut him up long enough for me to continue.

'The Court of Flowers know all about our stories. They know how we think, how we live.' I limped over to a broken column and leaned against it. 'These people . . . I'm telling you, they *plan* for defeat. In each failure, they plant the seeds for future victories. We think in terms of two-hour performances. Soldiers think in ten-day battles. The Court of Flowers . . . they plan entire generations ahead.'

'Forgive me,' Bida began, her slender fingers winding anxiously in the locks of her long blonde hair, 'but what do they want from us?'

I looked out beyond the rubble of the Belleza at this city. For most of my life, Jereste had been my entire world. I was only now beginning to understand how small a place it was.

Rhyleis started plucking the strings of her guitar, conjuring a melody dark and full of disquiet. 'They want it all. This city, this duchy – perhaps all of Tristia.' She struck an angry chord. 'Listen to me, all of you. What happened here in Jereste was nothing but an opening skirmish with the enemy. Chalmers, the First Cantor of the Greatcoats, sent me here because this is not the first evidence we have seen of their machinations.'

'But – but how do you know?' Bida asked. Roz's former understudy rested her hands on her belly, where the first swell of pregnancy was beginning to show.

'Because I'm a Bardatti Troubadour. Like the Greatcoats, we are part of the Dal Verteri: the twelve orders created long ago to defend this nation. When Tristia is threatened, when armies are insufficient to the task of protecting it, we are the ones who must act. And I'll tell you something else that will chill your blood: the Court of Flowers may be only one among many secret courts the enemy has sent to our shores.'

The Knights of the Curtain were the bravest people I'd ever known, but even they gasped at Rhyleis' words.

Ornella walked over to me and placed a hand on my arm. '*Dal Verteri* means "Path of the Daring" in archaic Tristian. Are you to be one of them now, Damelas? One of those who fight these shadowy forces we're facing?'

'I . . . I think perhaps I am.'

'Then how do you intend to defeat these other courts?'

Her question wasn't unanticipated, but I hadn't expected to see Ornella – the woman who'd been facing down bloody violence since before I'd even been born, just for the right to tread the stage – now looking at me as if I might have an answer worth hearing.

'Honestly, I'm not sure how to beat them,' I admitted. 'Politics and intrigue are as foreign to me as military strategy. All I know is that we only learned the truth about the Iron Orchids through the tale of Ajelaine, Corbier and Pierzi. If there really are other hidden conspirators sowing chaos throughout the country, then maybe the only way to uncover them is by seeking out other false tales.'

Ornella's head tilted as she considered my reply. 'So your plan is to travel the countryside searching for other historias to stage, in the hopes that your Veristor's gift will enable you to summon the memories of those involved in the actual events of the past, and use that information to outwit the impossibly sophisticated and devious schemes of these other insidious courts?'

Weirdly, it didn't sound completely mad when she said it.

Ornella squeezed my arm. 'I'm coming with you.'

I looked at her blankly. '*What—?*'

'You'll need actors, won't you? This Veristor's gift of yours – doesn't it require the ritual of the theatre? You'll be needing players to help you stage these historias so you can journey back into the past and learn the truth.' She nodded to herself. 'I'll pack tonight. We'll leave in the morning.'

'I can't ask you to—'

'Oh do shut up, you simpering swankpot!' Abastrini bellowed, striding forward. For once he wasn't accompanied by the usual cloud of alcohol. 'Do you seriously believe you would have lasted five seconds against the Iron Orchids without us?'

'No, but—'

'Silence, you talentless pissing pustule!' The blustering actor pounded a heavy, hairy-knuckled fist against his own palm. 'You would dare leave behind the great Ellias Abastrini while you chase after glory alone? Nay,

I say thee, nay, a thousand times nay! I've acquired a taste for remonstrating venomous arse-boils, and I weary of the audiences that infest this ill-educated parochial little burg. My talents demand a larger stage than fits inside a mere city, and so will I, by grace of my—'

'He gets it,' Beretto said, clapping a hand on Abastrini's shoulder and pulling him aside. 'You're joining our little troupe.'

'*Our* troupe?' I asked.

Beretto grinned. 'You think I'd let you have all the fun?' He took in a deep breath, as if the air were fresh instead of stinking of smoke and dust and decay. 'Ah, *this* will be the life. Voyaging from town to town, exposing foul conspiracies and beating the Hells out of blackguards and bully-boys. Of course, our plays may suffer from an excess of modesty if we've only four actors to stage them . . .'

Beretto's pause was drenched in unconscionable theatricality as he turned to the others and waited.

Oddly, it was Bida, shy, unassuming Bida, who came forward first.

'Are you sure?' I asked. The young understudy had a family here, a beau with whom she'd been considering marriage – and she had a child on the way. 'The life isn't—'

'You don't know what it's like,' she said, cutting me off with uncharacteristic curtness. 'They *murdered* Roz – they drove iron spikes into her skull and they left her hanging from a lantern-post. Even after she was dead, they left her there. And you don't know what we go through – what it's like to be—' She shook her head fiercely. 'I want to fight. I *will* fight.'

'So will I,' Cileila said. She was still gripping the bloodied hammer she'd wielded against the Orchids.

'And I,' declared Grey Mags. This time she gave the others a peremptory scowl to ensure none questioned her right to be among them, but others were already speaking up, some with merely a word or two, others – being actors – with attempted soliloquies. Abastrini's glares ensured those latter speeches were brisk and to the point.

By the time all those gathered in the ruins of the Belleza had spoken, every player, every stagehand and lighting rigger, carpenter, costumer and set-dresser was standing a little taller. Some of their vows were more bluster than anything else, brave words masking desperate anxiety, but their determination was never in doubt, not even when spoken by the particularly exuberant one far too young to be uttering such oaths.

'Don't you dare even think about leaving us behind,' Zina warned me, a smooth rock almost as big as her fist held high in one hand, the other on little Tolsi's shoulder. 'I can bean you with this from fifty paces, Damelas Chademantaigne. Do you doubt my aim?'

'Neither your aim nor your courage,' I said, unable to contain my smile. 'Besides, we can hardly have a travelling troupe if we've only Tolsi to play the little boy parts, now can we?'

'I'm a girl!' she huffed.

I ruffled her hair. 'No, you're an *actor*. You know what that means?'

'What?'

'It means you get to be whoever you damn well want to be.'

There was a sudden rumble of cheers at this, and Rhyleis and Shariza nodded to each other – then remembered how much they hated each other and turned away.

The jubilant mood was punctured by a figure lurking in the shadows cast by the Belleza's sole unbroken column.

'Saint Bubo-who-shoves-toothpicks-up-arses, are you all done yet?' he asked. 'This is worse than listening to one of Falcio's speeches.'

As one, the Knights of the Curtain turned on the mocking intruder, ready to deliver a hearty beating for his denigrating insolence.

'My fault,' I said, pulling Abastrini back before he bashed the archer in the head. 'I forgot to mention I'd invited a guest.'

Taking that as his cue, Brasti Goodbow stepped out from behind the soot-covered column. With his long leather coat and striking red-blond hair and beard, he cut quite an impressive figure among the ruins. The only real Greatcoat most of them had seen up close was my grandfather, who was well past his prime. Now they were gawking at this bold visitor in their midst with a mixture of awe and trepidation – all except for Beretto, who'd seen the coat, then the insignia of crossed arrows imprinted on the left breast, and promptly dropped to his knees. He looked as if he were about to faint.

'By all the saints,' he swore, 'can it really be—?' He hung his head. 'Forgive me, King's Arrow . . . or is it Queen's Jest now? I mean, we've a king and not a queen now, but your previous name was when you served King Paelis and now it's his son, King Filian, but in between—'

'Brasti is fine,' the Greatcoat said, then paused to reconsider. 'Actually, I prefer Brasti Godslayer, or Brasti the Handsome. Now that I think on it, I should really come up wi—'

'Mostly, people address him as, "Hey you, arsehole",' Rhyleis interrupted. 'Although, shouting, "Shut up, Brasti!" from time to time seems to work best.'

Beretto looked horrified, and I realised I'd never fathomed the true depths of his adoration for Tristia's swashbuckling magistrates.

How deeply it must have cut when King Paelis refused to name him to the Greatcoats, I thought.

After glaring at Rhyleis – not that it appeared to have any effect – Brasti gestured to Beretto, still kneeling before him, mumbling incoherently about the archer's various titles and accomplishments, and asked, 'He's the one?' He swung the polished wooden case up to rest it on his arm.

'He is,' I replied.

'What's your name, big man?' Brasti asked.

'Beretto, sir. Beretto Bravi of South Lankavir.'

The archer began opening the clasps. 'Well, Beretto Bravi of South—' He stopped. 'Hang on. Why do I know that name?'

Beretto reddened. 'Well, sir, I am an actor of some small reput—'

'No, that's not it.' Brasti stared down at Beretto, eyes narrowed. 'Saint Anlas' swollen balls! *You're* the one! The one who sent all those copies of that bloody play to Castle Aramor? *The Saga of the King's Heart*?'

Beretto's beaming face began to look a little uncertain. 'You've, er . . . read it?'

Brasti burst out in peals of laughter. 'Oh, I've read it, all right! Any time I want to wind up Falcio, I just pull out a page from your lovely play and start performing it for him until he runs out of the room swearing to hunt down the – and I quote here – "saintless lackwit who shat this pile of offal onto the page".'

'He . . . didn't like my play? I'd hoped to share with the world my deep admiration for his—'

The rest of Beretto's words were rendered inaudible by Brasti's chortling. 'Like it? We all thought you were writing satire! *No one* gives speeches that long – not even' – Brasti paused to catch his breath from laughing so hard – 'not even Falcio-fucking-val-Mond!'

Beretto was crestfallen. 'Well, the records are incomplete and I just thought . . .'

Brasti turned to me with a bemused expression. 'Does it really have to be him?'

I returned an ominous stare that would have done Corbier proud. 'Beretto Bravi will be as fine a Greatcoat as there has ever been.'

Brasti sighed. 'Very well, then. Beretto Bravi of South Whatever. On instruction of . . . actually, I suppose I should amend that to "with what I'm sure will be the eventual enthusiastic agreement of" Chalmers, First Cantor of the Order of Travelling Magistrates, and on behalf of King Filian the First – who's a right prick from what I've seen so far, I should warn you – I hereby call you to the Greatcoats.' He opened the wooden case and took out the coat, which was even more magnificent in the bright light of day than it had been in the dim glow of the tavern.

On the left breast of the coat was an insignia: an actor's mask and a rose. 'I name you the King's Player. Declare now whatever oath you choose that will bind you to the laws and people of this misbegotten country.'

Beretto was too busy blinking away the tears streaming down his cheeks to do anything but mumble incoherently.

'So much for the eloquence of actors,' Brasti said, and held out the coat for Beretto. 'Now will you get up off the damn ground? If Falcio finds out I let a Greatcoat kneel before me, I'll never hear the end of it.'

'Go on,' I said, when Beretto still hadn't moved, but something was wrong. The big man reached out, but his fingers never quite touched the coat he'd dreamed of wearing his entire life.

'Who knew all it took to finally shut Beretto up was a nice coat?' Teo asked with a smirk. This time it was Ornella who punched him.

I went over to stand beside Beretto, and only then saw that he was weeping, but not for joy.

'What's wrong?'

'If I take this . . . it would mean I wouldn't be able to join your troupe. And I can't—'

'*That's* what's bothering you?' Brasti asked. 'Didn't I explain about the—?'

'You didn't explain anything, you *idiot*,' Rhyleis said. 'This is why I asked Chalmers to send *anyone* but you.'

Brasti winked at her. 'I guess you must've pissed her off one too many times.' He turned back to Beretto. 'The First Cantor, knowing she was recruiting an actor' – he gave Rhyleis a sidelong glance – 'though not, apparently, *which* actor – anyway, Chalmers is apparently quite keen for us to have stronger ties to the Bardatti, and since no sane person can tolerate their company for long, you've been stuck with the job.'

'Really?' Beretto's face was aglow.

'Oh, you'll have to fulfil your other duties, of course: hear cases when you come across them; render verdicts; get your arse kicked periodically in duels. But this little travelling troupe Damelas thinks he came up with all by himself – because he hasn't yet figured out that it was a certain meddling Troubadour who put the idea in his head – actually makes sense. It will be a valuable source of intelligence for the First Cantor as she rebuilds our order and brings a little justice back to this wretched country of ours.'

Beretto threw off his old coat so fast you'd have thought it was filled with snakes instead of fleas.

Rhyleis insisted on helping him, first sliding the brown leather greatcoat over his shoulders, then doing up the buttons. 'There,' she said when she was done, patting his chest. 'Fits like a glove.'

Brasti's eyes narrowed. 'Which is odd, Rhyleis, since that might suggest that the measurements you sent the Tailor were clearly *not* for the person you told us the coat was meant for.'

The Troubadour ignored him. Beaming up at Beretto, she said, 'Try not to get blood on it, will you?'

Beretto, now blubbering openly, gazed down at her. 'You know all those dozens of men you claim fall in love with you every day?'

She raised an eyebrow. 'You imply that I exaggerate?'

'I think you've been undercounting.'

Brasti snapped the wooden case shut, then pointed a finger at me. 'A Bardatti Veristor.' His finger swung to Beretto. 'A Greatcoat.' And finally he looked at Shariza. 'And I'll be damned if you're not a Dashini.'

She came closer, moving casually, like a cat about to leap on a mouse. 'Now what would possibly give you that idea, *Trattari*?'

'Because my balls froze the moment I caught sight of you, which usually only happens with my fiancée.'

Shariza, for the very first time since any of us had met her, looked genuinely shocked. 'You're *marrying* a Dashini? And *she's* marrying ... *you*?'

Brasti grinned. 'I doubt I'll survive the honeymoon, but I can't wait to see who shows up for the wedding.' He put up a warning hand. 'And if you blow any of that fucking blue Dashini dust in my face, I swear to Saint Eloria, I'm going to vomit it right back over you.'

With that, the archer turned and walked over to Rhyleis. 'I expect an ode in my honour for this.'

The Troubadour patted his arm. 'Oh, believe me, I've already started composing it.'

Brasti paled, then, raising a hand in farewell, stomped away from the wreckage.

With the Greatcoat's departure, the playful mood that had overtaken us for those brief minutes faded, and the weight of what we'd all committed to descended over our now grim assembly.

'Can we really do this?' Teo asked. 'Can a bunch of players take on an enemy we can't even see?'

Everyone was watching me; even Shariza, who surely knew better than any of us the dangers we would face in this hopeless quest. She looked as if she was waiting for me to reassure her.

Saints, I thought, *I could really use some of Corbier's arrogance right about now.*

It turned out it wasn't the Red-Eyed Raven's memories I needed then, but the spirit of another, who was surely here among the ashes of the Operato Belleza. For better or for worse, it was up to me to take up the mantle of Directore Principale and try as best I could to live up to Hujo Shoville's example.

'"A bunch of players"?' I started, but it was a poor impression of the haughtiness Shoville reserved for such occasions. I'd have to do this my way. I slid my arm around Shariza's waist, pulled her close, and with the confidence and flair of a far more talented performer, loudly declared, 'We are *actors* – most beloved of the saints! Moreover, we are Knights of the Curtain. When we walk the boards, the earth rumbles. When we speak our lines, the gods themselves lean in close to listen.' I smiled at this motley assembly of players and crew: my friends. My family. 'And when we dig deep into the fertile soil of our art together, with the truth on our lips and the love we bear each other blossoming in our hearts . . . well, I do believe we can save the world every night we take the stage – twice if there's a matinee.'

The others cheered, Shariza kissed me, and I discovered I was no longer haunted by this unwieldy name my grandparents had given me. The first Damelas Chademantaigne had become a legend by judging cases no one else would dare take on, and then fighting duels to enforce his verdicts. I was an actor – a *Veristor* – and even without a blade and a leather coat, that made me a very dangerous man to those plotting to turn my people against each other. The trial about to unfold might be different from the ones my grandparents had faced, but that wouldn't stop me fighting for justice in my own way.

My enemies were no doubt far away at this moment, perhaps in some other country or even a different time. Still, I felt certain they could hear me when I whispered, 'Welcome to the Court of Shadows.'

THE END

ACKNOWLEDGEMENTS

Dramatis Personae

I've always wanted to have a *dramatis personae* for one of my novels. A listing of character names with a few clever words describing them makes a book look especially distinguished. There's really nothing stopping me from having one, actually; it's not as if my publishers would refuse. Yet every time I have a new book coming out, I find myself resisting the urge. Perhaps it's because I don't like to reveal any secrets about my characters until the right moment, or perhaps I'm just terribly forgetful. Either way, I've found the perfect solution, which is to place my *dramatis personae* here at the end of the book and use it to introduce an entirely different cast of heroes and villains.

Directore Principale

Jo Fletcher, a.k.a. 'The Inimitable Jo Fletcher', a.k.a. 'Jo Fletcher, Her Most Redoubtableness', a.k.a. 'God damn it all, Jo, stop trying to slip the word "sward" into my manuscript!': Renowned titan of fantasy publishing and the only person ever allowed to edit the Greatcoats. EVER.

Cantora Prima

Anne Perry: Our new First Cantor of the King's Order of Travelling Magistrates, whose championing and guidance of the Greatcoats begins with this first instalment of Court of Shadows and all the twists and turns to follow.

Dramaturges

Expert elucidators of narrative eccentricities:

Eric Torin: An enigmatic contemplator of themes and meta-narrative wizardry.

Christina de Castell: Inspirer of daring deeds, tolerator of authorly indecision, love of my life.

Assistant Directors

Someone has to make sure the script makes sense and the actors show up in the right place at the right time . . .

Lauren Campbell: Author's assistant extraordinaire, compiler of thousands of Greatcoats details. Lovely author in her own right. Terrible speller.

Sharona Selby: Proof-reader to the stars, much-appreciated spotter of errant commas and slippery typos.

Costumes

Dressing up a novel is a complex art demanding imaginative flair and meticulous precision.

Nicola Howell Hawley: Esteemed illustrator of fantastical theatre programs who designed all six of the gorgeous playbills accompanying the part breaks in this book – a feat made especially noteworthy when the author of said book forgot about the sixth one when writing the art brief.

Miblart: Talented creators of fantastical book covers. They performed a heroic number of alterations to the cover for me across more than twenty iterations, then subsequently asked politely if I could find a different design company for my future endeavours.

Pyrotechnics

Artificers of spectacular illusions to draw the eyes of the audience to the stage.

The redoubtable Ella Patel and Lipfon Tang, the publicist and marketeer who ensure news of this humble production reaches the ears and eyes of the great and good.

Technical Directors:

Without whom the entire production would surely come crashing down on all our heads.

Georgina Difford and Tania Wilde, who wield spreadsheets like weapons to ensure performances *will* begin on time, every time. Thanks also to Aje Roberts for conjuring an extra week for me to read the proofs. Now taking the baton (or rather, rapier) of assistant editing is Gaby Puleston-Vaudrey. Gaby, welcome to the Greatcoats!

Choreographers

An author's career is a careful dance. Thank goodness someone's kept me from tripping over my two left feet all this time.

Heather Adams of HMA Literary: Mystical counsellor wise and merry, drawn away from the destiny demanded of her by the fiction gods to pursue her own adventures at Oxford.

Jon Wood of RCW Literary: Fearless negotiator of exorbitant advances, tamer of undesirable contract clauses. Alas, too tall and too blue-eyed to be entirely trustworthy. Hair is also suspiciously close to ginger.

Fight Director

Special thanks to Christian (Miles) Cameron for giving the manuscript a read and making sure my fight scenes hadn't gone off the deep end.

Choir

Joe Jameson: Narrator without peer, creator of dozens of voices throughout this tale and so many others.

Critics

Brave souls who dare tell me that there might – might – *be a couple of things I should fix in my manuscript.*

Darryl Fuller: Long-haired ruffian and outstanding scribe who wrote the most detailed beta reader notes I've ever seen.

Kim Tough, Wil Arndt, Brad Dehnert and Peter Darbyshire: Knaves of the first order.

Allen Walker of the Library of Allenxandria: Expert in Latin and Ancient History, Debonair Docent of Literary Insight. I altered Paedar's duel just for you.

The Noble Margraves and Margravinas, Viscounts and Viscountesses, Lords and Daminas and even a few Valorous Alley Rats who make up our Esteemed Audience

I am forever grateful for the kind reviews I see posted across that mysterious landscape sometimes referred to as 'social media' and for the wonderful words of support in your letters, emails, tweets, and occasional shouts across a crowded airport. Hearing from you is always the best part of my day.

Your Humble Playwright
Sebastien de Castell
September 2022
Vancouver, Canada

Keep reading for an exclusive extract of the next adventure in the Court of Shadows series . . .

COURT OF SHADOWS BOOK 2

OUR LADY OF BLADES

SEBASTIEN
DE CASTELL

OUR LORD OF CORPSES

Rijou's rancorous Court of Blades falls silent as the duellist crosses the marble floor. Perched in the galleries above, the city's bejewelled lords and ladies lean precariously over gilded oak railings, a flock of splendidly attired geese craning their necks to admire his graceful, languorous passage. Crowded into rough wooden benches below, merchants and artisans clothed in drab browns and greys hold their breath as he nears. Even the colossal statues of War and Death whose outstretched arms form the archway into the courtroom seem diminished by his presence.

Indeed, our paragon stands taller than most men, though he towers above none; gangling height being no more advantageous to his vocation than excessive brawn. The sleeves of his billowing silk fencing shirt, white as a dove's feathers to expose any wounds he might suffer during the trial and bound with leather straps from wrist to elbow so as not to impede his blade work, reveal the powerfully corded muscles of his forearms. Likewise, the close-fitted black fencer's trousers draw attention to thighs and calves wound tight as coiled springs.

The duellist pauses thoughtfully at the edge of a twenty-foot ring of glittering ruby mosaic whose inner circle has been masterfully carved from a single slab of alabaster; the smooth texture is well suited to a fencer's complex footwork, the pristine white an excellent canvas for their blood.

Glancing around the courtroom as if only now aware of the audience's presence, he favours his admirers with a placid smile and faraway gaze that suggests indifference to the outcome of the day's proceedings. He even winks companionably at the hapless young gemcutter in the defendant's box who will, moments from now, be condemned to face him blade-to-blade in the circle. The defendant, not knowing what else to do, responds with a nervous wave of his hand, perhaps wondering whether he's being greeted by a long-forgotten acquaintance and all this talk of sharpened steel and verdict-by-combat is merely a misunderstanding.

No one else is fooled. Not the nobles gathered in their galleries nor the common folk huddled on benches. The magistrate seated atop his lofty throne has witnessed the scene about to unfold many times before, as have the black-clad advocates standing for the plaintiff and defendant at opposite sides of the dais. All those present know that there is only one talent for which this particular duellist is so richly compensated in Rijou's Court of Blades. He wears no crown nor sits on any throne, yet within the walls of this gilded palace of justice, he is more revered and beloved than any king.

Golden-haired, fair-skinned and black-hearted, his name is Dazidier Enguero, better known among those who can afford his services as Our Lord of Corpses. In a city famed for its fencers, he may well be the deadliest man to ever draw a sword from its scabbard. When the court clerk strikes the bell, his lunge will be as lightning from a cloudless sky: so sudden and merciless that those who blink will miss the moment when his rapier drew a crimson curtain over the trial.

Shh . . . Don't tell him yet, but Dazidier is about to have a very bad day.

PART I

THE COURT OF BLADES

A fencing match is like a chess game, won by strategy as much as skill, preparation as much as talent. But a duel? A duel is a magic trick. That's why the dead man always looks so surprised.

P.17 of The Hummingbird Bible,
family duelling manual of House Vauquelin

SLANDERS AND SECONDIERS

'My Lord Magistrate, this is nothing less than court-sanctioned murder!' shouts the defendant's advocate, punctuating his outburst with the pounding of his fists upon the bronze base of a throne that rises five feet above the dais before meeting His Most Eminent Sallo Calvino's ample buttocks.

'We will suffer no hysterics in my courtroom, Advocate Vicendi,' the magistrate warns perfunctorily. Well-manicured fingers slip a red tenderberry between the bars of a birdcage balanced on one arm of his elevated throne. An eager starling gobbles up the juicy morsel, trilling its appreciation, and Magistrate Calvino smiles for the first time since the trial began.

The lords and ladies in the gallery begin feeding their own caged companions, the living symbols of their noble houses. Enthusiastic warbling, chirping and squawking soon echoes throughout the courtroom, leaving the young advocate locked in an unwinnable contest for the magistrate's attention.

Vicendi's shabby court blacks lay bare his odds of victory: worn leather shoes and patched hose rise to meet the frayed hem of an ebony half-cloak that hangs limply over sloping, defeated shoulders. The scraggly curls of a black-powdered wig frame what might have been a modestly attractive face were it not already lined from despair at the futility of his profession.

Fortunes are made every day in the Court of Blades: by the fencers who fight the duels, the solicitors who secure them cases, the spectators wagering on the outcomes and, of course, the judges overseeing the trials. Alas, the same cannot be said of dewy-eyed advocates pleading for justice on behalf of penniless defendants.

'Must I cover myself in feathers to merit a moment of your Eminence's consideration for an innocent man's fate?' Vicendi cries out.

The vulgar outburst is met with hisses from the galleries and gasps from the benches below. Wagers over how long the defendant will survive in the duelling circle give way to odds being set over whether his advocate will precede him to the coffin.

Magistrate Calvino, having run out of tenderberries, frowns at this latest interruption. 'What motion would you have me consider, Vicendi? Surely you cannot expect the plaintiff to duel your client himself when he has only recently become afflicted with a most troubling ailment of the lungs . . .'

All eyes turn to the plaintiff's box on the other side of the courtroom. A middle-aged jewellery maker, luxuriously attired in a glorious new burgundy frock coat, is currently preoccupied with an inspection of its tourmaline-encrusted buttons. When he realises the court is awaiting evidence of his infirmity, he coughs unconvincingly before serving up the sort of smile typically found on the face of a cat in the process of digesting a canary.

'Clearly Master Jolen cannot duel today,' Magistrate Calvino concludes, though with obvious irritation at the jewellery maker's half-hearted performance, 'therefore this court has no choice but to rule that his secondier take his place.'

At the edge of the ruby-ringed duelling circle, the angelic Dazidier Enguero tilts his golden head left then right to loosen the muscles in his shoulders as he prepares to commit the entirely legal murder for which he's been commissioned. In response, Vicendi, who might, if he straightened his back and raised his chin – and if you squinted *just so* – appear *a little* heroic in his futile quest to save his client's life, sputters in outrage, 'You – you cannot call it justice for an untrained civilian to face Our Lord of Corpses in the duelling circle!'

'Cease your clucking, man,' Magistrate Calvino chides him. 'Have you forgotten that we are assembled this afternoon for a mere duella debtori? Trifling matters of unpaid financial obligations are fought to first blood only. By lunchtime your client will have returned home to his wife and child having suffered nothing worse than a nasty scratch and wounded pride – though admittedly somewhat impoverished by his intransigence.'

A smattering of knowing laughter drifts down from the gallery. Slouched in the defendant's box below, Opezo, the luckless young lapidarist whose gemstones Master Jolen has slandered as fakes to every reputable jewel buyer in the city, buries his face in his hands. Even Opezo knows that one does not hire Our Lord of Corpses to fight to first blood; they hire him to ensure that first blood is also last.

'A continuance!' Vicendi pleads the court as if from sudden inspiration. 'A week, no more! Surely the *honourable* Master Jolen will have recovered from his mysterious ailment by then and be prepared to fight his own battles!'

The spectators, rich and poor alike, groan at this latest tactic. They paid good money to witness today's duel. Now this upstart advocate would deny them their meagre entertainment? A smug-looking libertine in minstrel's blues comes to their rescue, rising from the commoners' benches to bellow, 'A continuance would be medically unsound, your Eminence!'

'What?' demands Calvino, peering across the courtroom at this latest unscheduled interlocutor. 'What bearing could any ruling of mine have on medical matters? Do you present yourself to this court as a physician, sir?'

The minstrel momentarily feigns concern before offering his audience a self-satisfied grin. 'Alas, only in the treatment of broken hearts. But it requires no medical training to diagnose the patient in this case, which is why I can predict with absolute certainty that a continuance will only serve to ensure that poor Master Jolen's cough persists unabated!'

Magistrate Calvino's booming baritone quickly puts an end to the merriment spreading through the courtroom. 'Sit you back down, sir!' He turns both his attention and his ire to the defendant's advocate. 'And I remind you, Vicendi, that it was *your* client who demanded trial by combat to dispute the debt filed against him. He cannot now rescin—'

'A debt levied in secret by the Court of Coins!' Vicendi counters. His hand shakes with barely contained rage as he jabs an accusing finger towards the gallery. 'A privilege afforded solely to Rijou's Ascendant Houses, which suggests that it was someone in this very chamber who contrived the charges against my client, not their puppet Jolen!'

The scandalous accusation sets off an indignant hubbub from the other side of the chamber. 'Unproven!' the plaintiff's sleepy-eyed advocate protests, wiping crumbs from the lustrous black velvet coat straining to contain his belly. 'Unseemly!' He adds, readjusting his ebony-powdered wig before turning to smile broadly at the audience, delighted to have at last contributed to the trial.

Magistrate Calvino's eyes flitter up to the gallery, no doubt seeking guidance from whichever of Rijou's illustrious noble citizens covertly financed today's ruling. 'A continuance in a duella debtori is highly irregular and would slow the wheels of justice.' Calvin's grumbling delivery suggests he is less than pleased with his own role in these proceedings. Nonetheless, he persists, 'Would you deny the right of your fellow citizens to a speedy trial, Vicendi?' Without waiting for an answer, the magistrate slams the ball of his ornately carved wooden sceptre against the bronze bell at his side. The discordant chime rings throughout the courtroom, setting the little starling to fluttering anxiously inside her cage. 'No, sir, I say no! Had you advised your client competently, he would have accepted the merciful verdict rendered by the Court of Coins. In appealing their decision, he has left himself no choice but to prosecute his case with steel!'

Vicendi's pale cheeks turn crimson. His upper lip curls in disgust. Those few in the audience sympathetic to his case watch in mute horror as he prepares to deliver his final objection. Reckless as he's proven himself throughout the trial, there is one line the young advocate hasn't yet crossed – one accusation that no lawyer in his right mind would dare put before the court.

'*Merciful?*' Vicendi asks through gritted teeth. '*Merciful?*' he repeats, louder this time. 'Has not the Court of Coins of which you speak with such admiration has rendered many such *mercies* of late, Eminence? Holding secret hearings on debts filed against master artisans, indenturing them to the plaintiffs, who then conveniently transfer their contracts to one of the Ascendant Houses seated in the gallery behind you? And should the artisan in question dare challenge the ruling?'

'We are not here to endure the opinions of a brash, unseasoned advocate regarding the rulings of our fellow magist—'

'Then *this* court provides those same Ascendant Houses the legal means to orchestrate the murder of anyone who refuses bonded servitude!'

Were he to utter not a single word more, Vicendi's transgression would already be sufficient to see him shackled in irons and dragged from the courtroom – or worse, into the duelling circle. Even so, he levels one final indictment upon the Court of Blades: 'What your Eminence calls mercy would be better termed *court-ordered slavery*.'

The accusation settles upon the crowded courtroom like a shroud. Slavery is the one penalty banned in Tristia since the country's founders freed themselves from the yokes of their oppressors. To suggest the nation's courts could be tacitly complicit in bringing back such a heinous practice is to bring doubt upon the entire judicial system.

'Would you accuse *me* of—?' Magistrate Calvino's fury gives way to an unusually grey pallor that creeps over his jowly features, as if he has just been made to swallow something poisonous to his soul.

Too late, Vicendi opens his mouth to retract his mad insinuation, but Calvino cuts him off with a slice of one meaty hand before turning to conspire with a trio of clerks holding weighty legal tomes. Dutifully, the clerks pretend to consult their texts before looking up and shaking their heads in feigned dismay. Calvino looks almost saddened as he concludes, 'I have no legal basis for a continuance. I will overlook your seditious slander, Vicendi, but your client must—'

'I, too, am sick!' Opezo the gemcutter declares abruptly, leaping up from his chair in the defendant's box.

The crowd jeers, and no one takes the objection seriously. Opezo can't be more than twenty-five years of age, and while clearly no fencer, the broad-shouldered lapidarist at least evinces the strength to hold a sword, unlike the foppish jewellery maker he'd expected to face in the duelling circle.

'You appear hale enough to me, Master Gemcutter,' the magistrate observes, squinting down at Opezo. 'Would you perjure yourself in my court?'

'But Jolen's the one who's lying!' Opezo insists, gesticulating wildly across the courtroom. 'I've never even done business with that crooked, counterfeiting bast—'

'Slander!' the once-drowsy plaintiff's advocate proclaims, beaming now that he's justified his fees with not one but *two* feats of legal wizardry.

Again, Magistrate Calvino slams his sceptre upon the bell. The ingenious design of the bronze half-globe is such that the harder it is struck, the more discomfiting the clang it produces. The entire courtroom covers its ears as the birds in their cages emit a cacophony of plaintive squawks and trills.

'Enough!' the magistrate growls. 'We will have our duel. Today. Now.'

The final act of the trial commences as Calvino turns to the pair of scales mounted on the right arm of his throne. He begins placing tiny silver weights upon them, one after another, as if each ingot were a particular element of the case. The ritual is more theatre than judicial process: by balancing the scales, the magistrate seeks to demonstrate to the gods that the duel has been impartially constructed and now it is for them to determine the outcome.

At the very last moment, though, still clutching the last silver weight needed to bring the scales into perfect balance, Calvino pauses. The audience watches, enraptured by this unexpected hesitation. This time, the magistrate's eyes don't flicker to the gallery, but rise ever so slowly to the thirty-foot-tall statues of War and Death standing guard at the entrance to his courtroom.

'It is my ruling that . . .'

Sallo Calvino goes quiet, the last silver ingot now clenched in his fist. He glances briefly at his beloved starling in its gilded cage. The bird cheeps adoringly, or perhaps hungrily, before preening its purple and yellow feathers. Magistrate Calvino then holds up the little silver weight for all to see. Gently, he places it upon the scales, bringing them into balance before proclaiming, 'In the interests of justice, it is the ruling of this court that the defendant may choose a secondier of his own to fight in his place.'

Mayhem erupts throughout the chamber. Accusations of corruption and bribery are shouted from the galleries with neither irony nor apparent fear of retribution.

Undaunted, Magistrate Calvino smashes his sceptre upon the bell until the clamour recedes. 'These are my terms for the duel and they are final!' His gaze descends upon Opezo. 'I suggest you find yourself a secondier quickly, sir.' He points to the massive clock at the opposite end of the courtroom held in the crook of Death's arm. The time is nearly noon. 'I grant you seven minutes to choose your champion.'

The gemcutter's eyes dart around the chamber in panicked desperation. 'Why are you just standing there?' he demands of his advocate. 'Find me a duellist, quickly!'

Vicendi doesn't bother getting huffy about being commanded to perform a task that is neither part of an advocate's duties nor possible to achieve in so small an amount of time. The process of securing the services of a duellist is a long and complex affair, often taking weeks. 'I cannot,' he replies simply, shuffling the papers inside his leather satchel as an excuse to avoid the gaze of his doomed client.

'Please!' Opezo begs as he runs around the courtroom trying to catch the eye of those few duelling stewards in attendance, hoping against hope that one of them will offer the services of their chamber's fencers.

One by one, grey-suited stewards turn away.

'I have money!' Opezo insists, holding out a sagging coin purse as if its mere touch might compel someone to fight on his behalf. Those he approaches lean away from him, or laugh in his face: they know full well that the only reason Opezo risked a debtor's duel in the first place is because the verdict rendered against him by the Court of Coins has already ruined him. Not even the potential fortune in duelling commissions that would surely come to their chambers from a victory against Our Lord of Corpses is enough for any of the stewards to risk the lives of their fencers.

Nonetheless, the desperate young artisan keeps pleading for someone – *anyone* – to take up his cause, right until Death's clock strikes the noon hour.

'I concede!' Opezo shouts, throwing himself at the massive bronze pedestal rising up to the Magistrate's throne. 'I accept the Court of Coins' most merciful sen—'

The hideous clang of the magistrate's bell sounds as Sallo Calvino, his grim features betraying some small hint of regret and perhaps even shame, strikes it twice more with his sceptre. 'An accusation of defamation and false debt made before the gods cannot be revoked. Only steel can settle the matter now.'

At the magistrate's signal, two representatives of the Guild of Weaponsmiths enter the courtroom, each bearing a red-lacquered case four feet long, six inches high and seven inches deep. The weaponsmiths approach the edge of the duelling circle. One stands before the plaintiff's champion, the other before the defendant. Their movements eerily synchronised, they unlatch the crimson cases and flip open the lids, revealing inside each one a single rapier resting on black velvet. The leather grips show the natural dullness of use, but the long, narrow blades are gleaming.

For a trial to be just, each blade must be newly forged, else wear in the metal could lend unfair advantage to the opponent – that's what the weaponsmiths' guild insists, anyway. At the end of the trial, the blades will be shattered so that they can never be used again. The manufacture of duelling weapons is one of the more lucrative industries in Rijou these days.

Dazidier Enguero, Our Lord of Corpses, draws his rapier, examines it carefully and nods to the first weaponsmith, who closes the red wooden case and withdraws. Master Jolen's advocate at last rouses himself off his arse to perform his one remaining duty.

With a swaggering, thumping gait he begins to stomp around the courtroom, whisking the tails of his long black silk coat as he heralds the champion. 'Observe you now, my most worthy lords and daminas, as a living legend binds to his hand the means of the gods' own retribution against those who bear false witness.'

Halfway to the defendant's side, he stops and turns to smirk at the shabby Advocate Vicendi and his client, the hapless gemcutter. 'And is any here so foolish as to doubt what their divine judgment will be?'

He spins on his heel – an elegant manoeuvre for so hefty a figure – and to the audience declares, 'For here have the gods sent to do battle their most beloved champion, the strong right arm of justice, Death's most sublime work of art . . .' He leans back now, his voice a thunderous bellow as he brings the audience clapping and whooping to their feet. 'His mother dubbed him Dazidier, son of the noble house of Enguero, but the gods and this courtroom know him by his true name . . . Our. Lord. Of. Corpses!'

The cheers are deafening. The advocate bows deeply, as though he has won the duel himself without even drawing steel. Dazidier Enguero gives a few quick swishes of the rapier. Anyone bothering to examine the blade will have noticed it is several inches too short for Dazidier's height, having originally been selected for his client, the jewellery maker. The golden-haired duellist isn't troubled in the slightest.

Master Opezo, tears of frustration and despair streaming down his cheeks, scrambles across the courtroom to drop to his knees before his opponent. He grabs for the blade of the other man's weapon in the vain hope that by cutting himself he can plead the duel has ended in first blood, even though this will ensure his indenture. Enguero is too fast, though, and whips the blade away before striking the gemcutter's wrist with the pommel.

Opezo cries out in pain. 'Please,' he weeps, at last accepting that Dazidier's employers will settle for nothing less than his death, 'make it quick.'

The beatific smile on the face of Our Lord of Corpses is unwavering as he gazes down at the defendant. 'Take up your weapon, sir.'

The gemcutter sobs, 'Just kill me now, damn you. Get it over with.'

Without warning, the duellist backhands him across the face. 'Take up your weapon, sir, or I will beat you until your bones snap and your internal organs burst within the worthless shell of your body. Even that will be no release for you, however, for I will leave your coward's hide unpierced until it becomes nothing more than a bloated sack filled with coagulated lumps of blood – these being no less rubies than the garish gobs of resin you have foisted as rare gems onto unsuspecting jewellers.'

Appreciative laughter fills the courtroom. In these refined times, a great duellist is rewarded not only for being a skilled fencer, but also a sharp-witted conversationalist.

Opezo rises to his feet, and only then does the audience see why he'd wanted to face death on his knees: along the left leg of his trousers, a dark stain of urine is spreading. The terrified gemcutter had hoped to die with a shred of his dignity intact. With even that grace denied him, he stumbles, legs shaking, to where the patient weaponsmith awaits, still holding the red case open for him.

With a trembling hand, Opezo reaches for the sword he will draw once, yet never see the use of. His fingers are about to wrap around the black leather hilt when a new voice breaks the reverential silence of the courtroom.

'I'll fight his case.'

As one, the audience leaps from their seats, peering into the shadows beneath the arch formed by the statues of Death and War, searching for the source of the irreverent feminine voice that dared interrupt a judicial duel.

My voice, as it turns out.

Are you ready, my darlings?

Watch closely now. Don't even blink because, as the old fencing bibles remind us, a duel to the death isn't a chess match.

It's a magic trick.

And I've waited seven long years to perform mine.

HYPOCRISY AND HYPOTHESES

A hundred pairs of eyes swarm over me like ants, scrutinizing every detail of my hair, my face, my clothes, my body. Every glance betrays a question:

Who is this woman?

How long has she been lurking in the shadows?

Is she really foolhardy enough to challenge Our Lord of Corpses?

And, of course, the most important question of all, the one that haunts every waking thought of Rijou's elite: *Could her presence interfere with my own schemes?*

I remain at the entrance, leaning impudently against one stone leg of the towering statue of Death, allowing the audience time to examine me. My hair is blue-black today, with elaborate curls draping down my cheeks to tickle the edge of my jaw. It'll be obvious to anyone watching that I am young, though a woman grown nonetheless. No doubt they will be surveying the planes of my face, the shape of my nose, the line of my neck, rifling through memories of the children of the noble houses of Rijou.

A second daughter, perhaps?

No, if so, my likeness would surely have appeared in the broadsheets, announcing some upcoming marriage alliance – or the scandal of why no such union was taking place.

A distant cousin, then? Someone less likely to be remarked upon?

Perhaps, perhaps . . .

The heat in the courtroom is stifling. Unbuttoning my long, reddish-brown leather coat to reveal the tightly laced duelling waistcoat beneath raises eyebrows. My figure is a trifle too slim to be fashionable.

The paupered child of a disgraced noble house, then?

A reasonable conjecture: the fortunes of aristocratic families rise and fall with the tides of Rijou's never-ending intrigues.

Those fitted calfskin fencing trousers, though . . . they reveal thighs that are unusually muscular.

Not very ladylike, I admit, but useful to a duellist.

Might the loose, billowing, ivory silk blouse partially obscured by her waistcoat be hiding similarly taut muscles underneath?

I keep my stance casual, almost indolent. It's easier than I expected, this posing and preening. I feel like a sixteen year old at the Swan Revel, presenting myself before lines of suitors in hopes of making a suitable match. It won't be kisses I'll be exchanging with them today, though.

Is she drunk? Is this all some churlish prank? I see the nobles in the gallery wonder as they try and fail to discern my identity, to place me within the ranks of some Ascendant or Rising or Falling House – to *rate* me. Soon, though, a rare flicker of despair reveals itself in the narrowing of their eyes.

What if her nonchalance is a sign of secret knowledge? What if a new piece has been placed upon the game board, this one neither a white pawn nor black, but a grey chevalier – one with cause to believe she can defeat the illustrious Lord of Corpses?

Death's clock has ticked away three long minutes since I made my entrance. It's only now that someone in the crowd notices the unusual design of my coat, the sturdiness of the leather and the way the slender, flexible bone plates sewn inside the lining give it the appearance of supple armour.

'A Greatcoat!' the fellow cries out.

'*Trattari*,' another declares before spitting on the floor.

Accusations of 'tatter-cloak', 'spy' and other less flattering terms spread throughout the courtroom. In the upper galleries, several of the nobles are shaking their fists at me. I notice other hands sneaking into the hidden folds of magnificent coats and gowns, reaching for hidden weapons that are supposed to be prohibited to the public inside the Court of Blades.

You need not fear the King's Travelling Magistrates, my lords and daminas. Upholding the law doesn't interest me in the slightest.

A quartet of Court Wardens, unsure what they're supposed to be doing but presuming it involves placing me in irons, begin a lurching march towards me. I casually duck under the outstretched arm of the first one and saunter into the ruby-ringed duelling circle to stand before the weaponsmith with his polished red-lacquered case. The wardens halt their approach at the edge of the circle. Duelling is a sacred thing in Rijou, after all, and the entire court heard Magistrate Calvino rule that the gemcutter was entitled to a secondier.

'Let's get on with it, shall we, sweetheart?' I ask Dazidier Enguero as I draw the plaintiff's rapier before turning back to salute the overdressed and excessively scented sewage who fancy themselves Rijou's elites. 'High time *someone* in this august chamber gets skewered, don't you think?'

The crowd gasps, the gemcutter gapes and the magistrate's clerks shuffle the pages of their ponderous legal tomes in search of a cause to prohibit my participation in the proceedings. Our Lord of Corpses merely narrows his eyes in contemplation of how best to end me. All the while I find myself occupied with a rather unexpected thought.

It's good to be home.

ABOUT THE AUTHOR

Sebastien de Castell had just finished a degree in Archaeology when he started work on his first dig. Four hours later he realised how much he actually hated archaeology and left to pursue a very focused career as a musician, ombudsman, interaction designer, fight choreographer, teacher, project manager, actor and product strategist. His only defence against the charge of unbridled dilettantism is that he genuinely likes doing these things and that, in one way or another, each of these fields plays a role in his writing. He sternly resists the accusation of being a Renaissance Man in the hopes that more people will label him that way.

Sebastien's acclaimed swashbuckling fantasy series The Greatcoats was shortlisted for the Goodreads Choice Award for Best Fantasy. the Gemmell Morningstar Award for Best Debut, the Prix Imaginales for Best Foreign Work and the John W. Campbell Award for Best New Writer. His YA fantasy series Spellslinger was nominated for the Carnegie Medal and is published in more than a dozen languages.

Sebastien lives in Vancouver, Canada with his lovely wife and two belligerent cats.

Praise for *Play of Shadows*

'The twists and turns of a story where theater genuinely is magic had me turning pages perhaps a little faster than I should have – but it was such a thrill to encounter sophisticated world-building mingled with nerve-wracking adventure and truly satisfying swordplay. De Castell's women are genuinely witty and intelligent, as well as hot as blazes . . . and I'm a sucker for any story with truth and friendship at its heart. Bravo, maestro! I eagerly await the next one'
Ellen Kushner, author of *Swordspoint*

'A fast-paced joy-ride from start to finish, filled to the brim with swashbuckling action'
Eleni A.E. at FanFiAddict

'Complex and enthralling . . . the novel's characters are expansive and full of verve. De Castell has a knack for comedic dialogue, with characters that are larger than life . . . I can't wait to find out what will happen next'
GeekDad

'Thrilling, complex, and absolutely addictive . . . It's not often a book leaves me speechless. This one pulled it off. *Repeatedly* . . . *Play of Shadows* is true to the spirit of the original Greatcoats in every way, and yet is utterly fresh and unique. From its humble beginning to its epic end, it stands among the author's finest works'
Andy Peloquin at FanFiAddict

'I'm still in awe. *Play of Shadows* is mysterious, enthralling, and just flat-out fantastic . . . the pacing was superb, and the climax had me gasping out loud . . . *Play of Shadows* is phenomenal and deserves a standing ovation'
Witty and Sarcastic Book Club

'Fast-paced, very dynamic and there are plenty of twists and turns . . . fantastic from the first page to the last'
Hobbleit

'Integrate[s] unusual locations and memorable characters into an exciting and engaging plot'
SF² Concatenation

'A fantastic romp revolving around the power of stories and how history is written by the victors'
Fantasy Book Nerd

By Sebastien de Castell

The Greatcoats Series

Traitor's Blade

Knight's Shadow

Saint's Blood

Tyrant's Throne

The Court of Shadows Series

Prelude: Crucible of Chaos

Play of Shadows

Our Lady of Blades (coming soon)

The Spellslinger Series

Spellslinger

Shadowblack

Charmcaster

Soulbinder

Queenslayer

Crownbreaker

Way of the Argosi

Fall of the Argosi

Fate of the Argosi

The Malevolent Seven